GARDEN of DREAMS

LAURA SIMON

BERKLEY BOOKS, NEW YORK

GARDEN OF DREAMS

A Berkley Book / published by arrangement with
the author

PRINTING HISTORY
Berkley edition / December 1992

ISBN: 0-425-13559-4

A BERKLEY BOOK ® TM 757,375
Berkley Books are published by The Berkley Publishing Group,
200 Madison Avenue, New York, New York 10016.
The name "BERKLEY" and the "B" logo
are trademarks belonging to Berkley Publishing Corporation.

PRINTED IN THE UNITED STATES OF AMERICA

10 9 8 7 6 5 4 3 2 1

For Jimmy

With many, many thanks to all those people who graciously contributed their time and knowledge to this book. In particular: Susan Simon, New York City; Contessa Nally Bellati, Milan, Italy; Deanna Slayton, Growing Enterprises, Nantucket; Keith Crotz, The American Botanist, Chillicothe, Illinois; Lois A. Stringer, Vegetable Research, W. Atlee Burpee Co.; R. D. de Jager, Vanhof & Blokker, Heiloo, Holland; Geke Eisinga, International Bloembollencentrum, Hillegom, Holland; Ans Schickler, New York City; Harrie Wagtenveld, Grass Roots, Nantucket; Gary Irving, Natick, Massachusetts; Lawrence Spaulding, Jr., Orleans, Massachusetts; Walter Oleszek, Washington, D.C.; and, of course, Roger.

= 1 =

Castle Garden, Port of New York
November 1887

Nina turned for only a moment, her attention captured by a sprig of paper violets on a bonnet brim. After being at sea for two bleak weeks, the bright bouquet was a welcome sight. But when she turned back, with a smile of delight, her family was gone.

Her mother, her father, and her six younger sisters were swallowed up by the crowd on the pier. By the hundreds of people streaming off barges, ferried from German and Irish and Italian ships at anchor in New York Harbor. Her family had disappeared among the thousands of people lugging boxes and bags and battered suitcases. Among the masses of people pressing forward toward the circular fortress called Castle Garden, where cannons once defended the fledgling United States, where Jenny Lind, the Swedish Nightingale, later sang to adoring audiences, and where, now, half a million immigrants a year were checked and inspected and admitted to a new future in America.

A prick of concern chasing away her smile, Nina scanned the faces around her, searching for the familiar ones of her family. She saw only strangers. Strangers wearing strange costumes and speaking to their children in strange languages. Strangers whose grave expressions reflected a mixture of apprehension and excitement, of confusion, fatigue, and hope. Strangers propelled forward by the human tide. Strangers pushing Nina forward, too.

Increasingly alarmed, she tried to resist, twisting first one way and then the other, her bundle of possessions clutched to her chest. *"Devo trovare la mia famiglia,"* she explained to the woman next to her as she stretched on tiptoe to look above the sea of people. Uncomprehending, the bleary-eyed woman with a blue kerchief tied under her chin shoved forward, and Nina was thrust through the entrance of Castle Garden.

If the crowd had seemed vast outside the fortress, against the broad horizons of the sky and the harbor, trapped inside the round walls it was overwhelming. The multilingual murmur of voices, dampened by the raw autumn air out on the pier, was loud and insistent in here.

Panic welled up in Nina's throat. Her family would be lost forever. *"Non spingermi!"* she cried in protest of the force that was pushing her deeper into the huge, packed hall. In a more frantic effort to extricate herself, she whirled to go back the way she came. And crashed into the person behind her.

The bundle in Nina's arms was thrown to the floor, and its contents spilled out of the black shawl wrapper: a travel-wrinkled dress and a pair of darned stockings, some mismatched hairpins, a comb with one broken tooth, and five little twists of paper.

"Neem me niet kwalijk," a voice apologized.

The foreign words were just part of the frightening babble. Ignoring them, Nina bent to retrieve her belongings. She raked four of the twists toward her with one hand and was reaching out for the fifth with the other, when a worn boot shuffled across it. The paper split open, and tiny seeds rolled out, scattering over the well-trod boards of the immigration hall.

"O Dio!" Nina wailed, falling to her knees, her fear forgotten in the face of this new crisis. Her hands darted between the plodding feet to rescue the seeds.

"It's no use," the voice spoke again. "They're gone. Even if we can pick them up, they're smashed and cracked. Quite worthless for planting." The speaker's tone was calm, his English was careful, and although his words were despairing, he knelt down, too. His long fingers skimmed across the floor, brushing the scattered seeds into a pile.

Nina heard him this time, but she didn't understand what he said any better. His actions, however, were obvious. He was attempting to help her. For half an instant her gaze flicked up. Then again. And froze in amazement. She found herself staring into the bluest eyes she'd ever seen. Wide and deeply set, they were a blue she couldn't describe. Darker than the sky, brighter than the sea. The color of a rare and magnificent flower.

In fact, his whole face was arresting. Cut in square, clean lines, it was nothing like the faces she'd left behind in her village in Sicily. Except for two rosy spots that looked almost scrubbed into his high cheeks, his skin was as lustrously pale as marble. Equally as wondrous was his hair. Thick and straight and silkily blond, it was swept back from his clear brow, neither pasted down with oils nor hidden by a hat.

As Nina continued to stare, transfixed by his fairness, the young man grinned. It was a slightly off-center grin with one end of his mouth rising higher than the other and a crease appearing in one cheek only, but it was a grin full of genuine amusement.

Suddenly aware of how she'd been gaping, Nina's gaze dropped and rosy color flooded her own cheeks. She scooped up the rest of her possessions, stuffing her clothes into the black shawl bundle and jabbing the hairpins, for good measure, into her bun. Just in time, too, because, as usual, the pins holding it on top of her head were working dangerously loose, leaving her dark wavy hair to frame her face in ever-widening ripples.

It was a striking face, and a strong one, with a bold nose and a firm chin. Big amber brown eyes, bright with curiosity, lit it up. And though still round and smooth with traces of childhood, full red lips and thick black lashes gave it a seductive hint. What really made it remarkable, however, was its expressiveness. Always animated, it was an open window to the emotions flashing inside her.

Right now it registered embarrassment and confusion, and she didn't look up when the young man spoke again. "I think that's all that can be saved," he said. "Here. Please take them."

Intent on scraping the trampled seeds on the floor back into the torn paper, Nina just gave a quick shake of her head. She didn't know what he said, or what language he said it in. Moreover, she wasn't sure she should be answering him. No matter how intriguing, he was still a stranger. Who knew what he wanted?

He showed her. Seizing her wrist, he turned her hand palm up, then trickled the salvaged seeds into it. "You must hold these for a moment," he instructed.

Never mind that Nina didn't understand his words, she barely heard him speak. Stunned by the hot shock that shot through her at his touch, she didn't even know there were seeds lying in her palm. She knew it, though, when he folded her fingers over them. His grip was warm and sure. Sensations she'd never before felt coursed through her body and seemed to cut off her breath.

"That old paper is no good," the blond stranger continued, apparently oblivious to the effect he was having on her. "We'd best make you a new packet." He let go her hand to reach inside the bag slung from his shoulder.

With her release, her breath returned, and Nina was finally able to look up. But as the young man pulled a journal from his pack, he gave her another crooked grin. It made her heart leap to her throat again, made it begin pounding uncontrollably. It was incredible that this could be happening. That this beautiful young man with hair like sunlight could be kneeling in front of her, talking to her patiently, folding a page he'd torn from his journal into a neat cone. It was incredible that, by some capricious stroke of fortune, they had arrived at the exact same spot at the very same moment from two divergent corners of the globe. That they spoke different languages and wore different clothes, but were brought together by the bright hope of flowers contained in a few spilled grams of seeds. Awe overcoming her excitement, Nina poured the seeds from her hand into the paper cone he extended. She sat back on her heels and waited while he twisted it closed and handed it to her.

"Move along, miss," a voice barked as something tapped her on the shoulder, shattering the glorious spell. "You can't sit here all day. Yer blockin' the way. Move along, now."

Again Nina didn't understand the words, but again she understood the tone. This time, though, it was stern. Looking up, she saw a barrel-chested policeman about to prod her with his nightstick. She jumped to her feet, her fear surging back. She was in a strange country, lost and unable to speak the language, and now a policeman was threatening her for some crime she didn't know she'd committed. Gripping her bundle in one hand and the prized packet of seeds in the other, Nina looked wildly around for her family.

"Move along, I said," the officer repeated more loudly, giving her another nudge with his stick. "I wish to Betsy that you people could understand plain English."

Nina's eyebrows knit together and she chewed her lower lip. What was he saying? Was he going to arrest her? Poised on the balls of her feet, she was ready to plunge into the crowd. But she didn't know which way to plunge. "*Santo cielo!*" she cried, near panic.

"Don't just stand there. Get moving." His command was harsh with irritation now. He poked her again, more sharply this time. Nina flinched, but pure fright paralyzed her where she stood.

"Sorry to be a problem," another voice spoke up, the voice of the blond young man. For a moment Nina had forgotten him, but now she whirled toward him, his calm and rational tone drawing her attention like a magnet. "We dropped some belongings, and it took a few moments to gather them together," he explained. "We'll move along directly."

"Hmph," the officer grumbled, his bluster deflating. At least this man could speak English. Even if he had an accent. "Well, see that you do." He moved off himself.

"That's that," the young man said, giving Nina his crooked grin and a wink, as well. "We've escaped the iron fist of tyranny for the minute."

Nina heard the dry humor in his voice and saw the smile on his face, but they only heightened her confusion. What was going on? What were these people saying? How was she supposed to respond? Then she burst into an explanation of what had happened, talking rapidly in Italian and waving her hands in additional description.

Nina had to look up to meet the stranger's eyes. Those blue eyes, as vivid—and distracting—as the violets. Though she was considered tall in her village in Sicily, she was no match for his long legs. Nor could she hope to match his elegance. Except for *il padrone*, the lord of the manor, she had never seen a man dressed so finely. His wool suit fit him perfectly, its jacket sitting squarely across his shoulders, its high-buttoned waistcoat hugging his lean chest. His collar was crisp, its tips carefully winged, and his tie was knotted with precision. His ankle boots were polished, his pants were pressed, and his cuffs were white and clean.

After telling him about her predicament, Nina fell silent, suddenly shy in the face of such splendor. She didn't notice that the elbows of his jacket were shiny and thin, or that the heels of his boots were worn down. To her, this fair stranger was incomparable.

Juggling her bundle and the seed packet, Nina attempted to straighten her own clothes, miserably aware of how inferior they were. Her brown skirt was coarse and her checked blouse was patched, its high neck wilted and stretched. When a few clumsy brushes brought no visible improvement, she yanked at the heavy shawl drooping off one shoulder, pulling it across the offending apparel to hide it from sight.

"It sounds like a desperate situation," the young man spoke again. There was the same dry hint of humor in his tone.

Forehead wrinkling, Nina glanced at him, but he was nodding gravely, as if he actually knew what she'd said. But how could he when she couldn't understand him? It was absurd, really, that they should keep talking to each other. That she should blurt out her problems, and that he should comment on them. Maybe he thought so, too. Maybe that's why there was irony in his humorous tone. Or maybe not. She shrugged and threw her hand in the air, letting it fall in resignation against her leg. "*Chi lo sa?*" she asked. Who knows what's happening?

"If you keep flinging those seeds about, you'll lose them for certain," came his voice in admonishment. "And I promise you, I won't go crawling around on the floor to pick them up. I only own one respectable pair of trousers, and I have to keep them clean so I'll look presentable when I apply for a job."

This time Nina stared at him. He was smiling again. That crooked smile added irresistible charm to his already fascinating face. It softened the cool, clean lines and made him seem less formidably foreign. It also made Nina's heart race. She swallowed.

"Well," he continued, hitching the strap of his pack higher on his shoulder, "no matter how tragic your story, if you're here at Castle Garden, it can only be for one purpose. I'll wager my first week's pay that you've come to find a better life in America than the one you lived in whatever country you left." He studied her a moment, his blue eyes squinting, before he added, "Italy, I would guess." Then he shrugged, too, dismissing the irrelevant detail.

"There's a long queue for that better life," he said, his smile coming back. He nodded toward the front of the hall, clogged with people. "Shall we join the queue before our police officer returns? I'm afraid he'll be quite vexed if he finds us here."

"*Non so cosa fare . . .*" Nina answered uncertainly, still unable to make heads or tails of his speech, but sensing that it required a response. She didn't know what to do. So many things were happening so quickly, and none of them were like anything that had ever happened to her before. She raised her hand with the intention of rubbing her brow. Halfway to her head, however, five strong fingers clamped around her wrist. She sucked in her breath, her dilemma—and everything else—forgotten. And when the young man tugged her forward, she followed unhesitatingly.

For several moments she was aware only of the hand grasping hers. Of that, and of the strange excitement rushing through her. Then she became aware of him speaking again. Her despair returned. What was he saying now? It was one word. He kept repeating it. "Wim."

She looked at him and shook her head. "*Non capisco,*" she said, telling him she didn't know what it meant.

In response, he took his hand, with hers entwined in it, and thumped it against the wool waistcoat buttoned high on his chest. "Wim," he said again.

Nina's eyes widened and her face lit up. So that was it. He was telling her his name. "Wim," she echoed. Then laughed. It felt so good to finally understand something he said. Especially something as particular as his name. Now he was no longer just a stranger, just another one of the thousands jamming the great hall. Now he was someone she knew.

"Wim," she said again, nodding in satisfaction. She liked it. Its odd, single syllable fit him. Somewhat more shyly she added, "Nina." With their joined hands, she pointed to herself. His answering smile made her glow with pleasure.

In the hours that followed, they made themselves understood on a great many more subjects. As they crept forward, the masses of people funneling down aisles, Nina and Wim "talked" with their hands. Although the descriptive gestures didn't come as easily or as gracefully to Wim as they did to Nina, he still managed to explain what was happening. He pointed out the doctors, a team of overworked men, who were examining the lines of immigrants, making chalk marks on the shoulders of those with head funguses or eye diseases or limps. And when they themselves passed the tired gazes of the doctors unmarked, Wim swiveled his pack around in front of him and fished for something inside.

"This calls for a celebration," he said.

"Eh?" Nina asked.

"Chocolate," he answered, pulling out a thick bar wrapped in a Van Houten Chocolade wrapper.

"Ah," Nina said, bursting into laughter. "*Cioccolato.*" She'd just understood her first word of English. She twirled her hand to make him repeat it once more.

"Chocolate," he obliged.

"Chocolate," Nina echoed in delight. She was speaking English.

"Very good." Wim seemed equally as delighted. He undid the paper and broke the bar in half. He held one piece out to her.

"*Aspetta.*" She lifted her hand, signaling him to wait, then shoved it into her bundle. After a few moments of worming around, she withdrew a plump orange. "*Arancia,*" she said.

"Orange," Wim corrected.

"Orange," Nina repeated with another ring of laughter. This was exciting.

As they inched along, sharing the last of the food they'd brought from the countries of their birth, Wim taught Nina more words of English. In no time at all she'd learned *hello* and *good-bye,* as well as *yes, no,* and *thank you.*

They ate standing up, their backs against the railing, surrounded by crying babies and restless children and harassed adults. It was hot inside, and despite a brief whiff of citrus when Nina peeled the orange, the air was sour and rank. Lunch was gone in a few gulps, but Nina couldn't remember when she'd enjoyed a meal more. Even the feast of Santo Stefano, last August, hadn't been as wonderful as the few slices of Sicilian orange and the few morsels of Dutch chocolate eaten in the company of this handsome, blue-eyed man. It was her first meal in America, and it was very nearly perfect.

But even though she was oblivious to the noise and the heat, Nina continued to fret about her family. While she practiced counting to twenty in English, she periodically peered into the crowd. "*Mia famiglia,*" she explained to Wim.

He nodded sympathetically. "Family," he said, laying a comforting hand over hers. Nina swung around, abandoning her search, as excitement again rushed through her at his touch. Her quick movement brought her closer to him, so close their shoulders bumped, so close she had to tilt back her head to stare at his face. A strand of silky blond hair had fallen across his brow, and a faint smile set a crease in the corner of his mouth. Nina drew in a breath and held it.

They stood perfectly still for a fraction of a moment, completely alone in the midst of the crowd. Then a look of surprise seemed to fill Wim's eyes. Dropping her hand, he took a hasty step backward, the rosy highlights in his cheeks even brighter than usual. "Well," he said, brushing the stray lock of hair off his forehead and hitching the strap of his pack higher on his shoulder. "Well."

Nina let out her breath.

"We're next. Do you see?" he asked, gesturing ahead, his composure restored almost instantly.

The banging in Nina's heart subsided more slowly, but she allowed her attention to be directed forward. They had reached the head of the line, and a clerk standing behind a high desk briefly beckoned to them. It was their turn.

Nina's heart began beating hard again and her throat was dry, though it wasn't shocks of pleasure and excitement that caused it this time. This time, she was extremely nervous. When Wim started forward, she clutched her bundle tightly and leapt to his side. They stepped up to the desk together.

Despite the knots in Nina's stomach, the clerk hardly seemed to notice them as he shuffled and sorted the stacks of paper on his desk. He wasn't much older than Wim, but his shoulders were stooped and his expression was as weary as the doctors'. When he finally looked up, the piles of forms arranged to his liking, his indifferent gaze flicked off Nina and settled on Wim. "Do you speak English?" he asked with a resigned sigh, as if he didn't expect even his question to be understood.

"Yes, I do," Wim replied promptly.

The clerk's eyebrows raised infinitesimally, and vague relief crossed his face, but he wasted no time in jubilation. "Name?" he asked, pen poised at the top of the form.

"Wim Pieter de Groot."

"Place of birth?"

"Haarlem, Holland."

"Age?"

"Twenty-one."

"Occupation?"

There was a pause. Looking from the clerk to Wim with each question and answer, Nina saw Wim's jaw momentarily tighten and a sober light flit across his face.

Without glancing up, the clerk repeated, "Occupation?"

Shrugging, Wim finally replied. "Since I left school, I've worked for the bulb companies." He paused again, then added, "Whatever job was available."

It was the clerk's turn to pause, though he still didn't lift his eyes. "Bulbs?" he asked.

"Yes," Wim said with another shrug. "You know. Tulips. Hyacinths. Narcissus."

Nodding, the clerk proceeded with his questioning. "Intended occupation in America?"

Wim laughed, his good spirits revived. "Whatever occupation I can find that will bring me success," he answered. "America is the land where dreams come true. Isn't that so?"

At last the clerk looked up, a hint of a smile easing the exhaustion on his face. He didn't offer an opinion, but there was curiosity in his voice as he asked, "And just what skills do you have to pursue your goal?"

Wim considered a moment before responding. "My mother taught me English and French and gracious manners," he said, rubbing his chin thoughtfully. "And my father taught me to work hard and to aspire to great heights. I can read and write and do figures." He shook his head and tossed up his hand. "Anything else I can learn."

The clerk absorbed what Wim said in silence, then looked back at his form. "Are you under contract, express or implied, to perform labor in the United States?"

A smile spread across Wim's face. "Of course not," he said. "Contract laborers aren't permitted entry."

Though he darted Wim a suspicious glance, the clerk continued without a comment. "Do you have any money, and if so, how much?"

"Sixty-nine florin," Wim answered, automatically sticking his hand in his pocket to check his wallet. "Twenty-eight dollars."

"Final destination in the United States?"

Wim laughed again. "Who knows where I'll finally find my fortune?" he said. "But for now I'll try my luck in New York."

There was no more curiosity on the clerk's part. His head remained bent over the form. "Have you ever been in prison?"

"No."

"An almshouse?"

"No."

"An insane asylum?"

"No."

"Are you a polygamist?"

Brow furrowing, Wim said, "I'm sorry. I don't know this word."

"Do you have more than one wife?"

"More than one?" Wim was startled. He shook his head. "No, of course not. In fact, I don't have any. I'm not married."

The clerk's head shot up. "No wife?" he asked. "Then who is this woman?" He pointed his pen at Nina and stared. Wim turned to stare, too.

Already tense from trying to follow this seesaw interview, Nina jumped when it suddenly tipped to her. What was happening now? Why were they looking at her like that? What had she done? Eyebrows knitting together, Nina hunched her shawl more tightly around herself. As her gaze moved from one young man to the other, she took a shallow step backward.

Wim turned to the clerk, his face filled with amusement. "This woman," he answered, "is a future American. Beyond that, I know very little. I think she's come from Italy and has lost her family in the crowd."

The clerk gave a long-suffering sigh and reached for a fresh form. "Does she speak English?" he asked, without much hope.

"No," Wim replied. Then he looked at Nina and grinned. "Not yet," he amended.

Though his obvious humor thawed some of Nina's fear, it also added to her worry. What was so funny? Smiling weakly in return, she took a tentative step forward.

After a short wait an interpreter arrived, a slight, bespectacled man with the same weary expression as the other immigration officials. Taking up a position next to the clerk, he began repeating the questions in monotone Italian. "Name?"

Shifting her feet, Nina replied, "Maria Antonina Colangelo."

"Place of birth?"

"Castel'Greco, Sicily."

"Age?"

"Sixteen."

"Are you accompanied by, or being met by, your husband or a responsible male relative?"

With that query, Nina again cast a desperate look around, wishing her missing family would appear. As she craned her neck, she launched into an explanation, almost pleading with the clerk to believe her. She spoke so rapidly and gestured so furiously, the interpreter had to race to keep up. It didn't take long for him to give up trying to translate word for word and to settle for a general summary instead.

"She says she's come from Sicily with her parents and six younger sisters, whose names are Lucia, uh, Serafina . . . uh, Bianca . . ." His voice momentarily trailed off. Taking a quick breath, he skipped over the other names and picked up the narrative. "She swears on her grandmother's grave that her family is here in the hall, that they were together when they disembarked from the *Bay of Naples* a few hours ago, but they got separated when she paused to admire some paper violets on a bonnet, which she did because she loves flowers."

With another gulp of air, the interpreter continued. "She also says that her father, Orazio Colangelo, is a very responsible male relative, as well as very hardworking. You can ask anyone in Castel'Greco if he didn't look after the gardens and the olive groves of the *padrone* as if they were his own, from the time he was a small boy until last June when the *padrone* died, leaving the estate to his oldest son, Franco, who didn't care a fig for either the land or its peasants, which is when her mother, Angelina Colangelo, said they should come to America, because her sister, Gabriella, came in 'eighty-four with her husband, Sergio Ruggieri, who found a good job on a farm in someplace called Long Island."

When the interpreter slowed to take another breath and to push his glasses back up on his nose, the clerk quickly interrupted. "Can you read and write?" he asked.

As this question was translated, Nina's chin lifted proudly. "*Si,*" she answered.

"Yes," the interpreter said cautiously, waiting to see if that one word was all she had to say on the matter.

It wasn't. "*Una volta c'era un ospite venuta dal padrone, veniva d'inverno per il tempo più dolce. Si chiamava Signora Klem Reginiano ed era generosa e sapiente,*" Nina elaborated, her hand circling through the air. "*C'ha insegnato tutti quanti, noi ragazzi.*"

"A woman, very generous and knowledgeable, who was a winter guest in Castel'Greco, taught all the children to read," the interpreter related. "Mrs. Klem Reginiano."

"*In fatti, Serafina, mia sorella preferita—*"

The clerk cut her off before Nina could explain how Signora Klem had also taught Serafina, her favorite sister, to make beautiful drawings of the flowers that Nina loved so well. "Read this," he said, thrusting a tattered page at her.

Shifting her feet again, Nina took it. Was she giving the wrong answers? Was she saying too much? Were the inspectors displeased? She darted a glance at Wim. He gave her a crooked smile of encouragement and a nod of approval. A flush of pleasure burned Nina's cheeks as she bent her head to the page. After clearing her throat, she read the simple text smoothly.

As they had done once before, the clerk's eyebrows raised infinitesimally. He encountered very few girls with Nina's background who could do so much as print their names. Also as before, though, that was the extent of his comment. He continued with his questions, ascertaining that Nina was neither insane nor an anarchist. When at last he was satisfied that she wouldn't be a burden to society, he looked up.

"You qualify for admission to the United States," he said, scratching his head with the end of his pen. "But it's against our policy to allow a young woman into the country unescorted. We're concerned not only with your character, but, even more, with your safety. Unfortunately, there are all sorts of unscrupulous and immoral ruffians waiting just beyond the door for innocent victims. I know you say that your father and the rest of your family is in the hall, but what if you don't find each other? Or what if they're denied entrance?"

Before the interpreter could translate the clerk's remarks, Wim interceded. "Will you stamp Miss Colangelo's papers if I give you my word that I'll stay with her until her family is located?" he asked, coming up to the clerk's desk and leaning one arm across its top. "I promise I'll allow no harm to come to her. No indecent proposals or tricks. I've heard about the swindlers who cheat immigrants with false offers of work or lodging. On my honor, I won't let her be bothered."

Tapping his pen on the desk, the clerk studied Wim as he considered his request. "Why?" he finally asked. "She's no relation to you. What if her parents are never found? What if you're stuck with a girl who doesn't even speak the same language as you do? Why are you making this offer?"

Wim looked over his shoulder and studied Nina as the clerk had studied him. She was balanced on the balls of her feet, her eyebrows knit together again, her full red lips pursed in concentration. Shrugging as if he weren't sure himself what had prompted his promise, Wim turned back to the clerk. "Because she deserves to be in America," he said. "She deserves to have her dreams come true."

The clerk considered a moment longer, then he shrugged, too. He'd already processed scores of immigrants today, and he was faced with the prospect of processing scores more before he could go home. "I'm making you her official guardian," he warned, writing Wim's name on Nina's papers. Then he stamped them, signed them, and shoved them across the desk without further looking up.

Wim grabbed the documents and Nina's hand, pulling her, surprised, from the hall. They squeezed past lines of people waiting to buy train tickets, and past more lines of people waiting to reclaim luggage from customs. Right by the exit another group milled, these people waiting to meet relatives arriving from the Old World. As Wim led her by them, Nina examined the faces, but saw neither Zia Gabriella, nor Zio Sergio, nor any of her cousins. The next minute they stepped out the door and into America.

It was still gray and cold, and the sound of a dozen different languages still reverberated as immigrant families wrestled with trunks or made deals with drivers of hacks. But the imposing profile of New York City loomed in front of them and a sense of excitement filled the raw air. Already thrilled by the feeling of Wim's hand gripping her wrist, this view of her new home sent a shiver down Nina's spine. *"O che bello!"* she cried.

"What?" Wim said, dropping her hand and looking where she gazed. "Beautiful, did you say?" he asked, eyeing the landfill that linked Castle Garden to Battery Park. Carriages laden with luggage trundled across the barren stretch of earth and wound down roads, past leafless trees.

"Your sight must be better than mine," he said, a smile poking a crease in his cheek. "It doesn't appear so very beautiful to me. In fact, America looks no different than anywhere else on a dismal November day. No fountains of youth and beauty. No streets paved in gold."

"Gold?" Nina asked, trying out a new English word.

"Gold," Wim repeated, his smile deepening. Because despite his professed disappointment, he was excited, too. "No streets paved in gold." He toed the packed earth in illustration.

"Ah." Nina bent to scrape a few crumbs of soil into her hand. "Gold," she said with a nod of satisfaction.

Wim laughed and waved a finger. "No, no," he said. "Now I've misled you. I certainly didn't mean to. This isn't gold. It's ordinary dirt."

"Gold," Nina said again, happily picking the word out of his speech.

"No." Wim was still laughing. "Not gold . . . Oh!" he cried as a sudden spatter of rain interrupted him. Grabbing her hand again, he led her back inside the fortress, steering her through the crowds to an empty spot in the waiting room.

As the hours passed, Wim whiled away the time by continuing the English lessons, pleased that Nina was such an apt pupil. Not only did she have a quick mind, she wasn't too shy or embarrassed to attempt the peculiar words, giving her hearty laugh when they spilled out in an unintelligible garble.

"I am 'ungry," she stumbled as the last bit of November light faded from the small windows in the fort. Though still glowing with excitement, she was a little light-headed from the hunger she was trying to express and from increasing fatigue.

"I am *hungry*," Wim corrected, slumping against the wall. He was growing weary, too.

"I am hun—" she started to repeat when something else caught her attention. "Mamma!" she cried, her whole face lighting up. "Papà!" In an instant she raced across the hall into the middle of her family, where arms hugged and hands flew and nine voices shouted at once.

"*Grazie alla Madonna Santa!*" her mother exclaimed, grasping Nina tightly around the neck. Her youngest sister, a toddler, yanked on her skirt, chanting, "Nina! Nina! Nina!"

"*Porca miseria!*" her father boomed, thumping her on the back. "*Dove sei andata?*"

Laughing giddily, her face flushed, her pulse pounding with a relief more profound than she'd ever felt, Nina tried to explain what had happened. While one hand held on to Serafina, the other fluttered in description. It wove around her head as she told her family about the hatful of violets, and it clutched her heart as she recounted her dismay at finding them missing. When she got to the part about Wim, she flung it from her, turning to indicate her rescuer.

She spun so quickly, she caught him in an unguarded moment. Standing a few feet away, his pack once again over his shoulder, and her bundle in his arms, there was an expression on his face that looked oddly like longing. It surprised her, but when she blinked, it was gone, his crooked smile filling his face with amusement, instead.

Not certain she'd actually seen that flicker of yearning, she turned back to introduce him to her family. And was even more surprised by the reaction she saw. Each and every one of them was regarding Wim with suspicion. Nor did it disappear when she blinked. Not even after she said, "Papà, *ti presento* Wim de Groot," and once again explained Wim's gallantry.

It didn't fade when Wim shook Orazio's hand and said, "How do you do, sir?" Or when he bowed to Angelina, or when he recited, "Lucia, Serafina, Bianca Maria, Benedetta, Rossana, and Maria Stella," correctly identifying the stepping-stone sisters. Despite his perfect manners, despite his fairness and charm, all eight Colangelos remained remote and cool, steeped in an age-old distrust of strangers.

Their suspicion jarred Nina to her core. It was the first time in her life she'd had a different viewpoint than her family's. It was the first time she'd ever stepped into the world on her own. It was a momentous step, she suddenly realized, and one that set her in front of her parents and sisters as they began the long and precarious process of making this new country their home.

"You see? I told you we'd find your family again," Wim said, interrupting her thoughts. She looked at him, astonished by this turn of events. "And now that you're safely reunited, I must wish you good luck and say good-bye."

"Good-bye?" Nina echoed, her astonishment turning into confusion. Did she understand the word right?

"Yes," Wim answered. "You have your family to gather you up, and I have my fortune to find. I've very much enjoyed our day together, but now we must go our own ways." His face sober and grave, he held out her bundle.

Even after her hours of English lessons, Nina had no idea what he'd said. The outthrust bundle spoke plainly enough, however. He was leaving.

"Good-bye, Nina," he said.

Her breath was suddenly tight in her chest as she took the bundle from him. "Good-bye, Wim," she responded in a voice barely above a whisper. "Thank you." She searched around in her mind for something else to say, some way to express her appreciation for his help. "You am good," she said more strongly.

The crooked smile leapt to his face. "You am, too," he said. Then he added, "Fix your hairpins. They're about to fall out, again.'' When her eyebrows knit together, he patted his own blond head, then pointed to hers.

Nodding, she bent her head and fumbled with the waves of dark hair. When she looked up, Wim was disappearing through the wide doors. A gasp rose up in her throat, and an icy sense of loss stabbed her heart. She was about to race after him, about to stop him from going. She put a foot forward. Then glanced at her family. They were staring at her, astounded. And not entirely approving.

For a moment, Nina hesitated. Then she pulled her foot back and reentered the circle of her sisters. Tossing her head, she told herself to forget about Wim. He had been kind to her, but he was a stranger. Not one of them. Not like her family. He was just someone who had passed through her life. As she joined in the happy chatter, though, she remembered her first sight of him. She remembered looking up from the seeds spilled on the floor and into the bluest eyes she'd ever seen. That image was frozen in her mind. For her, it was America.

2

Stamford, Connecticut
April 1895

"*Andiamo*, Nina!" Orazio urged, hurrying into the kitchen and pulling on his worn wool smock as he went. "Let's go! It's nearly seven o'clock, and you know that the Horticultural Society is expected at noon. On a nice day like this, they're bound to take a turn around the gardens before going in for lunch. We'll never get everything done if we fritter the morning away in here."

"*Si*, Papà," Nina responded, jumping up from the breakfast table, her toast in one hand, her cup of *caffè latte* in the other. Normally speaking, her father was a mild-tempered man, who requested nothing more from life than good food, the affection of his wife, and an occasional feast day filled with laughter, music, and wine. Today, however, he was plainly agitated.

Small and wiry, Orazio had the weather-beaten face of a man who'd worked outdoors all his life. And although it usually bore a genial expression, that expression was hidden by a bristling black mustache below his nose and bristling black eyebrows above it. Now, as he outlined the day's chores, those eyebrows worked up and down. "You'd better take the shears and trim the boxwood along the front walk—" he began.

"I did that last week," Nina interrupted him through a mouthful of toast.

"Do it again!" Orazio ordered, a scowl pulling at his mustache, too. "At this time of year the hedges are putting out new growth. The fresh shoots popping up look like four-day-old stubble. Mr. Blackwell wants them clipped as smooth as if they'd been to the barber." He patted his own lean cheek, scraped clean only minutes before.

"*Si,* Papà," Nina said without further protest as she jammed the last bite of toast into her mouth.

"Next I want you to go through the daffodil beds and deadhead. Some of those early doubles are looking brown at the edges. Mr. Blackwell doesn't want to see any flowers in his gardens that have gone past. Cut them out."

"*Si,* Papà," Nina said again, not bothering to remind him that she'd done that yesterday afternoon. That, in fact, she always kept up with it. She didn't like dead flowers, either.

Orazio rubbed his forehead. "Then I want you to come help me with the planters on the library terrace," he said. "They're all prepared and I'll carry them out from the greenhouse, but you'll do better at arranging them than I will. Mr. Blackwell trusts you."

This time Nina didn't respond, partly because she was gulping her coffee, but mostly because she knew it was true, and she didn't want to appear to undermine her father.

"I don't know what's gotten into him, lately," Orazio lamented, shaking his head. "He's impossible to please these days. Nothing is right. This coming November it'll be eight years that I've been his groundskeeper. Eight years since he found us at the Labor Exchange in Castle Garden. *Eight years!*" He shook eight fingers in the air. "In all that time there have never been any complaints. Well," he amended with a deep shrug, "not many.

Nothing to speak of, anyway. Certainly not like now. Now everything is wrong.''

Rubbing his forehead again, he muttered, "If I cut the grass, he wants it long. If I leave it long, he wants it cut. When I prune the grapes, he tells me I've cut them too much. Imagine. He tells me, Orazio Colangelo, who was practically born in a vineyard, how to prune grapevines.''

"Fff," Angelina scoffed, sweeping into the kitchen behind her husband. "The fault isn't your work. It's with Mr. Blackwell, himself. Ever since he retired at Christmastime, he's been like a wounded bear, growling at everyone who crosses his path." She settled into a kitchen chair, picked up a knife, and made a decisive slice through the currant-studded sweet bread that Benedetta had just pulled from the oven.

Larger than her husband, Angelina was an imposing woman with handsome, bold features and jet-black hair just beginning to show a few strands of gray. Her big coral drop earrings trembled with authority as she pointed the knife at Nina and said, "As for you, young woman, you'll ruin your digestion if you shove food into your mouth like that. Sit down and eat your breakfast like a civilized person.''

Nina sat.

"*O Dio!*" Orazio exclaimed as another thought struck him. "What if *il padrone* takes his guests through the new greenhouse?" He started massaging his temples. "The heat was left too high at night, and all the seedlings of the south bench are leggy. He'll be furious." Almost to himself, he muttered, "The only thing to do now is to dump them in the compost heap, then start new ones this afternoon after everyone has gone. *Mannaggia la miseria.*" He stopped massaging and clutched his head with both hands. "There's not enough time to do it all. We don't have enough help.

"Nina, never mind the boxwood hedge," he directed, peering at her around his fingers. "You did that last week. Take care of the seedlings instead. And clean up the greenhouse while you're at it. It looks like the *sirocco* blew around inside.''

"It looks like a working greenhouse," Nina said, finally objecting. The greenhouse was one of her favorite haunts. "Like a place where plants are being started for the summer gardens. And I don't think you should throw away the seedlings, Papà. They're perfectly healthy, they're just a little tall. When we set them out, we can dig them in deeper. They'll be fine. Otherwise," she added, "all those flowers will be three weeks late."

"Otherwise," Orazio corrected, "Mr. Blackwell will tear my head off. If he sees those seedlings, he'll turn purple with anger."

"No, he won't," Nina disagreed, though there wasn't a lot of conviction in her tone. "Mamma's right," she went on in a stronger voice. "It's not our work that's making Don Alberto so irritable. It's his retirement. He's beside himself with boredom.

"The New York Wool Company was his life," she said, leaning across the table to make her point. "It completely occupied his attention from the day he started it with a few bales of wool forty years ago, to the day he turned the huge brokerage over to his sons last December. Business was his only interest."

"That's not entirely true," Lucia said from the other side of the table. She seemed unmoved by their employer's sad fate. Feature for feature, she was the sister who most resembled Angelina. Nor did she seek to disguise the similarity, combing her black hair into a tight twist like her mother's and imitating the stately set of Angelina's shoulders.

"He has one other interest," she said, lifting her coffee cup with imagined majesty. "His gardens." She paused and looked around to assess the impact of her declaration. When she saw her family regarding her impatiently and Bianca Maria on the verge of speech, Lucia hurriedly forestalled her.

"Ever since you started filling his ear, Nina, he's been as besotted about plants as you." Her tone was crosser now. "You two always have your heads together, talking about gardens this and flowers that. You're as thick as thieves. Although," she said as an aside, "I don't know how you tolerate his grouchiness. Maybe his retirement is making him more unreasonable, but he was hardly a saint before. He'd come out from New York on the weekends and throw us all into a tizzy."

"He's always frightened me half to death," Rossana agreed. With a sallow complexion and adolescent awkwardness, she was the plainest of the sisters. Whereas Lucia's wide face was smooth and attractive, Rossana's were merely blunt. "Whenever he looks my way, I think he's going to holler at me." She gave an exaggerated shudder.

With an impatient gesture Lucia acknowledged Rossana's comment and returned to her original thought. "He's become obsessed with gardening," she accused. "Every time I turn around, you and Don Alberto have planted a new garden."

Sitting up straighter, Lucia sniffed. "You might think of poor Papà, occasionally," she said, pointing at Orazio, who was massaging his temples again. "You've created ten times more work for him."

Having heard this accusation any number of times before, Nina ignored it in favor of a snatched slice of sweet bread. Serafina, however, piped up in her defense. "Nina does her share of the extra work," she said loyally. "She helps Papà every day. And don't forget, Lucia, that when we first arrived, the Big House was barely a year old and ours was only half complete. The estate wasn't finished yet. It *needed* gardens and landscaping." She gestured out the window. "I think they've done a magnificent job," she said. "As many drawings as I've made, I always find something new to sketch."

Small and slender like Orazio, Serafina was almost delicately pretty. Her dark hair tended toward curly, and tiny tendrils of it escaped from her coil of braids to fluff against her face. Although her expression seemed shy and sweet, there was a keen light in her large brown eyes. As well as obvious admiration for her oldest sister. "Imagine what it would be like for Don Alberto if Nina hadn't aroused his passion for gardening," she said. "The poor man would be totally bereft in his retirement. No friend to talk to and nothing to talk about."

Lucia's answering shrug fully expressed her lack of sympathy. "He's a mean, grumpy old man who doesn't deserve any better," she said. "'If you sow bad seed, your crops will wither,'" she added, repeating an old proverb and thunking down her cup for emphasis. It seemed to be the signal for all the sisters to pile into the argument.

Round, jolly Benedetta, who had inherited her father's slight height, but her mother's ample width, disagreed. "Maybe the don is a little bit gruff," she said, disregarding Lucia's snort. "But I think he's been very good to our family. Remember, he hired Papà the day we arrived in this country. Before he could speak one word of English. And he's given us this wonderful house to live in. A house with *three* bedrooms and indoor plumbing." She paused to let the full force of that opulence sink in. "To say nothing of a big, warm kitchen with a superb stove." From her usual position, not far from its oven, Benedetta flicked her pot holder at the huge

Glenwood. "It's not like that dismal stone cottage *il padrone* gave us at Castel'Greco."

"Yes, but he's so *scary*," Rossana insisted, stirring a heaping spoonful of sugar into her coffee. "I remember when I was playing with my dolls once, in the orangery, he came running in, waving his arms at me and yelling, 'Shoo! Shoo!'" She waved her own arms above her head in demonstration, and the spoon she was still holding splashed a drop of *caffè latte* on the tablecloth. Guiltily she rubbed it with her forefinger.

"On the other hand," Benedetta countered, "when Maria Stella was playing in the big maple by the front drive last summer, and fell off the limb and broke her wrist, Don Alberto brought her to the doctor and paid for the visit. The best doctor in Stamford, too."

Maria Stella nodded vigorously, her thick black braids sliding up and down on her back. "It healed perfectly," she told her family, holding up her wrist for inspection. "Don Alberto even bought me an ice cream afterward. He said it was a bribe so I wouldn't whimper on the way home." Her round cheeks bunched in a smile. "I didn't, either," she said proudly.

"I don't know how you can call him that," Rossana said, with another shudder.

"Call him what?" Maria Stella was puzzled.

"Don Alberto." Rossana pronounced the name gingerly.

"That was Nina's idea," Lucia broke in, her voice full of scorn. "She started it years ago. As if he were a real Italian don." She snorted again.

"Exactly," Rossana agreed. "We should call him Mr. Blackwell."

"No, Nina's right," Serafina quickly spoke up. "'Mr. Blackwell' doesn't sound friendly enough. And it wouldn't be respectful to call him Albert. 'Don Alberto' is nice."

"Nice." Lucia spat the word out. "Ha!"

"Well," Bianca Maria said, entering the discussion for the first time. "It was certainly nice of him to buy all of us those challis shawls last Christmas. They're the most beautiful ones we've ever owned." Just the opposite of Benedetta, Bianca Maria had inherited her mother's height, but her father's slender build. Artful curls of hair, faithfully copied from the illustrations in *Harper's Bazaar*, framed a finely shaped face, fresh with her youth.

Lucia gave a grudging shrug. "He took Nina with him," she

muttered, sweeping a few crumbs off the table with her finger. "She picked them out."

Bianca Maria shrugged, too. "He didn't have to do it," she reminded her sister. "Nor did he have to buy such elegant ones. Although," she added with more resentment, "stuck way out here between the dairy farms and the hayfields, we never have the chance to wear them."

Her clear brow clouded and her pretty mouth turned down in a pout as she shoved her empty plate out of the way and leaned her arms on the table in their place. "We never see anyone," she complained. "No other people our age." She didn't say so, but everyone knew she was specifically referring to young men. "We never go anywhere, either," she went on. "We rarely even go to church on Sunday, because all the Catholic churches in Stamford are Irish. I swear, we're going to grow old and die among the cows without ever having any fun."

Forgetting her defense of him only seconds before, Bianca Maria now griped, "Whatever possessed Don Alberto to build his country home in the middle of nowhere? All the other fashionable homes are on Strawberry Hill, or, better yet, on Atlantic Avenue, in town. Why did he have to decide to put his estate miles away?"

"Just to be contrary," Lucia answered promptly, sitting up straight once more. "And to annoy his two sons. Next to business and gardening, the thing he loves most in life is annoying his sons." She reached for the coffeepot and poured the last few drops into her cup. "It's the same reason he accepts the invitation whenever Nina invites him to come for Sunday dinner, you know," she said as she reached for the pitcher of hot milk and wrung out its last few drops, too. "He enjoys the shock he's creating by dining with the gardener's family." Her voice quavered with indignation.

"*Basta!*" Angelina ordered, slapping her hand on the table. "That's enough of that sort of talk. You should be glad he decided to put his estate out here. If he had a house in town, with a tiny yard, there'd be no work for your papà. Besides, Mr. Blackwell is *il padrone*. He's entitled to build his home wherever he chooses, and for whatever reasons. It's impertinent for you to criticize him." After a pause she added, "It's also bad luck." Then she crossed herself to ward off any evil spirits her daughters might have evoked.

Lucia opened her mouth to object, but was cut off before she could speak by her mother's magisterial glare. "Another thing I'll have you know, miss," Angelina said. "Mr. Blackwell comes to dinner on Sundays because he likes my cooking. He knows he'll always get a good meal here." Lucia closed her mouth.

Taking advantage of the silence that followed, Orazio spoke again. "Let's go, Nina," he urged as he had before. "The morning's slipping away, and you're sitting here drinking coffee and eating cake."

Retracting the hand that was creeping toward the sweet bread, Nina jumped up for the second time. "*Sì*, Papà," she said, racing around the table and grabbing her smock off its peg by the door. "I'm ready."

"This isn't right, Orazio," Angelina warned, shifting her body in her chair, along with the focus of her attack.

"What isn't?" Orazio asked with the air of one who knew the answer. He edged away from the table.

Warmed up by the squabble that had just taken place, Angelina wasn't easily put off. "Don't pretend you don't understand what I'm talking about," she said, her earrings bobbing dangerously. "I'm talking about Nina. She shouldn't be treated like a hired laborer. It's one thing for her to help out in the greenhouse, occasionally, or to do some hoeing in the kitchen garden. But it's quite another matter for her to do garden work on a regular basis. She's a grown woman, after all." Her finger jabbing the air, she delivered her parting salvo. "She should be married and raising babies. Not sweet peas."

"*Bè*, Angelina, *ciccina*," Orazio responded, both his shoulders and his fierce eyebrows lifting. "Not now. *Mannaggia*. The Horticultural Society is going to be here at noon." He spread out his hands.

Angelina spread out her hands, too. "And your daughter is going to be twenty-four years old next month," she retorted.

Orazio tossed his hands in the air, his eyes rolling skyward.

For her part, Nina very carefully slipped her smock over her head, as if by her slight movements she would avoid her mother's notice. It was a fine April morning. She couldn't bear the thought of being trapped inside. Holding her breath, she crept toward the door.

"Am I talking to the air?" came Angelina's stinging question, stopping Nina where she stood. "To the walls? To the table?" Her fist pounded down on it, making the plates and cups rattle.

Nina's shoulders rose as her father's had. "Mamma," she said, turning toward her mother, "The Horticultural Society . . ."

"The Horticultural Society," Angelina repeated in scorn. "Today it's the Horticultural Society. Yesterday it was feeding the orchids in the solarium. The day before that the broccoli seedlings needed to be set in the ground. *Madonna mia,* Nina!" she cried, clasping her hands beneath her chin and shaking them hard. "Do you mean to spend the rest of your life digging in the dirt? Don't you *want* to get married?"

Shifting from foot to foot, Nina shrugged. "I like digging in the dirt," she began. When her mother sucked in her breath, however, Nina went no further. She fumbled with her hairpins while she tried to decide what to say next. "I like living here," she said finally, her eyes wide with sincerity. "With all of you. You're my family."

"Nina, *bambina.*" Angelina's head fell to one side in despair. A coral earring grazed the shoulder of her black muslin dress. "It's time for you to have your own house. And your own family. It's time for you to get married."

"Who am I going to marry, Mamma?" Nina shot back, wildly seizing Bianca Maria's complaint. Her throat felt tight. "We never go anywhere or meet anyone. The only young men I know are the stable lads. And they're *English*. You know you'd throw me out in the street if I married a foreigner."

"Of course not them." Angelina was appalled. "But you could find a nice Sicilian *ragazzo,* if you put your mind to it. What about that Carmelo di Pasquale who works at Mr. Rossi's grocery? I noticed that he waited on you ahead of Mrs. Mangano the last time we were in."

Nina's eyes shut as she tried to imagine living above Mr. Rossi's grocery with the squat, hairy Carmelo di Pasquale. Of spending all day, every day, in a tiny apartment, washing and ironing and scrubbing the floors. Of serving him his meals. Of darning his socks. Of crawling into his bed at night. Her eyes flew open as cold horror welled up in her throat.

"He seems like a steady boy," Angelina coaxed. "He works hard and Mr. Rossi told me he's very thrifty."

"That means cheap," Bianca Maria scoffed. "He's the type who would rather shiver all winter than spend money on coal." She fluffed the curls around her face. "He's also ugly and dull," she added. "Marriage to him would be worse than being in jail. *I* would never do it."

Nina nearly gasped with relief. "Neither would I," she seconded, immensely grateful for her sister's unwitting support. "Bianca's right. He's not very generous. If you don't watch him carefully, he'll try to give you short weight. And it's not even his money at stake."

"Besides, he's mean," Maria Stella spoke up. "He once slapped my finger because I was touching a bolt of silk that was lying on the counter. I only wanted to see if it felt as smooth as it looked," she explained.

Flashing her youngest sister a smile, Nina said, "You see, Mamma? He's no good."

Angelina sighed. "All right. He's no good," she conceded, dismissing Carmelo with a wave of her hand. "But there are others," she insisted. "If you really wanted to, you would have a husband. When I was twenty-four, I was married with three babies. And Serafina was on the way."

Another silence followed that remark as they remembered who the three babies were. Nina, Flavio, and Lucia. Flavio. The son. He had caught a chill during his third winter in the damp stone cottage and had died before spring.

"Hurry up, Nina," Orazio said, finally breaking the silence. His voice was no longer entreating, but grim and harsh. "There's work to be done. If I have only daughters, then a daughter must help me do it."

Wringing her hands, Nina glanced at her mother. Angelina nodded. "Go, *bambina*," she said softly. "Go help your father." Nina went.

As she closed the door behind her, she could hear Serafina saying, "Anyway, in America, girls don't get married so young. They wait until they're in their twenties."

"Perhaps." Lucia's tart rebuttal floated across the porch. "But we aren't Americans. We're Sicilians."

3

"Aha!" a voice barked. "I knew I'd catch you up to something."

On her knees by a stone wall, attacking the weeds and grass in an overgrown bed, Nina looked up, unalarmed. A bandy-legged man in his seventies was approaching her across the broad lawn. He walked aggressively, with his head and shoulders thrust forward, a combative look on his face. As he came nearer, it was easier to see the baggy pouches beneath his unsentimental brown eyes and the baggy jowls under his stubborn chin.

"Good morning, Don Alberto," she called back, waving her trowel. There was a musical accent to her clear speech.

"What the devil are you doing now?" Don Alberto demanded, coming to a halt in front of Nina and ignoring her greeting. "For God's sake, girl, you know damned well the Horticultural Society is due for lunch in an hour. That bunch of purse-lipped women and rheumy-eyed old men is going to be poking its noses around every square inch of these grounds. I can just imagine what snippy remarks they're going to make when they come across this bed all chewed up, with nothing but lumpy topsoil for show."

As he ranted, Don Alberto continued to lean over Nina, his body as belligerent as his words. With hardly a break in her quick, sure rhythm, though, Nina went on weeding, calmly listening to his tirade. "What were you thinking of?" he groused, rubbing his thin chest. "Why did you have to rip this open today, of all days? We could've gotten away with the weeds that were there. Up against that wall they looked . . ." He paused, searching for the appropriate Garden Club term. "Oh, so pastoral," he finished in a mocking falsetto.

"Good God, Nina," he went on bitterly, kicking the exposed earth, "why are you making this mess instead of smartening up the terrace? They'll all be standing around in the library after lunch, drinking those prissy little cups of coffee. If they saw one of your spectacular displays out the French doors, it would make their double chins drop.''

"Papà and I did the terrace first thing," Nina responded, banging her trowel against the root end of a clump of weeds to knock out the loose dirt. "The tall urns are crammed full of white azaleas and forsythia, and I grouped dozens of cachepots of purple primula and Lord Beaconsfield pansies at their bases." Tossing the spent weed into the wheelbarrow, she sketched a descriptive circle with her trowel.

"The long planter is filled with grape hyacinths," she went on, plunging her trowel back into the ground, "and with white and yellow Hoop Petticoats—the dwarf narcissus." She yanked a weed from the soil and beat it as she had the last one. "We also set out a few tubs each of white heather and Mme. de Graf daffodils, and Papà brought a pair of topiary trees from the orangery." Sitting back on her heels, she considered a moment. "It looks lovely," she decided, satisfaction lighting her face. "I don't think your guests will be disappointed."

Don Alberto absorbed her words greedily, then nodded his head. "Good, good," he approved. "I'll bet it looks ten times more impressive than Mrs. Palmer's terrace did at lunch last week. All she had were some urns of ivy and a few pots of lilies," he said with derision. The strong sense of competition that had served Don Alberto so well in business carried over into every aspect of his life. "This'll show up Mrs. Palmer and her gardener for the unimaginative dabblers that they are." He gave a cackle of laughter. "You did it again, Nina," he congratulated her. "I can always count on you."

The next moment, though, he remembered the bed in front of him and the glower returned to his face. "You may have a talent for plants," he said, the annoyance back in his voice, "but I sometimes wonder about your sense. What was going through your head to make you tear this up now?" Rubbing his chest again, he complained, "It's just an ugly strip of dirt."

That made Nina rock back on her heels for the second time. "Dirt is not ugly," she said. "It gives life to everything that grows." She wagged her trowel at him. "If your guests are really gardeners, they'll understand that and agree," she told him. "The earth *should* be visible now. "You *should* be able to see it, rich and moist and full of worms. You should be able to smell it, too."

Snatching up a handful, she held it to her nose and took a blissful sniff. "Ahh," she sighed. "Springtime."

"For God's sake, Nina," Don Alberto warned. "Theatrics aren't going to make up for your wretched mistake. You should have waited until after lunch to start this."

"No," Nina protested. "It's not just theatrics. The soil is precious." A softer note crept into her tone as she added, "When I first came to America, I thought the word for dirt was *gold*." Raking her fingers through the bed, she looked down, seemingly watching the small furrows she was making, but actually seeing a fair young man laughing in her mind. She shook her head to get rid of the old image. "Maybe the word is wrong," she said, "but the meaning isn't."

"What nonsense!" Don Alberto jeered. "What romantic piffle. We've always gotten along, you and I, Nina, because you're as bright as a new penny and you don't affect any of those silly notions or vaporish airs most females favor. So don't get goose-brained on me now. Dirt is dirt." He rubbed his chest harder.

"And don't think I've forgotten that gold business," he continued, disgusted. "Someone planted that idea in you so deeply, it took me weeks to root it out." He shook his head, too, also clearing out an old memory. "I never could understand why you had such trouble with that word when you picked up English as easily as you did. I only had to say something to you once or twice and you would repeat it back letter perfect. Retain it, too." He shook his head again.

"Not like the rest of your family," he growled. "I still can't make your father comprehend more than half of what I'm saying. Orazio's a good worker, and he's got a farmer's respect for the land, but I tell you, Nina, if you weren't around to translate, I don't know how we'd get anything done."

He stopped rubbing and wrapped his arms around his chest instead. "Normally speaking," he added, "I'd also say that if you weren't around to make suggestions, the grounds would be as boring as Mrs. Palmer's terrace. But after this disaster"—he stabbed his toe into the offending soil again—"I don't know what to think."

Nina's head had remained bent throughout Don Alberto's latest outburst, not because of embarrassment or modesty, but because of the odd ache in her heart. After all these years, she still felt a sad twinge of loss when she thought about the "someone" who had planted the wrong word on her tongue. Wim. Now that she was finally able to understand him, he was gone forever, leaving only his name on her immigration papers. And a vivid picture of him in her mind.

When Don Alberto turned his ill temper back to the bed, however, Nina's head lifted. "This is not a disaster," she said, tapping her trowel on the ground for emphasis. "This is the beginning of a beautiful garden. One that will twist through the rhododendrons and brambles that are already scattered on either side of the wall and add bright splashes of color all summer long. It'll make a lovely first impression as you drive up Newfield Avenue. Besides which," she said, with a final jab of the trowel, "it will look far more pastoral than these dreary weeds."

Don Alberto peered at her. "Oh?" he said, his curiosity temporarily overcoming his querulousness.

"Yes," Nina answered. "You're going to like it, I know. It's not going to be too fussy or formal, which would drive you into a rage. Just the opposite. The bed will seem almost as if it had sprung up on its own."

"Maybe," Don Alberto said, his fingers drumming on his crossed arms. "Why don't you tell me what this masterpiece is going to be, so I can decide for myself whether or not I like it."

Unaffected by his sarcastic tone, Nina launched into an explanation. "When I went outside this morning," she said, "the sky was just the shade of blue that it is in Sicily in the springtime. The air smelled the same, too. Sweet and sunny, with a background hint of hayfields being plowed." She closed her eyes and took a deep breath to catch the tantalizing scents.

"Yes, yes! Get to the point, Nina!"

"I am," she soothed. "In April and May, you see, there are stone walls in the field around the castle that are practically blanketed in wildflowers. Vines of white morning glories climb up their sides, and clusters of pink valerian have taken root in the cracks between the stones. Then there are clumps of purple nettles and bunches of scabiosa, whose tall, skinny stems and lavender pompons sway in the breeze."

As she talked, the trowel wove through the air, and her face, always animated, seemed even more alive. The softness of her childhood had long since fallen away to reveal a compelling beauty. She was an immensely appealing woman with a noble nose and strong, round limbs, a woman whose full, lush lips parted readily in laughter and whose wide, amber-colored eyes shone with delight. Though striking and graceful, she could never be considered pretty. She was too vibrant. Her attraction was an almost palpable force.

"So you want to re-create that planting here?" Don Alberto interrupted again. But more eagerly this time. And his expression was avid, as it had been when he'd listened to her description of the terrace display.

"Almost," Nina answered, rising up on her knees, her enthusiasm further aroused by Don Alberto's interest. "I'm going to train morning glory vines along the wall, and I'm going to set out some perennial scabiosa, but I'll substitute for the nettles. They bloom quickly and are gone," she explained, her fingers whisking away in demonstration. "We want something that will make a show all summer."

"Salvia farinacea!" Don Alberto pounced. "That deep blue flowering sage we got from Miss Lippincott's Seed Company. The one you always put in the library garden. It blooms until frost. Eh, Nina?"

"Yes, that would be effective," Nina agreed. "Although I was thinking of Emperor William bachelor's buttons. They stay until frost, too, and the flower has a more nettle-like look. Besides, it's taller. The scale is better."

"Good, good." Don Alberto's head bounced up and down. "Now, what about the valerian? What will you do for that?"

"We have an enormous patch of it by the side of our house," Nina said happily. "It needs dividing, anyway. I'll move it over here."

"That's right." Don Alberto smacked his forehead as his memory was jogged. "I always meant to ask you about that patch. Where did you get the plants? I've never seen that color before."

"I brought the seeds with me from Sicily," Nina replied, suddenly more subdued. She remembered those tiny seeds as they lay strewn across the floor of Castle Garden, and the long, strong fingers that helped her scrape them into a pile. A tingle went down her back as she remembered looking up. And into the bluest eyes she'd ever seen.

"You're incorrigible, Nina." Don Alberto chuckled, intruding on her thoughts. "I think you were born with flowers in your veins where the blood is supposed to go."

Pushing away the memory, Nina gave him a smile. "I wish that were so," she said. "I'd much prefer to bleed rosebuds when I cut myself."

"Not rosebuds," Don Alberto corrected. "Valerian."

His eyes raced back and forth, seeing the new plantings in place. "This is going to be a corker," he decided. "Wait until the Horticultural Society casts its beady eyes on this." He chuckled again, though it was a less humorous sound this time. "My turn comes up next in July. Won't they be stunned when we take our post-luncheon stroll along here! A Sicilian pasture. Ha! They'll be struck dumb," he gloated. "This'll stand them on their collective ear."

"Yes, it'll look nice this summer," Nina said, still smiling. "Although it'll look even more beautiful next summer. You know how it takes at least a year for perennials to establish themselves and fill in."

The gleeful smirk vanished from Don Alberto's face. "At least a year?" he repeated. "Do you mean to say you've made this hideous gash across the very front of my property and it won't even be healed over this summer? That every person who comes here for the next *year* is going to be greeted by this eyesore?" He pointed his finger at Nina and shook it furiously. "What the devil is wrong with you, Nina?"

"Nothing is wrong with me!" Nina shouted, her patience finally snapping. She shoved her trowel into the ground and jumped to her feet. "*You* are the one who's being outrageous." Then, with an effort, she lowered her voice, though her tone remained vexed as she told him, "You should be ashamed of yourself. Your behavior lately has been unforgivable."

"What?" Don Alberto shrieked, rubbing his chest again. "What are you saying?"

Nina's attempt at restraint ended abruptly. "I'm saying," she yelled, "that you've been impossible ever since you retired! You've been rude and unpleasant for no reason at all, scolding everyone who works here for completely imagined mistakes. Mamma says the cook is ready to quit, and the maids are driven nearly to tears. If you go on like this, you'll find yourself with no staff at all."

Punching the air with his clenched fist, Don Alberto screamed, "I've half a mind to fire them all, anyway. They're a lazy and incompetent gang of layabouts. The only thing they know how to do is gossip and complain." The bags under his eyes puffed angrily and the jowls under his chin shook. "You can tell your mamma to let them know I mean to boot the whole lot out the door if they don't pull themselves together. I'll hire some people who don't mind working."

Nina jammed her hands on her hips and glared at him. "You already have people who don't mind working," she snapped. "But you simply won't be pleased. Nor will you be satisfied with anyone else that you hire if you don't change your ways. You're bored silly, and you don't know what to do with your time but find fault with everyone you employ."

"I can give you the sack, too, you know," Don Alberto threatened, wrapping his arms tightly across his chest. "Don't think your tenure here is inviolable."

"I couldn't possibly think that," Nina replied, exasperated. "I don't even know what those words mean. But I do know that you can't fire me, because I've never been hired in the first place. Whatever work I do is to help Papà. And you." She hesitated, then shrugged and admitted, "And because I enjoy it." After another pause, she added more severely, "Except when you act like a cornered hornet."

Hopping from one foot to the other, Don Alberto shouted, "How dare you speak to me like that? And after all I've done for you and your family. It's a scandal, do you hear me? It's a travesty!" He practically spit the invectives at her. "I always knew you were a disrespectful minx," he raved. "Where did you ever learn such cheeky behavior?"

Her own temper cooled as quickly as it had flared, and Nina faced him calmly. Folding her arms across the front of her smock, she replied, "I learned it from you. You're an excellent teacher on this subject."

For a long silent moment it seemed as if Don Alberto would explode. His hard brown eyes bulged and his ears turned bright red. Then his fury suddenly dissolved, and he let out another cackle of laughter. "And you're an excellent student," he said, still chortling. "Too good. You'd be well advised to forget some of those lessons. There aren't too many people besides me who will tolerate such insolence."

"Fff," Nina scoffed, though a smile was spreading across her face. "There aren't too many people besides you who *provoke* such insolence," she told him. "In general, my manners are quite acceptable."

"Yes, I suppose they are," Don Alberto agreed, with another chuckle. "But say, is that true?" he asked. "That I've never hired you, I mean. Or was that something else you learned from me? Bluffing is the oldest trick there is."

"It's true," Nina replied, bending to retrieve her trowel. "Papà is the only Colangelo on your payroll. Though all of us lend a hand in some seasons. Even little Stella helps in the kitchen garden."

"How can that be?" Don Alberto said, almost to himself. He stroked his chin as he considered the surprising situation. "Your sisters might give a few hours now and then, but you do the work of ten people around here."

"Oh, yes," Nina said, raising her hand. "That brings up another point."

Don Alberto groaned.

Ignoring it, Nina continued. "Papà and I do the work of ten people *each*," she said. "And that's only a slight exaggeration. It's no exaggeration at all, though, to say that we can't keep up anymore. It's too much for us to do alone."

With Lucia's breakfast lecture in mind, she told Don Alberto, "It was one thing when we first came here and there were only the lawn and a few hedges to trim, but now that the grounds are so well planted, we need more help. We can't be everywhere at once. In the greenhouse. In the solarium. Powdering the roses. Pulling the weeds in the walk." Her trowel made wild circles in the air. "It's impossible," she concluded.

"We went over this last month," Don Alberto replied, irritation creeping back into his tone. "At your insistence, I hired someone else. Then, a week later, you told me to let him go. Make up your mind, Nina."

"He was an idiot," Nina retorted. "He barely knew which end of a shovel went down. I caught him watering the seed trays with a bucket. Naturally, the force of the pouring water made huge ruts and washed out the seeds. I had to start them all over again." She rubbed the back of her hand across her forehead, still appalled when she remembered the incident.

"Besides which," she added, looking back at the don, "he was Irish. He couldn't understand anything that Papà said, and when I translated, he wouldn't take orders from a woman." She shook her head. "He was no help at all. We need someone with experience."

"So I have to find you a person with a degree in horticulture and fluency in Italian, is that it?" Don Alberto groused. "You like spending my money, don't you, Nina? First you get me to put in all these fancy gardens, then you get me to build two greenhouses so we can stock the gardens, and now you need a trained staff to take care of it all.''

For a moment, Nina was silent with guilt, then she remembered to whom she was talking. There was no one on earth who could manipulate Don Alberto into doing something he didn't want to do. Especially if it involved money. He made the gardens and built the greenhouses because he enjoyed it.

"Don't forget the pansy competition,'' she reminded him, her conscience completely clear. "You're desperate to win the first prize from Miss Lippincott's Seed Company. You know that you admire gardeners who excel. How many times have I heard you talk about Otto Otis Schrock, who developed a red snapdragon and sold the seeds to Burpee? But we can't grow a prizewinning pansy if we don't have enough time to do our regular chores.''

"Now you're resorting to blackmail,'' Don Alberto complained. "I'm surprised you haven't thought of going out on strike. This would be the ideal moment, you know,'' he told her bitterly. "The greenhouses are full of seedlings. I'd be left in the lurch.''

"I have thought of a strike,'' Nina responded, laughing. "I couldn't bring myself to do it, though. I'd feel too sorry for the poor plants.'' Still laughing, she reached out and gave his shoulder an affectionate pat.

"Don't be angry,'' she coaxed as he fixed her a black look. "Mamma always says it's bad for the digestion. Listen. She's making *panelli* tonight. That's one of your favorite dishes. Why don't you come for supper?''

"*Panelli*,'' Don Alberto repeated, squinting. "Which are they?''

"The chickpea fritters.'' With the trowel still in her hand, Nina made a rectangular shape with her fingers to show him. "They get crisp and crunchy on the outside and stay hot and creamy inside. Remember? And Mamma usually makes *salsiccie al ragù* to go with them. You know. Sausages.''

"It doesn't matter what they are,'' Don Alberto said, his voice saturated in self-pity. "I can't come. My two beastly sons have decided to pay me a visit this evening, and they're bringing along their unbearable wives.'' He started rubbing his chest again.

"I can't imagine what motivated them to invite themselves,'' he growled. "They must want something, or they would never make the trek way out here. They never miss an opportunity to whine about how far from 'civilization' my house is. I can't make them understand that that's the whole idea."

"You can come for supper another evening, then," Nina said. "Mamma will make the *panelli* again." She was about to kneel in a renewed assault on the weeds when a grimace twisted the don's face. Looking more carefully, Nina thought that the grim lines around his mouth seemed more deeply etched than usual. And that his pallid skin was a little more ashen. She suddenly realized that it wasn't his habit to rub his chest, either. Shocked that she had been standing there for twenty minutes without noticing his poor coloring and his peculiar behavior, she reached out her hand again. "Don Alberto," she said, "what's the matter? What's wrong?"

In a fresh fit of pique the don pushed her hand away, snapping, "The only thing wrong is your mush-brained decision to tear up my front lawn moments before the Horticultural Society is due for lunch. If this is a ploy for me to hire another gardener, it won't work, Nina. You should know by now that I won't be blackmailed and I won't be bullied."

"*Santo cielo!*" Nina cried, whirling away. She threw her trowel in the dirt and stomped a few feet off, trying in vain to contain her anger. "You're a cranky old man," she accused him, whirling back, her finger wagging in reprimand. Then she stopped. Stunned.

His face deathly pale, his arms gripping his chest, Don Alberto collapsed to the ground, unconscious.

"No," she heard herself whisper, as if from a distance. The world seemed frozen in time. For the longest moment her limbs felt wooden and her breath was stifled in her throat. She was vaguely aware of the stillness on the wide lawn, and of the cloudless canopy of Sicilian-blue sky. Nothing moved.

From the big maple by the drive came the sound of robins chirping, their songs sounding eerie in the silence. Then Nina gasped and heat surged through her body. Her heart started hammering wildly. "Papà!" she screamed, as loudly as she could, praying her voice would carry to her father. "Papà! Papà! *Aiuto!*" Help! she thought, falling to her knees and easing Don Alberto's head into her lap.

Tears were streaming down her face as she stroked his sparse hair and wiped a blade of grass from his haggard cheek. With fumbling fingers, she unsnapped his collar and pulled his jacket across his scrawny chest. Bending over him, she picked up one of his hands. It was ice cold and crabbed like a claw. Sobbing anew, her own head sank until it was touching his and her hot tears soaked his brow. *O Dio,* she thought, pain tearing her heart. What have I done?

=4=

"Harry! Hello!" Wim called, waving at the large, middle-aged man crossing Fourteenth Street toward him.

"Wim! What a surprise!" Harry Beale boomed as he came striding up, the corner of his cashmere overcoat catching in the April breeze, his rubbery lips stretched in a smile. He thrust one gloved hand forward in greeting while the other held on to his top hat.

Clasping the extended hand, Wim said, "It's been so long since I've seen you. Why, it must be several years at least." He shook his head, amazed at how quickly time evaporated.

"Longer than it should have been," Harry agreed, pumping Wim's hand. "Although it's mostly your fault, de Groot," he added, his grin stretching even farther. "If you hadn't given up wholesaling flower and vegetable seeds when you bought the company from your former bosses, I could still be selling you seeds from my cabbage farm. I tell you," he declared, "I've never enjoyed as cordial relations with anyone else I've dealt with in business. And that includes in my manufacturing business here in New York." He nodded in admiration. "You've got a way about you, de Groot," he said. "At such a young age, too. I'll bet you're not even thirty yet."

"I will be in September," Wim replied, a smile stretching across his face, too. It crinkled the corners of his blue eyes and tugged at the clean, square cut of his jaw. "I'll officially cross the threshold of maturity then. Although, in my opinion, it's not how many years I've been alive that counts, but how many years I've been working. And there are quite a few of those."

"Hmph," Harry scoffed, dismissing Wim's claim with a flap of his hand. "There can't be that many. I've known you since you started at Wylie and Becker, which is how many years ago? Four? Five?"

"Seven," Wim answered calmly. "I'd been working in an office across the street when they came to ask my help in translating a letter they'd received from a bulb dealer in Holland. It was at the time when they were just adding spring-blooming bulbs to their seed inventory, and they were a bit unsure of what they were doing. So when they learned I not only spoke Dutch, French, and English, but also knew all about the bulb industry, they doubled my salary and hired me on the spot." He shrugged again and added, "I suppose it wasn't very loyal of me to quit my first job abruptly, but opportunity knocked."

Harry Beale's hand flapped for a second time. "That's business," he assured Wim. "It happens all the time. But I don't have to tell you how it's done. Not after the success you've made of Wylie and Becker."

"W. P. de Groot," Wim corrected as another smile nudged his mouth. The first thing he'd done after signing the papers was to change the name of the company. And almost six years later he could still feel the tremendous surge of pride that had swelled in him when he'd seen his own name on the door.

It was something he'd dreamed about and longed for since the first day he'd started working as a boy. Since the first day he'd been reprimanded for not performing his tasks fast enough. Since the first day he'd followed orders that didn't make sense. He'd always been certain he could run a business better than those who'd hired him. All that he needed was the chance.

"Right, right," Harry apologized, adjusting his top hat against another gust of wind. "It's most decidedly your business now. Though I'll have to admit I was more than slightly doubtful when you decided to give up wholesaling seeds. In fact, I was convinced you were tossing away the strongest element of the firm and concentrating on the weakest. But you've built an excellent reputation wholesaling bulbs. I don't know of anyone with other than praise for your merchandise and service." Giving his hat a final tap on his large head, he acknowledged, "No question, you've proved me wrong."

"Believe me, Harry," Wim said, "it wasn't my intention. I had no wish to prove anything to you." His smile deepened as he added, "Only to myself."

For a moment Harry Beale regarded the man in front of him. Having made a fortune in the shoe industry, Harry could judge both shoes and the person who filled them in an instant. Now he assessed Wim's ankle-high boots. A classic style, but made of the finest calfskin and cared for superbly. Completely in keeping with their wearer, Harry decided, his eyes traveling up Wim's English wool overcoat and coming to rest on his face. The spring breeze ruffled his blond hair, but neither the breeze, nor anything else, seemed to ruffle the steady light in his eyes.

"Well," Harry said, giving Wim a clap on the shoulder, "whatever you were proving, or to whomever you were proving it, it's obvious you made the right choice." Then he shook his head in wonder and said, as he had before, "So young. And just off Ellis Island. I tell you, Wim, it's a remarkable feat for a young immigrant to buy his own business."

Though Wim's expression remained unchanged, he didn't immediately reply. He knew that Harry was fishing for a clue to his success, a gossipy tidbit about his financial backing. But straightforward and honest though Wim might be, it wasn't his nature to divulge personal information. It went against his grain to think of Harry repeating the story of his business coup all over town, no matter how complimentary a light it shone on him.

Simply put, Wim told himself, it wasn't anyone's concern but his own that Wylie & Becker had been near bankruptcy when he'd bought the company, that the old owners had been only too glad to escape from under the burden of their debts—with a small dividend in their pockets to boot. He knew they'd considered him a greenhorn, a pigeon ripe for plucking. But he hadn't let their assessment influence him then, anymore than he was going to let Harry Beale's flattery influence him now. *Ga uw eigen gang,* he thought. Do it your own way.

Out loud, though, he remarked only, "Not Ellis Island, Harry. Castle Garden. It was the port of immigration back then."

"Of course! You're right," Harry smacked his forehead. "I tell you, I forget things faster than I can say them these days. It must be old age. It does something to a man's mind to see his children all grown up. It's—yipes!" Plunging his hand between the buttons of his coat and extracting a big, gold watch, he moaned, "Ten past one. I'm supposed to meet my daughter, Penelope, for lunch at one. Now I'm doomed. She'll look at me with those blue eyes and take me roundly to task.'' He stuffed the watch back under his coat, the picture of despair.

"It's hardly a dire fate," Wim said, laughing. "If I remember correctly, those blue eyes are very pretty."

"Indeed," Harry said proudly. "She's a beauty. Say, de Groot," he added, brightening with an idea. "Why don't you join us? Penelope would be delighted, and so would I. It's just at Luchow's." He pointed down the street. "It won't take you more than five steps out of your way."

"I wish I could," Wim responded. "Unfortunately, I have an appointment myself. It won't be nearly as enjoyable, I'm sure, but I hope it'll be profitable."

"I understand," Harry assured him, holding out his hand again. "I'll let you go, and be off as well, but you must promise you'll come out to our house on Long Island some weekend soon. For pleasure, this time, since my cabbage seeds no longer interest you professionally."

"It's a promise," Wim said, shaking the proffered hand.

Harry Beale bounded away to meet his daughter for lunch, but Wim walked slowly back to his office. In truth, he didn't have an appointment any time that afternoon, but for some reason, he hadn't felt like joining the genial Harry and his lovely daughter. Maybe it was the memories crowding his mind, the images of his childhood in Holland and his years in the United States. The memories of the day he arrived here, with a worn suit, twenty-eight dollars, and tremendous hope. Maybe he just wanted to savor his triumph again, to revel in that burst of pride once more.

Or maybe it was the Italian girl he was thinking of. The one with the flying hands and the animated golden eyes. Nina. The girl whose rich laugh came easily and whose lively emotions illuminated her face. Not for the first time, he wondered what had become of her, how she and her family had fared. He hoped she wasn't trapped in a tenement on Mulberry Street, married, with a brood of small children clutching her skirt. She was too vibrant for a fate like that. Far too full of life.

Wim shrugged again, then straightened his shoulders and took a deep breath. It was a beautiful spring day. The sky was a wonderful shade of blue.

"Nina, *bambina,* you've hardly touched your food," Angelina chided, though her tone was more anxious than scolding, and her large bosom heaved in concern. "You haven't eaten enough to nourish a sparrow," she said, eyeing the chickpea fritters that Nina was pushing around on her plate. "It won't help Mr. Blackwell if you starve yourself, you know. You'll only get weak and worn out and invite a fever. And tell me, please, what sense does it make for you both to be sick?"

"None, Mamma," Nina admitted as she set down her fork and quietly folded her hands in her lap. "I'm sorry. I'm just not very hungry."

If the pile of *panelli* still on the platter was any indication, neither was anyone else. On any other night the fritters would be long gone by now, devoured, along with the sausages in *ragù* and the zesty salad of young dandelion greens, amid talk, laughter, and noisy, but rancorless, arguments. Tonight, however, the atmosphere around the table was subdued. Everyone ate mechanically. And in near silence. Even Lucia was grave.

"*Per carità,* Angelina," Orazio spoke up, his hands and eyebrows both rising. "Don't badger her. She's not going to fall ill if she misses a meal or two. She has no appetite. She's worried about *il padrone.*" He poked at his own dinner, then he, too, set down his fork. "So am I," he added. "He looked terrible when we carried him into the house. Like the angel of death was standing at the foot of his bed."

Angelina crossed herself. "*E va bene,*" she conceded, excusing Nina from the table with a wave of her hand. "Go, *bambina.* Go up to the Big House and see if there's any news."

Nina was on her feet before her mother finished speaking. "I won't be long," she promised, dashing for the door. "I'll just find out how he's feeling, and I'll come right back." Her words were half mumbled, as if she were apologizing for the icy fear knotting her stomach and making it impossible for her to eat.

"Take a lantern," Lucia suggested. "It'll be full dark by the time you return."

"Good idea," Angelina agreed, her earrings bobbing. "And come back in and wrap up," she ordered as Nina took a step out the door. "Once the sun goes down, it still feels wintry."

Nina reached her hand inside and snatched her thick shawl off its hook, convinced as much by the sudden rush of cold air as by her mother's command. "I don't need a lantern, though," she called over her shoulder. "It's a clear night and the moon is nearly full."

Shutting the door behind her, she heard Serafina add, "Besides, Nina could find her way home from there blindfolded."

It was true. She'd gone between the Big House and the grounds-keeper's cottage hundreds of times, and not just to arrange pots of pansies on the terrace, either. Hurrying along the lane, Nina's throat swelled up and tears rose in her eyes as she thought about her frequent visits to the Greek revival mansion. In his own gruff way Don Alberto had always welcomed her. For that matter, he'd actively insisted that she spend her winter afternoons there, reading to improve her English.

In the years before his retirement, she'd go to the Big House during the week when Don Alberto was in New York. She'd select a book from the library, then wander from room to room until she found a cozy corner to curl up in. On the weekends, and in recent months, when Don Alberto was in residence, he'd invariably ring for tea and cakes, then they'd pass an agreeable hour or so discussing horticultural articles they'd read in *Garden and Forest* or *Vick's Magazine*.

Maybe it was an odd association, he being a wealthy American businessman and she being the daughter of Sicilian peasants, but because they shared a passion for plants, it felt perfectly comfortable. And despite the grandness of the Big House, despite its antique sideboards and Persian carpets and layers of silk drapes that cost more than her father earned in a year, Nina was as at home there as she was in the New England farmhouse at the end of the lane where she lived with her family.

In fact, every inch of the estate was familiar to her. The boundaries of possession had merged in her mind until it seemed to Nina that all fifty-eight acres were hers—in a manner of speaking. Granted that forty-five of those acres were leased to local farmers for hayfields and that she had very little contact with the stables and carriage house, or with their English groom and lads, but she cared for and fussed over all the grounds.

She had, almost single-handedly, designed the series of gardens and parks that spread out from the Big House, each connected to the next by leisurely paths and gracious lawns, and all dotted with benches in the most serendipitous locations. She had wheedled and cajoled until a small greenhouse had been built next to the kitchen garden, then, a year later, the gazebolike orangery, and finally, last spring, the splendid structure of wrought-iron and glass, informally referred to as the Nursery. No question about it, the Blackwell estate was her domain. Hers and Don Alberto's.

With the lump still hard in her throat, Nina entered the Big House, as she frequently did, through the kitchen. After the frosty night air, the huge, tiled room felt hot. She paused a moment, both to acclimate herself and to regain her composure. It took her several tries, but she finally managed to say, "Good evening, Mrs. Watkins."

From her station beneath a rack of gleaming copper pots, the pear-shaped cook broke off her instructions to the two Irish maids doing the after-dinner cleanup and looked around at Nina. "Well! Good evening, dearie!" she exclaimed, her small eyes almost disappearing in a smile. Then, seeing the stricken expression on Nina's face, she remembered such cheer was inappropriate. The smile vanished.

"It's a sad pass, isn't it?" she intoned, clasping her pudgy hands in front of her. "So trying. And I know how fond you and him are of each other." She clucked sympathetically. "I was telling Fiona, not five minutes ago, that Nina was going to take this hard, for sure. Wasn't I, Fiona?" she prodded.

Fiona looked up from the basin full of dirty dishes to give Nina a quick, cold glance. "If you say so, Mrs. Watkins," she responded, looking back at the sudsy water.

Mrs. Watkins sighed. "Don't mind her, dearie," she counseled Nina. "She's just upset by the turn of events. It's been a rough day for everybody."

"Yes, it has been," Nina agreed with a flare of annoyance, glaring at Fiona's back. "Especially for Mr. Blackwell." She knew that Fiona barely cared if Don Alberto lived or died. That his suffering caused her little distress. Her dark glance had been prompted by deep-seated animosity, plain and simple. The Irish maid resented having to serve tea to the daughter of the Italian gardener.

When neither her pointed remark nor her glare brought any further response, Nina shrugged in disgust. She'd been confronted by that attitude since she'd arrived in America, but she didn't have the time or the inclination to combat it this evening. At least, though, the momentary flare of anger had served to steady her quavery emotions. Returning her attention to the most important issue, she asked Mrs. Watkins, "Is there any news?"

It was the cook's turn to shrug. "Nobody told me any," she sniffed. "The doctor left a little while ago, after sitting down to dinner. Ate hearty, too. Mary says"—she nodded at the other maid, who was replenishing the silver salt cellars—"that they talked about some new drama the youngest Mr. Blackwell and his wife saw last week. Not a peep about that poor man upstairs." She shook her head tragically.

While Nina suspected that Mrs. Watkins's reaction was a trifle exaggerated, she was also sure that the stout woman had more feeling for her employer than Fiona. Nina nodded. "Maybe there was nothing new to talk about," she suggested. "Maybe Don Alberto was asleep. The doctor probably gave him some strong medicine." Her own words encouraged her.

"That's probably what happened," she went on more eagerly. "He often has trouble sleeping, you know. Most likely, the doctor gave him a powder to make him rest. After all," she said, "if there was really dreadful news, you would have heard it." A note of uncertainty crept into her voice. "Wouldn't you have?"

Mrs. Watkins shrugged again. "Maybe," she answered. She didn't look at Nina as she rearranged the wooden spoons in a jar on her worktable.

Nina's brief surge of hope plummeted, leaving her more deeply worried than before. "I suppose I ought to go find one of his sons," she said, though she stood where she was, rubbing her forehead. As desperately as she wanted to find out about Don Alberto's condition, the idea of talking to either of his sons wasn't awfully appealing. In general, she avoided both Edward and Reginald Blackwell whenever possible.

"Better you than me," Mrs. Watkins declared, looking up. "I wouldn't ask those two—or their wives—anything more than what time they wanted breakfast. They'd just as soon spit on me as talk to me civilly. Not that *our* Mr. Blackwell is such a Diamond Jim," she added. "It's easy enough to see where the sons get their mean ways."

"Don Alberto is *not* mean," Nina replied, leaping to the don's defense.

"Hmph," was Mrs. Watkins's only comment.

"Well," Nina conceded, after a moment's consideration, "perhaps he can be a little short with people."

"Hmph," Mrs. Watkins said again.

But Nina had retreated all she intended to. "He is *not* mean," she insisted. Then she burst out, "Not like his sons, at any rate. His sons have no hearts. They don't care about anyone but themselves. Certainly not about their father. And nothing gives them a drop of pleasure." Shaking her head, she said, "I feel sorry for their wives."

"It's a waste of time to feel sorry for them," Mrs. Watkins said, acid dripping from her voice. She leaned forward to point a plump finger at Nina. "They deserve every bit of what they got. I've never encountered two such high and mighty madams in all my days. And believe you me, I've cooked for the best of them." She hoisted her bulky bottom onto a nearby stool.

"Yes, sir," she went on, her double chins quivering as she settled in for an enjoyable session of backstairs gossip. "They are, all four of them, perfectly matched. Those two Blackwell men have hearts of stone, just like you say. It's unnatural, is what it is." She leaned forward again, a look of curiosity on her face. "I hear that's because their poor mother died when they was young and *he* never paid them a spot of attention until they was old enough to come into his business. What do you know about that?" she asked.

Too late, Nina realized she'd said more than she should have. That she'd let herself be drawn into making indiscreet remarks by her own apprehension and dread. Don Alberto's unflattering description of his sons, and the opinions she'd formed from her few personal encounters, should never have been aired. Especially not in front of this audience. Ignoring Mrs. Watkins's question, Nina repeated, instead, "I ought to go find one of his sons." Only this time she didn't stand indecisively in the kitchen but went on through to the main part of the house.

She poked her head into the dining room, though she was sure it would be vacant, its long mahogany table already stripped of its embroidered cloth. More politely, she knocked before entering the library, but no one was in Don Alberto's oak-paneled sanctuary, either. Her heart beating faster, she approached the drawing room. The doors were closed. First she licked her dry lips. Then she cleared her throat. Finally she tapped lightly and waited.

When, after a long minute, no response came from within, Nina slid the doors a few inches apart and peered inside. The damask-covered divans and velvet-cushioned chairs were empty. No one stood next to the Italian marble mantel, toasting himself by the dying fire. No crystal glasses or porcelain cups rested on any of the lace-draped tables. The silk-tassled lamps were off. Surprised, Nina slid the doors closed.

"They must have left with the doctor," she murmured to herself as she crossed the foyer and started up the wide, curving stairs. "He probably gave them a ride to the station."

"Just where do you think you're going, my girl?" an icy voice rang out, freezing Nina in midstep. Her heart suddenly banging, Nina looked up to see Edward Blackwell descending the staircase. He halted several steps above her. "Well?" he demanded. "What possible excuse can there be for such brazen behavior?"

Head tilted back, Nina tried to swallow, but her throat was too dry. Edward made a formidable figure. Although he lacked Don Alberto's aggressive energy and thrust, he was taller and broader than his father, and far more rigid. His features were regular, and at age forty not yet eroded, but an utter absence of humor in his expression made his face disagreeable and imperious.

"Can't you speak?" he snapped, further irritated by Nina's silence. "Or are you too shocked? No doubt you expected to creep up the stairs and steal whatever you could while my father lay sick and unable to stop you. But my presence has foiled your plans."

"No!" Nina finally cried, her hands flying out in protest. "No! That isn't true."

"Isn't it?" Edward folded his arms across the waistcoat of his well-tailored suit and let his cold eyes travel the length of her.

Suddenly aware of how dirt-stained her hands were, Nina jerked them back from view. Burying them in the folds of her shawl, she said again, more softly, "No." Her shoulders twitched from the frigid force of his scrutiny as she realized how she must appear. Her skirt, a serviceable serge that had long since done its duty, had muddy patches at the knees. The early spring sun had turned the clear skin on her face an unfashionable rosy brown, and her dark hair, as usual, was rippling loose from its bun. She looked, and felt, like the peasant she was.

"I'm not come to steal," she said, tripping over English as she hadn't done in years. "I mean, I *haven't* come to steal," she corrected. "*Voglio dire che . . .* No, no." Unbidden, a hand shot out to erase the Italian words she'd spoken by mistake. She took a deep breath and started again. "I mean to say, I was looking for you. To ask you about your father, that is." Her accent, usually light and lilting, now sounded heavy. She rubbed her forehead but faced Edward's unflinching stare. "I want to know how he is," she explained.

"You *want* to know?" Edward's tone was bleak. "Who are you to *want* such information? And how dare you climb these stairs, bold as brass, to ask your impertinent questions? There are proper ways for servants to make inquiries. If, in fact, you are a servant here." He gave her another scathing examination. "The staff will be informed of Mr. Blackwell's condition when it's deemed appropriate," he told her.

This time the wave of humiliation that Edward's reprimand provoked was tinged with a flash of anger. "Of course I work here," she said, her tone tight. He knew who she was and that she was more than just a servant to Don Alberto. "I help my father with the gardens."

"Oh, yes," another voice spoke up. "You remember her, Edward. She's Father's little pet."

Nina jumped at the sound of the second voice, which, if anything, was more unpleasant than Edward's. Tilting her head even farther back, she saw Reginald on the upstairs landing, hip cocked and leaning on the railing. He was younger than Edward by three years, but his receding hairline made him look older. And while Edward's ordinary face was humorless and cold, Reginald's was humorless and petulant. "She's the one who was with him when he had his heart attack," he added.

The accusation in his voice made Nina cringe, completely squelching her small flare of anger. During the long hours since Don Alberto had collapsed, she'd been tortured by self-reproach. Why had she callously argued with him, especially after she'd seen that he was unwell? Why hadn't she held on to her temper for once in her life? Undoubtedly, the wrath she'd provoked had made him worse. And why, above all, had she been too thick-headed or blind to see him massaging his chest? If she hadn't been so busy rhapsodizing about flowers and springtime, she would have known he was in pain. Now it took only Reginald's tone to revive all her guilt. Her eyes blinked in misery.

Edward's eyes, on the other hand, narrowed speculatively, assessing the open emotion on Nina's face. "Yes, that's right," he said slowly. "Our only witness." His pause was so long and his stare so intense, Nina backed down a step. "Tell me, my girl," he finally said, the ring in his voice arresting her escape. "Exactly what did you see this morning? What happened?"

Nina studied the designs in the carpet on the stairs. "He fell down," she said in a low voice, answering Edward's question literally. "He was rubbing his chest. Then he fell down." Her hand appeared again and made a rotating motion on top of her shawl.

"I know he fell down," Edward said, annoyed by her simplicity. "What happened to bring the attack on? Was he lifting something heavy? Did you persuade him to do some of your work? Perhaps some spading? Or carrying big sacks of grass seed?"

"Oh, no, no, no!" Nina exclaimed, looking up as her hands, again, flew out in protest. "It wasn't like that. I didn't make him work. He was just standing there. Talking." Then her hands fell and so did her gaze. She toed the rose on the edge of the stair tread. "Arguing," she amended softly.

"Aha!" Edward pounced. "I knew it! I knew you must have been exercising him somehow. What were you arguing about? Your wage? Were you browbeating him into increasing your wage?"

Without raising her eyes Nina shook her head. "No," she said, not bothering to explain that she didn't have a wage to increase. She wasn't trying to avoid any blame. "First we were arguing about soil. He said it was ugly, but I said it wasn't, that it was beautiful."

"What?" Edward was plainly startled. "Soil?" He didn't know what to make of that. For the first time he shifted his feet.

Still studying the carpet, though, Nina didn't see his uncertainty. Besides, she was responding more to her own sense of recrimination than to Edward's inquisition. "Then we argued about how grouchy he's been since he retired."

"Aha!" Edward said again, back on surer ground. "You were taunting him. Bullying him, no doubt. It's your natural instinct.

The way you people enjoy cockfights. You're not happy until you see blood. Or until someone dies.''

Nina's head sank lower. It didn't matter that she'd always abhorred cockfights, or that, moreover, the angry words she'd uttered could hardly be construed as bullying. The fact remained that she'd been arguing with Don Alberto so severely, he'd collapsed. "Then we argued about hiring another gardener," she said, barely above a whisper. "To help Papà and me with the grounds.''

"You were right, Edward," Reginald said from his position on the landing. "She was trying to weasel something out of Father. Instead of additional money, though, she was pressing him to make less work for herself. And most likely she'd only use that extra time to sit around eating macaroni," he added in disgust. He leaned over the railing. "They're all alike, you know," he told his brother. "They're all lazy and ambitionless, these immigrants.''

"Pathetically so," Edward agreed. "They're sly, as well.'' After a quick glance at his brother, he resumed his attack on Nina directly. "If I thought you had a sense of shame, I'd invoke it right now," he berated her. "You took advantage of an elderly gentleman's benevolence. Of his inexplicable fondness for you. Any person of normal morality would have been appreciative of his past indulgences and charity, instead of trying to wring more out of him. But not you.''

His stare was as bitter as his tone. "You're an ungrateful baggage," he said, "and were it my decision to make, you and your shiftless family would be sent packing immediately. You might fool my father, but you don't fool me.''

Too riddled with guilt to realize, as she had this morning, the absurdity of depicting the don as a philanthropic old man ripe for exploitation, Nina could only look up at Edward and say, in a voice choked with tears, "I didn't mean to hurt him. I would *never* hurt Don Alberto deliberately.'' She shook her head to show the depth of her regret.

Her heartfelt expression was like fuel on the fire, however. Edward's rage flamed. "That's enough!" he snarled. "I've heard enough of your insolence. I don't know where you get the nerve to overstep your place like this!''

"Outrageous," Reginald agreed from above. "The very idea of calling Father by his first name. And even worse, twisting it up in that vulgar language of hers.''

Edward nodded. "You'd be wise to remember that his name is

Mr. Blackwell,'' he warned Nina. ''Now get out of this house.''
He raised a ramrod stiff arm and pointed down the stairs. ''Get
out,'' he repeated. ''You've done enough damage for one day.''

Without another word, Nina turned and fled. She felt sick. She
was too anguished even to resent the brothers' hateful slurs. All
she could think of was Don Alberto lying gray-faced and
unmoving on the grass. And of her burst of temper that had
brought about his heart attack. As she stumbled along the lane
toward home, hot tears streamed down her face again, stinging her
cheeks in the cold night air.

$$=6=$$

Despite the pile of seed catalogues sitting in her lap and the book
held open in her hands, Nina wasn't reading. She couldn't
concentrate. It had been over a week since Don Alberto's collapse,
but she was as upset as she'd been when it had happened. In fact,
every day that passed with only rumors and gossip to inform her
of his condition added to her distress. Finally today she'd come to
sit in the Nursery, seeking the tranquillity and peace she always
found in the big greenhouse.

She loved it in here, in the warm, moist air, surrounded by baby
plants growing. She loved the longs rows of benches that held
trays full of seedlings, all stretching eagerly toward the sun. When
the greenhouse was first built, she used to come and just stand,
letting its sights and smells sink into her soul. Gradually she
carried in her magazines and gardening books, seeking a less noisy
spot than her house to read them.

After Don Alberto had found her leaning on a bench with *All
About Sweetpeas* propped against a pot of gloxinia, he had gone up
in his attic and unearthed a dilapidated armchair, covered in a
threadbare chintz, and a battered old cabinet with a broken door.
He'd had them installed in one corner of the greenhouse, and,
henceforth, had referred to the area as Nina's office. Now, seated

in her office, staring off in the distance, there was a degree of calm
on Nina's face for the first time in days. There was a quiet light in
her amber eyes. But she still couldn't concentrate.

A slow tap, tap, tap on the slate floor of the greenhouse brought
her back to the present. Turning to see what was making the
sound, Nina was greeted by a growl that made her heart soar. "I
knew I'd catch you in here," Don Alberto complained as he
approached her with the aid of a cane. "Diddling away a perfect
spring day when you should be outside preparing the gardens. Or
did you think I wouldn't know the difference? 'When the cat's
away, the mice will play.' Is that it?"

Overjoyed, Nina jumped to her feet, the pile of catalogues
spilling to the floor. "You're all right!" she cried, happily looking
him up and down. "You look fine. The same as ever. Maybe a
little pale." She cocked her head more critically. "And the cane.
That's new. Is it because you're weak?" Without giving him a
chance to respond, Nina reached behind her and patted the chair.
"Come sit down," she urged. "You mustn't tax yourself. You
should rest. Here, let me clear the way." In one swift move, she
scooped up the catalogues and stuffed them into the cabinet. "Sit
down," she repeated. "Rest."

"I'll sit," the don agreed, carefully lowering himself into the
armchair, "but don't think I'm too weak to know what's what.
Just because my legs are a little rickety doesn't mean my mind has
gone feeble. And don't start talking to me like that damned nurse
does. 'We musn't excite ourselves,'" he mimicked. "'We must
be good and take our medicine.' Treating me as if I were some
kind of slow-witted child."

"I won't talk to you like that," Nina promised over her
shoulder as she raced up an aisle to grab a stool and race back. "I
didn't know you had a nurse, though," she said, plopping the stool
in front of Don Alberto and plopping herself on it. Leaning
forward anxiously, she added, "Does she know you're here? Did
she say it was all right for you to be out walking around?"

"She didn't say yes, no, or maybe," the don announced with a
certain amount of triumph. "I fired her yesterday. Couldn't stand
the woman. And don't get that look on your face, Nina," he said
more sulkily. "She was a gargoyle. You wouldn't have been able
to stand her, either. She kept shutting the drapes in my bedroom
until it was as dark and stuffy as a tomb."

Relieved and delighted as she was to see Don Alberto in one

piece, and to hear his familiar grumbles, Nina couldn't help feeling alarmed by his announcement. "Was that wise?" she asked, her forehead furrowing in worry. "Firing the nurse, I mean. Perhaps she was annoying, but she has medical knowledge, and that's what's important right now. If she shut the drapes, it must be for a reason." One finger rubbed her chin as she tried to figure out what that reason could possibly be.

"To make me sicker," Don Alberto said. "That's her reason. So she'd be assured of a good stint of lolling around my house. That's all anybody thinks about these days. Their own pockets. How to do the least amount of work for the most amount of money. Which brings us back to my original point." He tapped his cane against the legs of her stool. "What are you doing in here in the middle of the day? This is the busiest time of year, and you're lounging around reading."

For another moment Nina remained full of misgivings, then, suddenly, a peal of laughter washed them away. If his health could be measured by his grumpiness, Don Alberto was in fine fettle. "It's Sunday," she reminded him. "I'm allowed to take some time off. Besides, I wasn't just being idle."

Randomly pulling one of the seed catalogues from the cabinet, she told him, "I was looking for some information on cleomes. I started the seeds two weeks ago, but they still haven't germinated." She ruffled through the pages of the D. M. Ferry Seed Annual. "I must be doing something wrong. I was hoping to get some helpful clues. Maybe warmer temperatures or wetter soil. Maybe less light." Shrugging, she tossed the catalogue over to the cabinet, where it landed with its back-cover illustration of a bright pink and green Sweetheart watermelon facing up. "I couldn't find anything about starting the seeds, though. None of the catalogues goes into detail."

Settling more comfortably into the chair, Don Alberto snorted. "You're not doing anything wrong," he assured her. "Never do. You know exactly how to make things grow. And anyway, you've been starting cleomes for at least five years now, without a single problem. Although," he added in a darker tone, "for the life of me, I can't understand why you want to plant them. I've never encountered a flower that had such a nasty smell."

"That's why I put them at the back of the border," Nina explained. "But they're tall and dramatic looking, and they stay in bloom all summer. Pretty shades of pink and mauve, too."

"Maybe so," Don Alberto conceded, though he then went on more contentiously, "I still say you're not doing anything wrong. If the seeds aren't germinating, it's because they're bad. Too old, probably. Or left in a damp warehouse someplace." He paused to stamp his cane on the floor. "That's the trouble these days," he griped. "There's no integrity in business anymore. No one has pride in his product. Just toss a load of rubbish onto the market and grab back as much money as possible. Greed, that's what it is. Unvarnished and unprincipled greed."

Well launched, he edged up on the chair and continued to rant. "No one cares about building a reputation today. And satisfying customers went out with whale-oil lamps. All anyone cares about is profit, and they'll lie, cheat, and steal to get it. Bah!" He shook his head in disgust.

"I won't tolerate that in my business," he warned, pointing a skinny finger at Nina. "The New York Wool Company has done nothing but grow since the day I started it," he informed her. "Even through these recent hard times it's continued to prosper. And that's because I built my business on a solid foundation. My customers trust me. They know they're going to get exactly what they pay for. If they pay for English down wool, they aren't going to get domestic merino."

"Yes, I know," Nina interrupted him before he could go any further. Having listened to similar harangues any number of times, she new Don Alberto could work himself into quite a lather. She was worried he'd get too excited now and overstress his recovering heart. Not to mention the fact that she still wasn't wholly convinced he should be out of bed and stomping around in the first place.

"It's a very good business," she said soothingly. "And you have every right to feel proud. But you mustn't let yourself get stirred up. It's bad for your health." She cut off the retort he was about to make by leaning forward and waving her finger in front of his face.

"Don't forget what the doctor told you last fall," she said. "You have to take life easier. Not chew yourself up with problems. That's why you retired, remember? It's time to let your sons fret about the customers and the prices and all the rest of it." Dismissing the various aggravations of business with a flick of her wrist, Nina leaned back again and cautioned, "If you don't leave it to them, you'll make yourself really sick."

As soon as those words came out of her mouth, Nina wished she could put them back in. She realized at once that they were a red flag in front of a bull. Hunching her shoulders, she waited for the charge. It came instantly.

"It's making me a lot sicker to watch those two insufferable nincompoops ruin the company I spent my whole life building!" Don Alberto yelled. "It was the biggest mistake I ever made to listen to that spineless sycophant of a doctor. What kind of nonsensical idea was it to advise me to retire? Just like that damned nurse, I tell you." His puffy eyes bulging with rage, he banged the floor with his cane.

"That snake-oil peddler *wants* to see me sick. He's trying to garnish his bank account at my expense. Well, I won't have it, do you hear me, Nina? I won't have it!" His face red, he started wheezing.

"Va bene! Va bene!" Nina cried, leaping to her feet in alarm. "All right!" Frantic to calm him, she picked up his hand and started stroking it. "Please don't shout," she begged him. "You're frightening me half to death."

"Bah!" Don Alberto scoffed, between gasps for air. Though he didn't withdraw his hand from Nina's grip. Rather, when his breathing returned to normal, he said, "You're the only one I can count on, Nina. If I didn't have you to talk to, this retirement would kill me within a week."

Surprised, Nina's eyes opened wide and a rush of emotion warmed her heart. Although Don Alberto had always been unequivocal in his praise of her gardening skills, and she knew, instinctively, that he enjoyed their teas as much as she did, he'd never before admitted his affection so candidly. Nor his dependence on their friendship. But even as the discovery touched her deeply, it also saddened her to realize how lonely he must be.

He didn't know the warmth and security of a big, noisy family like hers, crowding into a farmhouse at the end of a lane. He didn't sit elbow to elbow, laughing and bantering at every meal. Just the reverse, he inhabited his huge, formal manor all by himself. Unless a few uncaring servants could be considered company. Or the infrequent visits of his "beastly" sons. Much moved, Nina gave the hand she was holding an extra squeeze, though she didn't dare give voice to her sentiments. Don Alberto would only find them intolerably syrupy.

Instead, she said, "You're just saying that because you're

bored. If you had something to do that engaged your attention, you wouldn't sit around brooding." Giving his hand a final pat, she resumed her perch on the stool. "For now you have to concentrate on getting plenty of rest," she told him, "but when you're well again, you ought to find something to do to occupy your time."

"Like what?" Don Alberto demanded. "Pitching horseshoes? Playing croquet?"

"No, no." Nina brushed his derision away with both hands. "Not just a game to pass the hours, but something that interests you. Something that keeps your mind busy. That engrosses you as much as your business did, but without all the trouble."

"Bah!" Don Alberto scoffed again, his hand tightening around the cane until his knuckles shone white. "What nonsense!"

"It isn't nonsense," Nina protested, though her tone was determinedly mild. She had no wish to provoke another heart attack. "There must be any number of amusing activities from which you can choose." Her hand arced through the air to show the vast spectrum of gentlemanly leisure pursuits, though she became decidedly less definite when she tried to enumerate them. "You could, uh . . ." she began. Her eyebrows knit. This was a subject she knew very little about.

"Ha!" Don Alberto trumpeted. "You see?"

Nina shook her head doggedly. "There are lots of other retired businessmen," she reasoned. "They must do something with their free time." Her face suddenly brightened. "Don't they collect things?" she asked. "Model boats or stamps or paintings? Don't they go around to different shops, discovering rare and wonderful pieces to add to their collections?"

"For God's sake, Nina," the don snapped. "Where did you come up with such twaddle? Retired businessmen drop dead, is what they do. Which is what's apt to happen to me if I have to spend anymore time trapped in my bedroom."

Nina sighed but kept a firm rein on her temper. "I don't think it's twaddle," she said with studied calm. "I've read about wealthy businessmen who've bought enough artwork to build their own museums. But if that doesn't intrigue you," she went on, "then there's no point in talking about it anymore. Speaking of reading, though, maybe you could do more of that. No. Wait. I know!" She nearly hopped off the stool as an idea struck her.

"Instead of *reading* a book, you could *write* one," she said. "It's perfect! You could write about what you know best. About building a successful business. Thousands of people would want to read it.'' Her arm swept out to encompass the enormous audience. ''Everybody who has a business, or wants to start one, would be thrilled to read the advice of an expert like you.'' Lifting her hands, she repeated. ''It's perfect. Not only would you be filling your own days, but you'd be helping others as well.''

''No one helped me get started in business,'' Don Alberto responded, rejecting her idea with a stab of his cane. ''And I didn't learn how to make a profit by reading instructions in some foolish book. Wouldn't have trusted them if I had read them, and I can't say I'd much admire a man who would. Besides,'' he added in a deeper growl, ''I can't write. Don't have the patience.''

Nina's eyebrows rose and fell in resignation. ''All right,'' she said. ''It's true that not everyone can write. I know that I would never be able to.'' For a few moments, then, she was silent as she racked her brain for another idea. ''How about joining a gentlemen's club?'' she suggested. Her voice trailed off when she saw the expression on his face. ''I guess you don't want to join a club,'' she decided.

''Of course I don't want to join a club!'' Don Alberto shouted. ''Use your noodle. Why do you think I built my house way out here in the cow pastures?'' Angrily shaking his cane, he answered his own question. ''To get away from all those muddleheaded people, that's why. I'll be damned if I'm going to spend my last years on earth sitting in an armchair, gabbing with a bunch of old men. Twice a month with the Horticultural Society is bad enough.''

''Fine, fine,'' Nina said, on her feet once more. Her hands smoothed the air around Don Alberto, willing him to calm down. ''It was just a thought. All you have to do is say no, and we'll forget it.''

''No!''

Nina took a deep breath and tried to recall how happy she'd been to see him just ten minutes before. She sometimes wondered if Lucia and Rossana weren't right. If Don Alberto weren't a miserable crank without a single redeeming trait. As soon as it passed through her mind, however, she was ashamed of having the thought. She knew better than that. Don Alberto was just out of sorts because of his illness and the boredom that had brought it on.

Although never exactly an affable man, when he was in a good humor, Nina found it a pleasure to be in his company. For some reason, his bark had never bothered her. Rather, she'd come to appreciate his outspoken assessments and fearless opinions. Even more, she appreciated the fact that in all the years she'd known him, he'd never condescended to her, either because she was a woman or because she was an Italian immigrant. He'd always treated her as an equal person. And with gardening as a common denominator, their mutual respect had grown into friendship.

Another warm rush of feeling pushed away her irritation, and Nina redoubled her efforts to help her friend. "Let's see," she mused, backing onto the stool again, "There's bound to be something. We just have to find it." While she thought, she absentmindedly fiddled with her hairpins, capturing her dark hair before it sprang free from her bun.

"You're wasting your time," Don Alberto muttered from the depths of the chair. "I never should have retired, and that's that."

"You used to enjoy the trips you took for your business," Nina said, ignoring his comment. "Why don't you think about traveling? Remember when you went to England last summer? You came back in excellent spirits." Pleased with that idea, Nina sat up straighter.

"I was in excellent spirits because I made an excellent arrangement with an English wool broker," Don Alberto retorted. "It was when the Wilson Gorman tariffs went into effect and wool was placed on the free list. All that good English wool came into the country without a tax."

Despite her best intentions, Nina felt her irritation creeping back. He was being awfully stubborn. "Well, you've made other trips," she said, her tone a touch short. "And they all seemed to agree with you."

"Same reason," Don Alberto answered her, edging forward again, his tone equally abrupt. "I had business meetings to attend on those trips. There was a purpose to them. What kind of purpose do I have to take trips now? Some sort of high-flown cultural quest? Do you want me to go traipsing all over creation, peering at every church and museum ever built? No, thank you." As before, he thumped his cane on the floor for emphasis. Then he leaned back in the chair and added, "Besides, who am I going to go with? I prefer my own company to almost anyone I know, but I can't bear sitting in a hotel dining room by myself. Food is always revolting in those places, too."

Again Nina's annoyance was washed away by a surge of

sympathy. Just when she thought he was hopeless, Don Alberto proved to be human, after all. His desire for a tasty meal, and someone to share it with, struck a chord in Nina's heart. In her own life, mealtimes in the midst of her family were the center of her day. And good food, as Angelina never got tired of saying, fed not only the physical body, but also fed the soul.

Hooking her heels over the highest rung of the stool, she tried to think of a solution to this latest problem. After a moment she started laughing. She could just see Don Alberto setting off on a voyage, surrounded by her six sisters, all lugging hampers of Mamma's cooking.

"What's so funny?" Don Alberto demanded. "Do you find it amusing that I don't like hotel dining rooms?"

"Not a bit," Nina responded with a shake of her head. "I think it's very reasonable. It's just that I've thought of a trip you can take where you'd have mountains of delicious food and dozens of people to eat it with. No museums or statues to look at, either." She threw back her head and laughed again, her cheeks glowing with color. "Best of all, you'd get to hear a foreign language being spoken without ever having to leave American shores." Still laughing, she wiped one eye with the back of her hand.

Don Alberto's sparse eyebrows twitched in suspicion. "What?" he said. "Is this a joke?"

"Maybe a small one," Nina admitted, a smile spreading across her face. "Although it's a real trip. You see, my cousin Aurelia, on Long Island, is getting married next month, and we were hoping to go. If we were still in Sicily, it would only be the ceremony in the church and then a few glasses of wine afterward, to toast the bride's health. But Aurelia has taken the customs of America, so there'll be a big *festa*. Like on a saint's day." Nina's hands swung through the air to describe the party. "Everyone will be singing and dancing and eating till they burst. We'll see people we haven't seen in years. You can't imagine how much fun it will be. Bianca Maria has been talking about nothing else for weeks."

"Where on Long Island?" Don Alberto asked, his tone still suspicious.

"Near Oyster Bay," Nina replied. "Zio Sergio is the foreman on a big farm that grows cabbages for seed companies. But I was just teasing," she added. "I didn't mean you should really come. I only said it because it would be the exact opposite of a 'high-flown cultural quest.' Although you'd probably dislike it just as much.''

"Why?" Don Alberto's response was swift and sharp.

Startled, Nina looked at him more carefully. The sullen obstinance was gone from his pouchy face, replaced by his old alert shrewdness. "You're taking this seriously!" she exclaimed. If anything, she'd expected him to respond to her mock suggestion with increased pique.

"And why shouldn't I?" Don Alberto asked, assuming an injured air. "You've been nagging me for half an hour to do something. Didn't you invite me? Or are you now rescinding the invitation?''

"Oh, no, no." Nina waved both hands in denial, though she was becoming more and more incredulous. It was one thing for him to stop by their house long enough to eat Sunday dinner. It was quite another thing, however, for him to spend three entire days in their company.

"Of course I'm not rescinding the invitation, but I'm surprised that you would want to accept it, because everyone at the party will be . . . well, you know . . ." Her hands circled in a vain attempt to describe the awkward social situation. Finally she set them in her lap and looked at him earnestly. "Everyone will be Italian," she told him. "Immigrants."

"Yes," Don Alberto answered with the first hint of good humor she'd heard from him in months. "I was hoping the Vanderbilts wouldn't be there. Will your mother be cooking?"

For another full moment Nina stared at him, dumbfounded, then she again threw back her head in laughter. This time she laughed until the tears overflowed her thick lashes and rolled down her cheeks unheeded. She laughed until her stomach ached and until her breath came in hiccups. She laughed in relief of her long week of worry and in release of her annoyance. When she finally stopped laughing and mopped her face on the hem of her smock, she managed to gasp, "Yes, Mamma will be cooking. Along with Zia Gabriella and all of her friends."

The don looked pleased. "Good," he said. "It's decided. I'm going. I'm curious to see what a cabbage seed farm looks like, anyway." He settled back serenely, his hands loosely folded on top of the cane. That stately pose only lasted a minute, though. Then his eyes squinted, and he let out a hoot of wicked glee.

"Wait till Edward and Reginald hear I'm going to a Sicilian wedding," he chortled. "They'll faint dead away in shock."

Nina started laughing again. Don Alberto might still be weak and pale, but without question, he was back in form.

She did considerably less laughing at dinner that evening, when she informed her family that she'd invited Don Alberto to the wedding. "You did *what?*" her father roared, banging his fist on the table so hard Nina winced. *"Mannaggia la miseria,* Maria Antonina! What were you thinking of? How can I get drunk if *il padrone* is standing by my side?" He clasped his hands together and shook them at her. "How could you do this to me?"

"Per carità, Nina!" Angelina cried, her coral drop earrings trembling with passion. She waved her finger furiously. "This time you've gone too far, *figlia mia,"* she declared. "It's one thing to invite him to eat at your own family's table, but it's not for you to invite him to Aurelia's wedding."

Nina glanced at Serafina, but her usually staunch defender was silent, inspecting the cheese-stuffed raviolis on her plate. Uneasiness filled her. If even Serafina disapproved, she'd made a big mistake. She'd been so preoccupied with seeing things from Don Alberto's point of view, she'd neglected to think about her family's. Rubbing her forehead, she tried to figure out how that had happened. The moment had just carried her along.

"He's offered to pay for everyone's train fare," Nina said, hoping to conjure up some acceptance of the unwelcome guest.

"Who cares?" Lucia stormed. "He could give us a hundred dollars, and it still wouldn't be worth it to put up with that crotchety old man. Really, Nina. It's bad enough that our Sunday dinners are ruined by him. Having him at Aurelia's wedding will be unbearable."

"He'll probably holler at me the whole time," Rossana fretted, chewing her lower lip.

"We could run away and hide," Stella suggested. "He wouldn't find us under the porch."

"What's the point of going to the wedding if we're going to spend it under the porch?" Benedetta asked. She speared a plump ravioli and poked it, dispiritedly, into her mouth.

In the end it was Bianca Maria, of all people, who came to Nina's rescue. "If I recall correctly," she said, wrapping both hands around her water glass and choosing her words with care, "we never had any real plans to go to Long Island. It was just wishful thinking."

When her family stared at her with open mouths, she prompted, "Because we didn't think we could be gone for three days at this time of year. Remember? Because there's so much planting to be done in May. And transplanting. And pruning. And heaven knows what kind of fussing with plants. How many times did you tell me that?"

Her voice rose in resentment. "Doesn't anyone remember all the schemes we came up with to sneak those three days off? Planting the beans early and the potatoes late, or something to that effect?" One hand came away from the glass and floated vaguely in the air. "Everyone was so afraid of what Don Alberto would say if we went away. That he'd scream and shout and be upset." Upset herself, she paused to take a steadying sip of water.

"If you ask my opinion," she said, peering over the top of her glass, "if Don Alberto weren't coming to Aurelia's wedding, we'd *all* be staying home." She set her glass down decisively. "Now he's even going to buy our tickets. It's the best news I've heard in a long time."

Around the table, mouths clicked shut. Angelina lifted her eyebrows. *"E bè,"* she finally said, shrugging. One by one everyone else shrugged, too. This time Nina's smile was shaky with relief.

7

By eleven o'clock on the morning of the wedding, all lingering doubts and discontentment had vanished. Even as everyone worked to set things up, they were having a wonderful time. The day itself was sparkling and sweet, as only a day in May could be. Throngs of friends and relatives were arriving by wagon from nearby farms and by train from Mulberry Street in New York.

They came carrying wedding gifts and contributions of wine and food, some of it imported from the old country.

"I haven't seen olive oil like this since I left Italy," Angelina commented, wiping her hands on her apron and standing back to view the feast. A row of tables, their white cloths lifting in the breeze, had been arranged in the yard behind the Ruggieris' house. Platters of pasta and bowls of salad and baskets of fruit had been piled on top of them.

"I could eat just the olive oil with bread and salt," Nina agreed. She was holding a board full of coarse Sicilian bread that Benedetta had baked early that morning. While she looked for an empty spot to put it down, its aroma wafted up and made her mouth water. "Although everything else looks good, too," she added, eyeing the appetizing display.

On one table sat a pig that had been buried in a brick pit with rosemary and garlic and cooked to tender pink perfection. On another table was a lamb that had marinated in lemon and oil from yesterday afternoon until the time it was roasted at dawn. Although Zia Gabriella could take the credit for their ultimate succulence, they both had been provided by Mr. Beale, the New York businessman who owned the cabbage farm that Zio Sergio managed.

"It was a generous present, eh?" Angelina said, following Nina's gaze. She nodded appreciatively at the splendid roasts. "Aurelia told me he gave her fifty dollars, too."

"Mr. Beale was very kind," Nina agreed. She put down the breadboard, cramming it between a plate of fresh fennel the Colangelos had brought from Stamford, and a wheel of hard, salty pecorino cheese that had come all the way from Sicily. "It was also very nice of him to take care of Don Alberto."

"That's right, Mr. Blackwell!" Angelina exclaimed, looking around. "I'd forgotten about him. Where did he disappear to?"

"Mr. Beale whisked him off to join his other guests," Nina responded. "It seems he's having a little lawn party for the wedding, too. Zia Gabriella said she cooked enough for everyone, though Mr. Beale's friends won't eat here, with us. The maids will fix plates and carry them back there." Her hand waved in the direction of the huge, white clapboard country home, sitting behind a high hedge of privet, out of sight of the the cabbage fields and everything connected to their cultivation.

"Mr. Beale has Don Alberto installed in a wicker chair stuffed full of striped cushions,'' Nina explained, prying a small piece of pecorino from the wheel and popping it into her mouth. Her eyes widened in pleasure. ''I think he'll be more comfortable there. Especially since everyone will be speaking English.''

Nina knew that as much as he wanted to scandalize his sons, Don Alberto didn't really want to gulp glasses of ink-red wine and clap in time with the dancers doing the tarantella. And as much as she cared about him and enjoyed his company, this wasn't a day for discussing horticultural reports in the oaken isolation of his library. This was a day for laughter and exuberant song. In Italian.

This was a day for young people to dance, for older women to gossip as they replenished the platters, and for men to get drunk and brag. It was a day for little children to race back and forth until their cheeks turned bright pink and to play catch-me games around the row of food-laden tables while the farmyard dogs and the small flock of chickens patrolled the ground beneath the fluttering white linen. It was a day for the parrot to squawk ''*buon giorno*'' from its cage on the porch every time someone ran up or down the steps.

''Nina, come on!'' her younger cousin Fabrizio shouted, dashing up and grabbing her hand. Tall and skinny, with features too big for his face, he was at an awkward stage. More than a boy, but not quite a man. ''They've started to play. It's time to dance.''

Even as he spoke, the first notes filled the air. Standing beneath a tree, a concertina player, a fiddler, and an old man with a reed flute struck up a lively tune. Yes, Nina thought, happily letting herself be pulled into the set that was forming. Today it was better that she and Don Alberto were on different sides of the hedge.

She danced with Fabrizio for that set and with his brother, Ettore, for the next, then a strapping youth named Giuliano Gullota, who worked on the farm, guided her through an extremely enthusiastic waltz. ''*Basta!*'' Nina gasped, when the ragged music finally died. ''Enough! I have to rest a few minutes.'' She didn't go searching for a bench or a chair but collapsed to the grass where she stood. Laughing and panting, sisters, cousins, and friends collapsed, too.

''We need to eat,'' Fabrizio decided, starting to rise. He was at an age when he was always hungry. ''I just saw Mamma put out the salamis that Enrico's family sent from Catania.''

''Not yet,'' Serafina objected, waving her cousin down. Still out of breath, her pretty face flushed with excitement, she leaned gracefully against Nina's shoulder. "If we eat now, we'll be too gorged to dance. I think we should wait a little while more."

"I agree," Bianca Maria said, smiling at a stocky young man with a gleaming black mustache and black hair plastered to his head. "Listen. They're playing 'La Siciliana.' We should dance until we have really big appetites. The food will taste even better then." She cocked her head engagingly, and the young man, whose name was Giuseppe d'Agostino, willingly rose and held out his hand.

"We could eat a little bit now and some more later," Fabrizio suggested. Caught on his knees, halfway to his feet, he looked longingly at the tables. "Before it gets spoiled," he encouraged. "For energy."

"O Fabrizio!" Bianca Maria sighed, slipping her hand into Giuseppi's and allowing herself to be lifted up. She and Giuseppe slid away to dance.

Nina laughed at her cousin's doleful expression. "*Va bene,*" she told him. "All right. Go get a plate of antipasto. Some salamis and cheeses and olives. And don't forget some of Mamma's *caponata*. She put it up last summer when the eggplant and tomatoes were at their peak. Get a big plateful, and we'll all have a taste." Fabrizio was up and off in a flash. Laughing again, Nina glanced down at Serafina. "I'm a little bit hungry, too," she confessed. "Besides, I can't resist the thought of all that good food."

In truth, she couldn't resist the spell of the day. The spring sun was gloriously warm, melting her muscles and tingling her skin. But the overriding mood was warm, too. Warm with the love of close relatives and friends and with the familiarity of a common heritage. The air was loud with the music and dialects of the Sicilian hills. It was redolent of its aromas and flavors. Arms straight out behind her, resting on her palms, her favorite sister leaning against her, Nina felt just about perfectly happy.

"*Ragazzi. Cari. Attenzione,*" Zia Gabriella called out, demanding the group's attention as she bustled up. She was shorter than her sister and not as majestic, though she had every bit of Angelina's strong will. "I want you to meet a friend of Enrico's. From near Catania. They grew up together." She pulled forward a slender young man with a startlingly handsome face. "This is Dante da Rosa," she introduced. "He just came over last month."

Dante had a fine, high brow and chiseled cheeks, like the Greek statues Nina had seen when she'd gone, once, to Siracusa. The cap of dark curls covering his head looked Grecian, as well. Most arresting, though, were his eyes. Large and brown, they were hauntingly sad behind long, sweeping lashes that were gorgeous. Dante seemed unaware of his remarkable looks, however. If anything, he seemed shy.

"Let me make known to you my niece Maria Antonina Colangelo," Zia Gabriella continued, tugging at Dante's sleeve. "Nina will introduce you to everyone else. Won't you, *cara?*" She prodded Nina with her toe, making motions for Nina to get up. "She's a dear girl," Zia Gabriella said, turning back to Dante. "And a great comfort to her father, who, unfortunately, has not been blessed with a son. But Nina lends him a hand whenever she can and, like a good daughter, helps to ease his burden."

For a moment she paused as another thought struck her. Then she excitedly thumped Dante's shoulder, saying, "Didn't Enrico tell me that you're a gardener? What a coincidence. So is Nina. Eh, Nina?" She glanced quickly at her niece and again motioned for her to rise. "That is to say, her papà is the groundskeeper at Mr. Albert Blackwell's estate in Stamford, Connecticut, but Nina knows all about flowers and trees and such. She's like Orazio's right hand."

When Zia Gabriella paused again, for breath this time, Dante finally spoke. His voice was soft and his tone was quiet. "I *was* a gardener," he said. "In Sicily." He nodded over his shoulder, in the direction of the country he'd left behind. "I worked in the almond groves and the vegetable gardens, but here I work in a stable in New York. They pay me a dollar a day to clean the stalls." He shrugged apologetically. "It's a job," he said.

Zia Gabriella hesitated, reassessing him in the light of this new information. A dollar a day bought a room in a crowded tenement. It hardly supported a family. Then she shrugged, too. "You'll do better once you learn English," she said. "I can tell. You're a hard worker. And you're still young. What? Twenty-four? Twenty five? Just like Nina."

"Twenty-three," Dante corrected, even more apologetically.

"*E bè.*" Zia Gabriella tossed up her hands. "It's all the same," she said. "But today isn't the time for thoughts of work. Today is for enjoyment. Nina, get up. Make our guest feel welcome while I go back to the kitchen."

Nina laughed but still didn't rise. Instead, she tapped the grass with her heel. "We're worn out from dancing," she explained to Dante. "Come join us down here." She knew very well what her aunt was up to. It couldn't have been more obvious. Every time the two families got together, Zia Gabriella chided Angelina for not having married Nina off. For not having picked a husband for her, arranged the marriage, the way they did in Sicily, if Nina weren't going to follow American customs and find a husband herself.

Half an hour ago, Nina would have been made uneasy by her aunt's attempt at matchmaking, but right now she was too blissful to be bothered. Besides, she'd felt drawn to Dante immediately. It wasn't as if her heart were throbbing or she were "seized by rapture," like the heroines in the stories Bianca Maria read, but Nina found his quiet manner appealing. And he was a gardener. "You're the answer to my prayers," she told him.

Her words hit Dante as he was folding his legs and sinking to the ground by Nina's feet. He landed with a thud, a bright red blush shooting up his neck. "Pardon me?" he asked, choking.

Although she managed to suppress another peal of laughter, Nina couldn't hold back a smile. Apparently Dante was an unwitting participant in Zia Gabriella's scheme, too. "I only meant that Papà and I have more work than we can keep up with," she explained. "And it would be my dream come true to have an experienced gardener to whom Papà could speak in Italian."

Looking relieved, Dante was about to reply when Giuliano Gullota interrupted. "That's the trouble with this country," he said, snatching a blade of grass from the lawn and flinging it back to the ground. "An experienced gardener has to clean stables! These Americans treat us like dogs. Like the dirt beneath their feet. We get the worst jobs, at the lowest wages, then they accuse us of filthy habits because all we can afford are the tenements."

"This doesn't seem so bad," Dante said, looking around in surprise. He took in the big farmhouse where the Ruggieris lived, and the clean, green yard leading out to neat fields. "Not bad at all," he repeated.

"Maybe not here," a young man named Andrea spoke up. "But I saw a sign last week, advertising for workers. It said, 'A dollar fifty White Men, a dollar twenty-five Negroes, a dollar fifteen Italians.'" He thrust out his chin.

"What are we talking about?" Bianca Maria asked innocently. The dance was over, and breathing hard, a happy smile on her face, she dropped down next to Serafina.

"We were talking about how terrible it is for us here in America," Giuliano answered, still angry. "They have no respect for our customs. They make fun of our food. They even laugh at our church." He spat. "We never should have left Sicily," he concluded.

Shocked that her casual question had brought such a harsh response, all Bianca Maria could say was "Oh!" But Giuseppe, kneeling behind her, was more forthcoming. "How stupid," he scoffed. "How can you make such a ridiculous remark when you're stuffing your pockets with American dollars? You can make something of yourself here. You can have a home. You can give your children an education. You can own more than one pair of pants." He ticked off each advantage on his fingers, then threw up his hands.

"Who cares if they laugh at us?" he asked, scraping his chin with the back of his hand, a centuries-old gesture of contempt. "Who cares if they make fun of our food? You should hear what I have to say about theirs. Boiled beef and potatoes." He gave an exaggerated grimace. "Ugh."

His expression broke the tension that Giuliano's outburst had caused. There were a few tentative chuckles as everyone relaxed. "I don't even remember Sicily that well," Ettore confessed. He was sprawled on his back, staring up at the cloudless sky. "I was only four years old when we left. The only memories I have are from other people's stories."

"I remember Sicily," Nina said, finally entering the discussion. "It's beautiful. The hills and gorges are indescribable. Especially in the spring when the wildflowers are in bloom."

"I remember Sicily, too," Dante said, his quiet voice commanding attention. "I left in February when the almond trees were in blossom. It was magnificent." He nodded in agreement with Nina. "The hills looked as if they were covered in lace. And when you took a deep breath"—he took one in demonstration—"you could smell both the blossoms and the salty air from the Ionian Sea." There was a slight hesitation before he added, even more quietly, "But you can't eat beauty. And there wasn't much else to eat. Just bread and onions."

A chill ran down Nina's spine, despite the heat of the sun. The image of poverty that Dante's brief statement evoked was a powerful one. The perfect day might have been ruined, after all, if Fabrizio hadn't picked that moment to return, a heaping plate in each hand and Stella trailing behind him with a basket of bread. "Did I hear someone say eat?" he asked, squatting down in the midst of the group. "We can start with this."

"*Bravo!*" Giuseppe applauded, clapping loudly and breaking the somber mood for the second time. Released, everyone started shouting gaily and grabbing food, all at once. Her spirits soaring as quickly as they'd sunk, Nina reached out, too. Her abrupt move unbalanced her sister.

"*Aiou!*" Serafina cried as she fell over backward.

"*O la!*" Nina laughed. She juggled a slice of salami and a chunk of bread so she could come to Serafina's assistance. Too late. Dante leaned across Nina and offered Serafina his hand, easily pulling her upright again. Nina's eyebrows lifted in admiration of his chivalry.

Then, tardily remembering Zia Gabriella's instructions, she said, "Oh, yes. Dante, please meet my sister, Serafina."

"My pleasure," Dante responded in his quiet way, giving the hand he was holding a little squeeze before releasing it.

"My pleasure," Serafina echoed, almost simultaneously, pink with embarrassment at her ungainly flop.

"This charming young lady holding the bread basket is Maria Stella," Nina went on, grinning at her youngest sister, who grinned back. "And Giuliano. Giuseppe. Andrea," she said, pointing with one hand while the other stuffed bread and salami in her mouth. "My cousins Claudia and Marina, Fabrizio with the food, and lounging on the ground is Ettore," she introduced between chews. Shifting around, she finished, "And behind Serafina is another of my sisters, Bianca Maria." She took a big bite of the bread.

"My pleasure," Dante murmured again, nodding to each person in turn.

They all nodded back, except Bianca Maria, who looked at him coyly and said, "I've always heard that the men from Catania are the handsomest in all of Sicily. Now I can see that it's true."

"Bianca!" Nina gasped, horrified by her sister's boldness. Dante, again, turned bright red.

Unconcerned, Bianca Maria just shrugged. "The music is starting for another set," she said. "Isn't anybody going to dance?" Eyebrows arched invitingly, she stared at Dante until he awkwardly rose. Before he could open his mouth, however,

Giuseppe stood up, hauling Bianca Maria up with him. Without asking permission, he led her off to dance.

As it did before, relief cleared the blush from Dante's neck. But he was already on his feet. His glance slid over the rest of the group, finally coming to a stop on Nina. "Will you do me the honor?" he asked shyly.

"Absolutely," Nina answered. With every minute that went by she was liking Dante more. He seemed sincere and kind, and his simple gallantry impressed her. She took the last bite of bread and salami, wiped her fingers on the grass, and started to push herself up. Bending toward her, Dante held out his hand.

For a startled moment Nina just stared at him, meeting the steady gaze of those beautiful, sad brown eyes. Then she chewed furiously, swallowed, and put her hand in his, allowing him to help her up. His grasp was warm and firm and filled Nina with the same sense of peace and pleasure as did his quiet manner. She smiled at him. Yes. She liked him a lot.

She liked the way it felt when his hand circled her waist and he whirled her through a jubilant dance. She liked the way he thanked her profusely at the end of the set but diplomatically led Zia Gabriella through the next one. She liked the way he brought plates of food when she rested on the ground again with Serafina. He was thoughtful and considerate, and when he finally smiled, his entire face lit up.

She liked him, and she liked the day, alternately dancing with everyone from Ettore to Orazio, and eating course after course of sumptuous food. When she wasn't dancing, she was singing exuberantly or hugging cousins or telling stories. In fact, caught up in the festivity and the sky-high spirits, she couldn't think of a way she could possibly enjoy herself more. Until she turned around at the end of a dance, holding her side from exertion and laughter. And looked into the bluest eyes she'd ever seen.

Wim.

8

Wim was standing not three feet away, the glass of red wine in his hand untouched. He stared at her. Stunned, Nina stared back. The music that had seemed so lively only seconds before suddenly seemed remote. Instead, the loud sounds that filled her ears were the banging of her heart and her great, raw gasps of breath.

He was almost exactly as she remembered him. He was still tall and lean, still elegantly dressed. And though his face seemed firmer, more mature, it was still cut in clean, square lines and was still arresting. His cheeks still looked scrubbed to a rosy glow, and his hair, that incredible silky blond hair, was still pushed carelessly away from his fine brow. Even after eight years in America, Nina still found Wim's fairness dazzling. Her breath came back, but her heart continued to pound.

Then he smiled. It was the same off-center grin he'd given her that day on the floor of Castle Garden. The grin that lifted one corner of his mouth slightly higher than the other. The grin that put a crease in one rosy cheek but left the other one smooth. The grin that was filled with so much charm and amusement, Nina felt herself flushing even hotter. Her pounding heart leapt to her throat. As she had on that day eight years before, she bent her head and studied the ground.

"I must congratulate you on not having lost a single member of your family, in all this time," he said. "Quite the contrary, it would seem you've managed to collect a few new ones."

His voice was the same, too. The same calm tone with the same hint of ironic humor. Only this time Nina understood what he said. A bubble of laughter rushed up through her, lifting her head before bursting out. It was as much a release of the giddy pressure building inside her as it was a reaction to his words.

"I've only gained one new cousin—by marriage—and only as of today," she told him, holding up one finger in corroboration.

"Otherwise, the original numbers are unchanged. Two parents, six sisters, one each of an aunt and an uncle, five cousins, and a dozen or so relatives, many times removed." Her fingers shot up or folded as she counted off, ending in a flutter.

It was Wim's turn to look astonished, then he burst out laughing as well. "You've learned to speak English!" he exclaimed. "And perfectly, too. If it weren't for the very lovely accent you give to your speech, I would think that you'd lived in America all your life."

His compliment made her glow even more. "Thank you," she said. Her thick fringe of lashes swept down in an uncharacteristic show of shyness. But only for a moment. "You have an accent, too," she said, staring at him again, wide-eyed in amazement. "I never even knew it. Well, for that matter, I barely knew what language you were speaking," she admitted, lifting her shoulders and turning her hands palm up. "But I like it very much," she told him. "It's distinct. And very . . . um . . ." Her eyes narrowed in thought. "Very distinguished," she decided with a nod and a final flourish.

"Now I must thank *you*," Wim said, tipping his head toward her. A smile pulled at the corner of his mouth. "It's a pleasure to be described so grandly." He could no longer contain it. The smile came out full force. "Although," he added, "I think my pleasure comes less from your English words than from the very fact that you learned them. And without losing that wonderful fluency with your hands." His own hand waved in a pale imitation of her flourish.

"Whenever I recall the day we arrived in America," he went on, "I always see your hands swooping and darting as you explained yourself in Italian. I was completely taken by this marvelous means of expression." His smile broadened. "To tell the truth," he said, "I still am. So I'm glad that whoever taught you English didn't also insist you keep your hands folded demurely in your lap. What a loss to language that would have been!" He nodded, too. "Whoever taught you was very good."

Nina was utterly thrilled. Like him, she wasn't sure if her pleasure was caused by his charming words or simply by the fact that she understood them. Probably some of both, she thought, taking a big gulp of air. Without a question, hearing that he'd had an image of her in his mind, too, was enough to make her pounding heart swell. Still, she managed to shrug and say,

"Actually, *you* were my first teacher. Don't you remember? The first thing you taught me to say was 'chocolate.' ''

"Oh, yes. I do. Of course!'' he said, raising the glass of wine he was holding to toast the memory. "Chocolate,'' he repeated. "That's right. Then I taught you to say 'orange.' It was our entire lunch.'' His smile became a laugh.

"Well, what do you think?'' he asked with his usual irony. "Was I correct in my judgment of your teacher? Was he good?''

Nina laughed, too, though she wasn't joking when she answered him. "Yes, he was,'' she said. "Very good.'' Then her blush faded as another thought occurred to her. "Do you suppose,'' she mused, "that I learned to speak English with a Dutch accent? Or that my Italian accent has a Dutch twist?'' She hesitated a moment, her eyebrows knitting. "You are Dutch, aren't you?'' she asked.

Though he didn't quite laugh this time, Wim's smile was wide. "I am, indeed,'' he responded. "But I doubt that it has had the slightest effect on your speech.''

"Good,'' Nina said, relief relaxing her face. "I mean it's good to finally know that you're Dutch,'' she said, holding up her hands to ward off any wrong impressions. "Because I was never absolutely sure, you see. It was one thing to pass me a piece of chocolate and tell me what the English word for it was, but it was much more difficult to understand details that had no form.'' She grabbed fistfuls of air to illustrate how elusive some information was. "Like your nationality. Or why you came to America.'' Shaking her head, she told him, "There are so many things I've been wondering about all these years.''

"For example?'' Wim asked, crossing his arms on his chest and studying her with curiosity.

"For example . . .'' Nina hesitated again, her blush returning. She couldn't really tell him most of what she'd wondered. How she'd longed to know what thoughts had made the light in his blue eyes turn serious when he'd stared at her in the crowded hall, his hand resting gently on hers. Or what thoughts had chased the dry humor from his tone when he'd said his sober words of farewell. No, she couldn't tell him that she often spent hours wondering about him, singing softly to herself as she transplanted seedlings or clipped bunches of flowers. Who he was. Where he was. What his life was like. Instead, she smiled and answered his question lightly. "For example, why did you teach me that the word for *dirt* was *gold?*"

Wim looked startled. "What?" he asked. "Gold? Did I do that? It can't be. I don't remember it at all."

"You did," Nina insisted. "It took me months to sort out the difference."

"If that's the case, I certainly apologize," Wim responded. Mystified, he ran his fingers through his hair. "I wonder what I could have been thinking," he said, almost to himself. Then he looked at her and grinned. "Poor Nina," he sympathized. "You've spent all these years puzzling over my motives, and now that we meet again, by incredible chance, I can't even begin to enlighten you."

"Oh, well," Nina murmured, her gaze lowering again. She'd been unprepared for the ripple that had run down her back when Wim had called her by name. It seemed intensely personal to hear it on his tongue. To hear him say "Nina" in his calm, clear tone. She swallowed hard.

"Perhaps I'll do better answering your other questions," Wim continued. "And I hope you can answer mine. I've often wondered about you, too, you know. Where you'd landed. If you'd adjusted to this country. That sort of thing. Though from the sight and sound of you, your new life has gone very well. I think America agrees with you."

Nina took a deep breath to steady herself before attempting a response. "Yes, life has gone well for us," she said, lifting her chin. "We've been quite lucky. Papà has an excellent job, and we're all in the best of health and very happy." She thought a minute, then shrugged and amended. "Well, all except Bianca Maria, who'd rather live in town. And maybe Lucia." Her eyebrows knit. "It's hard to know if she's happy or not."

Wim unfolded his arms and laughed. "I want to hear all about it," he told her. "I want to hear all the 'details that have no form.' About your father's job and Bianca Maria's complaints and about all your other sisters." He bit his lip guiltily. "I've forgotten their names," he confessed. "No, wait. Isn't one of them called Sofia?"

"Serafina," Nina corrected, extremely pleased that he'd gotten it almost right.

"Serafina," Wim repeated, knocking his head with his knuckles to lock the name in place. "Good. You can tell me all about her, too. She was your favorite sister, wasn't she? Are you still so close?"

Nina nodded vigorously, but before she could elaborate, Wim held up his wineglass again. "I have an idea," he said. "Why don't we fill two plates with this delicious-looking food and take them someplace quiet where we can eat and talk? I noticed a glider beneath the trees." He gestured with the glass to a spot beyond the hedge. "We wouldn't have to shout over the music and singing, or be interrupted by all the activity. What do you think about that?"

Without thinking at all, Nina stepped forward. She didn't notice the astonished expressions on her cousins' faces as they darted glances her way. She didn't notice Bianca Maria standing with her mouth hanging open, or Giuliano Gullota fuming. She didn't notice the noise and activity that Wim was afraid would disturb them. Already intoxicated by the wedding merriment, now she was nearly floating.

"I've eaten enough so far today to keep me alive for a month," she told him. "But I'll gladly take a glass of lemonade for company while you have lunch."

"You won't mind if I eat in front of you?" Wim asked, walking with her to the tables. "I know it's rather rude, but I had breakfast very early this morning, and these smells are driving me mad." He surveyed the demolished remains of the feast with a look of anticipation. "What do you recommend?" he asked, without removing his eyes from the food.

"Everything," Nina answered promptly. "If you want a very Sicilian dish, try the *fasoli cu la menta*." She pointed at an almost empty bowl of white beans with mint and olive oil. "It tastes particularly good with a slice of roast lamb and a helping of steamed fennel. Here," she said, seizing a clean plate and starting to spoon *fasoli cu la menta* onto it. "Would you like me to fix it for you?"

"Yes, please. Why don't you do that?" Wim said, grinning as he moved aside to give her more room. When she looked over her shoulder at him, to see if he was teasing, he forced the grin away.

"I nearly didn't come today," he went on conversationally. "Harry Beale invited me out for a little lawn party, but he never mentioned that all this would be going on." He nodded at the festivities. "So when business kept me in town until almost noon, I was on the verge of canceling. Especially when I realized I'd have to wait an hour for a train. Then I saw what a beautiful afternoon it was and decided it would be far better to pass it in the country than sitting in New York City. Now I can't tell you how glad I am that I made that decision.''

Nina twisted toward him again, the wooden spoon she was holding suspended in midair. Was she imagining it, or had there been extra fervor in his voice when he'd made that last declaration? Her turn was so sudden, she caught him staring at her, studying her almost with surprise. Letting the spoon drop back in its bowl, she put her hand to her throat. "What is it?" she asked, her cheeks feeling warm. "What do you see?"

There was a pause, then he answered her simply. "You."

The warm pink on her cheeks turned to burning red, and her heart started pounding again. "Me?" Nina responded. At least she meant to. What actually came out was a whisper. Clearing her throat, she tried again. "Have I splashed something?" she asked. "Do I have tomato sauce on my shirtwaist? I hope not. It's brand-new." She ran her hand down the tucked front of her blouse.

The humor returned to both his face and his voice. "You may rest easy," he reassured her. "You've been a model of neatness. Your clothes are spotless. And quite becoming, too." He didn't seem to hear the sharp breath she took, or to see the way she nervously smoothed her blue linen skirt. Instead, he looked at her more critically and added, "However, I'm afraid I have to tell you that your coiffure is in grave danger. Apparently the hairpins that are made in America are no sturdier than the Italian ones. They're about to fall out. As usual."

Her hand flew to her head, capturing a hairpin just before it slid to the ground. "It's from the dancing," she explained. After fumbling singlehandedly for a moment, she thrust the laden plate at Wim. "Take this," she ordered.

"Thank you," he murmured, doing as he was told.

This time Nina ignored her suspicion of his tone while she jabbed the hairpins back into her hair. "I'll just get something to drink," she said, giving her dark hair a final pat. "Then we can go sit down." Under a tree was a washtub full of lemonade with chunks of ice and thick slices of lemon bobbing on the surface. Using a dented enamel ladle, Nina dipped out a frosty glassful.

"Even that looks unusually good," Wim commented when she returned to where he was waiting. Walking next to her, he started down the path toward the hedge. "If I weren't so eager to hear all your news, I could pass the afternoon very pleasurably in this yard,'' he told her. ''The food is so tempting and I've been enjoying the band very much. Especially that old man with the huge mustache who's playing the flute. He intrigues me. Is he one of your relatives?''

Nina tipped her free hand back and forth. ''More or less,'' she answered. ''Actually Signore del Vecchio is Zio Sergio's uncle, but since Zio Sergio and Papà are third cousins, he's some sort of blood relation to us, too.'' She looked at Wim and admitted, ''I'm not too clear about how, though.''

''It's enough to know that he's connected to you,'' Wim said. He cast a glance back at the scene they were leaving. ''I think that's what I like most about being here,'' he decided. ''The feeling in the air. You're not only celebrating a wedding, you're celebrating being a family. And if it makes an accidental guest like me feel good, I can imagine how much happiness it gives you.'' They reached the hedge, and he stood to one side so she could pass through the narrow archway.

But Nina paused a minute to take a more careful look at him. Although she was nearly oblivious to all else around her, to the songs and the laughter and the astonished mutterings of her cousins, she was keenly aware of Wim. Of his every gesture, his every look, every inflection of his tone. Now she thought she heard a hint of loneliness in his words. It made her suddenly remember the flicker of longing she'd seen on his face eight years ago, at Castle Garden, when she'd been reunited with her family in a flurry of hugs.

''Yes,'' she agreed at last. ''My family is the heart and soul of my life.'' She stepped through the opening. ''But what about yours?'' she asked. ''I don't know the first thing about your family. Is it big? Are you close, too?''

Since Wim was behind her now, Nina couldn't see his expression, but there was something about his hesitation in answering her that *felt* grim. Then they were through the hedge and side by side again, walking across the spring green lawn. When Wim finally spoke, his voice was calm, as always, but there was neither amusement, nor any other emotion, in his tone. ''I had only one brother,'' he said. ''Hans. He and my father died when I was eight years old. My mother died when I was sixteen.''

His stark statement jarred Nina to the core, but it didn't invite either questions or condolence. While she struggled to figure out an appropriate response, Wim led her to the glider. "Here we are," he said smoothly. "Isn't it a perfect spot? Look. You can just see the water." He pointed his glass of wine across the lush expanse of lawn and trees to the distant shimmer of Oyster Bay. Then he set the wine on the grass and gestured for Nina to sit down.

She sat. "It's lovely," she said, willing to be distracted, though she still felt the impact of his words. With almost exaggerated interest, she studied the surroundings, then smiled politely and repeated, "Quite lovely." She shrugged imperceptibly, privately thinking that Don Alberto's grounds were much more impressive.

Then Wim sat down next to her, sending the glider gliding and sending her thoughts into a spin once more. The din of the wedding party was muffled by the hedge, and even the more sedate sounds of a badminton game on Mr. Beale's back lawn seemed distant. They were all alone, floating in space, so close Nina could see every fair hair as it swept off Wim's clear brow, so close she could smell the clean scent of soap on his scrubbed cheeks. She took a hasty swallow of lemonade.

"Mmm. You were right," Wim said, tucking into his lunch. "This has a wonderful flavor." He pointed with his fork. "How do you call it again?"

Nina inhaled slowly, "*Fasoli cu la menta*," she answered as levelly as she could, while wondering why she'd never noticed the tiny dot by the bridge of his nose.

"Excellent," he pronounced. There were a few moments of silence then as he took a hearty bite of the lamb. And as Nina shut her eyes, desperately trying to steady herself, she felt both excited and confused.

"Are you falling asleep? Am I boring you?" His light questions penetrated her daze.

"No, no!" Nina exclaimed. Her eyes flew open and her hands shot up in denial. "I wasn't sleeping, I was thinking. I was just, um . . ." For a frantic moment she cast around for an excuse. "I was just remembering the day we first met." She nodded, pleased with that response. Although it didn't begin to explain her fluster of emotions, it certainly wasn't a fib. More evenly she added, "It was a long time ago."

"It was," Wim agreed, impaling a fat macaroni with his fork. "And a lot has happened in that time. While I eat, why don't you tell me all about it? I want to know everything. Did you come at once to Long Island?''

Nina leaned back in the glider. "We don't live on Long Island, if that's what you're thinking," she said. "We're just here for Aurelia's wedding."

"Oh?" With his mouth full of pasta, Wim couldn't say more, but his eyes opened wide in question.

"We live in Stamford, on Mr. Albert Blackwell's estate," Nina told him, pointing across the distant water at the invisible Connecticut shore. "After you left us at Castle Garden, we went next door to the Labor Exchange, and Don Alberto came up to us almost immediately and offered Papà a job. You see, he'd just finished building his house, and he was looking for someone to plant a few bushes and make the lawn look less like a field."

"And did he manage to do that?" Wim asked, setting his plate on his knee while he took a breather.

"Oh, yes. The grounds are beautifully planted now." Her hand waved descriptively. "From May till October they're really quite spectacular. If you saw them, I know you'd agree."

"I'd like to see them," Wim said, catching her hand as it sailed past. He turned it over to inspect the strong, stained fingers. "Although, from the looks of it, your father hasn't done it all alone. I would guess that he's had your help. Am I right?"

Nina yanked her hand away, her heart beating so fast it cut off her breath. She hadn't been expecting him to seize her wrist. Or to feel the hot shock of pleasure that had gone through her when he did. A flush crept up from her high lace collar and burned its way across her cheeks. Jamming her hands underneath her knees, out of sight, and out of reach, she answered him in a barely audible voice. "Yes," she whispered. "I help Papà."

Unperturbed by her swift withdrawal, Wim picked up his plate and started eating again. "What is it that you do to help him?" he asked. "Do you weed the gardens? Mow the lawn?"

Nina cleared her throat again. "Usually Papà mows the lawn," she said, her voice still a trifle shaky as she tried to organize her whirling thoughts and remember exactly what it was that she did. "I spend a lot of time in the Nursery," she said. "That's our big greenhouse that has running water and windows that open in the summer to vent the heat." Her hands emerged from under her skirt, and she stretched her arms far apart to show him how big the greenhouse was.

"You can't believe how wonderful it is inside," she told him, her voice growing stronger. "Especially in the early spring when the tiny seedlings appear." Her thumb and forefinger barely touching, she measured the baby plants. "You can practically watch them growing," she said with a satisfied sigh. "It's incredible."

Although Wim had a forkful of fennel, he paused to study her before carrying it to his mouth. "You like this work," he stated. The amusement in his tone was replaced by surprise.

Nodding enthusiastically, Nina said, "Yes, I do." She might be confused about his presence and thrilled speechless by his touch, but there wasn't a hint of a doubt in her mind about her enjoyment of gardening. "I love to see things grow," she said. "And thankfully, Don Alberto does, too."

Wim chewed thoughtfully. "This Don Alberto," he said, saying the Italian term cautiously. "Would he be the Mr. Blackwell I met when I arrived at the party?"

A line of worry began to form on Nina's brow. "Yes," she said, sitting on the edge of her seat again.

"Hmm."

"Why do you say 'hmm'?" Nina asked anxiously. "Was he rude to you? He's been ill lately. Sometimes he's a bit impatient."

"No, no." Wim waved his fork in the negative. "He was perfectly civil. In fact, I rather liked him. But I never would have suspected him of a passion for flowers. He seemed, uh, shall I say, businesslike?"

"I know, I know," Nina admitted, sinking back on the seat. "And you needn't soften your words. He can be very brusque, at first. Even difficult." Then she sat up straight again and came to the don's defense. "But underneath all that barking there's really an extremely decent man," she said.

"If it weren't for Don Alberto, I wouldn't speak English half as well as I do. Nor would I be able to read it. He took a liking to me," she explained. "Probably because of our shared interest in gardening. Whatever the reason, though, he's always treated me well. He's pushed me to read all sorts of books and every horticultural magazine he subscribes to. I can't tell you how many times he's hammered at me to improve my English and to broaden my knowledge. It's the path to success in America, he claims."

Nina stopped suddenly and stared at Wim, her head slightly cocked. "If I remember it right," she said slowly, "you told me the very same thing. You even had the interpreter translate it so I'd be sure to understand.''

Finished with his lunch, Wim set his plate on the grass, his crooked smile creasing one cheek. ''I don't precisely remember that,'' he confessed. ''But I believe you if you say I did. It's the truth. It sounds like advice I would give.''

It was Nina's turn to pause and study Wim carefully, her arms folded against the tucked front of her blouse. ''From the looks of *your* hands,'' she finally said, ''and from the looks of your clothes, I would guess that you've followed your own advice.'' Taking in his perfectly tailored suit of fine summer weight worsted, and the fact that his snow-white collar was crisply starched cloth, not paper, she nodded. ''You look quite successful,'' she decided.

Wim's smile became a laugh. ''I've done well,'' he acknowledged.

Settling back on the glider, Nina nodded again. ''Tell me,'' she demanded.

''Yes, madam,'' Wim agreed with another laugh. He, too, settled himself more comfortably. ''Let's see. I suppose I should tell you I spent my first six months in America working at a very dreary clerk's job. Then America's fabled opportunity knocked.'' He rapped his knuckles on the seat of the glider. ''I was offered a new job where all my years of experience in the bulb industry proved very valuable. You see, this company wholesaled seeds and spring-blooming bulbs.''

Already attentive to his story, at this information Nina sat bolt upright. ''Bulbs?'' she interrupted. ''Do you mean tulips and daffodils? That sort of bulb? Irises? You have experience with them?''

''Yes,'' Wim replied, somewhat startled. ''Yes to all your questions. Didn't you know that?'' Before she could answer, though, he slapped his palm against his forehead. ''*Stom!*'' he reproved himself. ''No, of course you didn't. You couldn't understand what I told the immigration officials.''

When Nina shook her head, he smiled and said, ''So. Now I must tell you that I was born in Haarlem, which is the center of the bulb-growing district in Holland. Really, the entire economy of the region is based on bulbs. Either you work in the bulb industry— growing them or sorting them or selling them or clerking in the offices of the exporters—or else . . .'' He let his deep shrug finish the sentence. There were no other options.

"How marvelous!" Nina exclaimed, clapping her hands together. Although she had no idea what Holland looked like, a whole region full of flowers had to be breathtaking. It sounded like a fantasy come to life. "How lucky you were to grow up in such a splendid place," she said with a trace of envy. "I can't understand why you would want to leave it to come here."

The amusement in Wim's tone became dryer than usual as he responded, "I left for the same reason, no doubt, that your family left the splendid place where you were born. Because I was poor. Because there was no chance to make any money unless I owned land and no chance to own land unless I had money. Does this sound familiar? How many feasts did you have in Sicily as grand as the one your family is having today?" He looked at her, waiting.

"*E bè*," Nina conceded, somewhat deflated. "Not many, it's true." Then she shrugged, too. "None," she corrected.

"Exactly," Wim said. "Which is why I left Holland. Always hard work without any reward."

"But now you have a good job, right?" Nina asked.

Wim beamed. "Now I own the company," he answered.

"What!"

Laughing, Wim told her, "I bought it from my former employers six years ago last week."

Nina shook her head in wonderment. She'd never known anyone who'd owned his own business before. Except Don Alberto, of course, which wasn't the same thing. She knew Don Alberto because he'd hired her father. He was *il padrone*, and his wealth and success was an established fact. He wasn't someone she'd met on the day they'd both arrived in America. Someone, apparently, who'd been as poor as she was. Granted, Wim had looked elegant and important, even then, but he'd been a steerage-class immigrant, nonetheless. She, too, tapped her knuckles on the seat. "Opportunity knocked," she said, full of awe. "And you answered."

"I did," Wim replied with decided pride. "The first few years were a bit rough, I admit, but I slowly built up the business. When the florists and nurseries and horticulture retailers realized that I go to Holland once a year, that I speak directly to the growers in Dutch, and contract for the finest quality bulbs in the widest variety, they gradually became my customers."

This time Nina's reaction was not at all reverent. In fact, it was extremely excited. "You sell bulbs to florists and nurseries?" she burst out. Now he was talking about something she knew. Not about opportunities or contracts, but about flowers. About beautiful things that grew. This put business in an entirely different light.

"That's where I bought our bulbs last fall," she told him, her hands whirling through the air. "At George L. Waterbury in Stamford. Do you sell to him? These are excellent bulbs. Much better than the ones we got through the mail in the past. The tulips are just coming up now and look *magnificent*. Especially the ones called Couleur Cardinal. They're a brilliant shade of red. Do you think they're yours?"

Almost bouncing, she sat forward on the seat, knocking the glider into motion. "Wouldn't it be wonderful if they were?" she asked, grabbing the side rail for balance. This news not only put business in a different light, but put Wim in one as well. Or, more accurately, it brightened the light already around him. It heightened his dazzling appeal. Then her hands flew again as she unleashed a torrent of questions.

"Do you use bone meal when planting?" she demanded. "What is meant by a 'species' tulip? And oh, how frequently should the narcissus be divided? What—"

"Whoa!" Wim said, laughing. For the second time that afternoon he reached out and caught her hands in midswing, this time, though, in an attempt to slow her tumble of questions. It worked. Actually, it stopped them dead cold as her heart once again leapt to her throat and cut off her speech.

"One question at a time, please," Wim said, still laughing. He gave her hands a gentle shake but didn't let them go. "And make it an easy one, or after all my bragging about how much I know, you'll show me up to be a dunce. So. Which one will it be?"

Nina didn't answer him. She couldn't. She hardly heard what he said. For one long, silent moment she looked down at his fingers. They were wrapped around hers in a warm, secure grip. Then she looked up. Up into his blue eyes. Bluer than the sky and brighter than the sea. Only now they weren't sparkling with amusement, laughing at some secret joke. Now they were serious. Intensely so.

"Nina," he said as he drew her closer. "Nina." His voice was low and nearly hoarse.

She had just enough time to take a short swallow of air. Just enough time to let her own eyes fall shut. Then Wim leaned forward and his lips brushed hers. It was only a touch, barely grazing her mouth, and then it was gone. But Nina gasped and her eyes flew open, though she remained where she was. She was powerless to move, paralyzed by the sensations rushing up through her body and flowing out her limbs. Completely overwhelmed, she could only stare at Wim.

He smiled. A tender smile meant only for her. Her heart gave another leap, and her lashes swept down as Wim leaned forward and kissed her again. It was a longer kiss this time, unhurried and smooth. His lips slid across her mouth, pressing and letting go and pressing once more. She could feel his face next to hers, feel the clean, rosy glow of his skin. She could feel his breath on her cheek. A lock of his silky hair fell against her brow, and her nose filled with the faint scent of his soap.

Nina had no idea how long they sat there, how long their knees touched and their fingers intertwined. It could have been minutes. Or hours or days. Or seconds. She only knew that when he finally pulled away, she felt a deep sense of loss, a wrench of regret. Involuntarily her fingers tightened around his, and his tightened around hers in response. She stared at him again, only inches apart, wanting to tell him about the feelings flooding her heart. Wim stared back, his lips moving to form words, his blue eyes bright with surprise.

= 9 =

Whatever Wim's words were, whatever might have come next, never got said or done. Instead came the sound of her name again, though brusque and impatient as this time it was called out by the don. "Nina!" he shouted, stumping toward her across the lawn. "There you are at last. Good God, I've been looking for you everywhere. What are you doing here?"

It wasn't only Nina's heart that jumped at the sharp tone. So did the rest of her, too. In less than an instant she yanked her hands

free of Wim's and was on her feet, her wits scattered in a dozen
directions and her cheeks burning red. What had happened? What
had she done? And what was Don Alberto shouting? Giving her
head a shake, she tried to clear her thoughts. "*Che cosa*?" she
asked as the don approached.

"I said I've searched everywhere for you," Don Alberto
repeated, coming to a halt in front of her and planting his cane in
the grass. "Where've you been? Why are you hiding over here?"
He gave Wim a hard glance. Not suspicious, just assessing.

Although Nina was too flustered to tell the difference, or to
make a reply, Wim seemed to have no trouble collecting himself.
"Mr. Blackwell, we met earlier," he said, holding out his hand.
"I'm Wim de Groot. Please forgive me for stealing Nina from the
party, but we were exchanging news. You see, we haven't seen
each other since the day we both arrived in New York, nearly eight
years ago. It was a happy coincidence to find her here today."

"De Groot, eh?" Don Alberto said, placing a limp hand in
Wim's and giving him a second, squinty-eyed look. "Doesn't
sound Italian," he commented.

The corners of Wim's mouth twitched but didn't break in a
smile as he firmly shook the hand he was holding. "Nor is it, Mr.
Blackwell," he replied with his usual calm. "I'd be pleased to be
from a country with food as fine as I've eaten this afternoon, but
the truth is I'm Dutch."

Don Alberto spent another moment looking from Wim to Nina
and back to Wim, as if he were trying to decide how a Dutch
immigrant had come to meet an Italian one. In the end, though, he
dismissed the matter with a stamp of his cane, insufficiently
curious to pursue it. "Yes, yes," he said, before turning to Nina
again.

"You've got to come see this, Nina," he told her, pointing
toward an opening in the hedge at the far edge of the lawn. "I've
been talking to Harry Beale about his seed business, and you can't
believe how fascinating it is. Come on. He's going to show us
the seedhouse." He snagged her arm and gave it a tug. "That's
where the cabbages are processed," he explained, starting off
across the lawn again. "Well, come *on,* Nina," he said, stopping
and looking over his shoulder when she failed to move. "Why are
you standing there like a cement statue? I'm telling you, this is
tremendously interesting."

Nina took a deep breath and forced herself to think, to sort out the talk of cabbages from the kiss she could still feel. It wasn't easy. Nothing like this had ever happened to her before. She'd never even realized it could. "I'm coming," she finally said, although she still didn't budge. She didn't want to disappoint Don Alberto, but how could she just walk away from Wim?

He solved that problem, too. "If you have no objections," he said, slipping her arm through his, "I'll join you on this expedition. I've seen the seedhouse, and others like it, a number of times, but Mr. Blackwell's right. It's an interesting business."

If Don Alberto had any objections, he didn't voice them. More likely, he hardly even noticed Wim. "Beale's just out here on the weekends, mostly," he told Nina as he started for the far opening in the hedge once more. "He lets your uncle take care of the daily routine. But when it's harvest time, he comes out more often. Likes to get his hand in. Says it's a welcome break from his New York office."

"I see," Nina murmured, keeping pace with the don. She nodded thoughtfully, although she hadn't absorbed a single word he'd said. Whatever concentration she'd finally managed to muster had fled the minute Wim had taken her arm. It was impossible to pay attention to what Don Alberto was saying with Wim's firm grip linking her to him. Nor was it solely the pleasure caused by his touch. Rather, Nina found everything about him intriguing and marvelous.

Peeking sideways at him, she thought, as she had eight years before, that he was the very essence of America. Strolling easily on his long, lean legs, he seemed confident of his place in the world. Just like America. He was honest and ambitious, with a sense of humor. He was fair-haired and blue-eyed and smart. Just like America, he was intensely appealing, and yet, ultimately, just like this enterprising young country, there was something about him that was foreign.

"Beale told me he gets three hundred and fifty to four hundred *pounds* of seed per acre," Don Alberto was saying. "Can you imagine that? And what do we buy every year in those little packets? Half an ounce? Do you know how many cabbages that represents?" He pointed his cane at the field out of sight on the other side of the hedge.

"Beale said that nationwide almost *half a million* pounds of cabbage seed were produced last year. Phenomenal, isn't it?" He paused for her exclamation of astonishment, but when none was forthcoming, he turned to glare at her. "Nina!" he snapped. "Are you listening to me? Have you heard anything I've said at all?"

The familiar bark jolted Nina, and some semblance of composure returned. "Yes," she answered, her forehead furrowing with determination. "Yes, I've heard what you said. You were talking about cabbages, isn't that so?" Sure that she'd got it right, she looked at him for approval.

But Don Alberto snorted. "Of course I was talking about cabbages," he said. "For the past ten minutes. Although you haven't got the faintest idea what I've said about them."

"No, that's not true," Nina responded, holding up her free hand in protest. "I heard you. You said . . ." Her fingers squeezed into a fist as she strained her mind and memory. "You were talking about cabbage seed. Yes, that's it. Cabbage seed." Her brow cleared and she flashed him a smile. "Three hundred and fifty or four hundred pounds to an acre, you said. Let's see. Sixteen ounces to the pound times three hundred and fifty is . . . No, four hundred pounds is easier. Four hundred times sixteen is, um . . ."

"Six thousand four hundred ounces," Wim supplied.

Nina nodded. "Right," she agreed. "And the packets we buy are half an ounce each, so that's . . . *Santo cielo!*" She stopped abruptly and stared at Don Alberto, her attention fully captured at last. "That's twelve thousand eight hundred packets of seed per acre! *Dio mio!* It must make a million plants!"

"That's what I've been trying to tell you!" Don Alberto shouted in triumph. "This is an amazing business. Simply amazing."

"Actually an acre of cabbage will produce far more than *one* million plants," Wim spoke up. Both Nina and Don Alberto turned toward him sharply. His mouth quivered again, but again he kept a straight face. "An ounce of cabbage seed should make approximately five thousand plants," he told his rapt audience. "Which means that four hundred pounds, or an acre's worth, will, in theory, propagate well over *thirty* million plants."

Nina gasped and looked back at Don Alberto in disbelief.

He shook his head and muttered, "Simply amazing."

"Well." Nina's hand flopped open as she tried to comprehend this wonder. "Some of the seed gets wasted," she rationalized. "More than half the shoots get thinned out. Some don't germinate."

"It's still a lot of cabbage," Don Alberto said solemnly.

"Yes, it is." Nina's tone was hushed. Nature was an awe-inspiring force.

It was Wim who started them moving again, ambling across the lawn. At the hedge he disengaged his arm from Nina's so she could step through the opening. Although she felt another surge of loss at the separation, the sight of the working farm on the other side of the privet distracted her. She and her family had come to Long Island half a dozen times before, but their visits had always been in winter when the fields lay under layers of straw mulch and there hadn't been much to observe. Now, however, her interest was piqued.

There was an enormous greenhouse, three times the size of the Nursery, some barns, a shingled office, endless rows of cold frames, and the building they'd come to see. The seedhouse. It, too, was wooden, but with bands of big, double-hung windows running around both floors, and a weathered door, wider than a wagon, smack in the middle of the building. At the moment it was tightly closed and barred, but a smaller door next to it was open. Harry Beale was standing in the doorway to welcome them.

"Hello! Right this way!" he boomed, beckoning to them. "Glad you found your helper, Blackwell. How do you do, Miss Colangelo? And I see you've picked up this young rapscallion as well." He clapped Wim on the shoulder. "But he's a good lad. Even though I can't sell him seed anymore, I still like him. Eh, Wim?"

"Perhaps we'll be able to do business again one day, Harry," Wim responded. "So your compliments won't have been a waste of time."

Harry Beale let out a short bray of laughter, then his face got serious. "You thinking of wholesaling seeds again?" he asked. "Have you got something up your sleeve, de Groot?"

"Nothing," Wim answered, still smiling and holding out his elegant arms for inspection. "At the moment I have no plans even to think about wholesaling seeds again, I promise you. But you never can tell when opportunity will knock." Rapping his knuckles on the doorframe, he looked at Nina and his smile deepened.

Nina felt a glow go all the way down to her toes. That comment, and its accompanying rap, were directed at her. While bantering with Harry Beale, Wim was telling her he remembered the moments they'd spent alone. His smile had an intimate warmth.

"It's too bad there's not much going on right now." Harry Beale's hearty apology wafted through Nina's reverie. "Now we're just waiting for things to grow. The new seedlings have gone into the ground just this last week, and last year's cabbages were dug out of their winter trenches and replanted in April. Cabbage is a biennial, you know," he said. "It takes two seasons for it to flower and make seeds. But at least I can show you the equipment in the seedhouse and tell you how it's used. Come in. Come in." Waving again, he gestured them inside.

The interior was light and airy, though one side was partitioned off. "This is called the bag room," Harry explained, pushing open its door and letting them file in. "We keep our tools and supplies in here."

Nina's attention returned to the seed business as she scanned the room, crowded with the paraphernalia of the trade. Bales of bags, in assorted sizes, were stacked against one wall. Against another were propped various paddles and sieves and toothless rakes. On a third wall hung dozens of stencils bearing legends such as Early Jersey Wakefields and Bridgeport Drumhead and Henderson's Succession. Taking a sniff, Nina smelled a mixture of cabbages, paper, and ink. It stirred the imagination. "How many varieties do you grow?" she asked, full of curiosity.

"Twenty-two," Harry answered promptly. "Though never all at the same time. If the varieties are to be kept pure, they mustn't be allowed to cross-pollinate. So we rotate. While a field of Marblehead Mammouth is in flower, for example, the field next door is full of Early Oxheart seedlings. And when that's in bloom, a year later, we've got a savoy in the other field."

He turned then and led them back out to where they'd entered, explaining that the wide corridor and barn doors enabled wagons loaded with sun-dried cabbage flowers to be driven directly inside. "Ask your uncle if that doesn't save a lot of heaving," he said to Nina. "Those stalks start to weigh after a while."

Next he showed them the threshing area, a smooth, tight floor where the round, black cabbage seeds were flailed free of their flowers. A series of hand-powered fans stood ready to blow the chaff away from the tiny prizes.

"Same process for all vegetables?" Don Alberto asked, experimentally poking the floor with his cane.

"Essentially." Harry nodded. "Anything that's got a dry covering gets some variation of the threshing and fanning routine.

There's a clever machine available that crushes small, delicate pods like balsams, but the principle's the same.''

"What about vegetables like tomatoes?" Nina asked as she bent down to run her fingers over the floor. It was satiny to the touch. "I should think they'd make a huge mess."

"Yes. There's a different process for pulpy vegetables. Don't know much about it." His tone grew vague and he motioned them toward the stairs. "Come up and see the drying racks," he invited.

Nina straightened quickly and followed their host, hoping she hadn't been too inquisitive. Suddenly intrigued by the whole concept of commercial seed growing, though, questions just popped out of her mouth.

"Tomatoes aren't threshed but put through a grinder and left to ferment," came Wim's calm voice behind her.

She turned, halfway up the stairs, and looked at him. "You know about *that,* too?" she asked.

"Of course," he answered with another smile. "I managed to acquire a certain amount of knowledge during my time in the seed business. Enough to know that fermentation will make the vegetable pulp separate from the seed. Then it can be rinsed and sieved until it's ready for drying. There. Now you know as much as I do," he said, putting his hand under Nina's elbow as a hint for her to keep climbing. "Satisfied?"

Nina didn't answer, just smiled back. Then she turned again and bounded up the rest of the stairs.

"Well, well. I thought you'd got lost," Harry Beale greeted her. "I was showing Mr. Blackwell the drying racks," he said, his hand sweeping around the room. Tall wooden racks stood out from every inch of the walls, interspersed by open windows. "We spread the seeds on canvas-covered frames to give them their final drying," he explained, "then slide the frames into the racks. Each frame has its own numbered slot. A smooth fit. The last thing we want is a lot of jiggling or banging to get the frames in or out. Imagine that?" He laughed. "The seeds would end up scattered all over the floor."

"How long do you keep them here to dry?" Don Alberto asked, ignoring the extraneous natter. He was all business as he leaned on his cane and peered around the room. "Do you ship them as soon as the seeds are ready or do you have to store them, too? How many times do the seeds get handled before they leave here?"

If Harry Beale ever answered those staccato questions, Nina

never knew. Because the next instant his daughter came up the stairs and slipped over next to Wim. "So this is where you've all been hiding," she chided sweetly. Her remark was addressed to everyone present, but her eyes rested longest on Wim.

They were baby-blue eyes in a round pink and white face, and they were fringed by long, curly lashes. Miss Penelope Beale was soft and pretty, with light, fluffy hair piled on top of her head in a bun. Though in her early twenties, her freshness and innocence gave her the air of someone much younger.

"I might have known," she said, tilting her head up at Wim and giving him a conspiratorial wink. "Every chance Papa gets, he drags our guests out here to show them this dusty old building. You'd think it was Windsor Castle." When Wim responded with his crooked smile, she turned to her father and shook a delicate finger. "If you keep kidnapping our company like this, no one will ever come to visit us again," she declared.

"Now, honey, I didn't kidnap this lot," Harry replied with a chuckle. "Fact is, I've never had a more willing tour group. They've been hammering me with more questions than I know how to answer. Isn't that right?" Still chuckling, he looked around at his guests, saying, "Help. You've got to save my life here."

However, Don Alberto, disgusted by such coyness, could only grind his teeth and twist his cane against the floor. Nina had her back to everyone as she examined the racks on a far wall. In the void, Wim spoke up. "I'm afraid that he's right, Penelope," he said, nodding his head in regret. "This time it's we who kidnapped him. But if you promise to forgive us, we promise to restore him to the party at once. What do you say? Will you be merciful?"

Penelope laughed, a merry, lyrical sound. "Only if you come, too," she countered.

"Done," Wim agreed instantly. "We're on our way."

While Penelope laughed again, Nina shut her eyes against the pain. It had come tearing through her, destroying her happiness, when Penelope had winked at Wim, and Wim had smiled in return. That same off-center smile that always made Nina's heart soar. That same smile full of charm and humor she'd imagined to be so intimate. That same smile she'd first seen on the floor of Castle Garden and seen again today on the seat of the glider. That wonderful smile that he'd smiled at her, he'd also smiled at the pink and white confection that was Miss Penelope Beale. The thought was devastating.

She'd had to turn away, feigning fascination for the empty stack of frames, when, in fact, she couldn't even see them. Her eyes were blurred with tears, and there was a knot in her stomach that was rising up to strangle her heart. It had been almost more than she could bear to hear Wim's even voice behind her, to hear the usual wryness in his tone. To hear him chatting familiarly with Penelope. To hear him say her name.

"You must come immediately," Penelope insisted, reaching out to lightly tap Wim's arm. "The Italians' music is drifting across to our lawn, and some of us are starting to dance. It's so much fun. They're such a happy people."

"Of course they're happy," Wim responded. "It's a wedding. It's a happy occasion. Coming, Nina?"

Somehow Nina composed her face and somehow she got down the steps. When she saw the open door in front of her, though, she lunged through it to gulp huge breaths of air outside. The bright and breezy seedhouse suddenly seemed intolerably close. Without a word she fell in at the rear of the group as they started back toward the hedge. At a fork in the path, however, she veered off sharply and went her own way.

"Wait, Nina! Where are you going?" Wim called after her as soon as he realized she was gone. But Nina was already well down the road to the Ruggieris' house and only lifted her arm in salute. She didn't turn around.

"It's all right," came Penelope's voice. "She's going off to be with her friends."

Nina wasn't, though. After the others disappeared through the hedge, she veered again and headed out toward the fields. The gaiety of the party seemed unendurable, too. Instead, she walked a long way across the flat, open field, following the rows of bolting cabbage. Their heads were split apart, their leaves were ripped and splayed, and weedy-looking stalks were growing up through their centers. They looked as battered as Nina felt.

Finally halting at the end of a row, she buckled her knees and sank to the dirt with her back to the world. Her high spirits were extinguished, her giddy bliss completely quashed, crushed to dust by Miss Penelope Beale. With her porcelain complexion and baby soft hands, she looked as if she belonged next to Wim. She was pretty and graceful, wore beautiful clothes, and probably passed her days sipping tea with equally refined and fair friends. If it wasn't a match made in heaven, it certainly was one made in America.

Fists clenched against her stomach, Nina rested her head on her upturned knees. Don't cry, she ordered herself. No tears. You don't deserve the absolution they bring. You were stupid. A fool. *Un'imbecille.* She continued to heap on the scorn. *Cretina,* she told herself. What did you expect? What could you possibly have been imagining?

She told herself she was an idiot to have believed, even for a minute, that Wim was really attracted to her. Those long looks she'd invested with such serious meaning were just his way of assessing her. And that kiss. Well. That was no more than a reaction to the excitement of the day. A response to the music and the laughter and the coincidence of encountering her again after all these years. He was just being kind to her, as he had been at Castle Garden, and, as he had at the end of that day, he would disappear from her life after this one.

Although they no longer communicated with gestures and pantomimes, they were, undeniably, still worlds apart. They had nothing in common except a few hours spent together, except a lunch eaten while leaning against the rails of an immigration queue. Remembering the orange and the chocolate, each split in half and shared, Nina, despite herself, choked on a sob.

Stop it! she commanded, willing herself to face reality. The truth was inescapable. Wim was a calm and cool businessman in a finely tailored suit, a successful, educated, and handsome man who fit flawlessly into America. And while she could speak and read English, thanks mostly to Don Alberto, she remained dark and Sicilian. A poor immigrant girl with dirt-stained hands and noisy, ignorant relatives. She had only to listen to Penelope guilelessly referring to "them" and "us" to be reminded that the gap was unbreechable. It didn't help to acknowledge it in her head, though. Where it hurt was in her heart.

It was late afternoon when Nina heard the soft padding of feet behind her. Even before she peeked over her shoulder, she knew from the sound of the tread that it was Serafina. Sure enough, her sister sat down next to her, drawing up her knees and resting her head on them, the same as Nina. "I saw you walk out here, so I thought I'd come and keep you company," she said.

Her quiet voice and affectionate sentiment were an instant balm on Nina's wounds. "*Grazie, cara,*" she thanked Serafina. As she turned to give her a weak smile, she was surprised to see a shadow of melancholy on Serafina's lovely face, and a wounded look in her keen, brown eyes. Another surge of warmth thawed the coldness in Nina's soul. Serafina must have sensed her mood and was sympathetically assuming it. Nina reached over and took her sister's hand.

"I can't think of anyone else's company I'd rather have right now," she said with all sincerity.

"Nor can I," Serafina responded with equal sincerity, giving Nina's hand a gentle squeeze. "The party is wonderful, but after a while so much festivity is exhausting. It feels good to be alone with you, sitting here tranquilly."

Nina looked at her sister again, studying her delicate features and shy expression. On an impulse, she pulled her into an embrace and planted a kiss on her coil of braids. "How lucky I am to have you," she told Serafina. To herself she added, and Mamma and Papà and all my sisters. And Don Alberto and the days I spend in his greenhouses and gardens. How lucky I am to have the life that I do. Really, what more could I want?

$$=10=$$

In the days following their return to Stamford, Nina resumed the lucky pattern of her life. It was May and the perennials were coming alive, and the annuals were bursting out of the Nursery. Flowers and vegetables were clamoring for her attention, and with increasingly revived spirits, she gave it. Most mornings she was hard at work immediately after breakfast and didn't return to the congenial clutches of her family until light faded after eight.

As time went by and plants started to bloom, the ache twisting her heart began to diminish. Only a bed of late double tulips hindered the restoration of her happiness. Every time she walked past, or even caught a glimpse of them from a distance, the vivid

Dutch flowers reminded her of Wim. Then that terrible pain would shoot through her again. Until it was squelched by a wave of self-disgust.

Basta! she would tell herself, fiercely rubbing her brow. Enough! It was all a mistake. A dumb misjudgment made in the magic daze of the day. But now it was over. Finished. Dissolved and vanished like a dream at dawn. Now it was time to stop brooding.

As she knelt in the newly tilled earth of the kitchen garden one afternoon, it seemed she was finally obeying her own orders. The sun was baking into her bones, and the fresh, green smell of the tomatoes she was planting filled her nose. She felt contented and even hummed a Sicilian love song while she stuffed the sturdy plants into the dirt. It wasn't a particularly happy ballad, telling the tale of two lovers who were separated, but at least she was humming.

Her musical offering was interrupted by the muffled thump of Don Alberto's cane, though she didn't stop working as he approached. She did look up, however, and was somewhat surprised to see him stomping along with more force than usual. His movements had been slow and creaky since his heart attack, the labored efforts of an old man. But today there was drive in his step, the forward thrust of his former self.

"You've got to listen to this, Nina," he told her, halting by the end of the row. He kicked over a crate just emptied of tomato plants and lowered himself on top of it. "Do you hear me?" he asked in an animated voice. "Stop fidgeting in the dirt and pay attention."

With a sigh Nina let go of the plant she was holding and rocked back on her heels. She fixed her gaze on the don's baggy face and folded her hands in her lap, the picture of attentiveness. "Tell me," she said. "I'm listening."

Ignoring the exaggeration of her pose, Don Alberto settled back on the crate and announced, "I've taken your nagging to heart and decided on an activity to occupy my retirement."

"You have?" Nina exclaimed, rising up on her knees. She didn't have to pretend to be interested now. "What is it? What are you going to do?"

Don Alberto lifted his eyebrows but didn't answer immediately, letting his dramatic silence build suspense. When he finally spoke, he said, in a satisfied tone, "I told you this was important."

It was Nina's turn to raise her eyebrows. And also her turn to be impatient. "Yes, yes," she said, circling one hand. "But what is this important decision?"

Unhurried by either her gesture or her prompting, Don Alberto draped both hands over the top of his cane. "I'm going to start a seed business," he answered.

"What!" Already on her knees, Nina could only straighten more stiffly.

"A seed business," the don responded, obviously enjoying her astonishment. "Didn't you hear me? I'm going to start a seed business." Then, unable to restrain himself any longer, he launched into an enthusiastic explanation. "I got the inspiration on Beale's farm on Long Island," he told her, leaning forward on the crate. "I've been thinking about it and researching it ever since we came back. And I've come to the conclusion that it's the perfect idea."

As Nina fell back on her heels, Don Alberto waved his cane at her. "Did you know that it's one of the few industries that hasn't stumbled through the hard times in recent years?" Without waiting for her answer, he went on. "In fact, it's actually boomed in the past decade." Giving a hard chuckle, he amended. "I suppose *bloomed* would be a better way of putting it. But whichever"—he jabbed his cane into the fluffy soil—"it's a good, strong industry, and I'm convinced it's the ideal occupation for my retirement. It combines the two things I know and like the most—gardens and business. Why, it's practically tailor-made for me. I'll have it running smoothly in no time." Having delivered himself, he leaned back and waited for Nina's reaction.

She didn't answer immediately, but her silence wasn't for dramatic effect as his had been. It was to gain time to compose herself. To control the sudden rush of anxiety she felt. It would never do to let Don Alberto see how utterly opposed she was to his idea. Especially since, as he had stated, she'd encouraged him to find something to do. Drawing a deep breath, she finally responded, couching her objection in positive remarks.

"It certainly sounds like the perfect business for you," she said with commendable calm. "I've no doubt that, given your knowledge and interest, you'd make a bang-up success of it, too." She paused and took another deep breath, then casually added, "But it does sound like an awfully active pastime for your retirement. I thought the reason you retired in the first place was to get away from that type of work. Didn't the doctor say that the pressures of running your own company were bad for your health?'' she asked in a mild tone. When she really felt like yelling that the doctor had warned him to give up his business or be prepared to give up his life.

Even before she could finish speaking, however, Don Alberto was leaning forward again. ''This is different,'' he said, pushing the doctor's warning to one side with a flapping hand. ''New York Wool is a huge corporation with holdings in a number of regions. All in all, I had close to three thousand employees to think about, besides the vagaries of the market to contend with. But this business,'' he said, pointing his finger at the fresh earth, ''this one would be small. There wouldn't be many employees to worry about, and there wouldn't be any pressure. This business would be fun.''

''Fun?'' Nina echoed, incredulous. ''*You* are going to run a business just for *fun*?''

''Well, all right,'' the don conceded, familiar irritation beginning to creep into his tone. ''I'd run it for a profit, too. But that doesn't mean it won't be amusing. There's no harm in making a profit, Nina. It isn't a dreadful disease, you know.''

''No, no. Of course not,'' Nina hastily soothed. The last thing she wanted was to trigger his temper. ''I just meant that there are bound to be problems with any business. Even a small one. And sometimes it's the little aggravations that can chafe the most. The doctor said you should avoid situations . . .'' Her voice faded as she saw his expression turn from slightly annoyed to riled. Quickly abandoning that argument, she tried a new tack.

''It's really an excellent idea,'' she said warmly. ''As you say, it fits you like a glove. I wonder, though, '' she added, idly raking her fingers through the dirt, ''I wonder if it could be made to work. After all,'' she said, scarcely daring to breathe, ''you haven't got nearly as much land as Mr. Beale. While it's more than enough for a splendid country estate, it might not be enough for a serious seed farm. I'm not sure you'll be able to turn a profit from just a few spare hayfields.''

To her amazement, Don Alberto neither growled nor sulked. Rather, he gave another chuckle. ''I don't need a lot of land,'' he told her. ''Come to that, I could do the whole business without ever stepping outside.''

''What do you mean?'' Nina asked, her eyebrows knitting

together and her hands stopping still in the dirt. "What kind of joke is that?"

Don Alberto's chuckle turned to gleeful laughter. "It's not a joke," he answered. "It's the plain truth. Because I don't intend to start a seed *farm*. I plan to start a seed *catalogue*." He paused a minute to let that announcement sink in, chortling again when Nina's mouth dropped open. Before she could collect herself, though, he edged forward on the crate to explain.

"Growing seeds is a nuisance," he said. "As you pointed out, I don't have enough acreage to make it worthwhile, just for starters. And then there's all that fussing around with planting and transplanting and threshing and storage. Too many steps. Too many opportunities for something to go wrong. One mishap and the whole year's profit is spoiled. No, no. Don't want any of that." He dismissed those risks with a flick of his finger.

"Besides," he continued, "there's nothing to *do* on a seed farm. At least not for me. Just sit around and watch the cabbage, or whatever, grow. Not much different from what I do now. Don't forget," he said, jabbing the same finger toward her, "Beale's got a business in New York to occupy his mind most of the year. He only looks in on the farm on weekends and at harvest time. I want something to keep me busy every day."

"Yes, but—" Nina started to say, having recovered enough from her shock to speak.

In his enthusiasm, however, Don Alberto bowled over her protest and kept on talking. "Had quite a productive session on Long Island," he went on. "I quizzed Beale and his associates at length. That Dutchman was particularly helpful. Knows his stuff, too. From what I gathered there, and with subsequent investigation, there are two essential ingredients for making this venture succeed.

"The first is good business sense," he told her. "Got to know how to organize the company, set sights, and realize them, so to speak. As far as all that goes," he said, without a trace of modesty, "I couldn't find anyone better than me. I built my fortune with precisely those skills.

"The second thing, though, is where you come in, Nina." There was genuine excitement in his tone as he leaned even farther forward. "The second thing needed for a successful seed catalogue is, obviously, seeds. Good ones. Not like those cleomes you bought that never germinated. Good seeds and a good selection of them. And as far as that aspect goes, I haven't met a single soul who knows more about plants than you. You've got an instinct for them, as strong as mine is for business. Fact is, Nina, we're a perfect team.''

He sat up straight and slapped his knee. ''Why, together we ought to be able to produce a catalogue that stands Vick's and Burpee's on their ears. You take care of the product, I'll take care of marketing it, and before you know it, we'll have a flourishing business.'' Almost flushed with triumph, he paused for breath and to hear Nina's response to his plan.

Because she didn't want to be responsible for another heart attack, Nina restrained herself, barely, from giving him her honest one. She didn't shout out that she thought it was a crazy idea, the lunatic fantasy of a bored old man. There was an undertone of annoyance in her voice, however, as she said, ''Papà and I can hardly keep up with the work we have to do right now. I don't know how you can possibly expect us to take on any more.''

''Simple,'' the don answered. ''We'll put on extra men. Already hired one who starts tomorrow, and we can hire as many more as we need.''

''What if they're idiots, like the last one?'' Nina fretted. ''What if they won't listen to Papà?'' She was more openly disturbed by his scheme.

Too excited to let her objections bother him, Don Alberto tossed his hand. ''Then we'll fire 'em,'' he said grandly. ''And keep hiring gardeners until we get the right ones.

''Listen to me, Nina,'' he demanded, twisting back and forth on the crate. ''There isn't a thing you can add to these grounds. You've gone as far as you can go. You've designed gardens and greenhouses, laid lawns, filled the solarium, set out hedges and borders without end. All that's required now is the maintenance of your creations, and there are plenty of drones who can tend to that. You're too talented to be weeding sweetpeas and fooling around with tomatoes.'' He poked his cane at a nearby Atlantic Prize. ''You should be out conquering the next horticultural horizon, and I'm telling you, Nina, this seed catalogue is it.

''Don't you understand?'' he asked. ''This is the ideal opportunity for *both* of us. It'll keep me from going mad, and it'll give you the ultimate boost up the ladder. We can make a success of it together. And we can enjoy ourselves besides. Look at what a good time we have when we go to the horticultural shows or on expeditions to botanical gardens. I guarantee this will be even better.''

Leaning over to straighten the leaves of the mistreated tomato plant, Nina struggled to frame a reply. The more the don talked, the more she realized he wanted her participation in this venture as much as he wanted to sell seeds by mail. In fact, she thought, gulping, her involvement was a major attraction of the business. The idea of doing a catalogue fit him so well because it combined not only gardening and business, but also her constant presence.

Still toying with the tomato leaves, Nina remembered the discovery she'd made a few months ago when they'd sat together in the Nursery. That Don Alberto was terribly lonely and depended on her for company. She was his only true friend, the family his ''beastly'' sons had never been. But despite the warm rush of affection that knowledge brought, her worry didn't diminish. The doctor had been quite specific about Don Alberto leading a more peaceful life.

''Perhaps that's the solution, then,'' she said, looking up at last. ''Perhaps instead of starting a business, we should just spend more time on our horticultural outings. We could go not only to the shows, but to nurseries and famous gardens as well. We could probably even find other seed farms like Mr. Beale's to visit.'' The light in her eyes was beseeching. ''Wouldn't that be as much fun?'' she asked. ''And it would be pure pleasure—without any responsibilities to chew away at us. After all, the doctor said—''

''Forget what the damned doctor said!'' Don Alberto interrupted in a roar. ''If I followed his orders, I'd be dead in days. From paralysis of the brain.'' Moderating his tone to a less thunderous grumble, he added, ''You know it yourself that I'm at my wit's end doing nothing all day long. I started working when I was nine years old, and after sixty-five years I can't just stop cold. The toll it takes is worse than any one of those years of work.'' He paused to shake his head in disgust. ''If that's what I have to do to keep on living, what's the point of staying alive?'' he asked.

''Because I'd miss you terribly if you were gone,'' Nina answered. She wasn't fiddling with plants or clumps of soil now.

For a moment Don Alberto seemed startled. ''Well,'' he harumphed. Then, typically, he took advantage of her tender declaration to press home his case. ''Believe me, Nina,'' he cajoled, ''this is going to be more satisfying than traipsing around to flower shows. Because instead of just drifting aimlessly, we're going to have a *purpose*.

"Listen," he said, excited again. "I've got it all figured out. For now we're going to run it from the library, but only while we're building a new building on the other side of the Nursery. It'll be a warehouse and a shipping department with offices upstairs. You're going to have your own office, Nina. Not just a dilapidated chair in a corner of a greenhouse, but a real office. And your own salary to match. You won't go unrewarded any longer. Or be considered an extension of your father."

"*O Dio!* Papà!" Nina exclaimed. Just when her opposition to Don Alberto's idea was starting to soften, a new problem reared its head. "I'm not sure that Papà will approve," she said with a sinking feeling. "In fact, I'm rather positive that he won't. The only reason that he lets me work at all is because he has no sons to help him. But it's one thing for me to work on the grounds, by his side, and quite another for me to have an independent job." She shook her head slowly, suddenly aware of how disappointed she was. "He won't like it," she warned.

For the second time that afternoon Don Alberto looked startled, though not very happily this time. A dark expression chased the excitement from his face. In such a low, gruff voice that Nina couldn't make out his words, he muttered, "Orazio. Damn. Never even thought of him."

"*Che?*" Nina asked, leaning forward in the dirt.

"I said, don't worry about Orazio," the don answered more loudly. "I'll have a talk with him." He nodded to himself, deciding on a course of action. "Don't worry, Nina," he repeated. "I'll make him understand that it would be a mistake to hide your light under a bushel. Or in an apron. Or wherever he wants to hide it."

Nina shrugged, her doubts about the whole scheme renewed. "Even if Papà agrees," she said, scooping up a handful of soil and letting it dribble through her fingers, "and mind you, I'm not sure that he will, even so, there are other disapprovals to consider."

"Like whose?" Don Alberto demanded, rapidly losing patience.

"Well, like your sons, for example," Nina answered, not able to meet his gaze. She scooped up another handful of dirt and crushed it. "They'd be upset if they found out I was part of your business." Her voice was smaller and more toneless than normal.

"They'd say I was an uneducated immigrant. That I didn't know what I was doing. That I was giving you all the wrong advice, and you were taking it because you liked me."

"Oh, for God's sake, Nina!"

"No, they'd be right," she said, finally lifting her head. Now the amber light in her eyes was dim with misery. "I *am* uneducated. I've never been to school. I've only had a few lessons with Signora Klem, a kind visitor from Milano. Really, all I am fit for is weeding sweetpeas and fooling around with tomatoes."

She shrugged again. "I think you're overestimating my abilities," she told him. "I don't know anything about seed catalogues except how to order packets for our own use."

"Bah!" Don Alberto snorted. "I'm not overestimating your abilities. Rather, you're underestimating them." He shook his cane at her and said, "You're as bright as they come, Nina. Quick and sharp. Besides which, you've read scores of books on the subject of plants and growing. Everything in my library. No question. I'd trust you to do this job above any so-called educated person you can name."

"I don't know," she said hesitantly, though she held her head higher. His praise put a flush in her cheeks.

"Well, I do," he replied. "You and I, working together, can make this catalogue a tremendous success. I don't care what anyone else says. Least of all, Edward and Reginald. Never have. And my advice to you is to do the same. Just ignore that pair of snobs and their insufferable remarks. Don't know why this little venture should matter to them anyway."

Nina sighed. "I don't know," she repeated as conflicting thoughts pulled her back and forth. On the one hand, she didn't want to disappoint Don Alberto by refusing her help, but on the other hand, she was afraid she'd disappoint him even more if her help turned out to be inadequate.

"Come on, Nina!" the don exhorted, punching his cane into the earth. "Stop being so wishy-washy. It isn't like you. Leave off all this worrying and just say yes."

Nina's mouth worked. On the one hand, she was anxious about her abilities, and still dubious about Edward's and Reginald's interference. She was concerned about the don's health and uncertain of her father's permission. But on the other hand, she didn't want to be disloyal to Don Alberto or to deny him her support. And he might be right. It might be fun. "Yes," she said.

* * *

Nina was still feeling stunned by the plans Don Alberto had unfolded so suddenly, and by her own agreement to participate in them, when she went in for dinner that evening. But instead of being comforted by the familiar routine of her family, she was confronted by another surprise.

"Nina! *Bambina,* look who's here!" her mother cried, throwing her arm around Nina's shoulders and dragging her forward.

"*Buona sera,* Nina," a quiet voice said.

Speechless with astonishment, Nina stared at the slender young man with dark Grecian curls and gorgeous brown eyes. Dante. She'd forgotten all about him. Overwhelmed at the wedding by the appearance of Wim, and distracted for days after by her thoughts of him, meeting Dante had slipped from her mind. Seeing him now, though, standing in the kitchen and smiling shyly, brought everything back in a rush.

"Dante's going to be helping with the grounds," Orazio announced in a pleased tone as he clapped Dante on the back. "Taking care of the greenhouses. Mowing. Trimming. Planting. Whatever needs doing. *Grazie a Dio,* I've finally got someone with experience."

"Of course!" Nina exclaimed, finding her voice at last. "Don Alberto said he'd hired an extra gardener." She banged her fist against her forehead. Rattled by the don's talk of the seed catalogue, she'd forgotten about that, too.

"Thanks to you, he hired me," Dante confirmed as bashful color tinged his handsome face.

"What did I do?" Nina demanded, her eyebrows knitting and her tone a bit wild. Too many things were being sprung on her today. There were too many disconcerting surprises. "I never said anything. How did I help?"

"*Bè,* Nina," Orazio cautioned, his mustache drooping in a frown. Nina spun around to stare at her father.

"He's being polite, *bambina,*" Angelina chided gently. "It's because you were the first one Gabriella introduced him to." Nina spun back to stare at her mother.

"No, not just polite," Dante insisted. His cheeks continued to flame. "You told me there was need of another gardener. Don't you remember, Nina? At the wedding. You said there was more work than you and your papà could keep up with. That it would be the answer to your prayers to have a gardener who could speak Italian.''

"You're certainly the answer to *my* prayers," Orazio said fervently. "We've needed a good man around here for years. Maybe now we can get caught up."

"*D'accordo,*" Angelina agreed. "It's a pleasure to have you here, Dante. For *all* of us." Beaming, she threw her arms around Nina's shoulders again.

"After dinner we can sit out on the porch and have a real talk," Orazio said. "I've got a bottle of wine that I've been saving for a special evening. I think it'll taste very good tonight."

"Mamma, the pasta is cooked," Benedetta interrupted from her usual station by the stove. "Shall I drain it?"

"*Si, si.*" Angelina nodded. "Nina, go wash up quickly," she ordered, patting her daughter's back in dismissal, then hurrying to the table to rearrange chairs.

"Dante, come sit here," she said. With a magisterial wave she signaled their guest to his place. "I'm putting you next to Nina. I know you'll get along well. And listen, I expect to see you here for all your meals." She wagged a finger at him in good-natured warning. "Never mind going up to the kitchen to eat with the rest of the help. All you'll get there is pancakes and mashed potatoes and a cold shoulder. *This* is where you belong."

"*Grazie,* signora. You're very kind," Dante said, coming to take the indicated seat. His voice was quiet and his beautiful lashes swept down shyly, but there was no mistaking the sincerity in his tone. "It feels good to be with a family again."

Angelina beamed again. "You have a big family, too?" she asked, taking her own place at the foot of the table. "Are they all still in Sicily? You must miss them, eh?" Before he could answer, her attention was distracted by Nina, still standing, dumbfounded, in the center of the kitchen

"Nina!" she said sternly, her handsome brow furrowing. "Why aren't you moving? *Via.* Go. Wash up and come to the table. Supper's ready."

"Yes, Mamma," Nina said, mechanically putting one foot in front of the other until she reached the sink. She felt dizzy as she opened the tap and reached for the bar of Ivory soap. During that astounding exchange, she'd turned rapidly from one speaker to another, trying to absorb what was happening. Her father, obviously, was thrilled by the idea of male companionship and assistance. There was even the hint that he preferred it to hers. If that was so, her gardening days were numbered. Especially if she'd interpreted her mother's actions correctly. And there was small chance she was wrong on that score. It didn't take a mind reader to know that Angelina meant "marriage."

Nina soaped up her hands and forearms, hardly noticing when the suds turned bright green. Usually she laughed in delight as the aftermath of touching tomato plants appeared under water, like invisible ink under light, but today she didn't even smile. Instead she attempted to assemble her thoughts, to assess her reaction to the third person who'd kept her pivoting. To Dante da Rosa. What, exactly, was he doing here?

Had he really come just for the work, as he claimed? Not that she blamed him for wanting to quit his job mucking out stalls, or for wanting to move out of the crowded, immigrant tumult of the tenements on Mulberry Street in New York. But were they the only reasons he'd come to ask Don Alberto for a job?

As she watched the green suds wash down her arms and suck into the drain, Nina was afraid that Dante had given some thought to Zia Gabriella's matchmaking efforts, after all. Although he'd undeniably been shocked and embarrassed when her aunt had pushed them together, maybe he'd since decided it wasn't such a bad idea. Maybe, upon further reflection, he'd decided that he wanted to get married. And that Nina would make him the perfect wife.

Leaning over the sink, Nina filled her hands with cold water and splashed it over her face. Again and again. She suddenly felt flushed, almost feverish. It wasn't because she disliked Dante. Quite the contrary, she still found, as she had on Long Island, that his unusual gentleness was appealing. It was just that the thought of marriage to him most definitely was not. Indeed, it seemed less inviting than it had at Aurelia's wedding. Actually, it was fair to say that the idea filled her with dread.

It's just because he startled me, Nina thought desperately. Because he popped up out of nowhere. And on an already crazy day. If I have some time to think about it, I'm sure it won't seem so terrible. Why should it? He's a very nice person.

She shut off the faucet and reached for the towel, burying her face among the linen folds. Time, she repeated to herself determinedly. I just need time. Time and tranquillity. That's it. After supper I'll go out to the Nursery and sit by myself.

"Nina!" came her mother's voice, making her jump. "What are you dawdling for? Finish washing up and come to the table. Your pasta is getting cold."

"Yes, Mamma," Nina said again, hastily blotting her forehead and hanging the towel back on its peg. She went over to the table and slid onto her chair, unconsciously sitting on its edge, as far from Dante as she could get.

"Dante was just telling us about his family," Angelina informed her. "Did you hear him with the water running? He's the youngest of twelve and the only one to come to America."

"Uh-huh," Nina murmured, picking at a few strands of spaghetti. Head bent, she gave a quick glance sideways, but Dante was studying his plate, too. His cheeks were bright red again. It was obvious that he was as uncomfortable as she was.

In an odd way, that discovery heartened her. It even softened her resistance to him. Setting herself more squarely on the chair, she twirled up a forkful of spaghetti with spinach and ricotta cheese. The delicious fresh flavors were reassuring. She'd planted the spinach herself. "Don Alberto has a plan for a new business," she said, stabbing her fork down for a second twirl. It seemed like an important topic to raise. And it had the advantage of avoiding any more pointed personal discussion.

"He told me about it this afternoon," Orazio said before Nina could continue. He wiped his mustache with the back of his hand and shook his head doubtfully. "I think he's gone too far, this time," he said. "Too far. It'll mean extra work and extra worry. Not to mention all the confusion it'll cause. This place will be upside down. See if it isn't." He stuffed a giant bite of pasta into his mouth, mumbling, "Too far. Too far."

"What's his plan?" Lucia demanded, her curiosity aroused. "What's he done now?"

"A bakery?" Benedetta guessed, one part hopefully and nine parts jokingly. She reached for the bowl of pasta for a second helping. "Has he decided to open the Albert Blackwell Bakery?"

"Bah!" Lucia scoffed. "That'll be the day."

"Maybe it's an ice-cream parlor," Stella speculated, picking up Benedetta's train of thought. "Wouldn't it be wonderful to have all the ice cream we can eat right here?" She tossed a black braid over her shoulder seconds before it dipped into her plate. "Without having to drive into Stamford, I mean."

"That's dumb," Rossana told her. "Who would come all the way out her for ice cream?"

"*Ragazze!*" Angelina warned. "*Basta!* Stop! You're being silly. Let Papà tell us what the business is."

"Fff!" Orazio said, taking another enormous bite of spaghetti while he waved his free hand disgustedly. Everyone waited with their eyes fixed on him as he chewed and swallowed and then pushed his empty plate away. "A seed catalogue," he stated, at last. "Mr. Blackwell has decided to sell seed packets by mail."

"What?" Lucia cried. "That's ridiculous. It's impossible. He'll kill you with work."

"Maybe he'll hire even more new men," Bianca Maria suggested, trying to catch Dante's eye.

"Then I'll have to watch them and check up on their work," Orazio said. "We have a good routine now. And with Dante to help, everything will go as smooth as silk. I don't know why he has to fool with that."

"And what about his health?" Angelina questioned. "I thought the doctor told him he had to rest. A business like this could make him sick again. All the work and tension could bring on another heart attack. Then where would he be?"

"He doesn't care," Lucia fumed, scraping her pasta into a precise pile on her plate. "He never cares. It's just another thoughtless whim of an unpleasant old man."

"It's *not* thoughtless," Nina spoke up. Although she'd used many of the very same arguments—albeit more gracefully worded—against Don Alberto only hours before, she now felt obliged to defend him. Especially since she'd agreed to give him her help.

"It's actually very well thought out," she went on with as much conviction as she could muster. "It's going to be a small business, so there won't be any of the pressures of his wool company in New York, though there will be enough activity to keep him busy. Look," she said, flinging out a hand. "Business is what he enjoys. And this is a business that also includes his interest in gardening. It can be run from his house, too. From his bedroom, if he wants."

"*A punto*," Lucia pounced. "My point exactly. While he's taking a leisurely nap, poor Papà will be working like a slave."

"Nina will be working, too, Lucia," Serafina chimed in from her seat on the other side of Dante.

"And we'll all be earning more money," Nina added, leaning forward to give Serafina a grateful wink.

"Oh?" Angelina asked, looking at her husband. Orazio lifted his fierce eyebrows and shrugged.

"I think it's a good idea," Serafina said stoutly. She set down her fork and folded her hands in her lap, leaving her portion of spaghetti almost untouched. "Everyone will profit."

"Everyone will work himself sick," Lucia retorted.

"I knew a man in Sicily who grew flowers for seed," Dante said. His quiet voice sounded as loud as a cannon. The entire family froze to listen. "It was a good business," he said simply. "The man lived well."

For a long moment there was silence. Then Angelina spoke. "You see?" she said triumphantly. "I knew you and Nina would get along well. You both see the same side of things. Two minds, one path." She signaled for Rossana and Stella to get up and clear the pasta plates and for Benedetta to bring on the salad and the roast chicken left over from lunch. "You've convinced me," she said. "I think it's a sound plan, after all."

"*Mannaggia la miseria*, Angelina!" Orazio sputtered. He clutched his head with both hands. "What are you saying?"

"What? Are you deaf?" Angelina asked, waving her hand impatiently. "I'm saying that I think this seed packet idea is smart. Didn't you hear Dante agreeing with Nina?" She gestured toward their guest, who was blushing furiously once more. He opened his mouth to say something, then shut it without uttering a word. "They both think that Mr. Blackwell is right," Angelina continued, never noticing Dante's discomfort. "And so do I." She stared at her husband again, and after a moment he again shrugged.

"*Va bene*," he said. "All right."

Released, the rest of the family shouted their opinions while Nina propped her elbows on the table and rubbed her forehead. How did things get so mixed up? She thought she'd been steering the conversation *away* from any discussion linking her with Dante, but her resourceful and determined mother had found a means of turning even Don Alberto's seed catalogue into proof of their compatability. What was more confounding was the fact that she'd felt forced to defend the don's plan to her family, and now that her family embraced it, Nina was more ambivalent about it than before.

All she knew was that she felt pulled apart, hauled in opposing directions by different desires. She felt tossed from the challenges Don Alberto presented to the family tradition that she enjoyed. From gardening to business to marriage. Nor was it as simple as Don Alberto on the one hand and her family on the other. America versus Sicily, New World versus Old. Up until now she'd been able to balance those elements. But that was before they'd gotten intermingled and entwined with Dante da Rosa and with the seed catalogue proposal. And before they'd all been thrown off track by the reappearance of Wim.

Nina shut her eyes and pressed her fingers over them. Wim. What was she going to do about him? How was she going to stop her heart from jumping every time she saw a tulip? How was she going to erase the blue eyes that were etched in her mind? If it weren't for Wim, she might be able to sort out the other pulls on her loyalty and her love, but with him tugging on her, too, the situation seemed impossible. And how could she hope to understand how he affected all the rest when she didn't understand why he affected *her* so much?

"Nina," Serafina said softly, bending close to her ear. "It's our turn to dry the dishes. Bianca's washing. Are you ready? Are you all right?

Nina raised her head to see her sister's delicate face, dimmed by the same melancholy that had shadowed it in the cabbage fields, the same somber light in her big, brown eyes. Touched now by Serafina's sympathy, as she had been then, Nina reached up and gave her hand a warm squeeze. "*Si, cara,*" she said as she got to her feet. "I'm ready. Let's go to it."

Well, that's that, she thought. No brooding session in the Nursery tonight. Just dishes and coffee and bed. Shrugging, she picked up a towel. Her musings would have to wait. Until then, she'd just have to keep going forward, hour by hour and day by day. She'd have to please, or appease, each person in turn.

As for Wim . . . *Fff*! she scoffed to herself. That's one distraction I can dismiss right now. After all, what good will it do to think about him? He's disappeared from my life again, just as absolutely as he did when he walked out the doors at Castle Garden. Only this time it's really final. Lightning might, one time in a million, strike twice, but it certainly never struck three times.

Nina plucked a wet plate off the drainboard and began to wipe it vigorously. Besides, she thought, raising her eyebrows, what if I should happen to see him again? I mean nothing to him. At least, nothing more than an amusing memory. An entertaining interlude in his normal life. Just a little foreign flavor, like the macaroni or the *fasoli cu la menta*. He belongs with someone who is tall and fair, as he is. Someone with soft hands and expensive clothes. Someone American. Someone like Penelope Beale.

=11=

"Good morning," a stranger greeted Nina when she walked into the library two days later. He was a young man, probably in his middle twenties, and only a head taller than she. His shoulders were broad, though, and there was something dashing about his looks, with his square-jawed face and very pale, clear skin.

When his dark eyes didn't quite meet hers, however, Nina felt a vague twinge of uneasiness, just enough to make her retreat toward the door. "Good morning," she replied. "I'm sorry. I didn't realize Don Alberto had a guest." As she turned to leave, she nearly collided with the don, who was hurling himself into the room.

"Good God, Nina!" he complained. "Watch what you're doing! Where are you going, anyway? Come back in here. We've got a lot to discuss." He gestured toward the stranger and added, "I guess you've already met my secretary."

"Your secretary?" Nina echoed, taken by surprise. Her uneasiness increased. Don Alberto certainly didn't need a secretary to keep up with his social engagements; therefore, this jaunty stranger could only mean the beginning of the seed catalogue business. She'd spent the last two days praying it would never happen, that Don Alberto would rethink the work involved and have a change of heart. Quite the contrary, though, it seemed he had plunged full speed forward. With a sigh, she turned toward the young man again. "We said hello," she finally responded. "We haven't actually met."

"No?" The don bustled over to his desk. "Then meet Gideon O'Shea, and Mr. O'Shea, meet Miss Nina Colangelo."

While he settled himself in his chair and pulled out appropriate folders, Gideon crossed the room to Nina and held out his hand. "It's a pleasure to meet you, Miss Colangelo," he said. His smile was charming and full of sparkling white teeth. "Mr. Blackwell told me we'd be working together. I gather you're quite an expert in your field." His voice had just a trace of an Irish accent, like a well-educated version of the housemaids' brogues.

Nina took his hand but glanced quickly at Don Alberto, hoping to get an explanation of Gideon's remarks. The don was busy shuffling his notes, however, and didn't look up from his desk. She glanced back to Gideon just as his eyes slid away. Feeling increasingly awkward, Nina shook his hand. "Uh," she said. "Thank you. It's a pleasure to meet you, too, Mr. O'Shea."

"Of course, my official title is Office Manager," Gideon continued. He released her hand and flicked a suggestion of lint off his sleeve. His dark gabardine suit was well pressed and the latest cut. "I'm not simply a secretary, you understand."

For a moment Nina stared at him, then she hastily held up both hands and declared, "Oh, of course. I understand." But she didn't really, and smoothed her heavy cotton skirt instead. There were dirt stains on it, she noted miserably, and a small, three-cornered tear by the hem.

"Yes, yes, titles," Don Alberto spoke up from behind his desk. It was a polished piece of mahogany furniture, perfectly suited to this paneled and book-lined room. "Everybody loves them. The bigger the better. I still have to give you yours, Nina." He leaned back in his leather chair and folded his arms on his chest. "How does Head Gardener strike you?"

Nina may have felt discomposed by Gideon's manner, or intimidated by his style, but she was completely undaunted by Don Alberto. In fact, she went up to his desk and leaned across it in exasperation, saying, "What titles? What is this? What are you talking about?"

With equal exasperation Don Alberto leaned forward and answered, "I'm talking about the Blackwell Seed Company, Nina. Come on. What else could it be? When you run a company, every job has to be spelled out so the duties attached to each position are clear. Get it? Now stop glaring and sit down." He waved his hand at some point behind her.

Turning, Nina saw, for the first time, that four chairs had been set up facing the desk. She turned back. "What on earth is going on?" she demanded, jabbing her hands on her hips. Things were happening too fast again, and she was getting tired of it.

But Don Alberto was getting tired, too. He slammed his hands down on the top of his desk and pushed himself to his feet. "We are having a *staff meeting*," he said, enunciating the words with icy sarcasm. "A *staff meeting* of the Blackwell Seed Company. And if you would do us the favor of sitting down, we could commence."

Barely grabbing on to her temper, Nina backed up to a chair. As she did so, she cast a glance at Gideon, who was already seated, his eyes darting between her and the don. His expression was so avid, Nina dropped to her seat without a further objection, suddenly horrified to think she'd been bickering with Don Alberto in front of this stranger. Clamping her mouth shut, she resolved not to make any more remarks.

"That's better," Don Alberto growled, somewhat mollified as he, too, sank into his chair. He picked up a pile of papers and tapped their edges on the desk, then cleared his throat portentously. "We were discussing positions," he began. "As O'Shea here has already noted, he's the Office Manager." He pointed the pile of papers in Gideon's direction. "As such, it's his responsibility to see that the correspondence, accounting, and clerical work are efficiently executed. In other words, he takes care of the paperwork. Any questions about that?" He paused to peer at his small audience.

Nina sat staring at him with her mouth screwed shut, but Gideon spoke up pleasantly. "I think I understand the general intent of my job, though I'm sure I'll be asking more specific questions as situations come up."

Don Alberto gave a curt nod, acknowledging Gideon, but essentially disinterested in this part of the operation. He expected it to function smoothly and, preferably, invisibly, but whatever their titles, secretaries bored him. "Now, Nina," he continued more enthusiastically. "You're going to be Head Gardener. I want you—"

"Impossible!" Nina interrupted, abruptly sitting forward, her resolution forgotten as quickly as it had been forged. "That's Papà's position." She shook her head firmly, quite sure of what she was saying. "I absolutely will not displace him."

Surprisingly, Don Alberto didn't snap back. Nor did he begin to wheedle. Instead, he let out a gleeful chortle, his old eyes gleaming as they always did when he'd maneuvered a coup. "You won't be displacing him, Nina. I promise," he told her. "But listen. This is very clever." He chuckled again. "I've figured out a way to keep your father from objecting to your role in the business. Are you ready?" He looked at her expectantly.

When she sat slowly back in her chair and gave a reluctant nod, he announced triumphantly, "I've given him a grander title than yours. Orazio Colangelo, Farm Manager. How does that sound, eh? And to make it even more important, I've given him an Assistant Farm Manager. That new gardener, whatever his name is."

His hand fluttered vaguely as he explained, "I've never yet met a man who didn't get his sense of power from the title of his job. You can give him double the wage and triple the responsibility, but if you call him vice-president instead of president, he feels inferior. You watch, Nina," he said, nodding wisely. "Orazio will have his title and his assistant and a few more men working under him, and he'll never even notice that you're doing other things."

Although Nina had started to surge up again, now she leaned back once more. She had serious doubts about her father being able to understand the subtleties of these various titles, given his shaky command of English. Come to that, she wasn't sure she understood the differences herself. But she didn't dispute Don Alberto. She was too aware of Gideon's gaze, still flicking back and forth curiously.

"Uh-huh," she murmured.

Don Alberto's eyes narrowed at her lack of response, but he didn't press the point. His tone was several shades cooler, however, as he said, "Before the others get here, I want to lay out your duties."

That made Nina sit up straight again, apprehension prickling the back of her neck. "What others?" she asked suspiciously. "What duties?"

"Your father and the new man, that's what others," Don Alberto answered, gesturing impatiently at the two empty chairs. "And if you'll stop interrupting me, I have just enough time to tell you what duties."

"Why can't you wait for Papà and Dante?" Nina demanded, half rising from her seat as her uneasiness increased. Ignoring the don's broad hint to cease her questioning, she asked, "Is there something you don't want Papà to hear? Is my job a secret? I thought we were all going to work together."

"Not exactly," Don Alberto corrected. His face wore as implacable an expression as she'd ever seen. "We are all going to work toward a single goal, which is the success of the Blackwell Seed Company, but that doesn't mean we all share the work equally. This isn't one of those Utopian colonies, you know. Or some sort of spiritual retreat. This is a business." He fixed her with a long, hard stare.

Nina sat down with a thump. It was even worse than she'd feared. It wasn't going to be like their trips to flower shows, after all. Not a horticultural adventure nor an oversized garden. Instead, it was a business. A strange, foreign, and unfriendly activity.

"Uh-huh," she said again, though her tone was less neutral this time. There was a nervous edge to her voice.

Don Alberto gave no sign that he heard it. "It's going to be your father's responsibility to turn the empty pastures into trial gardens," he told her. "We need a sample plat for every type of seed we sell. Orazio will plow, plant, fertilize, cultivate, and do whatever it takes to grow whatever seeds are decided upon. And in whatever design and under whatever conditions are decided upon." He took a slight breath before he went on, but his gaze didn't waver.

"It's going to be your job to make those decisions."

"What!" Nina gasped, leaping fully to her feet. This wasn't just strange and different, this was plain *pazzo*. It was mad. The don couldn't really expect her to give orders to Papà!

Apparently he could. At least he refused to recognize the fact that she was standing in front of him, gaping in astonishment. Without any indication that her exclamation of disbelief had ever registered, Don Alberto picked up his notes and continued. "Today is Friday," he said, glancing at her over the top of the papers. "I want you to spend the weekend working on a prospectus for the catalogue. We'll meet again Monday morning to discuss your ideas. I want the general draft finished one week from today. Next, I want—"

"Wait a minute," Nina broke in, holding up her hand. Her shock was rapidly turning to bewilderment. "I don't understand. What's a prospectus? What ideas are we going to discuss?"

With a long-suffering sigh, Don Alberto lowered his notes and said, "A prospectus is a report that outlines the guiding features of a business. In this case, of a catalogue. Before we can proceed, we have to know what we are proceeding toward. What the emphasis of the catalogue is going to be."

He began rattling off. "Do we favor flowers over vegetables? Vice versa? Or do we give them equal treatment? Do we sell fertilizers? Tools? Border collies? Burpee does. Do we call plants by botanical name or common name? It makes a difference in our image, you know. Do we capture our customers with no-nonsense listings, like Alfred Bridgeman or The Perry Seed Store Company? Or do we gush on about beauty and vigor, like Miss C. H. Lippincott? What's the size? The length? Do we use blue pages like Harris's? Multiple colors of ink like Vick's? In short, what is the final product going to look like?"

Don Alberto picked up his notes again, saying, "Now do you understand, Nina?" He didn't wait for a response but went right on. "O'Shea, you'll find a copy of the American Florist Company's directory on that first book shelf." He nodded in the general direction while continuing, "There's a list of all the catalogue companies in it. Pick out the ones that sell seeds and send for them. By my count, there's about one hundred and forty-five. Got to see what the competition's up to. That's rule number one."

"Yes, Mr. Blackwell," Gideon replied, jotting on the pad perched on his knee.

"You expect me to have this prospectus thing by *Monday*?" Nina interrupted again. She shook her head. This couldn't really be happening.

The notes hit the desk with more force this time. "For God's sake, Nina," the don said. "It's the thirty-first of May. We don't have a minute to lose. The truth is, we should have started this project six months ago or, even better, last fall. If we're going to have the 1896 issue ready by Christmas, we're going to have to work at double and triple speed. That catalogue has got to go in the mail no later than January one."

"*Santo cielo,*" Nina murmured, collapsing back in her chair.

"By the way, Nina, get yourself a notebook or pad like O'Shea has, so you can keep track of things," Don Alberto ordered, looking at his papers again. "And stop muttering in Italian." He pulled the top page off the pile and tossed it aside. "Next. We've got an appointment at Wallingford and Owens in New York on

Wednesday. They're the architects who are going to design the new building. Start getting together a few sketches of what you'd like, Nina. We'll do the preliminary meeting in their offices, but after that, they damn well better come to us.''

As Nina bent over, resting her elbows on her knees and clutching her head, she heard Don Alberto going on in that staccato tone. "We'll take the seven-forty train from Glenbrook. Be ready to leave here at seven A.M. sharp. O'Shea, you're coming, too. Need someone to take notes. We'll have lunch at the Grosvenor.''

Inside herself, Nina moaned. This was impossible. It wasn't anything like she'd imagined. She thought she'd be helping Don Alberto to relax and be happy. Instead, he was becoming an even brusquer monster. And while she'd known—in fact, worried—that this business would require a lot more work, she'd somehow thought those extra hours would be spent in the greenhouses or gardens. Not for an instant had she considered it would mean being handed problems far beyond her ability to understand, let alone to solve. And the idea that she would make decisions that Papà would carry out! That was just too ridiculous for words.

Don Alberto's endless instructions were finally cut off by the arrival of Orazio and Dante. They knocked deferentially, then entered the room and sat down quickly when Don Alberto gestured them to seats. Discarding another page, the don started afresh, giving them their titles and describing the trial gardens. As Nina had guessed, Orazio's new designation went right over his head. By the quizzical lift of his eyebrows, it was obvious that he didn't grasp the rest of Don Alberto's plan, either. Poor Dante, though straining to follow the don's every word, understood even less.

Through it all, Nina continued to sit rubbing her head, trying to decide how to undo this horrible mistake. It was too late to simply back out. Between Dante's endorsement and her mother's subsequent approval, this scheme had grown extremely complicated. Even though the catalogue, itself, was the major obstacle, it was hardly the only consideration. She had to think of Angelina's wishes and of Orazio's dignity. Of loyalty, traditions, and respect To say nothing of the unapproachable expression of Don Alberto's face.

When Nina dragged herself back to the library after lunch, though, and saw her battered cabinet full of catalogues from the

Nursery, the churning confusion inside her froze. The comfortable, overstuffed chairs and the handsome mahogany tea tables had been removed from the room. In their place were two functional desks. Gideon was seated behind one. The other, apparently, was for her.

Taking a deep breath, more to rein in her temper than to gather courage, she marched up to Don Alberto, arms folded in front of her. "I'd like a word with you, please," she said. There was an uncontrollable quaver in her voice as she added, "It's important."

The don looked up from the graph he was charting. "All right," he agreed. "Go ahead."

But Nina was no longer in a stupor. Even without turning around, she was well aware of Gideon's eyes darting from her to Don Alberto to the letters he was writing. They'd been busy all morning, those eyes, surreptitiously studying Papà and Dante, calculating, assessing. Before, she'd been too dazed to evade them, but now she was much more wary.

"A private word, if you don't mind," she said, keeping her tone pleasant. "It's a lovely day and the rose garden is just coming on. Why don't we take a walk down there?"

For a moment Don Alberto's hard eyes bore into her. Then he heaved himself to his feet and grabbed his cane. With a nod he motioned for her to lead the way. Nor did he say anything while they walked along.

It was Nina who finally broke the silence by commenting, "Have you noticed how beautiful these Duchess of Albany roses are?" Her hand brushed against a bush, and a lush pink bloom nodded. "They smell wonderful, too," she added, taking a breath of the fragrant air. "It's the first year they're showing, and I think they're going to be a sensation."

Don Alberto halted abruptly and turned to face her. "Do you mean to say you got me out here to talk about the roses?" he asked, banging his cane on the lawn. "With all the work there is to do, you want to discuss roses? Nina, I'm surprised at you. I don't think you're taking this business seriously."

"That's not true," Nina responded instantly, turning to face him, too. "I'm taking it very seriously. That's why I'm concerned. I thought there wasn't supposed to be a lot of pressure. That the whole purpose of this venture was *enjoyment*."

A puzzled furrow appeared in Don Alberto's forehead. "Yes,

that's right," he said. "That's what it was supposed to be, and that's what it is. I'm enjoying myself. Aren't you?"

At first Nina thought he was joking, then she remembered Don Alberto never joked. Rendered temporarily speechless, she could only stare at him. Finally she threw up her hands, spun away, and flung herself on a wrought-iron bench.

"No," she answered, shaking her head. "No, I'm not enjoying myself. How can I possibly be?" She thrust her hands into the air and shook them, too. "I don't know what you're talking about. I don't know about prospectuses or architects or sketching buildings. For that matter, I don't know about going to lunch in fancy restaurants. And I certainly don't know how to give Papà orders." Nearly shouting, she told him, "I don't know anything about doing business."

Stalking up to the bench, Don Alberto snapped, "You're not stupid, Nina. Don't act it." He plopped down opposite her, and a branch of blush-pink Baltimore Belles bobbed over and tapped him on the shoulder. Annoyed, he pushed it aside, saying, "You know more about gardening than anyone I've ever seen. I don't understand why you're being so difficult."

Nina took another deep breath, though this time she hardly noticed the perfumed air. "Look," she said in as reasonable a tone as she could manage, "I appreciate your trust in me. Truly I do. I'm very flattered. But I think it's misplaced." She leaned across the bench. "I'm not a businesswoman. I'm a simple girl from Sicily who was blessed with a green thumb. I belong in a field, not behind a desk. I can't do what you want me to do."

Don Alberto blinked, "Of course you can," he said. "I wouldn't be asking you to, otherwise." He poked her knee with the crook of his cane. "Listen to me, Nina," he said. "You were blessed with more than a green thumb, so don't start up with your peasant excuses. You've also got a larger than average share of brains and common sense. And that's the secret to success in business. Just take things step by step. Break every problem down to its most basic parts and solve one part at a time. There. That's lesson one."

He batted at the branch again, and a velvety petal fluttered down and settled on his shoulder. "After all," he continued, unaware of the decoration, "it isn't as if I'm asking you to engineer a bridge across Long Island Sound. This is a *seed catalogue,* for God's sake. You've read hundreds of them. If you spent half the time planning ours as you've spent weeping and wailing, you'd have the prospectus finished.''

"But I've never made a prospectus," Nina protested, holding out her hands. "I've never even seen one."

"Get O'Shea to help you with the writing," the don responded without a trace of sympathy. "That's what he's there for. And he's good at it. He comes well recommended. Lesson two: Fully utilize your staff's skills."

"But—"

"No more *buts*!" Don Alberto's patience was exhausted. "You've got what it takes, Nina. I'm sure of it. I'm never wrong about people." He lunged to his feet, but stood in front of her another moment. "Just watch me," he advised her. "Watch what I do. That's lesson three. Pick out someone successful and study his tactics." As he turned to stump off, he added, "This is quite an education I'm giving you. It'd be a shame to waste it." The rose petal on his shoulder sailed slowly to the grass.

Slumped on the bench, Nina gazed after him as he walked away. Half absently, she noted that his step seemed steadier than it had in months. That he used his cane more for an effect than for a crutch. She sat up straighter. Come to think of it, there had been faint color in his baggy face, too. Sighing, she buried her face in her hands. Maybe he really was enjoying this. Maybe it really was doing him some good. And maybe he was right. Maybe she could figure it out if she tried. She sagged down again. She'd better be able to. Too many people would be disappointed if she failed. Don Alberto, Mamma . . .

"Wait a minute!" she yelled, leaping to her feet. The don turned around. "What about Papà?" she called to him. "You didn't tell me what I'm supposed to do about him. How can I possibly give him instructions?"

"Hmph," Don Alberto snorted. "Same way you've been doing it for the past eight years," he replied. "You don't think all these gardens were his idea, do you?" He jabbed his cane at a rosebush, then turned again and continued on.

Nina bent over to pick up the pale petal that had drifted from Don Alberto's shoulder. He was right about that, too, she acknowledged to herself, running her finger across the delicate surface of the rose. She'd been telling Papà what and where to plant all along. But by the time she'd finished weaving together Italian translations of the don's wishes with horticultural advice she'd read in articles and her own suggestions, they'd never sounded like orders. To either of them. Amazed, Nina shook her head. Lesson four, she thought, starting back toward the library. Be politic.

The next lesson came later that afternoon. She had taken Don Alberto's first lesson to heart and was patiently reviewing her collection of catalogues, attempting to break them down to their basic parts. Midway through Peter Henderson & Co.'s, she remembered seeing, several years before, a slim biography of the company's founder. Hoping his life story might yield some helpful hints, Nina got up to look for it on the shelves.

"I'm going up for a short nap," Don Alberto said as she walked past his desk.

Pausing, Nina nodded. "Take a long one," she recommended. "It'll do you good to rest."

"I don't need a long one," the don retorted, rising. "Nor do I have the time to sleep the afternoon away. I'll be back in half an hour."

While he thumped out of the room, Nina shrugged in resignation and proceeded to the shelves. She found the little volume and thumbed through it, reading snatches here and there. The book absorbed her attention, so she was only vaguely aware of Gideon's chair scraping against the floor. Nor did she fully hear his soft footsteps until they halted behind her. Suddenly conscious of his presence, an eerie ripple went down her back, and she whirled around, heart pounding. He was standing not two feet away, a glittery look in his eyes.

"Oh," she said, pressing her hand against her heart. "You startled me."

Gideon leaned an elbow on a bookshelf, his eyes following her hand. "Sorry," he murmured without apology. He didn't move.

Nina's initial rush of alarm had started to fade, but now it surged up again. Why was he staring at her? What did he need? "Did you want to speak to me?" she asked tentatively. "Or am I in your way? That's it. You must be looking for a book." She took two quick steps backward, but found her path blocked by a potted palm on a pedestal. Then Gideon took three steps forward. Her heart leapt to her throat.

"*Che c'è?*" she asked, her voice scratchy and hoarse. She licked her dry lips and tried again. "What is it?" she whispered. "What do you want?"

The odd light in Gideon's eyes glittered brighter. "Just a token of your affection," he responded, moving even closer. The open edge of his jacket brushed against the tucks of her shirt. "Surely you'd prefer a strapping youth like me to that crotchety old man," he crooned, putting his hand on her arm. He slid it up her sleeve and cradled her neck.

For a fraction of an instant, Nina just stood there, her heart hammering in shock and fear. Then a cloying whiff of his bay rum tonic filled her nose and a wave of disgust rose up inside her. Her own hand flew out and smacked him across the cheek, leaving a bright red imprint across the pale white skin. "*Schifoso!*" she hissed, jamming the heel of her other hand into his chest and shoving him back. "How horrible! Where do you get the nerve to speak to me like that?"

"Why, you little Italian . . . !" Gideon cried as he cupped his bruised cheek. A flush of wrath was creeping up his neck. "You think I can't see what's going on? You think I can't see how cozy you two are? My mother didn't give birth to a fool, you know."

Nina's heart was still pounding, but it was pure outrage that made it bang now. "If your mother has a shred of decency, she'll be hanging her head in shame at the son she gave birth to," Nina said, leaning forward and wagging her finger under Gideon's nose.

"I don't know what put those nasty thoughts into your head, but I can tell you that you're very mistaken. Don Alberto may be a touch crotchety, as you say, but he's an extremely honorable man. And for your information, being Italian does not mean being immoral. Don Alberto and I are *friends*. Can you understand that?" She leaned back and stuck her hands on her hips. "Or does this word have a different meaning in Irish?"

For a moment it seemed as if Gideon would explode. The flush on his face turned to mottled fury. Then, apparently, some other thought took hold of him, and the choleric color receded as quickly as it had come. In fact, he burst out laughing in genuine merriment.

"I do apologize," he said. "I'm terribly sorry. I can see I've misjudged you completely. I can promise you, though, it won't ever happen again." Still rubbing his sore cheek with one hand, he held out the other. "Please say you'll forgive me," he begged. "We'll be working together. Let's do it in peace."

On the verge of slapping his outstretched hand away and telling him, in no uncertain terms, that his working days at the Blackwell

Seed Co. were numbered, Nina, too, had a second thought. Really, it was more like a flash of intuition. In the space of less than a second, she remembered Don Alberto saying that Gideon was good at his job. Then she realized she was going to need help in the days ahead. Lots of it. Wouldn't it be better, as her mother always said, to have the devil she knew than the devil she didn't? Especially since this devil would probably be extra helpful, in an effort to make up for his mistake. He'd laughed, but he had to know he'd made a serious miscalculation.

Her hand lost its angry swing and, instead, slipped into his for a friendly shake. She gave a laugh, too, though hers was forced and unnatural. The idea of pretending good will was going to take some getting used to. Lesson five, she thought.

It proved as valuable a lesson as the other four. As she had suspected, Nina needed lots of help as the project progressed. Surprisingly, though, it wasn't Gideon's familiarity with business that came to her aid as much as his comparative sophistication. She was discovering that her discomfort and ignorance came more from lack of exposure than from lack of ability. She needed to know how to act among businesspeople.

Hardly a day went by without some sort of meeting, either with salesmen or growers or architects. Deciding on plants, on paper, on printers, on plans. Discussing mailing lists, advertising, and equipment. Some meetings were in the library, others were in offices in New York, a few were even across linen draped dining tables. It was all foreign territory.

The first time Gideon helped her out of an embarrassing predicament was at their lunch at the Grosvenor. Nina had been silent, extremely awkward behind an array of silverware and the imposing menu. Being a curmudgeon, it hadn't occurred to Don Alberto that Nina might be in social distress, but Gideon had seen it and had offered discreet assistance. Disguised in polite small talk, he'd given her suggestions of what to order, then ordered the same thing himself. When the meal arrived, he'd shown her, by example, how to eat it.

Employing similar tactics, Gideon continued to help her. And taking the advice that was always carefully couched in casual conversation, Nina learned quickly. Her confidence grew with equal speed. It amazed her, however, that despite her gratitude and despite their increasing office rapport, deep down and after hours, Nina had no greater liking for him than on the day they'd met. She shook her head and shrugged. Business, she thought. What an odd world.

One Monday morning Gideon dropped a business card on her desk, saying, "I saw my favorite cousin yesterday, and she couldn't stop talking about her new dressmaker. To hear Edwina, the woman has magic in her fingers. She insisted on showing me every new gown and giving me a lengthy recitation of how the woman had designed it especially for her. When I finally managed to make my escape, Edwina pressed this card on me." Sliding behind his own desk, Gideon gave his merry laugh. "I certainly have no need for her services," he said. "But I thought it might amuse you."

Nina looked down and read MME. MATILDE SALLÉ, 42 SUMMER STREET, STAMFORD, CONNECTICUT. She picked up the card and tapped it thoughtfully against her cheek. Without a doubt, her wardrobe needed some drastic rehabilitation. The weathered skirts and comfortable shirts she wore for digging in the garden were completely inappropriate for business meetings. Even her Sunday clothes looked funny and provincial. But how did she know that Mme. Sallé's creations would be an improvement? How did she know that Cousin Edwina's taste was any more polished than hers?

Swiveling around, she confronted Gideon, once and for all. No tiptoeing. No tactful hints. No cautious chatter. "If you're so comfortable with formal dining and elegant dressmakers, why are you working as a secretary?" she asked. "It seems a rather common occupation for a man of your refinement."

"Tsk, tsk, Miss Colangelo," Gideon mocked, pulling a folder from his drawer and setting it in front of him. "Such boldness is acceptable in well-established businessmen, such as Mr. Blackwell, or in harmless eccentrics, but it's frowned upon in rising young executives. That's today's lesson."

Crossing her arms in front of her, Nina continued to study him. "I have the excuse of being a poor immigrant," she said. "I don't know any better."

For a moment Gideon toyed with the folder, annoyance pursing his mouth. Then he laughed again and shoved the folder away. "Very well," he said, sitting back. "I'll give you all the sordid details." He fingered a pencil as he began.

"I was born in Dublin to a man of decent means but ancient ideas. In other words, the major share of his wealth went to his oldest son, with the remainder going in diminishing amounts to the others. I'm the fourth.''

Gideon's eyes flicked over her. "After university, I thought to come here," he said. "My cousin had preceded me and had married a prosperous businessman. I thought I would find my fortune in America, as well. You can imagine my disappointment, therefore, when I discovered that the fact of my being Irish counts for more than the refinement you noted. Secretary, or rather *Office Manager*, is the best I can do." He pushed himself forward again and opened the folder. "The irony of it is," he concluded bitterly, "is that I'm a poor immigrant, Nina, the same as you."

Nina turned back to her own stack of papers but didn't immediately attack it. In her mind she saw another poor immigrant who'd come to America determined to find his fortune, too. Somehow he'd managed to overcome the obstacles. Somehow he'd managed to succeed. There was no bitterness in Wim's voice, no superiority in his manner. And his blue eyes didn't flicker and dart. They fixed on her squarely. Their steady gaze went straight to her heart.

With shaking fingers, Nina picked up a list from the Plant Seed Co. in St. Louis, Missouri, though she barely saw the words. Instead, she saw those blue eyes. Never mind that lightning didn't strike three times. The first two strikes had left their mark.

$$=12=$$

"Good morning, Mr. de Groot," the gray-haired clerk intoned. Without looking up through his visor, he held out a sheaf of papers.

"Good morning, Harris," Wim replied pleasantly. The older man always sounded inconsolably glum, his red-rimmed eyes and sunken cheeks reinforcing that impression. Wim sometimes wondered if he was responsible for it. If his own youth and success were a taunting reminder of how life had passed the clerk by. Then he gave an imperceptible shrug. He supposed it really didn't matter. Harris, despite his gloom, was very good at his job. Wim reached for the papers. "What have we got today?" he asked.

"A letter from the Parks Department in Pittsburgh requesting information and prices," the clerk recited. "A response from the insurance company regarding your inquiry into rates. An invitation from the Botanical Gardens to give a lecture as part of their evening series. Six customs forms that require your signature. And two cables from Holland. Something about a crop failure.

"Crop failure? *Verdomd!*" Wim swore softly, flipping through the papers to find the source and the extent of the bad news. He quickly scanned the cables. An outbreak of sclerotium tuliparum had decimated a field of parrot tulips. Wim sighed. He knew it was a particularly virile fungus that had not only ruined this season's bulbs but would spoil the soil for years to come. "Just a typical Monday morning, eh?" he remarked as he made his way toward his office.

Wim closed the door behind him, something he rarely did. For one thing, it was a modest-sized room, only as big as his needs, and he hated to feel shut in. But for another thing, he wasn't so far removed from life as a clerk that he didn't remember the cold, imperial picture that a closed door presented to those on the other side of it. It wasn't a picture he cared to perpetuate. One of the advantages to owning the company, though, was that he could modify the rules at will, his door policy among them. And right now, he wanted some privacy to think.

He tossed the papers onto his desk, then shed his jacket and draped it neatly on the back of a chair. With the door shut, the July heat was trapped in the room, even though he opened the lone window as wide as it would go. Sighing again, Wim finally sat down, tilted back in his chair, and put his feet on the plain oak desk. He picked up the cables and stared at them, but for some reason his mind refused to concentrate on the problem.

No, not for some reason. He knew very well what the reason was. It was a pair of big golden eyes in an animated face that belonged to a delightful young woman named Nina. She'd been haunting him for the last two months. Crowding into his head at the oddest moments, banishing all other thought with one of her engaging flourishes.

It was incredible how their divergent paths had crossed not once, but twice. How they'd found each other in this vast America.

What was even more incredible to him, however, was his own reaction to that second meeting. As clearly as if it had happened five minutes before, he could feel his immense relief on learning that Nina wasn't married. He could see her holding up her fingers as she counted off her relatives, and could feel his heart surge when he realized there was no ring on any of them or a husband among them. Until that moment he hadn't been aware that it mattered that much. But apparently it did.

Wim tucked his hands behind his head and stared at the ceiling. Honest with himself, as he was with everyone else, he now admitted that he found himself tremendously attracted to her. Not out of sympathy because she'd lost her family among a crush of strangers. Nor solely out of intrigue because her background and customs were so different and interesting. No, he found himself attracted to her, quite simply, because she was an utterly vibrant woman.

He'd never met anyone like her, anyone with such deep passions. She flung herself into life with the same grace and spirit as she flung her hands through the air to describe her feelings. There was an eagerness about her, a sense of excitement, that showed in everything she did. Even her clothes, which would seem shabby on another woman, seemed almost glamorous on her. They were a part of the way she lived, part of her style and purpose, part of her great love for plants. And her hair. Thick, dark, and wavy, and constantly on the verge of bursting free of its pins.

Dropping his chin on his chest, Wim rubbed his eyes with his knuckles. There was no question that she was a remarkable woman. No question that her strong face was beautiful. Rather, the question was why *he* found her so irresistible. He, Wim de Groot. He who was so calm and neat. He who rarely lost his temper. He who viewed the world with amused irony and based his life on logic, not emotion. Why couldn't *he* get through a day without thoughts of Nina distracting him?

Why had he been drawn, against all common sense, to seize her hands, to entwine her fingers with his, to kiss her? Why had he savored that kiss so much, feeling, even now, the sunshine on her smooth cheeks and tasting the faint trace of sugary lemonade on her full lips? And why, above all, had he felt shocked and hollow, when she'd veered off the path and sped away from him?

Wim wiped his own mouth with the back of his hand. He'd

come back from another stay in Oyster Bay only late last night. When Harry Beale had invited him for the weekend, he'd accepted with alacrity. Although he'd tried to tell himself he was looking forward to the fresh air and an escape from the steamy city, he knew he'd really been hoping to find Nina again. Or, at the very least, some echo of the wedding party. But apart from a brief chat with Sergio and a glimpse of Nina's cousins, there was no sign that the lively event had ever taken place. All was very decorously pleasant. And Penelope was very demurely lovely.

With another sigh and a brisk shake of his head, Wim forced his attention back to the cables that had fallen into his lap. He'd have to find a new supplier for the parrots. The showy tulips with jagged-edged petals were only a small portion of his business—and Roozendahl was only one of his growers—but he disliked disappointing even a few of his customers. It demonstrated an indifference he didn't approve of.

"*Verdomd!*" Wim muttered, loosening his tie and unsnapping his collar. "It's hot." His feet banged to the floor, and he rose to open the door. Then he rolled up his sleeves and got down to work, reaching for a pencil and pad to make a list of possible replacement sources. It was late in the season to be hunting for bulbs. Most of each year's crop was contracted for before it had even sprouted, often just after it was planted in the fall. Surely by spring.

If worse came to worst, he supposed he could always hire an agent to go to the Bovenkarspel. Named for the ancient town where it had been held for the past two centuries, this auction was the last hope for the grower who hadn't sold his bulbs. And for the buyer who had no other channels. The bulbs weren't the pick of the crop, though. Selection was hit or miss. Moreover, this method would cost him more than he'd make. But the Bovenkarspel was a sight to see.

Absently scratching his fair head with the end of the pencil, Wim let his attention stray again. He thought about how much Nina would enjoy the old auction. Even more, how much she'd enjoy spring in Holland when the flowers were in bloom. He could just imagine the rapture on her face when she stood in a field surrounded by thousands of tulips.

"*Zo is het wel genoeg,*" he told himself sternly with another shake of his head. That's enough. Get back to work.

=13=

Although Nina found her long hours behind a desk nerve-racking and her ever-increasing list of responsibilities exhausting, there was one aspect of the Blackwell Seed Co. she enjoyed immensely. The trial gardens. She loved escaping from the office with a clipboard under her arm and hurrying through the sunshine to the fields. Orazio, with the help of his new crew, had transformed them. Where weedy hay had once turned blond and dry, long, narrow beds now sprouted young green plants.

"It looks wonderful, doesn't it, Papà?" Nina said, shading her eyes to admire the far corners of the field.

"We got started too late," Orazio grumbled in reply. He had paused in his work to lean on a hoe and visit. "We rushed into this too fast," he told her. "You can't rush gardens. They have to be nurtured slowly. The soil has to be built up and prepared. It needs fertilizer and lime and a green manure crop that we can till in early in the spring." He toed a dry clump of dirt and shook his head. "All this haste isn't right. It's not good for the garden. And it isn't the way I like to do things."

Nina lowered her hand and turned to look at her father. Beneath the battered brim of his old straw hat, his eyebrows bristled irritably. "I know, Papà," she soothed. "The idea for this garden came about very abruptly and we didn't have time to do our usual job, but don't forget, it serves a different purpose. It's supposed to have just average soil and average care, so we can see how the seed will perform for the average gardener. It's meant to be a testing ground, not a showpiece. Although," she added, scanning the field again, "I think it's lovely. The sheer volume of plants is spectacular."

"I like it, too," Dante agreed, coming up behind her.

Nina spun around to give him a grateful smile, but Orazio wasn't moved. "Half this stuff will never make it," he worried.

"The perennials hardly ever show much the first year, to begin with, and a lot of the rest got started too late. You'll never see a single tomato from any of these plants, just for an example."

"I know, Papà. I know," Nina said again, though her tone was less patient this time. They had this discussion almost daily, but her father still refused to understand. "We'll have to make do with the results we get, for this year," she told him, checking the pocket watch suspended from a gold chain around her neck.

Eleven forty-five. There was a salesman from the Brown Bag-Filling Machine Co. coming at one. The architect was due at two-fifteen to inspect the freshly laid foundation. And she hadn't even begun her row by row examination of the trial plats. She kept a weekly log, making notes on her clipboard about any bugs or blights that afflicted the plants and generally charting their progress. As she realized how late it was, an increasingly familiar sense of pressure tensed her entire body.

Orazio shook his head, unaware of her schedule and stubbornly unwilling to compromise. "A bad beginning brings bad luck," he said superstitiously.

While Nina stamped her foot in frustration, Dante poked his hoe at a scrap of a weed. "Most gardens start awkwardly," he commented. "It takes a while for things to adapt. Both the plants and the people. You have to see what grows well, what methods work, what looks good." He gave a mild shrug.

"This garden might serve a different purpose, but the principle's the same," he said. "The first season you experiment, then you start adjusting." He thrust his chin out toward the long rows of plants. "Me, I'd like to see irrigation pipes laid out here next spring. And grass on the paths. It'll keep down the dust."

Shooting Dante another grateful look, Nina said, "See, Papà?"

"*E bè,*" Orazio muttered, his bushy eyebrows lifting in resignation.

For Nina, that growl meant a major victory. Delighted that her father had finally yielded, even a centimeter, she flung her free arm around him and grabbed him into a hug.

"*Ufa,* Nina," he protested, catching hold of his hat before it got knocked off his head. "*Per carità.*"

Nina ignored his protests as she laid a noisy kiss on his cheek. "Dante's right," she enthused. "We'll improve the garden year by year. We can plant winter rye this fall and spread the stable manure next spring. That'll bring the soil up several notches, at least.'' Still clutching her father's shoulder, she gave him another hug. ''I think irrigation is an excellent idea, too,'' she continued. ''I'll help you design a system this winter. The new building will be finished by then, and we can lay the plans out in the office. It'll be the perfect place to work without interruption.''

Orazio slipped his arm around Nina's waist and returned her hug. ''*Brava, bambina*,'' he said. ''You're a good girl. Don't bother about the irrigation, though. I've got Dante to help me with the plans and the five new men to install it. We can take care of it. You just help Mr. Blackwell.''

For a moment Nina stood as she was, too stunned to move. Then her arm fell away from her father and his words made a stab in her heart. Now that he had Dante and a crew of men, Orazio didn't need her. She was being dismissed. ''*Va bene*,'' she said, taking a step back.

She didn't have time to brood about it, though, because as she stepped, the heavy watch nudged her blouse, reminding her of the hour. ''*O Dio*,'' she murmured, checking the time again. Eleven fifty five. Tension stiffened her spine.

''I have to do my circuit,'' she said, excusing herself and backpedaling more rapidly. ''I haven't done a thorough log since last Tuesday. Although I'm afraid I won't get one done today, either. See you later, Papà.''

''*Arrivederci*, Nina.''

Orazio returned to his hoeing, but Dante moved forward. ''I'll come with you,'' he offered.

Resentment welling up inside her, Nina was about to brush him off. Then she glanced at him and her jealousy melted away. She wanted to dislike him and find his company unpleasant, but the truth of it was, she was growing fonder of him all the time. She was getting used to his quiet comments, actually listened for them expectantly. And where once she thought his subdued tone showed a sweet but passive temperament, she now knew that behind his shyness there was serious purpose and determination. She liked his involvement in gardening, and even more, she liked the fact that it wasn't just something he did for a living. It seemed to be a genuine source of enjoyment.

Not only that, she thought, glancing at him again, she also had to admit that Dante was very handsome. After a month and a half of working outdoors, his classic face was tanned and healthy. The glow it gave him made his huge, brown eyes appear less melancholy.

Unfortunately, none of this was enough to make her stomach unknot every time her mother hinted at marriage. But it was enough to make her forgive him for taking her place in her father's life.

"All right," she said, shrugging in agreement. "Come on. Though I don't know why you want to follow me up and down these rows. You see the plants all day long."

"I want to see what you're writing," Dante responded, falling in beside her as she started her inspection. "I want to see what you're looking for when you make your reports."

Bent over, about to examine some asters, Nina looked sideways at him, surprised. Hands on his knees, he was bent over, too, carefully studying what she was doing. "Why?" she asked. "Surely you know when a plant is doing well, or when it's got some sort of problem."

"Oh, yes," Dante assured her, meeting her sideways gaze, then straightening up as she did. "But I want to see what you're writing down. I want to know about how this"—he waved one hand wide across the field—"connects to that." With the other hand he pointed to the spot just beyond the stone wall where the Blackwell Seed Co. building was about to rise.

When he turned back and saw Nina staring at him in astonishment, a flush of color darkened his sunburned cheeks. "I can do my job better if I know how the whole business works," he explained somewhat bashfully. "Right now I'm like a horse with blinders on. I only know what's directly in front of me."

"But you want to learn this from *me*?" Nina asked, jabbing her finger into her chest. She looked over her shoulder at Orazio, peacefully hoeing the pansies. Her father would never ask her for a lesson.

"Yes, I do," Dante answered, puzzled by her surprise. "As far as I can tell, you're the only one who understands it all. Even *il padrone* doesn't know as much as you about the seeds and plants. And when I ask Signore Orazio"—he, too, glanced at the unsuspecting farmer, then shrugged apologetically—"he tells me to just do my work."

Hardly believing what she was hearing, Nina gave her head a sharp shake. "You think *I* know so much?" she asked. "You think I know more than Don Alberto and Papà?"

"Yes, I do," Dante answered again. Though his tone was firm, he cast another apologetic glance at Orazio. "Absolutely."

Nina threw back her head and laughed at the absurdity. She laughed hard, as she hadn't in weeks. She laughed until the tension washed out of her body and tears washed down her cheeks. "Well," she finally gasped, blotting her eyes on her sleeve. "If that's the case, the Blackwell Seed Company is in serious trouble."

A residual giggle escaped as she said, "Six weeks ago I didn't know a business prospectus from a boxwood hedge. If I had known any less, I wouldn't have known my own name. And now you think I'm more knowledgeable than my father, who's been a gardener for thirty years, and Don Alberto, who made millions of dollars selling wool? It's very kind of you to say so," she told him, dabbing her eyes and trying to stifle any further giggles, "but I think it's a bit of an exaggeration."

"No, no," Dante protested, waving one hand furiously. "I'm not just being polite, Nina. Don't forget, I was there at the beginning of this business, too. I saw how much you knew then, and I see how much you know now. You've learned a gigantic amount with lightning speed. It's almost as if you've absorbed an entire other person."

Hands by his side, he quietly said, "I've never met anyone like you before, Nina. I admire you very much."

Her laughter vanished. Rather, Nina shifted from foot to foot. Dante's declaration left her decidedly uneasy. Before she could ponder it, though, or even mumble a response, her attention was happily diverted. "Look who's here," she said, brightening instantly as she caught sight of her favorite sister. She was wandering along, drawing pad balanced on her crooked arm, stopping occasionally to make sketches of the young plants in their rows.

"*O la!* Serafina!" Nina called out. "Over here!" Still fiery red, Dante whirled around at the same moment that Serafina looked up. A startled flush leapt to her cheeks, too. "Come and join us!"

Serafina walked quickly down the path, waving to Orazio as she went past. "I didn't know you were out here, Nina," she said, coming up beside them. "You're hardly ever in the gardens anymore."

"Don't remind me," Nina said, reaching for Serafina's pad. She turned it around to examine the drawings. "Why, these are the poppies!'' she exclaimed. ''They look exactly like them. And the sweet William. And the delphiniums.'' She flipped through the sheets, delighted by each new sketch. With a few sure pencil strokes, her sister had captured the fledgling plants. ''Honestly, Serafina, they're wonderful. I don't know where you get this talent. None of the rest of us can draw a stick.''

''*Bè*,'' Serafina replied, rubbing her toe against a pebble in the path, her hands clasped behind her back. Though her eyes were lowered, the flush on her cheeks was heightened.

''Look at these, Dante,'' Nina said, passing the book across to him.

Too late, Serafina tried to grab it away in alarm. ''No!'' she burst out. ''They're just fast sketches. There's nothing to see.''

Although Dante gave her a grave look, he didn't give her the pad. Instead, he studied the drawings. ''It's true,'' he said, a hint of awe in his voice. ''These are very good. Really, they're excellent. They're not only accurate, they're very beautiful.'' He glanced at Serafina, and her outstretched hand fell away as the color in her face flamed hotter. Then he looked back at Nina and handed her the sketchbook, saying, ''You ought to have Serafina make drawings to go along with your progress reports. It would help you remember every little detail.''

''Perfect!'' Nina cried, seizing the pad again and staring at the sketches. ''What a perfect idea. I should have thought of that myself. You see, Dante?'' She looked up at him and nodded. ''You learn with lightning speed yourself. You understood the purpose of the reports completely.'' That reminded her. She checked her watch again. Twelve-thirty. ''I have to go back,'' she said, the tension returning. ''We don't have time to do the report today, but Serafina, please say you'll come out tomorrow afternoon and help me.''

''Of course, Nina,'' Serafina replied. Her blush was starting to fade, though a bewildered expression was taking its place. ''You know I'll help you. But I'm not sure what you want me to do. I don't know what report you mean.''

For a fraction of a second, Nina considered explaining, then she consulted her watch yet again. Twelve thirty-one. ''Here,'' she said, thrusting the sketchbook at her sister and giving her a push toward Dante. ''I have to go. Dante can tell you all about it, and we can set up a schedule tonight. I'll talk to you then. *Arrivederci*.'' She started back toward the Big House at a rapid pace.

"Nina!" her father shouted as she sped by. "Where are you going? It's time for lunch."

Nina just waved and kept on going. "I can't, Papà!" she yelled over her shoulder. "I've got appointments all afternoon. I'll see you at supper."

In the instant before she faced forward again, she caught a glimpse of the uncertainty and suspicion that crossed Orazio's face. She knew he didn't understand her haste, that he couldn't, for the life of him, comprehend what sort of business interrupted her lunch. She could almost see him wondering if he ought to question what appointments she had and whether he ought to object to them. Nina broke into a run, anxious to get out of earshot before he could make up his mind.

On the other side of the barn, out of sight as well as sound, she slowed to a walk, then halted under a huge elm and slumped, panting, against its trunk. It wouldn't do to arrive back in the office looking sweaty and disheveled, her face red from the heavy heat and running. She had to look composed and fresh for the salesman and architect. An attractive, assured businesswoman. As her hand automatically went to her hair, checking on its pins, she realized with chagrin that her father would be suspicious of that, too.

Taking a big gulp of air, Nina leaned her head back on the tree, closed her eyes, and waited for her breathing to return to normal. Life was getting more tangled lately, not less. It wasn't the first time she'd seen that look on her father's face, nor felt an increasingly uncomfortable gap growing between herself and her family. It made her remember that moment at Castle Garden when, after spending all day with Wim, she'd introduced him to her parents and her sisters. Their coldness had shocked her, and she'd known then that she'd taken the first step forward in America without them. Now it seemed as though they'd never caught up. That, in fact, they were falling farther behind every day.

Nina lifted her head, breathing more regularly, but her heart was as heavy as the heat. Her family was the center of her world, the anchor of her life. It was extremely unsettling to see the separation between them widening. "That's another reason why Dante's idea is so perfect," she announced to no one in particular. She pulled a crumpled handkerchief from the pocket of her skirt and patted her forehead while a pale blue butterfly fluttered by without response. In addition to the value of Serafina's sketches in recording the growth of the plants, having her sister involved in the Blackwell Seed Co. would help to narrow the disturbing gap. Yes, it was an excellent idea.

"Dante's idea," she muttered again, fanning herself with the clipboard. "Dante." She remembered to check her watch. Twelve forty-five. With a sigh, she pushed herself off the tree and started walking slowly back to the house. Dante. What was she going to do about him?

He had a perfect idea. He had a handsome face. He had a sweet manner and a serious nature. As their exchange just now had shown, he had a quick mind, curiosity, and ambition. But she could no more imagine being married to him than she could to Don Alberto.

"*Dio mio!*" she exclaimed. The very idea sent a chill down her spine despite the muggy July heat. Yet she knew it was what her family wanted, especially her mother, and she couldn't bear the thought of alienating them anymore. Maybe I just need more time to get used to it, she thought. Maybe with a little more time, it'll grow on me.

As she crossed the drive and started winding through gardens, only absently noting the beds in lush bloom, she told herself that it was just a question of time. It had nothing to do with a pair of incredibly blue eyes or rosy cheeks or a calm, but amused, voice speaking with a charming Dutch accent. It had nothing to do with sitting on a glider near the bay on Long Island and having her hands captured and held as they made flourishes in the air. It had nothing to do with the exhilarating touch of lips on hers nor with the clean scent and silky feel of blond hair brushing against her skin. No, it was simply a matter of time until she accepted, even liked, the idea of marrying Dante. It had nothing to do with Wim.

Still muttering and glum, Nina marched across the library terrace, kicked open the cocked French door, and stomped into the room. And stopped dead in her tracks. Bianca Maria was perched on the corner of Don Alberto's desk, one foot swinging prettily. Arms folded, Gideon leaned against the desk next to her. Both of them were laughing and flushed. Nina's heavy heart went cold.

"Hello, Nina," Gideon said, waving gaily. He turned halfway toward her, but in doing so, leaned closer to Bianca Maria. "You've been keeping secrets from me," he reproached. "And after all the help I've given you. Here I've told you my whole life story, but you never once mentioned that you have such a beautiful sister.''

While Bianca Maria giggled and dipped her fine chin, Nina stared with mounting horror. She didn't know why the sight of Gideon so close to her sister made her feel as though she'd been punched in the stomach with a fist. But it did.

''I have six beautiful sisters,'' she responded, her tone bleak and frigid. ''None of whom are any of your concern. What goes on in this office is completely disconnected from what goes on in my home. And vice versa. Do you understand?''

Gideon's eyes narrowed and angry color spotted his face, but before he could answer, Bianca Maria spoke up. ''Really, Nina,'' she said crossly, ''don't you think it's for me to decide who I talk to?''

''No.'' Nina snapped out the reply. A flash of hot temper thawed her frozen limbs, and she started across the room. Tossing her clipboard on her desk, she went to stand in front of her sister. ''You shouldn't even be here,'' she told her. ''This is a place of business, not a parlor. What on earth are you thinking?''

Sliding off the desk with an irritated thump, Bianca Maria glared back at Nina. ''I was *thinking* that I was being nice to you,'' she fumed. ''I was *thinking* that Benedetta baked your favorite *biscotti* because she felt sorry for you working so hard.'' She pointed an indignant finger at a plateful of crisp almond cookies on the desk. ''I was *thinking* that I'd bring you some because you're always missing lunch. But this is the thanks I get for *thinking* of you.''

As quickly as it had flared, Nina's temper died. In its place rushed real remorse. Just when she was lamenting the growing gulf between herself and her family, she'd actually made it worse. She'd let her own gloomy thoughts affect her judgment. She'd jumped to conclusions that didn't exist. One hand was stretched out and an apology was on her lips when Don Alberto burst into the room, head and shoulders first, as usual.

''You cut it close, Nina,'' he barked, making a beeline for his desk. If he saw Bianca Maria standing in front of it, he didn't acknowledge her. ''I hear a carriage out front, so that salesman must be arriving. I wanted to go over the projected print run with you before he got here, but we won't have time. Maybe there'll be a few minutes before the architect gets here. If I know him, he'll be late.''

He settled into his chair and shoved the plate of biscotti aside, spreading out information about the packing machine they were thinking of buying. "By the way, O'Shea," he said, not looking up, "book lunch for Nina and me in New York tomorrow. We're taking the seven-forty."

"What!" Nina exclaimed, her outstretched hand flying to her hip. Another wave of irritation washed over her, and she brushed past Bianca Maria to lean across the don's desk. "What kind of meeting do we have this time?" she demanded. "Honestly, I don't have a moment to get any work done between all these endless appointments." A trip to New York meant a whole day wasted, and she'd planned to do the garden log tomorrow. "At the very least, you ought to give me more than half a day's notice," she added.

Finally looking up, Don Alberto responded to her outburst, but instead of storming back, he chuckled. "You're not going to mind this meeting, Nina," he told her. "It's just what you've been wanting to do for weeks. Well, it took a bit of finagling, but I managed to arrange it. Ha! Maybe this will stop your whining."

"Who is it with?" Nina asked, her hands still on her hips. He could be so provoking, sometimes. He was well aware that she hadn't whined since she was a little girl. "What's it about?"

"It's about how this business is run," Don Alberto responded, sitting back in his chair. "And it's with the Alfred Bridgeman Company." He paused to let the full import of his words sink in before triumphantly announcing, "Tomorrow we're going to see one of the oldest seed companies in America, Nina. You and I are going to have a full tour of their operations."

For a moment Nina was speechless as her mood took another huge swing. Her hands dropped away from her hips and her annoyance disappeared. Then with an unexpected burst of excitement came an unexpected burst of words. "Bridgeman?" she repeated eagerly. "They've been around for over seventy years. Practically since the beginning of selling seeds by mail. And Alfred Bridgeman's *The American Gardener's Assistant* is one of the best guides I've ever read. Even if it was written before I was born."

Flinging her arms into the air, she clapped her hands and gave a giddy laugh. "Bridgeman," she said again, lowering her arms to lean her palms on Don Alberto's desk. "How did you ever contrive a meeting there?"

"You see?" Don Alberto chuckled again. "I told you that you wouldn't object to this appointment. Wasn't I right?"

"Yes, yes, you were right," Nina agreed, moving her hand in circles to urge him along. "But how did you do it? I can't believe they'd voluntarily throw open their doors to a man who's going to be their competitor." Another thought crossed her mind and she straightened abruptly. "Did you tell some sort of lie?" she asked, peering at him suspiciously. "Did you make up some fantastic story?"

Assuming an insulted air, Don Alberto lifted his jowly chin. "I did not," he replied. "I'm surprised you could even suggest such a thing. For your information, young woman, this is a classic example of how business works. I never made direct contact with Bridgeman at all, but arranged the whole thing through a mutual supplier."

Any further explanation on his part, and any further probing on Nina's, were cut off by the appearance of Fiona at the door. "Excuse me, please, Mr. Blackwell," she said, holding out a silver salver with a calling card laid across it. "Mr. Alexander Fuller is here to see you."

At the same moment Nina felt a faint ruffling of the air by her arm, then sensed a void beside her. Turning quickly, she saw Bianca Maria disappearing out the French doors. Too late she remembered their interrupted quarrel and the wave of regret that had come over her. Now a wave of guilt and embarrassment made her feel even more awful. How could she have let herself be distracted at such a crucial moment? What could possibly be more important than making amends with her sister? She took a step in the direction of the terrace door.

"Have him come right in," Don Alberto told Fiona. "Nina, are you ready?" he asked next. "Do you have your files in order?"

Nina hesitated, torn. She could see Bianca Maria, her striped skirt swishing, as she sashayed through the garden. Even from the back, Bianca looked fresh and saucy, a natural-born coquette. Affection tugged at Nina's heart. She took another step toward the door.

Then the salesman's footsteps came padding down the hall. With a sigh, she turned back to her desk and reached for her equipment folder. I'll take Bianca aside this evening, she promised herself. The minute I get home.

*   *   *

Despite Nina's complete sincerity at the moment she made it, that promise got broken, too. As Don Alberto predicted, the architect arrived late and, consequently, didn't leave until half past seven. By the time Nina raced into the kitchen, supper was on the table. After a fast pass of her hands under the faucet, she slid in next to Dante. He gave her a smile of welcome but didn't interrupt the animated discussion going on around them.

Conscience-stricken about Bianca Maria and nervous about Dante, Nina didn't interrupt the conversation, either. In fact, she was silent through the whole meal, not participating at all. Once or twice she tried to catch Bianca's eye, but both times her sister tossed her head and looked the other way. With each rejection Nina felt her discomfort growing. And when she tried to follow what the others were saying, she realized it involved an incident about which she knew nothing. Preoccupied with the concerns of the Blackwell Seed Co. in recent weeks, she'd lost the thread of family gossip. That discovery made the gap seem wider still. Terrible loneliness swept over her, and she sat motionless, marking the time until she could do her chores and escape to bed.

Even there she didn't find a refuge, however. No sooner had she turned off the light and climbed in next to Serafina than Bianca Maria spoke up from the other bed. "It's not fair," she complained. "You've got everything, Nina. You go to New York with Don Alberto all the time, and he takes you out to lunch in *restaurants*. You have new clothes made at fancy dressmakers, which you get to wear every single day. Linen skirts and a splendid suit and I don't know how many lovely waists. On top of all that, everyone knows you're going to marry Dante, who's handsome and kind and thinks you're the most extraordinary woman he's ever set eyes on. In a hundred years you couldn't have dreamed up a more wonderful husband. Your life is perfect. But instead of sharing your good fortune with us, you shoo us away when we get too close. How can you be so selfish?"

Under the sheet Serafina's hand found Nina's and gave it a comforting squeeze. "You should be ashamed of yourself, Bianca," she chided with rare force. "Nina works harder than anyone else in this family."

"She doesn't work harder than Papà," Lucia protested.

"Well, she works at least as hard as Papà," Serafina conceded. "Besides which, she has to learn all sorts of new jobs that Papà doesn't have to do. She's got meetings and appointments and . . .'' Her voice faltered as Serafina tried to think exactly what kept her adored older sister busy from morning until night. "*Un mucchio di cose*," she said in a stronger voice. "She has lots of important things to do. It's not a party, you know, Bianca. Nina's earning a salary. And she shares every penny of it with us."

"She did bring us a box of petit fours from the restaurant the last time she went to New York," Lucia added grudgingly. "You know she always brings something."

"A box of bonbons," Bianca muttered, angrily rustling their sheet. "Nina gets everything she could possibly wish for, and we get a couple of candies. That's some bargain."

"Don't forget Nina's older than any of us," Serafina scolded. "She's six years older than you, Bianca. That's six more years that she's been working, helping Papà and Don Alberto. Maybe when you're twenty-four, if you try as hard, you'll have as much good luck as she does."

Under cover of the darkness Nina let the tears welling up in her eyes roll down her cheeks unchecked. She clung to the delicate hand holding hers, but she didn't move or speak. She couldn't. What could she do or say? Could she tell her sisters that although she had "everything," she didn't want any of it at all? Could she tell them she didn't want to wear fancy new clothes all the time and spend long hours behind her desk? Could she tell them all the appointments gave her a headache and the meetings made her tense? Most of all, could she tell them that as handsome and good as Dante was, she didn't want to marry him?

One tear fell on her pillow, the other trickled into her mouth. What was worse, she didn't dare think about what she wanted instead. Or, rather, about who. The course of her life was decided, like it or not.

"If you could have your wishes come true, Bianca, what would they be?" Serafina asked into the unquiet silence that had fallen.

"Oh, that's easy," Bianca replied, her tone brightening perceptibly. "First, I'd want a silk dress. No, wait. I'd want several. One for daytime, or maybe two, and a beautiful one for evening. Then I'd want to go to a ball in a mansion on Fifth Avenue, and to that new Carnegie Hall everyone's talking about. If I could choose, I'd want to hear Rose Inghram, the famous soprano, singing in a concert. They say her voice is as clear and beautiful as an angel on a cloud. And after that I'd want to go to Delmonico's for champagne and oysters and chocolate cake.''

''How silly,'' Lucia scoffed. ''What a waste of wishes. All that would be over in a day or two, and then where would you be? Me, I want a husband and a family of my own. A good man, like Papà, who works hard and doesn't drink a lot. And lots of children. That would keep *me* happy for my lifetime.''

''*Bè*, maybe,'' Bianca said skeptically. ''But it doesn't sound like very much fun. How about you, Serafina? What would you wish for?''

Serafina's hand slipped out of Nina's as she turned to face the wall. Across the mattress, Nina could feel her shrug. ''I don't have any wishes, really,'' she said. ''I just want everyone to be happy. Then *che serà serà*.''

It was a noble sentiment and typical of Serafina, but there was a catch in her voice that made Nina wonder. Was her sister sensing her sadness, as she'd done that day in the cabbage field, or did Serafina have a hurt of her own? What could it be? And why didn't Nina know about it? This time frustration mixed with the wave of guilt, and she scrubbed her eyes dry of tears. It was bad enough to lose track of Stella's escapades or Bianca's latest daydream, but to be ignorant of what was troubling Serafina was entirely too much.

Nina turned in the same direction as her sister. It was too hot to snuggle up spoon fashion, as they used to do when they were little. Instead, she patted Serafina's shoulder and gave her nighttime braid a gentle pull. What was all this talk about wishes, anyway? She'd never before wanted anything but what she had. She'd been happy laughing with her family and sticking her hands in the dirt. No question about it, she thought with longing, it had been a much more contented time. Wouldn't she be better off returning to it?

I'm going to do it, she decided suddenly, nodding in the dark. I'm going to give up this catalogue business and go back to the way things were. I'll just ease off slowly, so I don't spook Don Alberto. I'll just do a little less every day. If I creep away, an inch at a time, he'll never even notice that I'm gone. And maybe it won't solve all my problems, but at least it'll be a good start.

Feeling enormously relieved by her decision, Nina drifted into the deepest, most peaceful sleep she'd had in weeks.

Although Nina woke the next morning feeling extremely well rested, she soon realized that nothing else had changed. The same worries awaited her, the same pressures and rush. Last night's resolute decision to ease out of the business seemed a little difficult to implement today. The trip to New York was already arranged, appointments had been made and confirmed. And to tell the truth, Nina was just as glad it was too late to cancel. The idea of touring the Alfred Bridgeman Co. had a very definite appeal.

She was curious to see how a real seed catalogue business was run, especially one with an acknowledged horticulturalist like Alfred Bridgeman at its head. Because despite her unending hours of work and despite Don Alberto's unquestionable financial expertise, Nina couldn't escape the uneasy impression that the Blackwell Seed Co. was an amateurish effort. When she looked at the other catalogues, at Jerome Rice & Co. or Michell's or Alneer Bros. or Wm. Henry Maule, they seemed beautiful and organized and informative. She couldn't imagine how a catalogue even half as enticing could emerge from the frenzy and confusion that surrounded the creation of theirs. Quite simply, she didn't know what she was doing, and she was certain it would show.

With only a small amount of reluctance, therefore, Nina postponed her decision, telling herself that first thing tomorrow, positively and for sure, she would start her planned withdrawal. In the meantime, she had to carry on as usual. That meant listening to Don Alberto in the carriage on the way to the train station in Glenbrook, complaining about her decision to offer grass seed to their customers.

"It's so bulky," he groused. "People always want large amounts of it, then we have to make big parcels. It's not neat like seed packets."

"Every company of any significance has grass seed listed,"

Nina countered, rummaging through the jumbled pages in her paper case for her notes on the subject. "If we're going to supply 'superior service,' as you say we must, then we have to be prepared to do the same. Don't forget that the reason seed companies have done so well in the past decade is because of the home gardener, not the commercial grower. Didn't you tell me that since 1879, seed catalogue sales have increased fifteen hundred percent? That's all due to individual families with a kitchen garden, some flowers by the porch, and a plot of grass. They should be able to find everything they need in our catalogue.

"Ah. Here it is." She pulled out the dog-eared page she was looking for and quickly scanned it. "Several people have recommended the Plant Seed Company in St. Louis. We're supposed to get in touch with a George Urquhart."

"All right, all right," Don Alberto agreed. "List it, but don't make a lot of fuss. Grass seed is so boring."

On the train to New York, Nina sat opposite him and listened as he held forth on the illustrations. "It's the most important feature of the catalogue, Nina," he told her, leaning forward and jabbing his finger at her knee. "We can have the best seeds in the world, but the sad truth is, if we don't have a showy cover and lithographs on every page, we aren't going to sell a single packet. People want to see pictures. They want to be wooed with pretty images."

Nina nodded. Even though Don Alberto sounded disgusted, it seemed perfectly reasonable to her.

"Stecher Lithographic Company is one of the leaders of horticultural lithography," the don went on. He settled against the worn velvet seat. "They've got over a hundred employees—artists and the like—and the most up-to-date equipment. They do a lot of work for *Vick's Magazine.* I've had O'Shea write to them. We want a company with experience."

"But they're in Rochester, New York," Nina objected. "It's so far away. We can't be running up there every time we want to check on what they're doing."

"That's what the U.S. Postal Service is for," Don Alberto said. "We can check on them by mail. Rochester is the center of the seed catalogue industry in this country, and Stecher is set up to service it. They're professionals, Nina."

Nina lifted her eyebrows but didn't press further. *"Va bene,"* she murmured. "If that's what you want."

They had a more heated discussion over peas while they clung to the sides of the hack and careened down Park Avenue. Don Alberto was in favor of offering a few of the standards, such as Alaska, Tom Thumb, Blue Peter, and Telephone, and being done at that. "They all taste the same, anyway," he grumbled. "Terrible."

Nina thought differently. "That's not true," she said. "In the first place, peas are delicious, especially when they're barely blanched and tossed with fresh mint. Mamma knows how to cook them perfectly. But in the second place . . ." She tapped her finger on her case to underscore her words, then hastily grabbed the door handle as the cab swerved. "In the second place, there *is* a difference in taste from variety to variety. And there's certainly a difference in maturing time. You don't want all your peas to come in at once."

Looking sulky, Don Alberto squinted at the ice wagon they were overtaking. "I don't want them to come in at all," he muttered. "I hate peas."

"Landreth's offers over forty varieties," Nina continued, ignoring his pout. "They've been in business since 1784, so they must know what they're doing." When Don Alberto neither responded nor turned her way, Nina shook her head and sighed. "I'll ask Dante to help me pick out a good selection," she said. "He seems to have an uncanny sense when it comes to vegetables."

It was only when they jerked to a halt in front of 37 East Nineteenth Street that Nina remembered the conversation that Fiona's appearance in the library door had interrupted yesterday afternoon. Don Alberto had never finished explaining how this tour of the Alfred Bridgeman Co. had been arranged, and between Bianca Maria's exit and the salesman's arrival, Nina had forgotten to inquire about their "mutual supplier." Now she didn't have to ask the question, because the answer was obvious. Standing on the sidewalk with a jovial smile of welcome stretched across his face was Harry Beale. And right behind him stood Wim.

Lightning did strike three times, after all, and this time it struck her dumb. Except for the wild pounding of her heart and a sudden feverish flush unrelated to the summer day, Nina sat frozen in her seat. The confident stream of opinions and information that had been pouring from her since they'd left home dried up and disappeared. She didn't know what to think, let alone what to say.

"Hello, hello!" Harry boomed, yanking open the carriage door.

"Glad to see you again, Miss Colangelo. By the way, your uncle sends his best. How are you, Albert? Did your journey into town go uneventfully? Was the train on schedule? Bet you hated to leave the country on a hot day like this one."

"Well, get out, Nina," the don said, nudging her foot with his. "Wake up. This is where we're going."

Prodded into motion, Nina accepted Harry Beale's outstretched hand and awkwardly descended. "I'm very pleased to see you, too, Mr. Beale," she murmured. Even as she addressed him, though, her eyes kept flicking to Wim.

"Say, do you remember Wim de Groot?" Harry asked, guiding Nina forward. She had stopped still again, blocking Don Alberto. "He was at the party for your cousin's wedding."

"I hope you're pleased to see me as well, Miss Colangelo," Wim said as he moved over to greet her. The familiar dry amusement in his tone sent a ripple down her back, but when he picked up her hand, a shock of excitement went all through her body. "It was just by chance that I bumped into Harry this morning and that he told me about his appointment with you. Before the words were out of his mouth, I invited myself along. I know I'm barging into your meeting, but it sounded too intriguing to resist. Will you forgive me?"

"Umm," Nina answered, trying to collect her thoughts, trying to decide what intrigued him: the premise of this meeting or the fact that she was there. The fact that Wim himself was so intriguing didn't make it any easier to think. His rosy cheeks were lightly tanned and his blond hair was bleached even lighter by the sun. It made his eyes seem brighter blue than ever. She rubbed her hands across her forehead.

"Yes, that's right. I do remember you," Don Alberto said, shouldering Nina over and sticking out his hand. "You're the Dutch fellow with the bulbs, aren't you?" While Wim nodded and shook the don's hand, he added, "I also remember that you seemed to really know the business. Not a lot of bragging. Just good, hard facts. I like that in a man."

"Thank you, Mr. Blackwell," Wim said. As he dipped his head in acknowledgment of the compliment, his crooked smile tugged at his mouth. "And as I remember, you are very direct yourself. I, too, find this admirable."

"Indeed, indeed." Don Alberto's baggy cheeks wrinkled in a way that might almost be construed as beaming. "You remember him, don't you, Nina?'' he asked, grabbing her upper arm. "He was on Long Island when we were there. De Groot, isn't it?" He looked back to Wim for confirmation.

"Yes, it is,'' Wim replied in his even tone as he plucked the paper case from Nina's numb hand. "Here, Miss Colangelo. I'll hold this. You're about to drop it. You might want to check on your hairpins, as well. They seem to be up to their usual mischief.''

"*O Dio!*" Nina exclaimed as her hands flew to her head, though her cry was caused more by confusion than by concern for her coiffure. It made her heart leap to see Wim standing in front of her, calmly organizing her as he had at Castle Garden. His manner was so personal, his gaze so direct, it almost seemed as if she truly occupied his attention. But hadn't she decided that Wim wasn't really interested in her? That he was simply being kind to her in memory of the long-ago day they'd shared? Hadn't she come to the conclusion that he belonged with someone as fair and elegant as he? Someone, for example, like Harry Beale's daughter, Penelope?

"Nina and I arrived in America on the same day,'' Wim explained to Don Alberto, reinforcing Nina's suspicion that he was thinking of her as the lost child she'd been eight years before. An ache of disappointment turned her pounding heart to lead as he went on.

"We met when I clumsily knocked into her and set her possessions—most important, five paper twists of seeds—sprawling across the floor of the immigration hall. Remember, Nina?" He turned back to her but didn't wait for an answer. "And now here we are, accidentally meeting again, and again because of seeds. Quite a remarkable coincidence, isn't it?''

So that was it. The intrigue he'd been referring to was just coincidence. Nina's mouth was dry when she finally responded. "Remarkable," she agreed without enthusiasm.

"You never told me this, Nina,'' Don Alberto complained, giving her a reproachful look. "You never mentioned that you've known de Groot for years.''

Right at the moment it seemed impossibly difficult to correct the don, to explain that he had been told this before, that he simply hadn't listened. Nina only shrugged.

"I've always said life is full of coincidences," Harry Beale chimed in in his hearty voice. "It keeps a person on his toes. But say, I think we should go inside. I made the appointment for ten-fifteen. We don't want to keep them waiting." Rather than moving, though, he leaned in front of Nina and gave Don Alberto a conspiratorial wink.

"I told them you were a friend of mine with a big estate in Connecticut," he whispered loud enough for half the world to hear him. "And that you wanted to give your gardener's daughter a treat by showing her where the seeds she planted came from. Is that all right?"

The frantic banging of Don Alberto's cane didn't silence Harry before Nina's sharp intake of breath. All her confusion disappeared as she focused on her suddenly aroused fury. "You did make up tales, after all," she accused, whirling to face the don. "You lied your way into Bridgeman, and then you lied to me when you told me that you didn't."

While Don Alberto shifted his weight against his cane and Nina stood there glaring at him, Wim looked from one to the other, a puzzled frown between his eyes. "I don't understand," he said. "What's untrue about your story? I thought that you do own an estate in Stamford and that Nina's father is your gardener."

"I do. He is," the don quickly confirmed. "You see, Nina?" he said, glaring back at her and waving his hand toward Wim. "I didn't lie. Everything about that story is correct. It's one hundred percent true."

"It's only half the story, and you know it," Nina retorted, tapping her foot angrily. If she weren't on a sidewalk in the middle of New York City, she'd be tempted to stomp away.

"Oh, dear," Harry Beale said. "I think I've opened a Pandora's box." He looked at Wim and grinned. "Albert is starting a seed catalogue, you see," he told him in the same stage whisper as before. "We're doing a bit of espionage."

Don Alberto cleared his throat loudly and pointed to the open windows in the Alfred Bridgeman Co. building, but Wim threw back his head and laughed. "That's wonderful!" he exclaimed, though again he didn't elaborate on what he thought was so splendid. Instead, he gracefully inserted himself between Nina and the don, threaded her arm through the crook of his, and started toward the door. "By all means, let's begin. This promises to be fun."

Given the fact that she alternated between hot flashes of outrage and flushes of pleasure, Nina hardly saw the inside of the seed company, let alone had any fun. A young clerk with thin, narrow shoulders and an even thinner and narrower mustache escorted them from room to room and floor to floor. His soft-voiced recitation barely registered.

He showed them the large office where mail was opened and the orders recorded, after which he led them to the order department, another large room whose walls were lined with rows upon rows of drawers. Women wearing aprons drifted around the room, selecting seed packets from various drawers and sticking them in their voluminous pockets. When an order was filled, they'd carry it across the hall to the packing department, where more women in aprons wrapped up the seeds, addressed the package, and tossed it into the mailbag.

Upstairs was where the big bags of bulk seed were sorted into packets, using a machine similar to the one Don Alberto was about to buy. Seed poured into the hopper on the top came out the bottom in measured amounts. The machine filled the brightly illustrated envelopes, then folded them and sealed them, at the rate of three thousand packets an hour. Young boys then brought them down to the order department and restocked the rows of drawers. There wasn't a lot of activity at this time of year, and the workers were moving slowly.

"Wait until late winter and spring," Wim said. "People will be racing around and packages will be stacked to the ceiling. That's what it's like in the bulb business in September and October."

Out on the sidewalk again, Nina took a deep, steadying breath. It had been close in the seed company, very close. Not only had the air been hot and still, but Wim had never left her side. Although he hadn't been able to keep his arm locked in hers among the aisles and between the worktables and machines, he'd always been within touching distance. It left her flustered and uncertain. She couldn't wait to gulp down lunch and get back on the train to Stamford.

"Did you see all that, Nina?" Don Alberto asked, hunching his shoulders and hurrying for the corner where he could talk out of earshot of the Alfred Bridgeman Co. "You should make some notes right away so we don't forget anything. We should have brought O'Shea with us," he said, then instantly changed his mind. "No, it's better that he didn't come. How would we have explained him?"

"You would have thought of something, I'm sure," Nina

muttered, still annoyed on top of everything else. Turning to Wim, she held out her hand. "May I have my case, please?" she asked. "My paper and pencil are in there."

Wim pulled the case from under his arm, where it had been tucked for the entire tour, but he didn't give it to her immediately. The top had popped open, forced by the mass of papers within. A smile lifted one corner of his mouth as he rifled through the crumpled pages spilling out. "A unique filing system," he commented. "Is it your own invention?"

"It's no system at all, is what it is," Don Alberto answered for her, coming to a halt by the crosswalk on Park Avenue. "It's a disgrace. I've told her over and over again that the key to success in business is organization, but she won't listen to me. I don't understand it. Her greenhouse would never be such a mess. You try explaining it to her, de Groot."

Snatching the case out of Wim's hand, Nina said, "Nobody has to explain anything to me. And there's nothing wrong with my filing system. I can find exactly what I'm looking for. Always."

"I'm sure you can," Wim replied. "I believe you absolutely."

Intent on cramming the errant papers back in the case, Nina looked up sharply when he spoke. Had she imagined it, or had there been an odd inflection in his tone? She couldn't quite tell what it was, though. His usual amusement. Or admiration. His calm stance, hands clasped behind his back, didn't give her any clues, and she looked back down.

"Well, whatever," Don Alberto said. "This isn't the place to debate that issue, and it's probably not the place to be taking notes, either. Someone might come by." He cast a quick glance behind him, but no eavesdroppers were in sight. In fact, anyone who could manage it was off the hot sidewalks and sticky streets in the middle of the day.

"We'll do it over lunch," he decided, pulling out his handkerchief to blot his forehead. "Damned hot out here." He stuffed the square of cloth back in his pocket, then addressed Harry Beale and Wim. "We've got a table booked at the Grosvenor. Will you gentlemen join us?"

Caught again in the act of straightening her case, Nina again stopped abruptly. This time, though, she didn't look up but held her breath and waited. She'd been counting on one of Don Alberto's usual cursory lunches, then a trip home to mercifully end the day. In addition to her other discomforts, she was boiling inside her linen suit. Bianca Maria was welcome to these "fancy" clothes.

To her relief, Harry Beale begged off instantly. "Wish I could, Albert," he said with real regret. "But I've got to meet a salesman in half an hour. Can you imagine? On a day like this, I've got to think about winter boots."

"Know how it goes." Don Alberto nodded. "I was always busy in the wool business in the summer, too. Well, another time, then." He held out his hand to Harry but scarcely glanced his way as the big man shook it, tipped his hat to Nina, and strode off. The don fastened his eyes on Wim. "How about you, de Groot?" he asked. "Will you join us?"

"I'd be delighted," Wim answered evenly while Nina's heart raced in panic. "I see an empty cab. Let me hail it."

Nina squeezed herself into the corner of the hack and, at the restaurant, sat silently at the table, not participating in the lunchtime discussion, which centered mostly around bulbs and selling them. On Long Island, she'd been thrilled to learn Wim was in the bulb business and had bombarded him with questions. Today, she couldn't think of a single thing she wanted to know. She was tired of business. Tired of thinking about a hundred details and solving a hundred problems. Silly ones, like peas, while the real problems went unresolved.

With a listless hand she poked her spoon at a melting scoop of lemon sorbet, then peeked across the table at Wim. Although explaining to Don Alberto about the Green Auction of bulbs in their fields, he was staring straight at her. She quickly looked back at her bowl.

In addition to all the other real problems that plagued her, now she had to think about Wim, too. It didn't help matters that Don Alberto seemed totally taken with him. Usually the don had little tolerance for people, let alone interest in what they did, but he absorbed everything Wim said, and eagerly probed for more.

"Not trying to put you out of business, de Groot," he said, after Wim had patiently and lengthily explained the many channels for buying bulbs, "but you'll have to tell me why all the florists and nurseries and stores you sell to can't buy their bulbs direct. Skip the middleman. Why I couldn't, for example, order my bulbs from the growers in Holland and sell them in my catalogue. You just told me how to do it, so what do I need you for?"

Nina tapped her spoon on the side of her dish in annoyance.

That was going a bit too far even for the don. However, a smile played around Wim's mouth, and he appeared completely unoffended.

"You may try, if you like," he answered. "I'll even wish you luck. And when you fail, I'll take you on as a customer with no hard feelings.

"You see," he continued, leaning back in his chair, "for all that it sounds like a sensible system, very straightforward and organized, it's actually quite complicated. There are layers and traditions that go back for centuries. Back almost to the time of Carolus Clusius, the botanist who brought the first bulbs to Holland late in the fifteen hundreds. Certainly back to 1637, which was the year the Dutch government put an end to Tulipmania—a period when tulips were still scarce and considered extremely precious and when the sums paid for single bulbs were staggering. With all that history, you have to be Dutch to understand it.

"Which is why," he said, his smile broadening, "Holland has a monopoly on bulbs. Over the years many have tried to break this lock on the market, both in growing and in selling, but no one has ever succeeded. Right now the Japanese are making an attempt." Still smiling, he shook his head. "I predict they'll have as little success as the others."

"Hmph." The don took a final swig of his coffee, wiped his napkin across his mouth, then tossed it on the table. "Kind of cocky, aren't you?"

Involuntarily Nina's hands flew up to cover her eyes, but again, Wim seemed unoffended. Relaxed against the back of the chair, he said, "You're testing my comprehension of the English language, but I believe a better word would be confident."

Don Alberto chuckled. It was a low noise that made Nina drop her hands and stare. He actually sounded amused. Her eyes grew even wider, though, with his next words. "I like your mettle, de Groot," the don said. "And I'd enjoy doing business with you. If there were any way I could take on bulbs, I'd sign up with you in a minute. Can't do it, though." Shaking his head, he set both bony hands on the table and rubbed the back of one with the other. "Just can't do it," he repeated. "It's too much."

For the first time in weeks, Nina really looked at him. Not to read his reaction to some catalogue suggestion or to gauge his irritation with some delay, but to really look at him. She had never before heard him admit that anything was too much to tackle, especially where business was concerned. He thrived on competition and challenge.

Studying him now, though, Nina was shocked to see how old and tired he appeared, how much of a drain these weeks had been, despite his relish of the activity. The bags under his eyes were puffier and his thin chest seemed almost sunken. It *was* too much for him. Too much work, too much pressure, too much heat. Her anger with his machinations and her aggravation with his rudeness gave way to great compassion.

At the very same moment, though, she felt an icy sense of doom. There was nothing she could do about the temperature, but there was something she could do about the work and the pressure. She could assume more of it herself.

As an invisible vise clamped around her, she blinked a few times but gave no other sign that she could barely breathe. This meant saying good-bye to last night's plan to retreat from the business, the plan that let her sleep peacefully for the first time in over a month. It meant hurrying even faster, being even later for dinner, seeing even less of her family then she already did. But it also meant saving Don Alberto. She had no other choice.

"I would enjoy doing business with you, too, Mr. Blackwell," Wim's voice intruded on her grim reflections. "And I'm sure it would be profitable for both of us, as well. Although, of course I understand that it's too much to undertake at the moment. You would have to do another catalogue to send out in the spring, and make preparations for another shipping season in the fall. Better to establish yourself with seeds first. But here." He reached into the breast pocket of his jacket, pulled out a smart leather case, and extracted a card. "When you get ready," he said, sliding it across to Don Alberto, "let me know."

"My word on it," the don promised, tucking the card into the breast pocket of his jacket. "It's a real temptation."

"I hope so." Wim smiled again as he extracted another card. "For you, Miss Colangelo," he said, pushing it toward her. "For your file."

For a moment Nina just scowled at the card, then she lifted her eyes and scowled at Wim, transferring all her anger and frustration to him. How could he, in good conscience, tempt Don Alberto? Couldn't he see how worn out he was? Apparently he couldn't, because Wim returned her scowl with a quizzical look. Sighing,

Nina picked up the card and jammed it in her case. "Thank you," she said, looking away.

"My pleasure," Wim replied, never taking his eyes off her. "I hope you won't lose it."

With that her gaze flicked back to him in surprise, but any further response was interrupted by the don. "Listen, de Groot," he said. "Even if we can't do business, at least we can have lunch again. How'd you like to come out to Stamford one day soon and take a look at what we're doing? I'd be curious to hear your opinion."

Nina scarcely had time to swivel around and stare at the don, stunned, before Wim gave his answer. "Nothing could please me more," he said. Nina swiveled back to stare at him. He raised his eyebrows at her but continued to address Don Alberto. "I doubt that my opinion has any great value, but I'm honored that you should ask it. And I'm very curious, also."

"Good," Don Alberto said, satisfied. "Next week? Shall we say Wednesday? I believe that's the twenty-fourth of July."

"Excellent," Wim agreed. "The twenty-fourth it is."

"I like him," the don announced as the train rattled back to Glenbrook. "That de Groot fellow's got what it takes. He's pulled himself up by his bootstraps." He wagged his finger at Nina, again sitting opposite him. "I admire that. It's what I did. And don't let that pretty face and nice manner trick you. He's got an edge to him that cuts right through the nonsense. I don't trust men without that edge. A bunch of buffoons and fools." He shook his head, disgusted with humanity.

"Not de Groot, though. He's all right. I like him," he repeated, then settled back on the seat.

Nina leaned her head against the window. "Yes," she said sadly. "So do I."

=15=

"Mr. de Groot?" a young man asked as Wim descended from the train. When Wim turned toward him, he plucked the cap off his head and said, "Mr. Blackwell sent me to fetch you, sir."

Wim looked at the groom, then looked at the empty carriage waiting just beyond him and felt a stab of disappointment. He hadn't really expected Nina to come to the station to meet him, but he'd been hoping just the same. Eyebrows raising slightly, he said, "Thank you. Shall we go?"

Half an hour later, when they turned off the road, Wim's eyebrows raised again. No wonder Nina seemed so unimpressed by Harry Beale's grounds, he thought. These were gorgeous. A wild riot of flowers in pink, blue, and white crowded the stone wall bordering Newfield Avenue. Hedges and trees and beds of flowers lined the drive. Sweeps of emerald-green lawn fell away from still more gardens near the house.

Wim was equally as impressed with the house itself. Mounting the wide wooden steps to the veranda, held up by four massive white columns, he felt a sense of majesty. This was a grand home, built in clean, classical lines. No fairy-tale towers and eaves dripping gingerbread trim for Mr. Blackwell, even if it was the fashion.

When the Irish maid showed Wim into the library cum office, his host stood up at his desk to greet him. From behind another desk rose a young man with a rather handsome face but shifty eyes. The third desk was unoccupied. Wim strode forward, holding out his hand, trying to ignore another, stronger, ache of disappointment. "Mr. Blackwell," he said. "How are you? I'm delighted to be here. And thank you for sending the carriage."

"De Groot," Don Alberto said, allowing his hand to be shaken. He himself always gave this ritual greeting a token gesture, but Wim's shake was long, brisk, and sincere. "Glad you could come," he said, finally freeing his hand. "Don't think twice about the carriage. Got to do it. No one could ever get here, otherwise. There's hardly ever a cab at the Glenbrook station, and the Stamford station is ten miles away. Yes, indeed. I built in the middle of nowhere. Drives my sons crazy." There was satisfaction in his voice as he made that statement.

"I can't speak for your sons," Wim responded, his usual smile poking at the corner of his mouth, "but in my opinion, you chose very well. And not just your location, but every detail of your estate. I was admiring the grounds as I drove up. They're magnificent."

"They look good, don't they?" Don Alberto agreed. "That's Nina's doing. Come on. We can take a walk around before lunch. I can tell you about most of it, but we really need Nina for a proper tour."

Grabbing his cane, he came around to the front of his desk. "I wonder where she's gotten to," he said. "Must have forgotten you were coming. Though it's not like her to forget an appointment. O'Shea, do you know what happened to her? By the way, de Groot, this is my secretary."

"Office Manager," Gideon corrected, acknowledging Wim with a dip of his head. Then he grudgingly answered Don Alberto's question. "I believe Nina mentioned the Nursery when she left." He shrugged. "I don't know anything more than that."

Although Wim's eyes narrowed, Don Alberto didn't seem to notice Gideon's pique. "That's my big greenhouse," he said, aiming himself out through the French doors. "I think they're potting up houseplants today. Got to offer them in the catalogue. We'll check there for Nina."

They crossed the terrace and descended a few steps along a bank carpeted in verbena and heliotrope, and accented by silvery shoots of lychnis. A beautiful bowl-shaped garden waited at the bottom, enclosed by borders of holly and barberry bushes, hydrangea and spirea. In between were four-o'clocks whose fragrant trumpets of flowers opened late in the afternoon. Around the edges ran bright blue salvia. Several dogwoods cast a lacy shadow.

"It's lovely," Wim remarked. "It looks so natural."

"Not tortured, you mean," the don said, chuckling with glee. "Can't stand all those damned formal gardens with the shrubs tortured into identical shapes. Neither can Nina. She's always got visions of the wild hills of Sicily in her head when she plans a garden.''

"I take it she's had an influence on the landscaping, then," Wim said with a casualness he didn't quite feel.

"Ha!" Don Alberto snorted, leading the way out of the bowl and down a path lined with pedestals holding plaster busts of poets and musicians and nearly overgrown by beds of perennials. "More than an influence," he said. "She's done it all. We let her father think he's the boss, but we all know it's Nina's orders we're following. Tells me what to do, too. And you know what?" He stopped still in amazement as he answered his own question. "I do it."

Wim also stopped, though he wasn't as surprised as the don. "She has an engaging way," he said. "It's hard to refuse her."

Don Alberto started forward again. "That's the truth," he declared. "I'll never forget the first time I met her. She was out here puttering in the dirt. Place looked dreadful back then. Raw. But she was sticking plants in the ground.

"I came up to her and demanded to know who she was and what the devil she thought she was doing to my lawn. Well, she could barely speak English, but she stood right up and told me she was Orazio's daughter and she was going to make my grounds beautiful." He shook his head and chuckled again, remembering that historic confrontation.

"We had quite a discussion. An argument," he admitted. "I let her know in no uncertain terms that I was perfectly capable of deciding how my property should look and that I liked it the way it was. I tell you, de Groot, that girl never backed up an inch. She stayed put, her arms waving like windmills, shouting her dozen or so words of English at me. And when the dust finally settled, not only did she go on planting, but I was down on my knees helping her. She's got spunk," he said admiringly. "I like that."

Hands clasped behind his back as he walked along, Wim absorbed every word Don Alberto said. In his mind he could see Nina perfectly, see her gesturing and unafraid. "I like it, too," he said. "She's an exceptional person."

"She certainly is," the don agreed. "That Orazio is a fool to yearn for a son when he's got her. Believe me, I know. I've got two sons, and I'd trade them for her in a minute."

Wim would have liked Don Alberto to continue talking about Nina, to hear more stories about her life. He found himself increasingly drawn to her, and he still didn't know why. But as he walked through this wonderland and listened to Don Alberto, Wim had the vague feeling he was on the verge of an answer. There was something about this setting that seemed to define her. Maybe it was the odd combination of the magical gardens she'd created and a grumpy old man's affection. Or maybe it was just because he was close to her home. Whatever caused the feeling, though, it enhanced her appeal.

Don Alberto, however, had exhausted his supply of praise. He dropped the subject completely and, instead, rattled off varieties as they passed through the rose garden. The roses were big and blousy this late in the season, still sweetly scented, but almost gone by. Wim nodded politely.

On the other side of the garden, and across a wide lawn, a huge structure loomed. The Nursery. Its ornate wrought-iron frame held thousands of panes of glass, many of which were propped open today. Inside, four men stood in front of benches, transplanting seedlings from flat trays into individual pots. The first thing Wim noticed, though, was a battered old armchair stuck in the corner. Somehow he knew, without being told, that it belonged to Nina. He could almost see her in it, happily slouched.

"Orazio!" Don Alberto shouted, stumping down an aisle. At the far end a man glanced up, startled, then wiped his hands on his pants and came toward them. Wim recognized him at once. Except for a few flecks of gray in his bristling eyebrows and mustache, the wiry little man looked the same as he had nearly eight years before. Nina's father.

"Good morning, Mr. Blackwell," Orazio said as the three men met in the middle of the greenhouse. He nodded a greeting at the don, but glanced toward Wim. His eyebrows beetled as he strained to place him.

"Hello, Mr. Colangelo," Wim said, reaching around Don Alberto with his hand extended. "I'm Wim de Groot. I met you at Castle Garden the day we arrived in America."

Orazio's brow cleared as the picture came together. "Yes," he said. "Now I remember." He shook Wim's hand, polite and respectful and, after all these years, still aloof.

"We're looking for Nina," the don said, peering at a flat of tiny gloxinia. "Know where she is?"

"*E no*, Mr. Blackwell," Orazio replied, lifting his shoulders in an elaborate shrug. "I have no see her all morning. *Aspetta.* I ask

Dante.'' Turning, he called out, "Dante! *Hai vista la* Nina? *Sai dov'è?*''

Wim watched as a young man set down his watering can and walked over to join them. He was slight, too, but extremely handsome, with dark, curly hair and soulful eyes. Something twisted inside of Wim. Aside from disapproving of Gideon's attitude, he hadn't given the secretary a second thought. But now he suddenly found himself wondering how much time Nina spent in the company of this young Sicilian, if she were attracted to his striking good looks. He was surprised at how much that thought hurt.

"È andata nel giardino," Dante answered Orazio. Then he looked at Don Alberto and, cheeks flaming, haltingly translated. "Is go in the garden,'' he said. "To the zinnias, I think.'' His gaze slid to Wim, almost as if drawn by the force of Wim's stare. Though still blushing, Dante met his eyes squarely.

For a moment the two men assessed each other steadily. Then Wim held out his hand again. "I'm Wim de Groot,'' he said. "How do you do?''

"Piacere," Dante replied. "I am Dante da Rosa.'' His handshake was firm.

"Let's go, de Groot,'' Don Alberto said, turning and stumping toward the door. "I'll point you in the direction of the trial gardens, but it's too hot for me to trek out there. You go tell Nina it's time for lunch.''

Wim didn't need any further urging. He said good-bye to Orazio and Dante, then turned, too, and followed the don.

Nina saw him coming out of the corner of her eye but pretended not to notice him until he halted in front of her. Even then she remained bent over, feigning scrutiny of a zinnia. Her show of indifference, however, didn't still the sudden banging of her heart.

"Hello, Nina,'' Wim said. "We've been looking everywhere for you. You've been hiding.''

"I've been working,'' Nina corrected, without looking up. She scribbled a note on her omnipresent clipboard, the tool that had replaced the trowel in her life. Then she pulled a wooden stick out of her pocket and shoved it next to a double zebra zinnia just starting to flower. Later, when it was cooler, Serafina would come out and make quick drawings of all the plants Nina had marked. She moved a few feet down the row to another plant.

"And I've been admiring your work," Wim replied, stuffing his hands in his pockets and strolling down the path parallel to her. "Mr. Blackwell took me through a few of your gardens. I felt as if I were in another world. A very beautiful and serene one. All I wanted to do was sit on a bench and listen to the birds. And to think I once thought you only mowed the grass and weeded the beans. You've done a splendid job, Nina."

Nina bent lower, ostensibly to push aside the leaves and check the soil at the base of a brilliant pink pompom zinnia, but actually to mask the brilliant pink that flushed her cheeks listening to his words. No one outside of her family, or Don Alberto, had ever complimented her like that before. Especially not someone whose opinion meant as much as his. Even so, all she said was, "Thank you."

"You're welcome," Wim responded easily, as if they were having a real conversation. "Although it would be more appropriate for me to thank you for the pleasure I received."

This time Nina said nothing, just fluffed the foliage back into place and moved on to the next plant.

Wim moved with her. "Mr. Blackwell . . . No. What is it you call him? Don Alberto?" he asked. At her barely perceptible nod, he went on. "Don Alberto sent me to fetch you for lunch. He seemed anxious for you to come in."

"All right," Nina said, inspecting a bud that was just about to burst into bright yellow bloom. "Tell him I'll be in shortly."

"I'll wait for you," Wim proposed in a pleasant tone. "We can walk back together."

Shrugging, Nina held a ruler next to the plant, then jotted down its height. She didn't see the frown that momentarily furrowed Wim's brow.

When he spoke, though, his tone was calm, as usual. "I have the impression that your Don Alberto relies on you heavily," he said, still conversing companionably. "That he holds your judgment and instincts in the highest regard. I was quite taken by his fondness for you."

Nina finally straightened up, one hand gripping her clipboard, the other massaging her back. This was an issue she could address head on, and she didn't hesitate to do so. "Listen," she said, "I hold Don Alberto in high regard, too. I'm fond of him, too. Which is why I'm angry with you for coming here today."

"What!" The word exploded out of Wim, propelled by pure

astonishment. His hands flew out of his pockets. "What are you talking about?" he demanded. "Do you think I came here to disrupt your friendship?"

"You came here to sell him your bulbs," Nina accused, shaking the clipboard at him. "More work. More problems. More pressure." She flung her hand up and the pages on the clipboard fluttered. "This whole business is too much for him," she said. There was a slight quaver in her voice. "He never should have started it, but now that he has, I'll never get him to stop. You don't have to make things worse, though. You don't have to tempt him to do more."

"Nina." Wim folded his arms in front of him and looked at her seriously. The shock had gone out of his tone, but the dry humor hadn't yet returned. "I didn't come here today to sell Mr. Blackwell bulbs," he told her. "That wasn't my intention at all. I didn't come here to make problems for him, or to tempt him to take on more work than he should. Actually, the reason I came here has very little to do with Mr. Blackwell." He paused, his blue eyes intent. "The reason I came here is you," he said. "I wanted to see you, Nina, and I didn't know how else to do it."

Nina's big eyes opened wider, but other than that she didn't move or reply.

"Nina," Wim said again, though there was frustration in his voice this time. He took a step toward her but was stopped at the edge of the bed by bright flowers coming nearly up to his knees. "I don't understand what's happened, Nina," he said. "You've changed. You've turned into a stranger. Into someone I hardly recognize. You were so quiet last week in New York. More than quiet. You were . . ." His arms unfolded and his fists clenched as he attempted to express her subdued state.

"It was as if someone had smothered the wonderful light inside you," he said, trying again. "As if someone had tied your hands together." He held his own out in front of him, wrist to wrist. After a silent moment he slowly lowered them, but his eyes continued to search her face. "Even today you're like this," he said. "Why? This isn't the Nina I know. This isn't the person I met at Castle Garden."

It took more than an instant to answer him. Nina had to lick her dry lips and swallow hard. "Castle Garden was a long time ago," she finally said, though her voice was hoarse and she looked away.

"I was young then. Not much more than a child. Now I've grown up. People do change, you know."

"No." Wim adamantly refused to accept her answer. He tried again to step closer and was again thwarted by the knee-high zinnias. "People don't change that much," he said, glancing in annoyance at the flowers. "Nor do they change so quickly. Not in five minutes. Not in the blink of an eye. Because that's the way it was with you, Nina. That's the way it happened on Long Island. One minute you were full of excitement and spirit. We were enjoying ourselves. Do you remember?" He paused to let her answer, but she only bit her lip and kept her head turned away.

"You remember," he stated. "I could feel the life in you. As soon as I touched you, I could feel the force inside." He paused again to shake his head. "Then it was gone," he said. "Bang. Shut off." His hand sliced through the air to illustrate the finality.

"I don't know what made it disappear." He shrugged. "I don't know what caused the change. We were talking about cabbages in Harry Beale's seedhouse. What possible offense could you find in that?" He turned his hands palm up, helpless. "We looked at the bag room, then the threshing floor," he went on, reviewing the innocuous tour. "Then we went upstairs to look at the drying racks. It was harmless. There was nothing . . . Oh, no! *Stom!*" He smacked his forehead, disgusted with himself as the mystery that had been haunting him for weeks was suddenly solved.

"Penelope," he said. "*That's* what happened, isn't it? Penelope came upstairs looking for us, to bring us back to the party. She wanted to dance. That's what's been bothering you, Nina. Am I right?"

For an answer Nina gave a shrug and stooped again to examine a giant zinnia. Just the mention of Penelope's name brought a renewed wave of pain.

Up above her, though, Wim tilted his head skyward and let out a great breath of relief. When he looked at her again, he said, "I'm surprised at you, Nina. I thought you were too sensible to act like this. I thought you were too sensible to be jealous."

That did it. It was the drop that made the dam overflow. All the disappointment and desire, all the hurt and hope, all the tumultuous emotions she'd been locking inside of her came bursting out. The restraint snapped, the smothered light flamed, and her fettered hands swept free.

"Sensible!" she shouted, straightening abruptly, her hand

waving wildly over the flowerbed. "Logical! Practical! Reasonable! Everything always has to make sense to you. It has to be neat and orderly and carefully thought out. Well, I'm not like that, do you hear me?" Her voice went up another octave as she beat the air with her fist. "You were wrong about me. I'm not sensible! I'm not reasonable! I don't even want to be. I'm Sicilian and Sicilians think with their hearts, not with their heads."

"Pardon me," Wim apologized, holding up both hands and taking a step back. Although his tone was solemn, the corner of his mouth twitched suspiciously. "I can see now that I've made a grave mistake. As you say, my judgment was wrong. You are *not* sensible." He paused and thoughtfully tapped a finger on his cheek. "Let me see if I can get it right this time," he said. "Does this mean that you *are* jealous?"

Hands jammed on her hips, shoulders thrust forward, Nina had her mouth open to make a heated reply when Wim's words registered. She blushed bright red. *Mamma mia!* What had she admitted? How had she managed to charge headfirst into that one? Clamping her mouth shut and hugging her clipboard to her chest once more, Nina turned and waded out of the flowerbed. Without another word, or a backward glance, she went striding down the path, her cheeks burning and her heart banging hard.

Wim watched her a moment, then followed at a more leisurely pace. The grin that he'd been repressing now spread across his face. "Nina," he called out softly. "Nina. Nina. Maria Antonina."

"What is it?" she cried, stopping short ten feet in front of him and whirling around. She tossed her hands in the air. "What do you want from me?"

"A kiss," he replied simply, never slowing a bit. And before she knew what had happened, he was only inches away. Then his hands cradled her hot cheeks, and he brushed his cool lips across her mouth.

"Oh," she whispered as her clipboard dropped, unheeded, to the ground. The instant he touched her, wave upon wave of pleasure pulsed through her body, filling her senses but banishing thought and movement. Except for her eyes, that is, which drifted shut.

"A kiss," he said again as his thumbs traced down the sides of her nose and outlined her mouth. "I want a kiss from you, Nina," he murmured, leaning forward to retrace the trail with his lips. "A kiss." He showed her what he meant.

His hands slid around to cup her neck and the back of her head as he buried his fingers in her thick, dark hair. Pressing even closer to her, the full length of her body, he kissed her again. Not a gossamer touch, this time, not a feathery graze, but a long, deep kiss that seemed to consume her entirely. She felt him crushed against her, felt the heat of his skin. She felt his breath tickle her and his silky hair sweep her face. The exquisite feelings made her ache with desire.

"A kiss, Nina," Wim whispered as he laid a path of them from her lips to her ear. "Give me a kiss."

She gave it. Her arms came up and wrapped around his back, holding him to her, clasping, straining. Rubbing her cheek along his, she twisted her head until their mouths fused again. Oblivious to everything else, to the place and the time, to the hot sun beating down and the bees buzzing from flower to flower, Nina kissed him. She kissed him as he had kissed her, deeply and at length. She kissed him with all the strong passion that throbbed through her soul.

"You're magnificent," he murmured when he rolled his head to one side for a breath, but never breaking away or loosening his embrace. Still so close, Nina could feel his lashes flicking over her closed eyes, Wim nudged her with his nose. His lips moved against the side of her mouth. "Don't be jealous," he said softly. "There's no reason to be."

It took a moment for his words to filter through the thrill of his touch, but when they did, they broke the spell. Nina's eyes flew open. "*O Dio!*" she gasped, dropping her hands and pulling back in his hold. Now what had she done? Though her lips still felt swollen and her skin was still tingling and taut, Nina was no longer unconscious of the world. Reminded of Penelope, she remembered all the rest, too. Churning one way, then the other, frantically searching the garden to see who might be watching, she struggled to get free.

Wim's cheeks were rosier than usual and his blue eyes were especially bright, but he didn't protest or plead. He let her go. "You're all right," he reassured her, his voice almost calm and his tone almost even. "No need for alarm. You're completely unharmed. You're fine." Then a smile creased his cheek and the humor returned to his tone. "In fact," he added, "you're even better than before."

Nina took several quick steps back, one hand kneading her brow. "You confuse me," she blurted out, looking at Wim accusingly. "I never know what to think when you're around."

Neither taking offense, nor taking advantage of her confusion, Wim smiled more widely. "That's good news," he decided, bending to retrieve her clipboard. "We're making progress. At least you don't despise me anymore." Then, tucking the clipboard under one arm, he linked the other with hers. "We should go in for lunch," he told her, tugging her forward. "Your don is waiting."

"Yes, of course," Nina muttered, stumbling along beside him. She shook her head to clear it, but that was almost impossible with their arms intertwined and their shoulders brushing. It was almost impossible to think when her senses were so aroused. "Lunch," she said, still muttering and massaging her head.

Wim gave her a glance, but, as before, didn't press his advantage. This time he even changed the subject completely, choosing one he knew she'd find comfortable. "Flowers," he said. "There are flowers everywhere I turn. You really enjoy them, don't you? Even paper ones on bonnets."

At his mention of the incident that had brought them together at Castle Garden, Nina ceased rubbing her forehead and looked up, surprise chasing away her confusion. "You remembered that?" she asked. "I didn't think you even understood what I was telling you."

"Of course I remembered that," Wim replied, laughing. "You made yourself perfectly clear. I can still see you pantomiming how those flowers distracted you." His hand circled his head in a pale imitation of her descriptive gestures. "I also remember thinking that they must have had a powerful appeal if you let them capture your attention at such an important moment. Here you were, in America for only a few minutes, at the very beginning of a whole new life, and what was the first thing you saw?" He looked at her, shaking his head in amazement, then answered his own question. "Flowers," he said. "You must love them a lot."

"Yes, I do," Nina said, stopping where she stood to return his stare of amazement. "I can't imagine any life, new or old, without them. But I don't see why this should strike you as unusual. It must be the same for you. Surely, you love flowers, too. Why else would you be in the bulb business?"

Wim laughed again. "Why else?" he asked, giving her arm a gentle yank to stir her to motion. She obliged by resuming walking, but she didn't remove her gaze from his face. "I'm in the bulb business," Wim told her, "because I was born and brought up in Haarlem and Lisse, the heart of the bulb district in Holland. It's what I absorbed from the cradle. Had I been born in Alkmaar, where they sell tons of cheese, most probably I'd now be a cheese merchant." Meeting her gaze, he gave a little shrug. "For me it's the business that matters," he explained. "Not the product. It's the business and the fact that I've made it a success."

Even more astonished, Nina stopped short again. "You mean you don't like flowers?" she asked. There was a note of horror in her voice. She couldn't comprehend such a state.

About to laugh once more, Wim took a second look at her expression and changed his mind. His tone was still light, though, as he replied, "Oh, no, I suppose I think they're pretty. Some of them have a delightful scent, too. And the way you've displayed them here creates a stunning effect. I'd have to be blind not to like your gardens." Giving her arm another pull, he said, "Come on, Nina. We're going to be late for lunch."

Although Nina started forward again, she was, by no means, through with this discussion. "How could you be so indifferent?" she said. "The bulb fields must be gorgeous when they bloom in the spring. How could you not notice such a beautiful sight?"

This time it was Wim who stopped and turned to face her full on. There was no hint of laughter in his tone when he spoke. "Yes, the bulb fields are gorgeous," he said. "But unless you own them, they only mean backbreaking work for wages that are barely enough to survive on. It's hard to appreciate the beauty when you're bending over the rows, for as many hours every day as there's light to see, cutting the tops from the stems."

"Cutting the tops?" Nina was aghast. "You mean the flowers? You cut the flowers off the stems?" Almost cringing, she made a decapitating gesture. "*O Dio*," she moaned. "What on earth for?"

"To make bigger bulbs," Wim replied matter-of-factly, although his grimness seemed to lessen watching her performance. He turned again and started to walk. "So the plant's energy isn't wasted on the bloom, but can go back into the bulb."

"Wasted?" Nina repeated in an undertone, though she allowed herself to be pulled along. It was beyond her to imagine a flower being wasted. "What do you do with the flowers when you cut them off?" she asked, almost afraid to hear the answer.

A trace of his smile reappeared as Wim shrugged and replied, "Dump them in the canals. Feed them to the cows."

Nina just shook her head, trying to understand such an incredible practice. They passed through the wall surrounding the trial gardens and were well across the lawn before she spoke again. "You didn't look like you worked in the fields," she said. "When we met at Castle Garden, that is. Sicilian peasants wear old, homemade clothes, but you were so well dressed. In fact, I thought you were the most elegant man I'd ever met." Glancing at him sideways, she didn't add that she still thought so.

Wim didn't seem to notice her glance, though, nor even hear her compliment. Instead, he stiffened and looked straight ahead. "When I was seventeen, I managed to get a job in the office of a bulb company," he said tersely. "The pay was only a little bit better, but at least I escaped the drudgery of the field."

This time Nina looked at him more closely. Only once before had she heard such austerity in his tone: when she'd asked him about his family, that day on Long Island. Her eyebrows knit as she studied his rigid profile. "You were lucky to get that job, then," she said, fishing for a clue to explain his soberness. "Usually, you need an education for a position in an office."

If Wim recognized her intent, he didn't object to her curiosity. Although, neither did he satisfy it. Rather, in that same terse tone, he said, "I had an education. My mother taught me. She went to school in London and Paris."

For the third time Nina stopped short to stare at him in astonishment. "Then you *were* well-to-do," she said. In Sicily, only the children of wealthy parents went to school at all. Never mind London and Paris. She'd never been to Holland, but she doubted it was very different. "My first impression of you was correct."

Wim finally looked at her, though his blue eyes were bleak and he let go of her arm. "No," he said, "I wasn't well-to-do. My grandfather was a rich man—in fact, still is. But he disowned my mother—cut her out of his life completely—when she married my father, who was poor."

"How dreadful!" Nina cried, her hands flying to her heart. She couldn't imagine Orazio banishing her, or any of her sisters, from the family no matter what they did. "Surely it was just a fit of

temper and he realized his mistake in time," she said, positive that
that was the case. "Surely he's renewed the ties."

"Never." Wim's voice was gruff as he turned away and started
walking once more. "Even after my father and brother died, he
never approached us. Never sent so much as a florin." Wim took
a deep breath, then added, without emotion, "He didn't come to
my mother's funeral, either. In my life I've never met the man."

"Madonna mia," Nina whispered. For a moment she stood
where she was, horrified, then she hurried to catch up. "What a
terrible thing." She slipped her hand through the crook of his arm
and gave it a consoling squeeze. "A grandfather is such a
wonderful person. My *nonno* used to carve dolls for me, and for
Lucia and Serafina, too. By the time Benedetta was old enough to
play with them, his fingers were too crippled to carve, but he made
us all share."

Looking down at the hand clutching his arm, the frozen light in
Wim's eyes started to thaw. There was sadness in his voice,
though, when he told her, "Not all families are as warm and
loving as yours, Nina."

Not knowing how to respond, Nina only nodded. At least now
she understood the flickers of longing she'd glimpsed when she'd
caught him watching her big, noisy family.

In total silence they threaded through the rose garden and down
the perennial path. They'd crossed the bowl garden and were
mounting the steps to the library terrace when Nina remembered
how this startling conversation had begun. For the last time she
stopped and turned to face him. "But you do like flowers, don't
you?" she asked anxiously. "I know you said you picked the bulb
business because that was what you knew best. And I understand
about how hard the work was in the fields. Still and all, don't you
enjoy flowers just a little?"

It took a moment for Wim to answer, but when he did his smile
emerged. "Yes," he reassured her. "I enjoy them. And now that
you've inspired me, I think I'll enjoy them even more."

Nina hadn't realized she'd been holding her breath until it
escaped in a huge sigh of relief. Her face lighting up, she returned
his smile.

"Now may we go in for lunch?" Wim asked.

"Absolutely," Nina answered. They swept across the terrace
and through the library door.

* * *

"It took you long enough," Don Alberto greeted them, rising from behind his desk. He was alone in the room, Gideon having gone off to eat. "I've been waiting forever. You must have come by way of Greenwich."

"I had to finish the zinnias," Nina said, unruffled. She pulled the clipboard out from under Wim's arm and tossed it onto her desk. "They're doing nicely. They don't seem to be bothered at all by their late start."

"Yes, yes." Don Alberto impatiently dismissed the colorful annuals. Instead, he waved a large envelope at them and crowed, "Wait until you see this." He came around to stand in front of them and thrust the envelope forward. "It's from Stecher Lithographic," he said. "Samples of cover art. They came in the morning mail. Glad you're here, de Groot. I'd like to hear your opinion, too."

"That was quick," Nina said, grabbing the envelope from the don's hand. "You just wrote to them." She took out four pages and laid them on the desk.

"I told you this was an efficient way to do it," Don Alberto reminded her. "I told you they knew what they were doing. Just look at those covers. Eh, de Groot?" He snagged Wim's arm and led him over to the desk.

Unlike early seed catalogues, whose covers merely stated their purpose in plain letters, catalogues in the past decade had become increasingly ornate. Since the color still life of onions that Landreth's had put on their 1880 cover, seed companies had been competing for customers' attention with ever-more elaborate chromolithographs. The samples on the desk were a perfect example. One showed a bucolic scene, with a pond, a meadow, and a barn. Another showed a fresh-faced maiden holding a bouquet bursting with flowers. Still another had an oval inset of a castle, surrounded by ribbons and roses. The fourth featured fat cherubs bearing baskets of vegetables.

"Very nice," Wim said obligingly as Don Alberto beamed. "Stecher has an excellent reputation. I doubt you'll be disappointed."

"Good man," the don approved, banging Wim on the shoulder. He turned to Nina. "Well?" he asked. "What do you think?"

Nina *was* disappointed, though. In the cavalcade of showy catalogue covers, these weren't anything exceptional. She shrugged. "They're all right," she replied, flicking one of the pages. Then she looked at him squarely and said, "I think Serafina's paintings are lovelier. And more unique."

The excitement on Don Alberto's face turned to thunder. "What are you talking about?" he stormed. "Who the devil is Serafina, and what has she got to do with us?"

"You know very well who Serafina is," Nina retorted. "She's my sister and a talented artist. I think our cover would be far more striking with one of her paintings on it than with one of these." She picked up the page with the cherubs on it and shook it at him. "These are fine for what they are, but they look like every other catalogue on the market. All that tells one from the other is the name scrolled across the front." Flinging the inadequate picture back on the desk, she said, "It seems to me that what we want is a cover that makes our catalogue both immediately recognizable and intriguing."

"Bah!" Don Alberto scoffed. "We want the cover to be recognizable as a *professional* piece of art. Not the ninnyish daubings of some amateur." When Nina made no further comment, just pursed her lips and turned away, the don looked at Wim and insisted, "Isn't that so, de Groot? You're in the business. Tell her that's the truth."

"Of course," Wim agreed, picking up the page Nina had discarded and studying it carefully. "I've always felt one should strive for the best possible quality in every phase of business. It gives customers confidence." Just as Don Alberto was about to wag his finger in triumph, though, Wim added, "But I've often gotten the best results from the least likely sources." Setting the cherubs back on the table, he suggested, "Perhaps before you make your final decision on the cover, Serafina should submit some of her work for consideration. It can't do any harm."

While Don Alberto looked sour and Nina smiled at Wim, Fiona stepped into the doorway to say, "Excuse me, Mr. Blackwell. Lunch is ready."

Before the afternoon was over, Don Alberto's good humor was restored. He enjoyed talking to Wim about seeds and bulbs and what it took to sell them. It was also apparent that, more and more, he enjoyed Wim's sense of irony, the "edge" he'd told Nina about on the train. By the time the carriage appeared by the front steps to take Wim to the station, he and the don were friends.

"When can you come out again?" Don Alberto asked as they stood on the veranda to say good-bye. "Another lunch next week? No. I almost forgot. My sons are having a do here on August tenth. Why don't you come for that?"

"Your sons?" Wim asked.

"It's Don Alberto's seventy-fifth birthday," Nina explained. "His sons are giving him a party."

"More like an excuse to show this place off to a bunch of their snobby friends," the don growled. "Need you here, de Groot, or I'll die of boredom before I reach seventy-six. What do you say?"

A smile creased one corner of Wim's mouth. "I wouldn't miss it for the world," he answered.

As Nina left the library and made her way through the gardens that evening, the day's extraordinary events played over and over in her mind. Especially that kiss. She could still feel the thrill it caused. Still feel the shimmering flush of desire. But in the aftermath, she could also feel its divisive pull. Her steps got slower the closer she came to her house. With all that was happening lately, she was no longer sure it was home.

=16=

August tenth was clear and sunny, playing into Edward and Reginald's plans. They'd had linen covered tables and beribboned chairs set out on the lawn, clustered in the shade of a dozen canopies festooned with yards upon yards of swags. Silver buckets of ice kept champagne bottles deliciously chilled while silver trays full of ice kept beautifully molded aspics from melting. It was obvious that the brothers perceived of the occasion as a patrician event and meant to celebrate it grandly. The estate, at the peak of its summer glory, lent itself perfectly. For once, both their irascible father and his inconvenient home served useful purposes.

Most of the guests, arriving in a caravan of carriages from the station, were either friends of Edward's and Reginald's or associates they wanted to impress. In recognition of the man whose birthday they were purportedly celebrating, however, they'd also invited a few of their father's acquaintances. Since he had no friends, or none that were socially acceptable, they'd had to ask Dr. Taylor, Don Alberto's physician, and Messrs. Brown and Haverford, his lawyers. They were taken by surprise, therefore, when one carriage pulled up and Wim descended. Followed by Harry Beale, his wife, Emma, and his daughters, Penelope and young Cecilia.

Nina was even more surprised. She was wandering around the lawn, not quite sure if she was guest or staff, disguising her uncertainty by peering at the plants in a way that could be interpreted as either innocent admiration or professional scrutiny. Straightening from her inspection of a particularly fine clump of godetia, she saw Wim coming toward her. Her heart leapt, only to sink the next instant when she recognized the people at his side.

"Well, well, well, Miss Colangelo!" Harry boomed, stepping forward with his hand outthrust and a huge smile on his face. He seemed oblivious to the shock on Nina's. "What a delight to see you again. How have you been?" While he pumped her hand he asked, "Do you remember my family?"

It was all Nina could do to look beyond his broad shoulders at the three female Beales. Her insides felt twisted and icy, despite the August heat. More than anything, she wanted to run away and hide. There was no escape, though. No escape from the anguish the sight of Penelope caused. As she smiled at Nina, without a hint of recognition, she looked as pink and white and pretty as ever. And her hand rested gracefully in the crook of Wim's arm. It tore Nina to pieces.

"Why, Harry, I think you must be mistaken," Emma Beale spoke up. "I don't believe I've met this young lady before. How do you do, my dear?" She too extended her hand, but she did it more delicately than her husband.

"How do you do?" Nina mumbled in return. She took Mrs. Beale's hand, but let it drop almost immediately. She didn't know how firmly to shake it, if at all. Besides, it was so soft and fragile feeling, she was afraid she'd clumsily crush it. Without a question, she felt awkward and coarse next to these women. Mrs. Beale's face might look slightly lined and tired, and Cecilia's wasn't quite mature, but all three exuded a gentility Nina couldn't hope to acquire.

"My gracious! How silly of me!" Harry cried, grabbing Nina's arm. "I thought you'd met the day of Aurelia's wedding. Well, then, please let me introduce you." Before Nina could nod numbly or the Beale women could murmur their pleasure, Harry added, "And I'm sure you've met Mr. Wim de Groot."

"Miss Colangelo," Wim greeted her, his eyes fixed on her face. Perhaps no one else noticed her stricken expression, but he was well aware of it. This time he knew what caused it, though. He viewed her with a mixture of frustration and sympathy, alternately wanting to shake some sense into her and to comfort her with kisses. Obviously he could do neither in the present circumstances, so he confined himself to saying, "You seem a bit wan. Are you unwell? Can I get you something?"

"No," Nina answered, grimly meeting his gaze. His familiar solicitousness was almost unbearable. "I'm perfectly fine, thank you. I don't need a thing." Even as she said it, though, she felt extremely lonely.

"Perhaps the sun is too strong," Wim persisted. Why was she being so stubborn? "It's terribly hot and you've neither a hat nor a parasol. Come. I think we should sit in the shade, and I'll go and get us some cold drinks."

"Excellent idea!" Harry agreed with enthusiasm. Still holding on to Nina with one arm, he offered the other to his wife, then marched them both under a canopy to an empty set of table and chairs. "Say, Emma," he said as he held out a chair, "I think I spotted the Boston Whitakers here. After we have some refreshments, we'll have to find them and say hello. I haven't seen John in ages."

"Yes, dear," Emma replied, sinking down with a relieved sigh. "It will be nice to see them again. Don't they have a daughter who is Cecilia's age? A pretty blond thing, as I recall."

"That's right," Penelope chimed in, letting Wim seat her. "Her name is Charlotte, isn't it? And she has an old sister called Lucy, who is very amusing. Oh, yes, and their handsome brother, Frederick. Do you suppose he's here, too?" Peering around the lawn, her eyes shining with excitement, she said, "We had such fun when he brought his yacht into Oyster Bay last summer. If he comes again, this year, we must introduce him to Lilian Hayes. She's mad about sailing. Do you remember her, Mr. de Groot?"

Looking up at him, she smiled a beguiling smile. "Lilian was at our party in May. She was the one who beat us all at croquet."

"I can't be sure," Wim replied, dismissing the subject with a shrug. He glanced at Nina. She was sitting stiffly, staring at the edge of the table. He sighed. "I see a waiter coming with some glasses of champagne. Does that appeal to everyone, or shall I search for some lemonade? Cecilia?"

"Champagne, please." Cecilia replied with a happy smile. She was a sixteen-year-old version of her lovely sister.

"Just one glass," her mother warned. "And sip it slowly."

"Lucky you, Cecilia," Penelope said affectionately. "I wasn't allowed even one glassful until my debut."

"That's not so far away," Cecilia replied, selecting a crystal glass from the tray being held in front of her. "I'll be coming out this fall, you know." She took a tiny sip of the champagne and let the bubbles tickle her throat. "I should have some practice before then, shouldn't I?" She giggled. "After all, I intend to dance and drink champagne till dawn."

"Won't you be tipsy!" Penelope laughed and took a sip from her own glass. "We'll have to carry you up to bed in a chair," she teased. "Like Aggie Miller at her debutante ball. She drank so much champagne she fainted dead away."

"Girls!" Emma admonished, holding a hand to her breast. "Such a conversation! What can Miss Colangelo be thinking of you?"

In truth, Miss Colangelo was thinking that she was very much out of place at this table. Far from being offended by tales of drunkenness, however, she was, instead, made extremely uneasy by the discussion of yachts, croquet games, and coming-out balls. As it was, she walked a tightrope between two separate worlds, one where her family lived and one where Don Alberto did business, but this chatter represented yet a third. The only sailing she'd ever done was from Sicily to Castle Garden in the steerage of a ship.

Despite all the strides she'd made since debarking from that "yacht," despite having mastered English and having read her way through Don Alberto's library, despite the knowledge and skills she'd acquired, and the assurance she'd gained, Nina was still a complete stranger in this gilded world. And despite the fact that Mme. Sallé's tasteful creations now replaced the garden-stained clothes she once wore, she still looked entirely different from the ladies and gentlemen promenading about the lawn or posed languidly under awnings.

Her face was much stronger, her expression more dramatic, her silky skin unfashionably golden from repeated trips to the trial gardens. Nor was her hair artfully curled and arranged beneath a bonnet, but was constantly on the verge of rippling free from its bun. That reminded her. Nina's hands flew up to check on her pins. All that was missing from this uncomfortable scene was to have one of them come sliding down her head and bounce into a crystal glass of champagne.

As she jabbed the pins into place, she caught Wim's eyes on her. Blushing, she quickly folded her hands in her lap and looked away. *He* fit into this elegant tableau. *His* face was fair and refined. *His* demeanor was gracious and *his* manners impeccable. Even though he'd sailed to America on the same type of "yacht," even though he'd arrived with only a few dollars in his pocket, Wim belonged in this world. It was part of his heritage. His mother had been educated in Paris and London. His grandfather was a wealthy merchant in Holland. He belonged under a canopy sipping champagne. He belonged in the company of Penelope Beale.

"Miss Colangelo has six sisters of her own, so I'm sure she's not the least bit surprised by this exchange. Isn't that so, Miss Colangelo?" Wim spoke pleasantly, filling the slight silence that had fallen.

Realizing she'd been expected to respond to Mrs. Beale's comment, Nina's blush deepened. They'd been waiting for her to make a polite demurral. Now she muttered, "Uh, yes. That's right."

"Six sisters!" Penelope exclaimed. "How divine! What fun you all must have trading clothes and jewelry. Cilia is constantly after me to lend her my jet earrings and necklace, and I'm always coveting the pearls she inherited from Grandmother. I can just imagine what it would be like if there were seven of us. Are your sisters older than you or younger, Miss Colangelo? Or some of each?"

"Younger." Nina's answer was brief. She didn't know what else to say. Should she tell Penelope that the only thing her *nonna* left when she died was a skillet, two pots, and some wooden spoons?

"Oh." Penelope's forehead wrinkled delicately. There was a puzzled light in her baby blue eyes.

"How nice that you're the oldest," Mrs. Beale said smoothly. "Do you have brothers, too?"

"No," Nina answered, feeling more awkward than ever. She knew she was supposed to elaborate, to make conversation. But for the life of her, she couldn't think of how to do it. "Just sisters," she said. "Six sisters."

"How splendid," Mrs. Beale said while Penelope and Cecilia nodded brightly.

"You've got male cousins, though, haven't you, Miss Colangelo?" Harry boomed. Without waiting for her answer, he leaned across the table and explained, "She's Sergio's niece, Emma. Fabrizio and Ettore are her cousins. They're good lads, too. Just like their father."

"Ah," Emma said. "I see." Although she didn't say what she saw, the look on her face, and on her daughters', made it clear enough. Their expressions had gone blank with horror. They were sitting at the table with one of Mr. Blackwell's servants. An immigrant from Sicily.

"Say, de Groot, that reminds me," Harry went on, unaware of the effects of his last remark, "what did you think of Bridgeman's operation? I never did get the opportunity to ask you. Did it strike you as being a tad run-down? I've the idea that they're being overwhelmed by these new companies with fancier catalogues."

"It's a slow season right now," Wim replied. "It's difficult to judge. Although," he added, a smile starting to crease his cheek, "you certainly make an argument for distinctive cover art. Wouldn't you agree, Miss Colangelo?"

At last there was a subject about which Nina could make an intelligent comment. Trying to pretend she was as unaware as Harry of the effects of his remarks, she said, "Bridgeman has a reputation—"

"Oh, Papa, you promised," Penelope said, cocking her head and pouting prettily, as if Nina had never spoken. "You promised that there would be no talk about cabbages today. It's a party and we should have gay conversation. Not boring ones about seeds. You too, Mr. de Groot," she scolded Wim. "You mustn't encourage him."

"My deepest apologies," Wim said, laughing. "I won't say another word about anything that grows. Shall we talk instead about Miss Rose Inghram's performance in Mozart's *Don Gio-*

vanni? I understand her Zerlina brought the house down when she sang the role this spring.''

"Do you admire her, too?" Penelope asked, turning toward him eagerly. "Her voice brings tears to my eyes. We have an opera subscription this winter. Please say you'll come with us when she sings."

"Gladly," Wim replied. "It would be a pleasure."

The blush that had flared at Penelope's interruption faded abruptly away, leaving Nina icy-cold again. They weren't to speak about anything that grew. That topic was boring and socially incorrect. Instead, she must sit and listen as Wim and Penelope made arrangements to attend the opera together. She looked around for an escape but, to her increasing dismay, only saw Edward Blackwell approaching the canopy.

He came to a halt by their table, his eyes flicking over Nina and settling on Harry Beale. "Won't you join us in the main tent for a toast to my father?" he asked. "My brother and I would like to say a few words in honor of his seventy-fifth birthday."

"We're on our way," Harry declared, surging to his feet. "I think your father's a remarkable man. It'll be a privilege to toast him." As he stepped behind his wife's chair, he didn't notice Edward lift his eyebrows before he moved on to the next table. "Come on, Emma," he said, pulling back the chair. "Girls. Don't forget your glasses."

Nina stood up quickly, before either Harry or Wim could help her, but she wasn't fast enough to avoid a hand seizing her wrist. While the Beales started across the lawn, Wim held her still. "Stop it, Nina," he hissed. "Stop looking so tragic. I won't accuse you of being sensible, this time, but for heaven's sake, please don't be stupid. Surely you realize that *I* didn't invite the Beales to this party. I just met them, by chance, on the train."

"I'm not being tragic," Nina retorted, her voice low and fierce. She yanked her arm free from his grip, though his touch, as always, sent waves of excitement shooting through her body. "And it has nothing to do with the Beales. I just don't want to be here. By all rights, I *shouldn't* be here."

"What!" Wim exclaimed, genuine surprise making him let her go without protest. "What on earth do you mean by that? Why shouldn't you be here?"

"You know why," Nina replied, lifting her chin in defiance, even as her cheeks burned in embarrassment. Was he going to make her spell it out in humiliating detail? Head high, she moved out of the shade and started across the lawn. Away from the party.

Her retreat ended as suddenly as it began. Wim fell in next to her and linked his arm in hers. It was an unexceptional gesture, outwardly decorous. Only Nina felt the iron pressure that clamped her to his side and steered her back toward the main tent. "I'm afraid I don't know why," he said. His voice was as calm as usual, but quiet enough so it wouldn't carry to other people strolling leisurely near them. "I can't think of a single reason for you not to be here. Unless you truly are sick or infirm. Barring that calamity, you're the person who has the *most* reason for being here and toasting Mr. Blackwell's health. Quite simply, Nina, you're the only one he cares about. And probably the only person who cares deeply about him. Your don will be disappointed if he doesn't see your glass raised in the air."

His words made an impact. Nina went limp against him, her resistance gone. It was true, she knew. Don Alberto enjoyed Wim's company, and he liked Harry Beale. Other than that, she was the only person in attendance he could tolerate. "This party isn't his idea, though," she muttered. "It's his sons'. Don Alberto would just as soon have a plate of Mamma's *panelli* on a tray in the library."

"I don't know what *panelli* are," Wim responded, "but if they're one of the things I ate at the wedding, I'm sure that's the wiser choice. Nonetheless, this is the way Don Alberto's seventy-fifth birthday is being celebrated, and he'll want you, of all people, to join in."

"Maybe so," Nina conceded, "but Edward and Reginald don't want me here. I look peculiar and I have funny clothes."

Wim stopped and turned to look at her, an amazed expression on his face. "Now what are you talking about?" he demanded. "There's nothing at all funny about your clothes. I think they're quite lovely. In fact, I meant to tell you that the last time I saw you. You've been to an excellent dressmaker." He looked her up and down, taking in her dotted silk gown with its finely tucked mousseline de soie basque. He nodded appreciatively. "Lovely," he repeated as Nina's face flamed. "I also think the person inside the clothes is very beautiful."

Nina's cheeks grew hotter still and her heart beat very fast. It was thrilling to hear him say those words to her, even if he didn't mean them. Even if he was just trying to coax her into staying.

"You're being very kind," she replied, gazing at a point beyond his head. "But it isn't necessary to flatter me. I know I'm not soft and dainty, like the other women here. I know I'm odd. After all, Wim," she told him, darting a glance his way, "I'm an immigrant. I speak with an accent."

Rather than seeing the wisdom of what she was saying, Wim gave her an exasperated shake. "Don't talk nonsense, Nina," he said in a voice measurably less calm and quiet than before. "I'm not just flattering you. You don't have to have a face like a porcelain doll to be beautiful. Quite the opposite. Your looks are far more striking. And so what if you're an immigrant? I am, too. I speak with an accent, too."

"Yes, but your accent is distinguished," Nina countered. She couldn't respond to his astonishing compliments, so she reacted to the impatience in his tone. "It gives you dignity. It makes you sound important." Then realizing what she'd said, she burned even brighter. "Not that you aren't important," she corrected. "You are, of course."

"Of course," Wim agreed, a smile wiping the uncharacteristic irritation off his face and restoring the amusement to his voice. "And now I must tell you that your accent is lyrical," he said, bringing his free hand across to cover hers as it lay in the bend of his arm. "It gives you grace. Not that you aren't already graceful. You are, of course. Very." He gave her hand a squeeze, then asked, "Shall we continue on before they make the toast without us?" Her head spinning from such praise, Nina followed his lead.

The small amount of pleasure Wim had succeeded in arousing disappeared completely as soon as they reached the main tent. On a podium, raised up above the crowd, stood Don Alberto, looking sour, and his two sons, looking pompous. Fanned out in front of them, chatting gaily, were the guests, but lined up behind them, silent and deferential, was Don Alberto's entire staff. Including Papà, Mamma, all her sisters, and Dante. The sight made her freeze.

If Nina had felt awkward and uncomfortable before, now she was rigid with misery. If before she had wanted to run away and hide, now she longed to vanish instantly. There was her family, not twenty feet away, but so far distant she felt she could never reach them again. The gap between them was as wide as an ocean. They didn't even see her. They didn't recognize her face at this gathering. Staring out at the well-dressed bevy of guests, they looked right through her as if she were invisible. Nina couldn't breathe. She couldn't swallow. Never in her life had she felt so alone.

Then Stella's face lit up. The big bow on her braids bobbed and her squeaky clean cheeks rounded in a smile. After a surreptitious glance at her parents, she lifted her hand and gave a little wave. Relief flooded through Nina as her breath rushed back. *Grazie a Dio,* she thought fervently. I'm saved.

"Isn't that your youngest sister?" Wim asked, leaning closer to Nina to see if she had the same view.

"Yes, it is," Nina said. She waved back at Stella, and Wim waved, too.

"Ladies and gentlemen, if you please," Edward called out, lifting his arms imperiously. He waited for the talk to die down, then he spoke again. "My brother, Reginald, and I have invited you here today to help us celebrate an extraordinary milestone in the life of an extraordinary man." He paused again, and a little patter of applause welled up. "Albert Blackwell," he pronounced. "Today we honor this man who has forged through three quarters of a century with unflagging vigor and indomitable spirit."

While more applause sounded, Don Alberto's eyes glittered dangerously. For the first time that day, Nina couldn't suppress a smile. "What's so amusing?" Wim asked under cover of the clapping. He leaned closer again, to make himself heard.

"He'll be furious," Nina whispered, leaning toward Wim, too. "This sounds like a eulogy. Don Alberto must hate it."

It certainly seemed so. The scowl on the don's baggy face deepened as Edward went on for another ten minutes. Then he turned the ceremony over to Reginald, who, with a great deal of flourish, proposed the toast. While all the guests lifted their glasses and murmured, "Here, here," Don Alberto looked ready to spit.

But it was finally over, and the crowd began to disperse. The guests went to peruse the buffet table, and the staff went back to their posts. Those employees not needed for the grand fete took the path to the groundskeeper's house where the Colangelos were having a party of their own. Once again Nina froze, not sure where she belonged. When Stella looked over her shoulder quizzically, though, Nina made up her mind. She took a step forward to follow her family.

"Don Alberto is signaling you," Wim informed her, pulling her back. "He wants you to come over to see him."

Nina sighed and gave Stella another wave, more forlorn this time, then she turned and let Wim escort her to the head table. It was large and set for ten. Don Alberto was hunched at one end, Edward and Reginald were flanking him. The other places were occupied by the brothers' wives and their most important friends. Extremely conscious of the cold gazes on her, Nina walked around to Don Alberto and said, "Happy birthday." She didn't know what else to add. She didn't even dare call him by name for fear of provoking his sons' rage.

"Yes, yes," the don said. "Don't you annoy me with that claptrap, too. Sit down and keep me company. You, too, de Groot."

"Sit down?" Nina echoed, glancing sideways. There were neither extra place settings nor extra chairs.

In the midst of taking a swallow of champagne, Edward choked. "Really, Father," he sputtered. "I'm afraid the table settings have already been laid. Regrettably, there's no more room. But I see a few empty spaces at the table across the way. I'm sure these people will be comfortable there."

Nina was perfectly willing to sit elsewhere. In fact, she was ready to leave that moment, but Don Alberto wasn't at all interested in that arrangement. "I want Nina next to me," he barked. "Either shove down and find some plates for her and de Groot, or the three of us will go have lunch in the library."

Although each of the three would have preferred that outcome, Edward and Reginald, trembling with rage, made space at the table. It was a mostly silent meal, the tension thicker than the lobster salad. Occasionally Don Alberto made a growling remark to Nina, and she made a strained mutter in reply. Occasionally Wim attempted to engage Reginald in conversation, though his efforts were, for the most part, in vain.

Nina could barely eat the plate of food Fiona set in front of her. Mostly because her stomach was tied up in knots, but also because she found the elaborate food hopelessly bland. She was wretched by the time Don Alberto pushed back his chair and announced he was going up for a nap. Again, the brothers looked apoplectic, but Nina jumped up with alacrity. "I'll walk you to the house," she volunteered.

"I can find my way by myself," the don returned, very grouchy.

"No one doubts that," Wim said, rising as well. "But it would give us both pleasure to accompany you."

"Hmph." Don Alberto stuck out his chin. "In that case, lend me your arm. It's damned hot out here. What an asinine day for a party." Wim immediately offered his arm for support, and the three of them finally made their escape.

Midway back to the house, Don Alberto waylaid one of the waiters hired for the day. "Bring us some ice cream with blueberries and cookies," he ordered. "We'll be on the library terrace."

"Yes, Mr. Blackwell," the waiter replied. "There's birthday cake as well, sir. Shall I bring that, too?"

"No," the don decided for everyone. "I hate those damned sugar roses Mrs. Watkins insists on making. Cakes are dry, too."

On any other day Nina might have reminded the don that Mrs. Watkins was working very hard to please, and he shouldn't insult her. Today, however, she had no such sympathy. "The salmon croquettes were also dry," she remarked. "Didn't you think so?"

"Terrible," Don Alberto agreed with relish. "And how about those tomato aspics shaped like seashells? They looked ridiculous, and they tasted slippery."

"It was a very unkind thing to do to delicious tomatoes," Nina said, beginning to feel better. "And the cucumbers deserved a better fate than being made into jelly."

"No flavor at all." The don punched Nina in the arm. "Did you see Edward's wife chasing it around her plate? What a ninny. She finally captured it and got it halfway to her mouth, then *boom!* It fell off her fork and landed in her lap."

Nina giggled. She was beginning to feel a *lot* better. "I missed that," she confessed. "But I did see the gentleman at the end of the table lift an oyster ever so delicately . . ." She demonstrated the gesture with her little finger extended. "Then the oyster slid off the shell and down the front of his shirt."

Chortling gleefully, Don Alberto said, "That was no gentleman. That was Arnold Wiggens. He made a fortune building tenements in New York City. I wouldn't trust him out of eyesight."

"You two are merciless!" Wim exclaimed, though he was laughing, too. "I'll have to remember to watch my step. I can just imagine what you say about me when I'm not listening."

"You don't have to worry, de Groot," Don Alberto assured him. "We can say whatever we have to tell you to your face.

You'll understand. Not like those twits with puffed-up heads. Bunch of conceited fools.''

"I think I've just been complimented," Wim said, still laughing. They reached the terrace and a small table set up in the shade of an umbrella. "I also think I've been admitted to a very exclusive club," he added, holding out a chair for Don Alberto. He made a sweeping bow. "I'm deeply honored."

"Ought to be," Don Alberto said airily as he dropped into the chair. "Eh, Nina?"

"Indeed," Nina agreed. Tremendously relieved to be away from the party, she was suddenly relaxed. She pulled another chair out and collapsed into it, stretching her legs in front of her. "The rules of the club are extremely strict."

"Oh, dear." Wim's forehead wrinkled in mock worry as he sank onto the third seat. "What must I do to remain a member in good standing?"

"Don't be an idiot," the don told him succinctly.

Then the waiter returned with three frosty bowls of peach ice cream, heaped over with blueberries, and a plate full of paper-thin gingersnaps arranged on a doily. For a pleasant half hour they ate ice cream and cookies while talking agreeably. The main topic was the one Don Alberto enjoyed most. Business. But perhaps he felt the momentousness of the occasion, after all, because in an unprecedented display of sentiment, he told them stories about his early days selling wool. Nina and Wim listened with interest.

"Well, that's enough of that," Don Alberto finally declared. He spooned up the last blueberry, popped it into his mouth, and pushed the bowl aside. He set his palms on the table and heaved himself to his feet. "Got to go take this coat off and unsnap this damned collar. I feel like I'm choking. No, no, don't get up, de Groot," he said as Wim started to rise. "I don't need any help. That ice cream refreshed me." In another astounding show of feeling, he gruffly added, "So did the company." Before either of them could reply, he grabbed his cane and clomped off toward the house.

"Don Alberto," Nina called, jumping up and racing after him. She caught him just in front of the library door.

"What is it?" he asked, eyeing her suspiciously.

Nina smiled. She put her hand on one of his cheeks and put a kiss on the other. "Happy birthday," she said. He flicked his wrist in disgust and disappeared inside.

Still feeling the glow of her affection for the don, Nina returned to the table but remained standing. "I'm going to go home," she told Wim. "My family is having a party, too. Would you like to come?" Then she remembered Penelope, and a cloud settled over her. Looking down, she ran her finger over the back of the chair. "Or perhaps you'd rather return to the lawn. I'm sure the Beales are wondering where you are. You shouldn't disappoint them."

Wim was on his feet in an instant. "The Beales are cozily settled with some friends from Boston," he said. "I doubt they're even aware that I'm gone. Besides, I'd much rather come with you."

"You don't have to say that," Nina insisted, gripping the back of the chair. "You don't have to feel obliged to stay with me now that Don Alberto's gone in for a nap."

"Nina." Wim came around the table to pry her fingers loose and take both her hands in his. Holding them up to his lips, he laid kisses across her knuckles. "I wish you would stop being so mistrustful of me," he said. "I wish you'd stop thinking I'm just being polite." He paused to study her face for a moment, and to again press her hands to his lips. "Why can't you understand that I enjoy your company?" he asked softly. "Like Don Alberto, I find it very refreshing."

He gave the hands he was holding a gentle shake. "I've never met anyone like you, Nina," he told her. "I've never known anyone with your spirit or charm. From the day I first saw you at Castle Garden, you've surprised and delighted me every time we've met." Bringing her hands up, he clasped them close to his chest. "Yes, I like Don Alberto," he said. "And I'm glad to join him for lunch on his birthday, but quite frankly, Nina, if you weren't here, I doubt I would make this trek to the far reaches of Stamford so readily."

With a final look into her eyes and a final kiss on her fingers, Wim let her hands drop to her sides. "Now shall we stand here and dither some more," he asked, his voice teasing again, "or do you think we can go to your family's party?"

Nina took a deep, shaky breath and gingerly wriggled her fingers as if they'd been trapped in a vise instead of tenderly cradled. "Yes," she answered him. "Let's go."

The party at the Colangelos' house was considerably livelier than the one on the lawn. In addition to the family, there were

Dante, Gideon, two stable lads, and the five new gardeners, plus their wives and friends who'd driven up from town. A young man Nina had never seen before was playing the harmonica, and three of her sisters were dancing.

"Bambina! Vieni!" Angelina cried, waving Nina to her. She was sitting in an armchair in the shade of an old elm, keeping track of the comings and goings. When Nina approached, she said, *"Finalmente, ci sei. Dai. Dammi un bacio."*

As directed, Nina placed a kiss on each of her mother's cheeks but told her, "Speak English, Mamma. This is Wim de Groot, and he doesn't understand Italian."

"It's a pleasure to see you again, Signora Colangelo," Wim said, bowing in her direction.

Angelina studied Wim another moment, then gave a majestic shrug. This tall, blond man was a stranger, but today was a special day. Today her home was open to all of *il padrone*'s employees and friends. *"Piacere,"* she said.

"In English, Mamma," Nina prodded.

Although she frowned at her daughter, Angelina sat up even straighter and complied. "'Ow do you do?" she asked.

"Very well, thank you," Wim responded. "I hope you are also well."

Nodding briefly, Angelina turned to Nina. She'd done her duty. She'd welcomed the stranger. But she didn't have to chat with him. *"Hai mangiato, bambina?"* she asked.

It was Nina's turn to frown. While it was true that Wim wasn't being greeted with the usual hostility, he clearly wasn't being greeted as a friend. To say nothing of a possible suitor. "Yes, Mamma," she replied a bit wearily. "We ate."

"Although I'm sure the food at your party was twice as good as what we were served," Wim said, peering across the yard to where the remnants of a feast lay across several tables. "No, make that ten times better," he immediately amended. "I remember the wedding on Long Island. What was that wonderful dish called, *Fasoli?*"

In spite of herself, Angelina beamed. *"Si, fasoli cu la menta,"* she said. If this Viking had complimented her beauty or her clothes, or even praised her children, she would have been impervious. But she couldn't resist someone who liked her food. "No *fasoli* today," she told him, slicing the air with the side of her hand. "Today I make *polpette di melanzane.* Very good." She bunched her fingers together and kissed their tips. "*Molto buono.* Eh, Nina? *Come si dice?*"

"Eggplant fritters," Nina translated. "Mamma makes them with fresh basil and grated cheese. They're really delicious."

"*Si,*" Angelina agreed, beaming again. "Delicious. Go. *Mangia.* Eat."

"They sound awfully tempting," Wim said, eyeing the food tables again.

"Come on." Nina beckoned to him. "We have to taste everything, at least, or Mamma will be mad."

"Oh, no," Wim said, falling in beside her without delay. "I don't want to make your mother angry. Not when she's finally smiled at me."

Though it was only fifty feet to the tables, en route they must have stopped a dozen times. Whenever she crossed paths with a sister, Nina had to exchange kisses and hugs. Whenever she came across a gardener, she had to be introduced to his wife. Wim inched along with her, shaking hands at the appropriate moments, and watching the whole scene with fascination. While Angelina was indisputably the grand matriarch of the family, Nina was obviously respected.

She was the one who'd found success in America, conquering the alien sounds of English and the strange customs along the way. She was the one who'd not only answered when opportunity knocked, but had, in fact, flung open the door. She'd taken giant leaps forward in this modern and prosperous new world, and she was pulling the rest of her family with her. Nina was an inspiration to every person present.

A smile creased Wim's cheek. She wasn't even aware of the deference shown her, but she moved through the crowd with the natural grace of a queen. As he watched her accept tributes and greetings, Wim felt as if he were a spectator in a royal court. Nina was the Monarch of the Yard.

"Stella, *piccina*," Nina called, signaling her little sister to her side. One hand settled across Stella's shoulders, the other accompanied her speech. "Listen, Stella," she instructed. "I want you to go get a plate of food for us to taste. *Taste.*" With her thumb and forefinger, Nina showed her sister the small size of the portion. "We've already eaten lunch, so if you give us too much, we'll burst." Her hand exploded through the air. "Understand?"

Stella's bow, limp and askew by now, nonetheless bobbed her comprehension. "*Si*, Nina," she said. "Just a taste."

"*Brava*." Nina gave Stella's braids a tug and shooed her on her way. "Don't forget the *polpette di melanzane*. Mamma wants Wim to try them."

Wim's smile broadened. Having dispatched the youngest lady-in-waiting, Nina now summoned the prettiest. "Serafina," she called this time, and a slender young woman, ten feet away, looked around for the source of the voice. When she saw Nina waving her over, devotion lit up her delicate face. Again Nina threw an arm across her sister's shoulders, both embracing her and drawing her into a quiet conference. "Tell me who some of these people are, Serafina," Nina commanded. "I've never seen them before. Who's the man talking to Lucia? The one without any neck."

Aha! Wim thought. It would appear that Serafina is the Royal Confidante.

Unaware of having just been so dubbed, Serafina cast a discreet glance at the party in question and turned back to her sister, giggling. "His name is Luigi Tagliaferro," she reported, peeking again at the solid young man whose large head seemed to sit directly on his massive shoulders. "He's from the same town as Salvatore Cascio, one of the new gardeners. In fact, they came over together. I think he said he has a job at Yale and Towne making locks." She rolled her eyes conspiratorially and added in a whisper, "He's been talking to Lucia all afternoon."

"Very interesting," Nina commented, whispering, too. "Is he married?"

Serafina giggled again. "You sound like Mamma," she said. "I don't know, Nina. I can't very well ask him."

Her amused reproach made Wim grin, but it made Nina laugh. "I'm just being careful," she said somewhat sheepishly. "I'm just being protective of my precious sisters." She gave Serafina a squeeze to show her what she meant.

"Speaking of which," she went on, her face suddenly darkening with concern, "how long has Gideon been hanging around Bianca?" Her eyes narrowed as she looked across the yard. Wim followed her gaze and saw Nina's middle sister coyly flirting with Don Alberto's secretary. Office Manager, Wim corrected himself wryly.

"He's been here all afternoon, too," Serafina answered, also staring at the pair. Her big, brown eyes looked worried. "Mamma hasn't said anything, but I know she's very upset. He wouldn't eat any of her food, except some bread and dessert."

As Nina's expression grew darker, Wim looked around for Stella and their plate of food. He didn't want to be similarly condemned for failing to eat. Stella was nowhere to be seen, but bearing down on them was Signora Colangelo with Dante da Rosa in tow.

"Nina, guarda che ho trovato Dante," Angelina announced, pushing the blushing young man forward.

While Wim watched, his own eyes narrowing, Nina's cheeks turned red, too, and her royal assurance vanished. She looked flustered for the first time since leaving the lawn. And for the first time, Wim himself felt uncomfortably anxious. It wasn't a feeling he was accustomed to, as uncharacteristic for him as Nina's nervousness was for her.

Wim didn't know what Angelina was saying and he didn't know what Nina was stammering in reply, but he didn't need to speak Italian to understand what was happening. It was plain as day that Nina's mother was eager to make a match between her oldest daughter and this handsome Sicilian. It was equally plain that they were both embarrassed by her tactics.

What wasn't clear, however, and what made Wim's stomach knot in dread, was how Nina and Dante felt about each other. He saw none of the uneasiness that had darkened Nina's face when she was peering across the yard at Gideon, nor any of the detached scrutiny she'd given Luigi Tagliaferro. He saw no signs of distaste in either of their expressions. Could those blushes, therefore, be the shyness of love?

Wim felt himself turn cold under the glare of the August sun. His square jaw clenched, and his blue eyes turned glacial. When Stella finally came back with the plate of food, he ate mechanically, hardly tasting the exquisite eggplant fritters. For all he knew, they could have been seashell-shaped aspics or cucumber jellies. The flavor had gone from the day.

=17=

In the week following the party, they didn't hear a single word from Wim. Since it wasn't like Don Alberto to discuss personal matters, and since Nina wasn't about to bring it up, total silence enshrouded his name. Nina tried to tell herself that she was just as glad, that her destiny lay with Dante, and that any time she spent with Wim was only a disruption.

As noble as those thoughts sounded, however, she had a little trouble believing them. Like her nighttime resolutions, which dissolved in the light of day, these rationalizations didn't stand up to reality. The plain fact of it was, she wasn't glad, at all. The plain fact of it was, she missed him. Terribly.

That didn't make any sense, she told herself. She must be imagining it. She'd seen Wim only five times in her entire life. How could she miss someone she hardly knew?

But if there was one voice in her head reproaching herself, there was another voice arguing back. She *did* know him, she insisted. Maybe she hadn't spent a whole lot of time in his company, but not an instant of that time had been wasted. From the moment they'd collided in the crowd at Castle Garden, she'd been intensely aware of everything about him, every move he made, every word he uttered, every nuance in his tone. So if she still didn't know that much about his background or business, about the daily routine of his life, she knew a lot about who he was and about that dry, ironic sense of humor with which he observed the world. That's what Nina missed most of all. She missed his amusement.

Even as she confessed that, though, she was busy making excuses. It was just because tension was so high these days, she tried to convince herself. Because they were racing to get a business started and a catalogue in the mail by the first of January. Because they were all feeling hot, tired, and strained. Not that

Wim could exactly relieve that strain. His humor didn't run to clown tricks and jokes. But his evenness and amusement would be a welcome counterpoint to the constant pressure of Don Alberto's testiness and Gideon's smirk.

Whatever the case, Wim occupied more of Nina's attention than she could afford to give him. When she was supposed to be writing descriptions of the eight varieties of pansies they were carrying, she found herself gazing into space, longing for Wim to appear. When she was supposed to be listening to the Planet Jr. salesman pitching seed drills and single-wheel hoes, she found her attention wandering, wondering where Wim was.

She was at her desk one afternoon staring at the list of fertilizers while trying to chase images of Wim from her mind, when her divided concentration was interrupted by someone saying her name. Still slightly absorbed, she looked up. Her head cleared instantly. "Dante!" she exclaimed.

He was standing at the edge of the open French doors, his straw hat in his hand. His collarless shirt was unbuttoned at the neck, his sleeves were rolled halfway up his arms. Deeply bronzed and fit from working outdoors, he looked like a pagan god of Nature's bounty.

"*Scusi,* Nina," he apologized. "*Posso parlare un momento con te?*"

"What's going on?" Don Alberto asked as he set down the letters he was signing.

"Dante wants a word with me," Nina explained, standing up quickly. She tried to sound casual, even though her heart was beating in alarm. What was so important it couldn't wait until he saw her at supper? Or was it too private to say in front of her family? "We'll just step outside so we don't bother anyone," she said, acutely aware of Gideon's darting eyes. "I won't be a moment."

"Excuse please, Mr. Blackwell," Dante added.

"Hmph," Don Alberto responded, returning to his correspondence.

"What is it, Dante? What's the matter?" Nina demanded as they crossed the terrace and descended the steps. Was he going to proclaim his ardor for her? Was he going to ask her to marry him? She could barely breathe.

"You seem upset," Dante replied. "Are you angry because I disturbed you at work? I'm sorry. I should have known better."

"No, no," Nina assured him, her hand fluttering as she tried to appear normal. "I'm surprised to see you, is all." She forced a smile. "You've never come to talk to me like this before."

"I've never had the courage before," Dante confessed. He returned the smile shyly while Nina's heart sank. Her legs felt wooden. "But at mealtimes I can never seem to get your attention," Dante continued. "With everything that's going on, I can never pull you aside. I finally decided that if I'm ever going to talk to you, I'd better come see you in the office. I didn't mean to interrupt your work."

"Don't be silly," Nina said, her hand waving again. "It's nothing that can't wait a little while longer." They paused in front of a bench made of wrought-iron vines, but Nina was too nervous to sit down. "Do you mind if we keep walking?" she asked Dante, her throat dry. "I've been sitting all day. It feels good to stretch."

"Of course not," Dante replied, instantly starting forward again. "In fact, if you want to walk, we can go out to the trial gardens. That would be the best thing yet. Then I could show you what I'm talking about."

"You can what?" Nina stopped abruptly to stare at him, confused. "Wait a minute," she said as an inkling of comprehension worked its way through the daze. "Just what *are* you talking about?"

Dante stopped a few steps later and turned to look back at her, somewhat surprised by her reaction. "I'm talking about the corn, Nina," he said. "It's coming in now, and some of it isn't as good as it should be. For example, the Stowell's Evergreen looks short-grained to me, and the Early Minnesota is uneven. Maybe, if it's not too late, you should try to find a new supplier."

It took a moment for his words to fully sink in, but when they did, Nina felt a lightness run through her that nearly lifted her off her feet. Dante didn't have marriage on his mind, at all. He had corn. First she hiccuped. Then she burst out laughing.

Even more startled, Dante looked at her uneasily. "I was right the first time," he decided. "I shouldn't have interrupted you in the office. You're too busy to think about the corn."

"No, I'm not," Nina gasped, trying to control her laughter. "Truly I'm not." Swallowing her last few giggles, she wiped her eyes on the back of her hand.

"I'm sorry, Dante," she said. It was her turn to apologize and she did it gladly. "I'm not laughing at you," she told him. "I'm laughing at myself. I was all prepared to hear some really dreadful news."

"I thought this *was* bad news," Dante said, scratching his forehead. "You haven't been out to do your log in over a week, Nina, and I thought you'd want to know the corn is doing poorly. It seemed important to tell you."

"It is important," Nina agreed, not bothering to explain her outburst any further. She started walking again, but at a leisurely pace. The anxiety that had driven her was gone. "Thank goodness you've been keeping an eye on the gardens," she said. "I've meant to check them on three separate days, but every time I start out the door with my clipboard, something else comes up." She let her hand hang loose, and her fingers brushed the tops of some lavender. "Maybe you should start taking the notes for me," she added, half joking.

Strolling beside her, Dante smiled, though a faint flush was visible beneath his tan. "I'll just tell you what's happening," he half joked in reply. "I can't write notes in English."

"All right," Nina said. "You can just tell me. Although I'll bet we could get Serafina to write the notes for you when she's out there doing the drawings. She's so good. She's always willing to help."

"Yes, I'm sure she would," Dante said, his flush deepening. He turned to look at Nina. "In the meantime, shall I tell you about the onions, too? They're nearly ready to harvest."

Nina laughed again. "By all means," she responded. "Tell me about the onions."

A second week went by and again there was no word from Wim. By now, even Don Alberto missed him enough to comment. "Must be up to his ears in business," he said gruffly, tossing a stack of invoices aside. "Must be getting ready for his big season."

"More than likely," Nina said, without looking up from the copy she was writing on sweetpeas. She tried to sound indifferent, though her voice quavered slightly.

For a moment Don Alberto drummed his fingers on his desk, then he swiveled around toward Gideon. "O'Shea," he ordered, "write him a letter. Tell him to come out for a weekend whenever he's able to get away."

"Yes, Mr. Blackwell," Gideon said, darting a glance at Nina.

Her cheeks looked a little pinker than usual, but other than that, her pencil was looping easily across the page.

Regardless of her outer composure, however, inside Nina was anything but calm. With each postal delivery that brought no letter from Wim, her inner turmoil mounted. Gone were her nighttime vows and denials. Gone were the excuses and logical plans. Gone was last week's self-reproach. What was left was a raw desire to see him. Nor did she any longer attempt to disguise it.

Because despite having been relieved to the point of laughter the other day, Nina wasn't lulled. Quite the opposite, she was alerted. She'd spent a pleasant hour touring the trial gardens with Dante, talking the entire time about vegetables. But just because he hadn't proposed between the stalks of corn, didn't mean he wasn't going to. Nina knew it was going to happen. She could see it in her mother's face, and she felt it in her soul. It was only a matter of time.

It was only a matter of time before he asked her to marry him, and only a matter of time before she accepted. Whatever her doubts and apprehensions, Nina knew it was only a matter of time before Fate cast her forever with Dante.

Sensibly speaking, she didn't know what difference it would make to see Wim again before it happened. But as she'd once told him, she wasn't sensible. She was Sicilian. She thought with her heart instead of her head. And in her heart she more than missed him, she yearned to see him, at least once more. The longing became more urgent the more he stayed away.

As the last days of August slid by, Nina grew desperately afraid that Wim was gone for good. That this time, for sure, he'd vanished from her life forever and that she'd never see him again. Never again see a crooked smile creasing his cheek, or look up, unexpectedly, into the bluest eyes she'd ever seen. She was afraid he'd finally realized what she'd known all this time. That she belonged with Dante, digging in the earth, and he belonged with someone fair and refined. Someone like Penelope Beale. The thought filled her with panic.

She ate without tasting and scarcely slept, but somehow managed to get her work done. Although she wrote about four-o'clocks and Mourning Brides, although she consulted with draftsmen and printers, if anyone had asked her what she'd written or said, she wouldn't have been able to answer. She was consumed with thoughts of Wim.

On the first day of September, Nina told herself enough was enough. The summer was over and Wim was gone. *Finito.* It was time to shake herself out and put him behind her. She had to put him back in the recesses of her mind where he'd been before Aurelia's wedding. It was much safer to think of him as just a fond, but ancient, memory.

Unfortunately, this resolution, like all the others, was more easily said than done. When her parents and sisters settled down for their Sunday naps, Nina felt too restless to join them. She decided it would be the ideal time to take her neglected log out to the trial gardens. The quiet plats, empty of human activity, would be certain to soothe her nerves. Surrounded by thousands of flowers at the height of their bloom, she couldn't help but feel much better. Just thinking about it had a balming effect.

Walking out the path, Nina's spirits started to rise. It had been months since she'd spent any time alone, especially in a garden. She took the time to check her favorite spots, peering at various beds and bushes along the way. The Nursery didn't lure her in, but the new building caught her attention.

Despite her early objections to it, now she rather liked it. It was a huge, two-story edifice, with enough rooflines and details to save it from appearing massive. Besides, Don Alberto had had it designed with separate offices for everyone, and now that Nina worked at a desk every day, the idea of an office of her own was appealing.

The exterior of the Store, as it was already called, was completely finished. Every clapboard was in place and neatly painted. But when Nina opened the door and looked inside, an entirely different scene greeted her. There were ladders and sawhorses and kegs of nails everywhere. Hammers and planes were strewn about. Levels leaned up against newly plastered walls, and the smell of freshly milled pine filled the air.

On an impulse, Nina entered the Store and went up to the second floor to take a peek at her private office. Although she hadn't been upstairs yet, she knew it faced the trial gardens and had floor-to-ceiling windows. Don Alberto had grumbled about the cost and grandeur, but, nonetheless, it was he who had planned the room. Aware that Nina didn't like being inside, he was trying to bring the outdoors to her.

Listening to the pleasant sound of her heels on the wooden floor, Nina poked her head into every doorway. The late summer

sun poured in all the windows and made the brand-new pine
planks sparkle. It was peaceful in here. Warm and bright and still.
For the first time in weeks, Nina felt the knots in her heart loosen
and felt her body relax. She started to hum.

"Pretty tune."

His words reached her at the exact moment that she entered her
office and saw him sitting on a pile of lumber, the windows flung
wide open in front of him. His jacket was off and his collar was
unsnapped and his boots and socks were stuffed in a crate. Though
his back was to her, he was looking over his shoulder, so the
crease of his welcoming smile was visible. Wim.

Nina's humming ceased abruptly and she stopped in the
doorway, though, curiously, she wasn't gasping in wild excitement. Instead, the peace that had been drifting through her, easing
away her tension, now settled deep inside her and spread through
her entire being. She felt completely serene.

"Thank you," she said, taking a few slow steps forward, until
she was close enough to touch him. The sun was catching in his
thick, blond hair and making it gleam. "It's a Sicilian song."

"I thought it might be." He spoke quietly and sat without
stirring, his arms lying still on his knees. Only his head dipped
slightly, dislodging a glistening lock of hair. It slipped across his
fine, clear brow and rested above his eye, a single strand as smooth
and luxurious as satin. Nina was suddenly overcome by the desire
to run her fingers across it.

"I hope you don't mind my being in your office," he said after
a moment of silence. Neither of them moved an inch. "When I
arrived from the train, Albert was napping, so I wandered out here
seeking solitude. It's quite restful, don't you find? And the view is
spectacular." He turned his head forward to stare out the window
at the trial gardens, bursting with color below.

"I came for the same reason," Nina responded, though she said
it almost absently and didn't even look at the flowers. Her
attention was fixed on the back of his head. On that head of
lustrous, fair hair. "My family is also napping, so I, too, came to
be alone." She had to touch it. Had to know if it felt as exotic as
it looked. Like the hair of kings and mermaids in fairy tales and
myths. Without even knowing it, her hand started to rise.

"Am I disturbing you, then?" Wim asked as he turned to hear
her reply. Startled by his sudden movement, Nina stopped her
hand in midair, and for a fraction of an instant Wim hesitated, too.

For as long as it took for her to draw a quick breath, he looked at her hand in surprise. Then his gaze flicked away and traveled to her eyes. His question didn't disappear, however. Rather, it gained significance. His expression as intense as she'd ever seen it, Wim searched her face for an answer.

The force of his stare momentarily unnerved her. It jarred the serene trance she was in. Practical thoughts started to filter into her mind. She started to think about what she was doing. With another sharp breath, her open hand closed. It began to retreat.

Then a hint of a breeze wafted through the windows, barely enough to feel. But it made the rays of sunshine shimmer as it ruffled Wim's hair. That hypnotic sense of tranquillity swelled up again, pushing rational thoughts aside. As her balled fist unfurled, Nina thought with her heart instead of her head.

Ever so slowly, her hand reached out and her fingers stretched toward his hair. Tentative at first, they touched a strand. Then she hastily pulled them back, half afraid she'd broken something fragile. When nothing happened, when Wim didn't flinch, when his eyes never left her face, she reached out again, and this time she buried her fingers in his hair. It felt clean and glossily smooth, like a cascade of silk from ripening corn.

Nina breathed deeply. "No," she answered in a husky voice. "You're not disturbing me." Every fiber in her tingled as she brushed his hair from his brow. "Am I disturbing you?"

In response Wim finally moved. He lifted his own hand and wrapped his fingers around her arm, drawing it down in front of him and placing a kiss on her palm. Surely and steadily, he unbuttoned her cuff and pushed her sleeve higher. Then starting at her wrist and following her pounding pulse, he laid kisses to her elbow. Nina felt every one shoot up her arm and explode inside her body. She arched back her head and breathed very hard.

"Come, Nina," he said, his voice low and gravelly. He pulled her arm until her knees buckled and she sank to the pile of boards. From either side of the wooden planks, they twisted toward each other. His eyes were unusually bright and blue, and the scrubbed spots on his cheeks were especially rosy. But even now a crooked smile tugged at the corner of his mouth.

"Have you satisfied your curiosity about my hair?" he asked in that same raspy voice, again bringing her bared arm to his lips. His kisses felt cool and moist against her increasingly inflamed skin. Inexplicably she shivered.

"Yes," she whispered, her eyes half shut, hoping he would never stop.

"Are you sure?" he murmured, lowering her arm and unbuttoning her other cuff. He repeated the pattern of kisses. Slowly, lingering over each one. The effect was even more powerful than before. Nina swallowed hard.

"Yes," she whispered again. "For now."

"Ah," he said, laughing softly against the tender skin in the bend of her arm. "I look forward to the moment when your interest is renewed." He placed a final kiss in the crease of her elbow and blew it dry with a gossamer breath. "In the meantime," he said, folding both arms in her lap, "I have to satisfy a question of my own."

Nina's eyes opened and her eyebrows knit. "What question?" she asked. She let her arms lay where Wim had placed them, fighting an urge to slide them around his neck. He'd released her only a second ago, but she was already aching for his touch.

Wim's smile appeared again as his hands reached toward her hair. "I've always wanted to know what would happen if you didn't catch your hairpins before they fell," he replied, pulling them free, one by one. A thick mass of dark hair tumbled down from her head and spilled around her shoulders in rippling waves.

"Beautiful," he murmured, filling both hands full and weaving his fingers through the shiny strands. "Even more beautiful than I imagined." With fistfuls of hair, he drew her toward him, unhurriedly, studying her in admiration. He swept the hair away from her face, plunging his fingers deeper to cup the back of her head. "Beautiful," he murmured again.

Holding her breath, Nina closed her eyes. And Wim bent forward to press kisses on the lids. Her breath whooshed out as the pleasure inside her soared. Unconsciously she leaned closer, silently willing him to run his fingers down her neck. To let them run down her back. She leaned closer still, wanting him to rub his flushed cheek against hers, wanting his cool, silky hair to slide across her face. She yearned to fill her nose with his clean, fresh scent and to feel the desire that had brightened his eyes. She wanted him to kiss her. Sensing her wishes, he did it all.

He nestled tiny kisses in the hollow behind her ear. Tenderly, just a touch. And when she inhaled sharply, he retraced those kisses with his tongue. Rolling his head slowly, his lips trailing across her cheek, he kissed her with a luscious lack of haste, tasting and savoring her smooth skin.

Then his head rolled a little bit more and his lips nudged against her mouth. His own breath sucked in as he found her awaiting him eagerly, as he felt her hands slip around his back and embrace him with intoxicating urgency. His fingers raked free from her hair and clutched her to his chest. Crushing his lips against hers, he matched the vibrant passion of her kiss.

When after a minute they paused, breathing heavily, Wim wrapped a hand around her waist. In a single fluid movement he scooped her across the boards and slid her into his lap. Startled, Nina's eyes flew open and she leaned back in his arm. His lips were bruised and his color was high and he was looking at her with glittering need. "Don't be alarmed," he said hoarsely.

Hot waves of longing flooded through her with a force greater than she'd ever known. She smiled, her own eyes bright and feverish. "I'm not," she said, relaxing.

Wim smiled, too. His breathing steadied. While he cradled her in one arm, he caressed her with his other hand. His fingers were feather-light as they floated over her face, brushing her dark eyebrows and outlining the full circle of her lips. They stroked the delicate skin under her eyes and followed the plane of her cheek as it curved and disappeared below her chin. Carefully then, his eyes never leaving hers, Wim undid the buttons of her shirt. Nina drew a deep breath, but she didn't stop him. She didn't want to. Her eyes fluttered closed.

Looking down at her, Wim smiled again, but he didn't quicken his pace. Still moving with deliberate slowness, he folded open her shirt and eased it from her shoulders. For a moment he let his fingertips glide over her naked skin, enjoying its satiny feel. Then he skimmed across to her arms again, slipping off the straps of her camisole and inching it down her body. His smile deepened when her breasts emerged, round and lovely, above the batiste. Bending his head, he kissed one, and then the other.

All the thrilling sensations Nina had felt since she came into the room dimmed by comparison with what she felt now. Shock after shock of pure pleasure engulfed her. She was wholly absorbed by desire. Winding her fingers around locks of Wim's hair, she held his head to her breasts, straining to get even closer.

Sliding off the pile of lumber, they landed on the new board floor. With pine-scented wood curls for a mattress and pillow, and mellow sunshine for a sheet, they made love to each other where they lay. Outside the windows, thousands of flowers nodded. A few birds called lazily across the fields.

Afterward, after their grand need had been sated, they remained, legs tangled together, on the fragrant floor. Nina felt a delicious languor spread through her, as warm and glowing as the late summer sun. It wasn't like the hot excitement of before, but in its way it was as wonderful a feeling. Maybe even better. What she felt, as she lay in the circle of Wim's arms, was satisfied and blissfully happy.

Turning her head, she pressed her lips against the first bit of Wim she encountered. As it happened, it was his chest. It was so pale. His skin was as white as marble. Almost reverently, she brushed her fingers across it.

Wim laughed and hauled her on top of him. "I won't break, you know," he said, running his hands the length of her round, strong limbs. "I'm not a precious object."

Inches above him, Nina touched his face. She traced a line around the features that defined him, from the crease in his cheek to the tiny dot by the bridge of his nose. "You are to me," she said softly.

Wim reached up with both hands and smoothed the hair away from her face, twisting it into a neat knot behind her head. Then he placed a hand on either cheek and shut her eyes with a sweep of his thumbs. Pulling her to him, he kissed her gently, but with profound feeling. For a long time Nina lay on top of him, basking in contentment. There wasn't a single flaw in the afternoon.

It was only late in the day, when they were getting dressed, that Nina remembered to ask him where he'd been. She was sitting on the floor, leaning against the lumber and fastening the buttons of her shirt. "It's been weeks since we've heard from you," she said. "Was something wrong? Why haven't you come for a visit?"

Seated on the stack, putting on a sock, Wim hesitated in mid-motion. He glanced down, but saw only the dark jumble of her hair, barely held together with a few salvaged pins. Turning back to what he was doing, he finished slipping the sock over his foot, then jammed it into his boot. At last he answered her. "I was afraid you didn't want to see me again," he said simply.

Nina lifted her head quickly, her golden eyes wide. For a stunned moment she watched him pull on his other sock, then, with wonder in her voice, she asked, ''If that's so, why did you come today?''

Wim set down his foot and studied her carefully, finally running the back of his hand across her cheek. ''Because I was afraid I'd never see you again,'' he told her, then looked away and picked up his boot.

Her heart swelling too much to respond, Nina could only continue to watch him. When both his feet were shod, he picked up his tie and began to knot it around his neck. Still wordless with happiness, Nina resumed her buttoning but let herself fall sideways and rest her head against his knee. Wim leaned down to set a kiss at the base of her neck before it was covered up by her blouse. Without looking up, she knew he was smiling, because she was smiling, too.

Nina's bliss lasted exactly four minutes from the moment she left Wim at the fork in the path. While he turned one way to thread through the gardens toward an early supper with the don, Nina turned the other way toward home. Walking along, her arms swinging aimlessly, Nina felt less hurried than she had in months.

About to amble past the Nursery, on impulse, she turned off the path and headed toward it. What better place to revel in her happiness than in the big greenhouse where she always found peace? She stooped to pluck a scarlet four-o'clock from one of the urns on either side of the entrance, took an appreciative sniff, and stuck it between the buttons of her shirt. Then she stepped through the door. And froze in horror.

Halfway down the center aisle, almost hidden behind some potted ferns, Bianca Maria was pressed against a bench. The person pressing her was Gideon. Gideon's mouth was glued to Bianca's, his thighs thrust against her hips. One of his hands was behind her, rubbing up and down on her rear. The other was snaked beneath her shirt and was rhythmically kneading her breast. Nausea rose up in Nina's throat and nearly made her gag.

''Stop it!'' she cried, advancing down the aisle toward them. ''Stop it this instant! What do you think you're doing?''

Halting in front of them, she clutched her face in shock, but when the couple pulled apart, they seemed more annoyed than remorseful. Gideon's eyes were hard and glinting, his pale skin was flushed and shiny. Wiping his mouth with the back of his hand, he took a few steps away. Flushed, but defiant, Bianca fixed her disarrayed hair and tucked in the loose tail of her shirt.

"Don't make such a fuss, Nina," she said. "There's no harm been done."

"No harm?" Nina gasped, twisting her hands together. "How can you say that? This is . . . this is . . ." she stammered, feeling dizzier and dizzier. This is what she had been doing half an hour ago. Only worse. "This isn't right," she finished faintly.

"You sound like an old lady, Nina," Gideon said. His eyes had darted between the sisters, assessing the situation before he'd spoken up. "This is America. It's 1895. It's not some medieval village in Sicily. You heard Bianca. There was no harm done. It was all in fun."

If Gideon had come to the conclusion that Nina could be embarrassed into retreating, his judgment couldn't have been more wrong. This wasn't a question of coaching her on her clothes or her social skills, this was a question of family. When it came to her family, Nina was absolutely immune to criticism, threats, or ridicule. In fact, rather than intimidating her with his comments, Gideon succeeded in focusing her wrath.

"How dare you pretend there was no harm done?" she shouted, jamming one hand on her hip and wagging the other in front of Gideon's nose. "I don't care where we are and I don't care what year it is, do you hear me? We could be in China or Brazil or on the moon!" she cried. She flung her hand in a descriptive arc. "There is *no* time when you can treat my sister as you've done and *no* place where your disgraceful behavior is acceptable. If you had any decency at all, you'd be begging Bianca's pardon instead of standing there making shameful excuses."

It didn't take much to make Gideon's temper flare, and this had certainly exceeded it. The flush on his face turned an ugly red as he watched her finger jab at him accusingly. "I don't beg," he snarled, stepping past her hand. "And I don't listen to lectures from women." He strode part of the way down the aisle before he turned to shake his fist. "Keep out of my private life, Nina," he said harshly. "And save your preaching for someone else. I don't give a damn about your high-toned opinions. I'm not interested in your sermons."

"Then stay away from my sister!" Nina shouted, punching the air for emphasis. "Don't ever come near her again!"

About to turn toward the door again, Gideon, instead, wheeled back to face her. "Don't tell me what to do!" he screamed.

"Gideon, please," Bianca said softly. Casting wary glances at Nina, she patted the air imploringly.

Again Gideon looked from one sister to the other, not assessing this time, but contemptuous. In the end he spat on the floor, whirled, and stormed away.

"Good riddance," Nina muttered at his disappearing back.

"Oh, Nina!" Bianca Maria exclaimed angrily. She knew better than to contradict her older sister in front of strangers, but now that they were alone, she let her annoyance show. "Why did you have to do that?" she demanded. "Why did you have to interfere? Why couldn't you have left us alone when you saw that we were in here?"

"Leave you alone?" Nina repeated, spinning to stare at Bianca. "I could no more leave you alone with Gideon than I could with a wounded panther. Don't you see?" she asked. "He's no good. He'll destroy you. Eat you alive. He doesn't care who he hurts. His only concern in life is for himself. You should leave *him* alone, Bianca. Forget about him. Otherwise, I'm afraid you'll regret it."

"*Fff!*" Bianca scoffed, lifting both her shoulders and her eyebrows in a shrug. "How did you get to be such an expert?" she asked. "What do you know about men? The only thing *you* care about is gardens and flowers.

"Honestly, Nina," she said, fidgeting with her hair, "sometimes I think you're positively unnatural. Here you are, twenty-four years old, without a husband or even a proper *fidanzato*. And every time Dante goes near you, you get rigid." Snapping up straight and stiff, she demonstrated Nina's posture. "It's as if you had Benedetta's rolling pin in your spine." She relaxed and flapped her hand in disgust. "You're a fine one to be giving advice on men."

A bright blush shot up Nina's neck and suffused her cheeks. Bianca Maria's remark hit home, but not for the reason she'd cited. Quite the opposite. Nina had to clear her throat several times before she could speak.

"I may not be the ideal person to be giving you advice on men," she began, a trifle unsteadily, "but I do think I'm qualified to give you advice about Gideon." Her voice picked up strength now, and she clasped her hands together and shook them beneath her chin. "Bianca, I've worked with him every day for the last three months. Believe me, I can judge his character."

Bianca Maria didn't reply, just regarded Nina with narrowed eyes. Encouraged, Nina went on. "He's very good at his job," she said. "He's sharp and efficient when it comes to all that paperwork." Her hand waved vaguely. "And he can be charming and helpful when it comes to people. But only if it's in his own best interest. Do you understand what I'm saying?" she asked her sister. "Gideon isn't to be trusted."

"*Fff,*" Bianca said again, and again gave an elaborate shrug. She started walking down the aisle, swishing her hips defiantly. At the door she stopped, though, and when she turned to look at Nina she didn't seem as grand. "You won't tell Papà about this, will you?" she asked.

Nina thought about it a minute, then wearily shook her head. "Not if you stay away from Gideon," she promised.

After Bianca Maria left, the silence in the Nursery was enormous. Suddenly sagging, Nina stumbled down to the end of the aisle and collapsed in her old chintz chair. Now that her anger was gone, there was nothing left to support her. She felt totally drained. Devastated beyond description. Who, indeed, was she to be moralizing when she'd lain naked in Wim's arms only minutes before?

Nina put her hands over her face and pressed her eyes, but the images wouldn't go away. She kept seeing Gideon rubbing lewdly against her sister, kept seeing the glint of lust in his eyes. Is that what she and Wim had looked like? The heavy, sick feeling again welled up in her throat.

"*O Dio,*" she moaned as her hands fell away and lay limp and lifeless in her lap. How could she have been so blind, deaf, and dumb to let what had happened happen? How could she have let herself be so mesmerized by the sunshine shimmering in his blond hair that she'd willingly let Wim seduce her? And then, as if that weren't bad enough, to have enjoyed it. To have gloried in it. Nina's hands balled up and banged against her chest in anguish. How could she be so stupid?

She'd cautioned Bianca against Gideon, warning that he wasn't to be trusted. That he only acted in his own self-interest, complimenting and being charming when there was something in it for him. But was Wim really any different? How did she know that his gracious manners weren't part of a similarly selfish game?

After all, hadn't he tried to kiss her every time he'd found her alone?

Moaning again, Nina clutched her stomach, sickened to think that she'd played into his hands. Ha. Into his arms was more like it. It mortified her to remember how she'd responded to his caresses, straining toward him, aching for his touch. For that matter, who knew but she had started it herself by running her fingers through his hair.

"*Che miseria!*" she wailed, rocking back and forth in the chair. In a burst of rage, she'd accused Gideon of disrespectful behavior. All because he'd kissed her. If that were the case, what should she say about herself? What honor was left to her? Nina's rocking stopped as her heart broke and sobs convulsed her body.

She cried for a long, long time, until she didn't have the strength to cry anymore. She cried for the honor she'd lost and for the happiness that had been hers so briefly. But mostly she cried for the innocence that was gone forever, for the sweet faith she'd had in life. More than anything, she cried for the childlike trust she'd left behind her on the pine-plank floor.

With bleary eyes Nina stared into the distance as thoughts moved sluggishly through her head. This was America, Gideon had said. It was 1895. The New World. The land of opportunity. This was the country where dreams came true, where miracles happened every day. Where a lost girl from Sicily could look up from the floor at Castle Garden and into the bluest eyes she'd ever seen. America. From the moment she'd arrived on its glorious shores, the symbol of America, for her, had been Wim.

Hot tears ran down her face again. Another dream lay shattered.

=*18*=

If Wim had been around in the days that immediately followed, things might have developed differently. If Wim had been there before the horror was indelibly set, he might have been able to erase it. He might have been able to seize her by the wrist and heal her with his logic and calm. His clean, fresh looks might have balanced out Gideon's unsavoriness. The wave of shame and disgust that roiled up every time Nina looked across the library might have ebbed away if Wim had been there to make it.

But he wasn't there. He was meeting the bulbs. Tens of thousands of tulips and narcissus and hyacinths that were arriving right now from Holland. Because he was busy ushering the bulbs through customs, he didn't have time to come to Stamford. And because he wasn't there, Nina hardened against him. By the time he finally returned, she didn't want anything to do with him. Not ever again.

It was on a Saturday, almost at the end of September. Nina had been working demonically these past three weeks to finish the first draft of the catalogue. Despite the emotions tearing at her heart, she'd had to fix her head on the job in front of her. She'd had to forget about being Sicilian and concentrate on being American.

At eleven-twenty on that foggy morning, she plopped the thick manuscript on Don Alberto's blotter. Then she returned to her chair, collapsed with her arms sprawled across her desk, and rested her head on top of her arms. Staring dully out the French doors, Nina waited while the don read through the draft. Her eyes felt gritty, her back was stiff and sore, and every muscle in her body ached. She'd worked until midnight yesterday and was at it again by seven this morning. As she gazed out at the gray autumn day, Nina tried to count how many family lunches she'd missed recently, but couldn't remember. She did know, however, that she hadn't had supper at home since Monday. She felt exhausted, battered, and miserable.

"I don't like it."

For a moment Nina remained as she was, watching a few leaves drift down from a dogwood. Then she sat up slowly and looked at the don, her fingers drawing into a ball. "You what?" she asked, hoping she hadn't heard him correctly. Hoping she'd imagined his disagreeable tone.

"I said, I don't like it," Don Alberto repeated, slamming a fistful of papers onto his desk. "For God's sake, Nina. Didn't you hear me? I don't like it. It's boring. Dry. Like every other damned catalogue in circulation. It looks like you put them all through a grinder and came up with this one."

"That's what you told me to do!" Nina cried, surging to her

feet, hands flying. This couldn't be happening. Not after all her hard work and sacrifice. He couldn't possibly be rejecting it. "I followed your instructions exactly!"

"My instructions?" the don barked, also pulling himself up behind his desk. "Never! I never told you to copy the other catalogues. If that's all I wanted, I could have had O'Shea here do it." Tossing his head in Gideon's direction, he added bitterly, "From you I expected something original."

"No!" Nina was shouting now and banging her palm on the desk. All the pressures inside her suddenly burst and came pouring out with fury. "No! No! No! You didn't tell me that at all. You didn't give me the slightest hint that that's what you wanted.

"You sat right out there in the rose garden," she raged, flinging her hand at a point beyond the door, "and told me that I'd read hundreds of seed catalogues and therefore should be able to plan one for us. 'Break it down to its most basic parts,' you said. 'Solve one part at a time. That's lesson one.' And that's exactly what I did! I went through every single catalogue that Gideon sent for and analyzed it page by page."

"How could you be so featherheaded, Nina?" Don Alberto shouted back. "Never in a hundred years did I imagine you could act so stupid. I told you to take the *job* step by step!" he yelled at her. "The whole problem. The overall goal. I didn't tell you to dissect our competitors' products like some damned biology experiment, then reassemble the various parts as our own. I expected you to use your noodle. To do something clever."

"Then you should have said so," Nina stormed, slapping the desk again, unspeakably angry. "You should have told me precisely what you were thinking. With everything else you demand I do around here, I can't also read your mind."

"It doesn't take a mind reader to know that I want everyone to give their best effort at all times," the don bellowed. He grabbed up his cane and brandished it at her. "I've hardly made a secret of my policy."

"No, you haven't!" Nina agreed in a savage shout. "You want everyone to give *more* than their best effort. You want the impossible. I've put every bit of thought and energy I possess into that catalogue, and now you tell me it isn't good enough.

"Well, that's too bad. Do you hear me?" she cried, clenching both fists in the air and shaking them. "It's not my fault. I did absolutely all I could. But you want more than I can give you.

Your expectations are too high. You keep insisting that I'm someone I'm not.''

"Bah! Now you're getting hysterical," Don Alberto spat out, sounding highly agitated himself. "You're acting as if this were the Spanish Inquisition and I'm the one cranking the rack. For God's sake, Nina. Get a grip on yourself. I haven't asked you to work any harder than I'm working myself. And I'm fifty years older than you."

About to scream back that she was, indeed, being tortured, his last words echoed in her head. He was fifty years older than she. Fifty-one, to be precise. And he'd already had a heart attack. Her clenched fists opened and her hands fell to her sides as she looked at Don Alberto in sudden fright. His eyes were bulging and his lips were flecked with spit. He seemed on the verge of choking. *O Dio,* she thought, one hand flying to her throat. I didn't mean it. Please don't let him die.

In the same flash of an instant that her rage disappeared, Nina remembered that Gideon was in the library, too. Even without looking at him, she knew his eyes would be darting between them, gleefully recording their every move. Her hand lifted to her forehead and she massaged her brow as she realized what a spectacle they must have made, poised behind their desks and shrieking across the room. She wished she were anywhere else. "Let's talk about this later," she muttered.

"May I offer a suggestion?" The voice was calm and even and pleasant.

Astonished, Nina whirled toward its source and saw Wim standing in the doorway. In the gloom and grimness of this gray fall morning, his blond hair shone like sunshine and the reason in his tone was like oil on tempestuous waters. Despite herself, her breath caught in her throat. Even as the sight of him brought back devastating memories, even as she closed her heart against him, Nina felt herself fill with longing.

"How long have you been standing there, de Groot?" Don Alberto snapped. Nina's fury might have fizzled, but that didn't mean his had, too.

Wim crossed his arms on his chest and thoughtfully stroked his chin. "Perhaps longer than I should have been," he admitted. "No one came to the door when I drove up, so I took the liberty of letting myself in." He spoke quietly and chose his words carefully.

Nonetheless, given the current state of Don Alberto's temper, Nina waited for him to rip into Wim. Arms still crossed, regarding the don gravely, it was obvious that Wim waited, too. Don Alberto surprised them both, though. Instead of dressing Wim down, he pulled him into the argument without a break in stride.

"Then you know that it's rubbish," he fumed. "You heard me tell her the catalogue's no good." Now that he had someone else's ear to fill, he refused to look at Nina or even to call her by name. Nina's good intentions started to dissolve and her irritation rekindled.

"We've got to bring it to the printer by October first," Don Alberto groused. "We've got to have a finished draft nine days from now, and what do we have so far?" Beating his fist on the offending manuscript, he answered his own question. "Rubbish! Might as well toss the whole thing in the trash and be done with it!"

While Nina drew in a sharp, angry breath, Wim took several steps into the room. Again picking his way delicately, he said, "Apparently the catalogue isn't what you envisioned." He unfolded his arms and clasped them behind him, instead. "I can well understand your frustration. You must be extremely disappointed."

Victorious, Don Alberto glared at Nina, who shifted her feet and scowled.

"But even if it doesn't meet with your approval as a whole," Wim went on, still speaking neutrally, "no doubt there are parts of it which are salvageable. I find it hard to believe that Nina's information could be inaccurate. Surely, after you've had a chance to go over it again, you'll find that's the case."

"I don't need to go over it again," Don Alberto retorted, his triumph forgotten. "I can tell the first time through whether it's going to make money or not. This is a loser." He thumped the manuscript. "I didn't build a good business by dithering over every decision that came up, de Groot. And I'll wager you didn't, either. Here." He picked up the stack of pages and thrust them at him. "You read it and tell me if I'm wrong. It may be accurate, but so is an encyclopedia."

Wim took the catalogue, but before he had a chance to read past the title, Nina marched around her desk and snatched it from him. He looked at her, startled, but she ignored him as she clutched the manuscript to her chest and turned to face the don. "You've made your point," she told him in a voice quavering with anger and genuine hurt. "I heard you the first time. You don't like it. All right. I'll tear it up myself. But you don't have to parade it past every person who enters the room. It's none of their concern."

Since Wim was behind her, she didn't see his eyes open wide, but she could almost feel the force of his astonished stare. She didn't care. It didn't matter if he was shocked or confused, or even if his pride were bruised. In fact, it was probably better that way. She wanted him out of her life, and the sooner he felt unwelcome, the sooner he would leave.

"De Groot's not just any passing stranger," Don Alberto replied. "He knows a few things about doing business. This business in particular. He can back up my judgment." Then he hunched his shoulders and added darkly, "But if you agree to throw the damn thing away, it isn't necessary for him to read it."

"Fine." Nina whirled toward her desk and its nearby trash can. Before she could move forward, however, Wim sidestepped quickly and blocked her way. It was her turn to be startled.

"Just a minute," he said, taking advantage of her momentary surprise to pry the disputed manuscript out of her arms. His voice had lost its blandness, though its usual amusement was still absent. "I believe you're both getting carried away. It's irrational to think that three and a half months of work is totally useless."

Holding it just out of Nina's reach, he ruffled through a few pages, scanning the text at random. When he glanced down from a description of potato varieties, he found Nina's fierce gaze fixed on his face. Raising his eyebrows slightly, he clapped the pages closed and tucked them under his arm.

"I think you need an objective opinion," he said. "Albert's quite right. A third view is required." Tapping the manuscript, he said, "I'll read it after lunch and tell you what I think." When Nina's eyes narrowed, his eyebrows raised again.

"I was about to suggest that you postpone any further discussion until after you've eaten," he added. "A good meal might improve everyone's disposition." Though he spoke to the room in general, he seemed to be addressing Nina specifically.

"Suppose it can't hurt," Don Alberto conceded. "All right, de Groot. We'll adjourn until after lunch. We'll hold a staff meeting then." Chafing his hands against the autumnal chill, he said, "I hope Mrs. Watkins has soup on the menu."

Nina made a quick sidestep of her own, skirting around Wim to grab her shawl from the back of her chair. Throwing it over her shoulders, she headed for the French doors.

"Hold on, Nina!" the don yelled. "It's time for lunch. Where're you going?"

"Home," Nina answered, without looking back or slowing her pace. She opened a door and stepped out on the terrace. "I'll see you in time for the staff meeting," she said, closing the door behind her.

When Nina returned at half past one, she brought her father and Dante with her, for moral support. The truth of it was, she felt as if she were throwing herself to the lions. Don Alberto hated the catalogue and would be merciless at the meeting now. And Gideon would be only too happy to bear witness to this scene of her humiliation. Although he'd been the very model of civility since their confrontation in the Nursery, his smoothness didn't deceive Nina for a minute. He was lying in wait for his moment of revenge, and this afternoon's fireworks were sure to please him.

As for Wim, the third lion in the den, well, it might seem he was on her side, but Nina was definitely suspicious. Hadn't she come to the conclusion that, when all was said and done, he wasn't much different from Gideon? Hadn't she realized that while he was splendid to look at and while his manners were charming, he used them to callously further his own interests? His attention and flattery were for one purpose, and one purpose only. Himself. It was a custom that was distinctly American. Nina shuddered. She was a fool to have trusted him.

Even as she reminded herself of that fact, though, she knew she wasn't being wholly honest. Deep down inside she knew that more than mistrusting Wim, she mistrusted herself in his presence. She was afraid her resolve to lock him out of her life would come to the same end as similar resolutions had. That it wouldn't last out the afternoon but would melt away beneath his blue-eyed gaze.

And she didn't dare let that happen. Not this time. Not after the searing shame of that Sunday in the Store. Not after sobbing until her body ached and her heart broke, sitting in her old chintz chair. Not after the pain and disillusionment he'd caused.

This time, for sure, she had to free herself from his spell. After all, what good would it do to remain enchanted? Even if, by some stray chance, he meant the things he'd said, it was still an impossible situation. From the color of their hair to the countries of their birth, they were as different as two people could be. They had nothing in common. Certainly, they had no future together. But the more involved with him she got, the more she put her own future at risk. If she hadn't destroyed it already. Glancing at Dante, she turned hot with guilt.

"What are they doing here?" Don Alberto demanded as soon as she entered the library with her father and Dante.

"It's a staff meeting, isn't it?" Nina answered in an astringent tone. "We're the staff. *Sediati*, Papà." She motioned her father to her chair. While Orazio sat down and Dante took up a position next to him, Nina crossed her arms and her ankles and leaned against the corner of her desk. "We're ready," she announced. "Let's go."

Her performance brought a smile to the corner of Wim's mouth as he stood browsing through the books on a shelf, but Don Alberto, in his customary seat behind his own desk, was plainly unamused. "I don't know what you think you're doing, Nina," he said, "but it isn't going to work. Having your family in here isn't going to distract from the fact that your catalogue is a failure. That it's indistinguishable from a hundred others."

"Now it's *my* catalogue," Nina said, straightening up a little bit. She didn't want to be responsible for another heart attack, but he made it very difficult for her to hold on to her temper. "If it were a masterpiece, I'm sure you'd call it *yours*."

"Of course I'd call it mine!" the don shouted, pounding his fist on a pile of papers. "My name is on the cover, isn't it?"

"It certainly is!" Nina shouted back, uncrossing her ankles and arms and leaping up. "In big gold letters right above the most forgettable painting I've ever seen. A painting that is 'indistinguishable from a hundred others.'" She jabbed the finger of one hand into the palm of the other. "If you want to talk about giving this catalogue a distinct appearance, you ought to talk about changing the cover. It's the first thing everyone sees, and what they're seeing here is boring. I told you that in July."

"You're trying to distract attention from the real problem again," Don Alberto retorted, also coming to his feet. He gripped the edge of the desk for support as he thrust his head and shoulders toward her. "The cover has nothing to do with the fact that the contents are dull. Admit it, Nina. You did a second-rate job. It's like reading a shopping list or a bill of lading."

"It's a catalogue, for heaven's sake!" Nina cried, banging her fists against her sides. "It's not a novel. It's *supposed* to have lists."

"It's *supposed* to convince customers to buy seeds from us," Don Alberto corrected. "It's *supposed* to make our seeds seem superior to all others."

"It certainly seems I guessed wrong," Wim interrupted. "I can see lunch wasn't very helpful, after all." Literally coming between them, he settled himself, in the same position Nina had assumed, on the corner of the don's desk. "It makes me rather hesitant to recommend sleeping on the problem for a night."

The cool humor in his voice doused Nina's hot temper instantly. Remembering Don Alberto's heart, she clamped her mouth closed, wrapped her arms tightly across her chest, and dropped back against the desk. Her flush of anger turned to a flush of embarrassment as she realized, for the second time that day, how ridiculous she and Don Alberto must have looked.

The don, apparently, made no such realization. Although he, too, sat down in his chair, he continued to grumble. "Don't need a night's sleep," he muttered. "Need to knock some sense into her head."

"Yes, you're right," Wim agreed, staring straight at Nina, his eyebrows again slightly raised. When she pursed her lips and flicked her gaze aside, he gave a little shrug. Looking over his shoulder at the don, he added, "Although I think she has a valid point, too. I must confess, I don't think the cover is as inspiring as it might be. As Nina pointed out, it's the first impression potential buyers have of your company. You might want to consider something a bit more unique."

"Unique?" Don Alberto repeated querulously. "Where am I going to find something more unique? And at this late date. Stecher is the best in the business. You said so yourself."

"I did, didn't I?" Wim responded, scratching his chin as he searched his memory for that particular conversation. After a pause, he asked, "Wasn't Serafina supposed to submit some paintings, too? Weren't you going to consider using hers?"

Don Alberto rattled some papers. "Never did them," he said.

"That's not true!" Nina exclaimed, jumping to her feet again, momentarily forgetting her self-imposed restraint. "Serafina painted four exquisite pictures for you to choose from. One was more beautiful than the next. Isn't that so, Papà?" She whirled toward her father for confirmation.

"*Che?*" Orazio asked foggily. "Serafina?"

Nina snapped her wrist impatiently, too wound-up to stop and translate. "Dante, don't you remember the paintings?" she asked, holding out both hands, pleading.

Miming a paintbrush moving across a canvas, Dante nodded. "Paintings?" he said. "Yes, yes. Serafina."

"You see?" Nina whirled back to face the don. "Serafina made the paintings. You just refused to look at them."

Don Alberto cleared his throat. "Hmph," he said, squaring the papers in line with his blotter.

Refolding her arms and leaning back against the desk, Nina gave a triumphant nod. That incomprehensible grunt signaled a concession. She'd just won round one. At the next staff meeting Serafina would be in attendance with the title of Staff Artist.

Wim also must have felt the issue was resolved because he nodded, too. "Good," he said. "Now that we have the covers decided, we should discuss what goes between them." On that cue, both Nina and Don Alberto surged forward, ready to restate their cases. But before either of them could speak, Wim quickly came between them again.

"If you won't think me presumptuous," he said loudly, as if he were already speaking over their argument, "I'd like to offer a suggestion that I believe will please each of you." That caught their attention, and he was able to lower his voice and continue. "It'll retain Nina's work," he said, bowing his head in her direction, briefly furrowing his brow when she glared in return, "and add something extra." He turned to dip his head toward Don Alberto.

"Aha!" the don pounced. "I knew you'd agree with me," he said. "You're a businessman, de Groot. I knew you'd see this catalogue's a disaster. That it needs something impressive to grab the customer's attention and something distinctive to hold it in place."

"I'll agree that it needs a little more work," Wim admitted. "But I think the catalogue already has something with both the qualities you mentioned."

"What?" Don Alberto demanded, disbelieving.

"The Head Gardener," Wim answered, again staring straight at Nina. "Maria Antonina Colangelo."

While Nina's mouth dropped open, Don Alberto gave an unsentimental snort. "Maybe everybody in this room knows that," he granted, "but how the devil are the catalogue subscribers going to know Nina's any different than the boy down the block who mows the lawn? They'll certainly never guess it by what they read. It'll put them to sleep."

"If you'll permit me to make my suggestion?" Wim let the question hang in the air.

"Of course, of course," the don replied, dismissing Wim's politeness with a flap of his hand. "That's what you're here for. If we didn't want to listen to your suggestions, we'd boot you out. Now fire away, de Groot."

But first Wim turned again. "Nina?" he asked, cocking his head.

A warm flush crept up her cheeks and Nina felt her heart start to pound. Angrily suppressing the rush of feeling, she looked out the doors and nodded. "*Va bene,*" she consented, refusing to give him even the consideration of speaking in English.

"*Grazie,*" Wim thanked her in stiff Italian, seemingly unaware of her rudeness. Although when Nina wouldn't look at him, he was forced to address himself to the don. "It occurred to me that there are two great assets, in particular, that Nina brings to her position," he explained to him. "The first is a tremendous knowledge of horticulture, which is well documented in the text she's already written."

"Like a damn schoolbook," Don Alberto growled.

Again Wim seemed unperturbed by the remark as he glanced around the room, nodding pleasantly at Orazio, Dante, and Gideon, including them in this meeting. Then he turned back to Don Alberto and continued. "The second asset," he said, "is Nina's rare and quite wonderful talent for creating spectacular gardens. Gardens that both excite the imagination and soothe the spirit. Gardens that seem to possess a magical aura. That transport the observer to another world. One very pure and beautiful."

He paused again, but this time no one uttered a word. Chin thrust out and eyes squinting speculatively, Don Alberto waited for Wim to go on. Dante and Orazio didn't understand all the words, but they heard the admiration in Wim's tone, and extremely curious, neither of them moved a muscle. Gideon, sensing the suspense, remained absolutely still. Only Nina stirred, turning away from the doors to stare at Wim, surprised.

Wim turned, too, and met her gaze, holding it for a long, silent moment. Then his eyebrows lifted another time, and he quietly revealed his idea. "I think Nina should design some gardens," he said. "Gardens that can be planted by the average homeowner to enhance his yard, using the Blackwell Seed Company seeds. I think some of Nina's magic should be incorporated in the catalogue."

"Perfect!" Don Alberto shouted.

At the same moment Nina jumped up and yelled, "You must be mad!"

Ignoring both their outbursts, Wim went on to explain his scheme. "As I envision it," he said, "there could be five or six different designs to fit various conditions or situations. For shade or full sun or a hillside or a tiny plot." He waved his hand, gesturing toward Nina. "I'm sure you know more about that than I," he said, also ignoring the frown on her face.

"In addition to maps of the gardens, perhaps Serafina could make illustrations of them in full bloom," Wim continued. Now he was addressing himself mostly to Nina, despite her obvious resistance. "It would help people visualize the results they could expect.

"A column or two of 'Advice From the Head Gardener' might be helpful, as well," he added, absently tapping the desk. "The majority of catalogue customers are people relocated from cities, you know, and they have no horticultural experience. You see a lot of companies attempting to solve that problem by writing about hot beds and sowing and the like, but if you were to go a bit further . . ." Again, he waved his hand through the air. "What to plant where, for example, I'm sure you'd create a loyal following. Not too much, of course," he cautioned, lifting both hands in warning. "People don't want to read volumes of instructions. Just a few subtle suggestions tossed in amongst the pictures."

"Perfect!" Don Alberto shouted again. "No one else has a feature like that. It'll set us apart immediately. Give us a recognizable style. You're sharp, de Groot," he congratulated, rising halfway out of his chair to slap Wim on the back. "I like your idea. I like it a lot."

"I don't," Nina said, jamming her hands on her hips. "I don't like it at all."

"Why not?" the don demanded.

"Because," Nina replied with a decisive nod. It wasn't much of a response, she knew, but she couldn't very well add what she was thinking. That her entire reason for rejecting the idea was because

Wim had proposed it. Because she didn't want anything to do with him anymore, or with anything he'd thought up.

"Because?" Don Alberto's voice was dripping with scorn. "What kind of an answer is that? Because why?"

"Because . . ." Nina said, shaking both hands in front of her. "Because . . ." She was keenly aware of Wim studying her, and she was having trouble concentrating. "Because I don't," she finally snapped, flinging her hands high. "I don't have to have an explanation for every little decision I make. I'm trusting to my instincts. That's what you told me successful businessmen do."

"I also told you that successful businessmen use their heads," Don Alberto retorted. "Which you very plainly are not doing. You left your head at lunch, Nina. This isn't a 'little decision.' This is a big one." His hands stretched wide apart to show how huge it was. "It's also a brilliant one." His hand came down to whack the desk. "We're going to do it," he announced.

"Just like that?" Nina held out her hands, palms up, as her shoulders also lifted. "Just like that it's 'Nina, design some gardens and write some advice'?"

"Just like that," the don confirmed, unsympathetic.

"Perhaps it's too big a task," Wim suggested. Although his tone was very mild, his gaze was extremely intense. "I apologize. I should have been more considerate of your time and talents. I should have realized it might be more than you can accomplish."

Even as she took the bait, Nina knew she was being hooked. She also knew it was impossible for her to resist the challenge he was laying down. She'd have to accept his idea just to spite him, just to prove that he was wrong. "I can do it," she said, staring back with equal intensity. Round two went to Wim.

His eyebrows raised and he dipped his head in mock salute. "*Brava,*" he complimented her in Italian.

For once the amusement in his voice didn't please or charm her. Rather, it made her angry. "But I want help," she added, striking back. She had to show him that although she'd accepted his idea, she hadn't accepted him. That he was a stranger and that she preferred the company of Italians. "Not only Serafina's, but also Dante's." It worked. The smile disappeared from the corner of Wim's mouth, as well as from the light in his eyes. Giving a small nod of victory, Nina struck harder.

"I can't do it without Dante," she said, talking to Wim but looking at Don Alberto. "I depend on him a great deal for support and assistance. We're comfortable discussing problems that come up, and we can work them out together. There's a good understanding between us." Pausing, she peeked at Wim. His expression was grim. With a toss of her head, she concluded, "I think that Dante should be promoted to Vegetable Manager. And he should have a column, too. Serafina can help him with the English."

"Titles," Don Alberto muttered to himself. "Fine," he said in a louder tone, whacking the desk again. "Done. We've got a bargain."

For another hour or so they haggled over a few more details, then Orazio and Dante got up to leave. Dante had had a blush on his cheeks since he first heard his name being mentioned. It deepened when Nina explained exactly what she'd gotten him into. As he went out the door, Nina threw on her shawl to follow.

"Where're you going?" Don Alberto asked. "We've got a lot of work to do. I can buy a little more time at the printer, but there's only so much time to buy. We've got to have the finished catalogue in our hands before Christmas."

Glancing at the clock above the mantel, Nina said, "It's a quarter to four. I'm going home to put my feet up and to spend the rest of the day with my family. I've barely seen them recently."

"There's time for that after the catalogue goes to press," Don Alberto objected. "Until then, we've got to give every waking minute to getting it done. Success requires a little personal sacrifice, Nina. You can't expect rewards without effort."

"Monday," Nina said, unmoved, going out the door.

She had descended the terrace steps, crossed the bowl, and gone around the first bend in the perennial path when Wim caught up to her. "Just a moment, Nina," he said, seizing her wrist so hard she was forced to stop and confront him. He sounded very disturbed, and when she looked up at him, Nina could see the agitation on his face.

"I think you owe me an explanation of your behavior," he told her, giving her wrist a shake. "And don't think I'll be satisfied with a dramatic 'because,' and that nonsense about trusting to your instincts. Your don might believe that excuse, but it doesn't convince me in the least. Something's happened since I last saw you to upset you tremendously, and I want to know what it is."

Instead of answering him, Nina just struggled to free her hand. "Let go of me," she insisted. "You're hurting."

Wim loosened his hold but refused to release her completely. "If I let you go, you'll run away from me," he said. "Like you did at lunchtime and a few minutes ago. I don't know what I've done to make you act like this. It's as if you can't bear to be in the same room with me. As if you despise me. For heaven's sake, Nina," he said, giving her wrist another shake, "you can't even look me in the eye."

Although his intention was different this time, the challenge was the same. Nina lifted her head and looked at him squarely. Her face felt hot and her stomach felt cold and her heart was pounding like mad, but she met his gaze steadily. "There," she said. "Now let go."

"No," Wim answered instantly, actually grabbing her other wrist, too. He held both hands up in front of him, manacled together by his grip. "Not until you tell me what's happened," he said, searching her face for a clue. "Three weeks ago you kissed me a hundred times and told me I was precious to you. You smiled at me and ran your fingers through my hair and you lay with me in the sun."

When Nina inhaled sharply, aghast at his bold descriptions, he shook her hands again. "Don't gasp," he ordered. "You enjoyed every minute of that afternoon. I know you did. Don't think I can't read your face, Nina. It's like a window to your soul. And three weeks ago it was radiant with happiness. Today it's sour with gloom. For God's sake!" he cried. "*You've got to tell me what happened!*"

A dozen thoughts raced through Nina's mind, but she was unable to tell him any of them. She couldn't tell him about Bianca and Gideon, and she couldn't tell him about sobbing until her strength was gone. She couldn't tell him about the waves of horror and shame, or the revulsion that choked off her breath. She couldn't tell him about her heartbreaking disillusionment, about the tender innocence she'd lost on the pine-plank floor. She couldn't tell him anything, because that would have meant accepting him long enough to do it. And she'd already locked him out of her life. So she just continued to look him in the eyes and not say a word.

"Are you angry because I haven't come to see you in so long?" he finally asked, probing for the reason. "I told you I wouldn't be able to," he answered into the silence. His voice was ringing with frustration. "When we parted on the path, just up ahead, I kissed you good-bye and told you I wouldn't be able to come out to Stamford, and you told me you understood. Don't you remember?''

Nina didn't need to be reminded. Every bit of that day was crystal clear. "I'm not angry," she said at last. It was true. She wasn't.

"Then what is it?" Wim asked more gently. Sliding his fingers up, he encased her hands in both of his, then brought them to his lips.

Nina reacted as if she were stung. Crying out in pain, she ripped her hands free and hid them behind her back. "Don't," she said in a voice full of tears. "Don't do that. Don't touch me." Stepping quickly, she moved a few feet away.

"Why not?" Wim asked, now more worried than annoyed. He didn't try to grab her back, but stood still so as not to frighten her. "I don't want to hurt you, Nina. You must know that. You've got to. I only want to help you. I want to bring the happiness back to your face. It's so becoming." He held out his hand, tentatively.

"How can I do that if I don't know what happened to destroy it?" he asked. "There's something terribly wrong, and I don't know what it is. Please, Nina. Tell me."

"Nothing happened," Nina finally blurted out. She knew she had to say something, or he'd never cease his questioning. She had to make him stop before he wore down her resistance. "I just realized that it was all a huge mistake. That afternoon, I mean." Her face flamed, and she gulped before going on.

"I was giddy from the wine I drank with Sunday lunch," she explained, no longer meeting his eyes. "You see, I was overtired from working so much, and then I went out in the hot sun. The wine just went to my head. I did things I never should have done." Her voice was small as she stared at a last brave phlox, crimson bright in the autumnal gray. "I never meant to do them. And I truly wish I hadn't."

It was Wim's turn to be silent as he stared at her. After a long time, he spoke up. "I don't believe you," he said. His tone was even, as always, but his voice was vibrant with feeling.

Nina shrugged and backed up farther. "It was a mistake," she repeated. "A big, big mistake. It won't happen ever again."

For another instant, Nina just stared at him. Then she sidestepped and walked hastily away. Before she could escape, though, she felt his hand clamp around her wrist again. She lurched to a halt so rapidly, the momentum spun her around. When she lifted her head in alarm, his face was only inches above her and his blue eyes were boring down.

"You've run away twice today, and you can run away now," he told her. "But you can't avoid me forever. I promise you, Nina, I'll be back again and again until you tell me what's wrong. Sooner or later, you're going to say what's troubling you, if for no other reason than to get rid of me for good. I'm not going to leave you alone, though, until I know what happened to upset you. Believe me, I can be just as stubborn as you."

$=19=$

Wim was as good as his word. Over the following weeks he turned up repeatedly, a hack arriving at the door and disgorging him when she least expected it. Nor did he confine himself solely to Saturday visits, but appeared on Tuesday mornings or Thursday afternoons, once, even, on a Monday evening. It happened to be the evening Nina had promised to have dinner with Don Alberto, too, although how Wim had found that out, she never knew. Trapped, she had to spend three hours in his company. Every time she looked up, his eyes were on her, questioning. By the time she got home, Nina was truly unnerved.

Not that she had much spare time to brood about it. There was still a lot to do. And she was actually enjoying her work now. Writing the column and tossing bits of horticultural wisdom among the lists of seeds was a chore, but designing the gardens was a joy, pure and simple. It was what she did best, in all the world, and what gave her the greatest satisfaction. She could spend hours contentedly daydreaming, imagining different combinations of flowers. Reluctant as she was to admit it, she was glad Wim had suggested the idea.

At the end of September they moved into the Store, and then life improved considerably. In her own private office, with a door that closed, Nina could shut out Don Alberto's constant prodding and Gideon's darting eyes. Dante built an easel for Serafina, which they set up near the big windows. So, while Nina dreamed out loud and Dante talked about vegetables, Serafina painted beautiful pictures. It was extremely congenial.

It was, in fact, like having a family within her family. No longer did she feel uncomfortable at the supper table, out of step with the conversation, because now Serafina and Dante shared her daily experiences. When she wasn't listening to Lucia's speculation about the baby Aurelia had announced she was expecting, Nina could lean over and say, in a low voice to Dante, "Remind me to check on the Duchess of Edinburgh sweet peas tomorrow. We may not have enough seed to be promoting it in one of the gardens."

Then Serafina would lean over from the other side of Dante and giggle. "He doesn't know one sweet pea from the next," she said, gently teasing, "but ask him about green peas and he can recite the characteristics of a hundred different varieties."

"That's because I can eat green peas," Dante explained, wiping up the last tomato sauce on his plate with the last fat macaroni. "And for your information, signorina," he added, "there aren't a hundred different varieties of green peas. Probably not more than fifty." He popped the morsel into his mouth.

Nina laughed, feeling safe and secure, happy in the warm glow of home. At that very moment, in the midst of supper, listening with one ear to Dante reciting pea varieties to Serafina and with the other ear to Lucia predicting that the baby would be a boy, in the midst of watching Mamma toss a fresh, green salad and Benedetta slice a crusty loaf of bread, at that very moment Nina knew she was absolutely right to have rejected Wim. This was where she belonged.

Her future lay here, with people she knew. With Sicilians. People whose concerns were the same as hers. Family and the earth. That's what mattered the most. Life was measured by aunts, uncles, brothers, sisters, parents, and cousins. It was sustained by wresting bounty from the soil. It wasn't spent in single-minded pursuit of success. It wasn't an exercise in doing business. It was a good life. And as soon as she fulfilled her obligation to Don Alberto, she was going to resume that life full time.

On the strength of that conviction, Nina sailed through October, sending the final draft of the catalogue to the printer on November the sixth. The proofs came back several weeks later, and once they were read and corrected, she had to turn her attention to what came next: getting ready to mail out the catalogues and getting ready to sell seeds.

They advertised for, interviewed, and hired a staff. Six fresh-faced young women and one fuzzy-cheeked young man, all of whom looked to Nina for instructions. Startled, she gave them. It amazed her to realize she was *la padrona*. The Boss.

A week before Christmas, the catalogue arrived from the printer. *Grazie a Dio*, it was finally finished. Every last detail had been attended to, every phase of its production was done. All that remained now was to admire it, and, awed, Nina did just that.

Picking one off the top of a huge stack in the hall outside her office, she stared at it with unabashed pleasure. "The Blackwell Seed Co." was emblazoned across the top of Serafina's painting. Inside, on real bound pages and printed in professional type, were the words and ideas she'd written herself. It was all there. Her garden designs, Dante's vegetable advice, and Serafina's artwork, captured forever for everyone in America to see. The peasants from Sicily had made a mark.

Smiling, she looked up to find Don Alberto watching her, an almost warm expression on his baggy face. "You did a good job, Nina," he told her gruffly. "You ought to be proud."

Nina looked at the catalogue in her hand, then over at the stacks lining the wall. She listened to the sounds of their employees working downstairs, diligently following her orders. Turning again, she nodded. "I am," she said. And threw her arms around him, giving her don a heartfelt hug. "You know," she added, "I think you might be right about business. It's awfully satisfying, isn't it?" Six months of toil and anguish vanished in a minute.

"Knew you'd come to your senses," Don Alberto muttered, giving her shoulder an awkward pat.

For the next several days Nina went about her work serenely, steeped in her new sense of satisfaction. It even enhanced her usual contentment when she stole a few hours, one afternoon, to putter in the Nursery. She hadn't had her hands on any plants in ages. Her fingers had barely touched dirt. It was extremely rewarding, therefore, to tidy up the overwintering perennials and to pot some Christmas roses in urns.

She was humming a Sicilian love song and standing back to examine her work when she heard the door rattle open and felt cold air rush past her legs. Looking over, she saw Dante just shutting the door behind him.

"Oh, good. Hello," she called out as he started down the aisle toward her. "You've come at the perfect moment to give your opinion. Come look," she said, waving him on. "Do you think these will be nice beside the hearth in the Big House parlor?"

"*Si, si,*" Dante replied, hardly glancing at the lovely white flowers sticking up from shiny green leaves. "Very nice." He came to a stop not far away and stood nervously twisting his cap. The frosty air had whipped color into his sculpted cheeks and had tousled his curly, dark hair.

"Or do you think they'll be too low?" Nina went on, giving the soil an extra tamp. "They're pretty plants, but they're short and they might get lost sitting in that huge, grand room." She stood back again to view them critically, cocking her head one way, then another.

"Maybe they would be better at our house," she mused. "Don Alberto will come to us for Christmas dinner, anyway. He always does." Looking toward Dante for approval, she asked again, "What do you think? Should we bring them home with us, then just string some garlands of holly around the Big House parlor when his sons come to visit next week?"

"Che?" Dante asked, then shook himself and said, "I mean, yes. That is . . . uh, yes." He took a deep breath and stood up straighter, jamming his cap in his pocket. "Yes," he answered more positively. "I think that's a fine idea." He took another breath before plunging on. "Listen, Nina," he said. "Can I talk to you?"

"Talk to me?" Nina repeated, leaning forward to pick a withered leaf from the base of one of the plants. "Aren't we talking now?" She was studying the leaf more closely, checking it for disease or parasites, when she suddenly realized that Dante wasn't answering. In that fraction of an instant, her pleasant reverie was shattered, and icy apprehension struck her heart. Even as her head jerked up and her fingers curled numbly around the forgotten leaf, she felt a premonition crawl along her skin. A catastrophe was coming. One look at Dante confirmed it.

He was standing very still, the light in his beautiful brown eyes serious. And despite the blush on his windswept cheeks, his stare was determined. All at once she felt both hot and cold, in alternating waves. Her pulse was racing so fast it made her dizzy. This wasn't going to be a casual conversation. She knew that as surely as she knew her own name. He wasn't going to ask her to suggest a Christmas gift for Mamma or make some remarks about the catalogue. He wasn't even going to engage her in a horticultural discussion, as he had on that day last August. This time it wasn't corn that he had on his mind.

"Of course you can talk to me, Dante," she said. At least, that's what she meant to say. What actually came out was a scratchy whisper. Her eyes blinked shut, and she took a shuddery breath. This was it. He was going to ask her to marry him. The time had come for him to make his proposal. Opening her eyes slowly, she swallowed and tried again. "Yes, Dante," she said, only a little more clearly. "You can talk to me." Then she shrank back and waited for the words.

It took Dante a moment to begin as he shuffled his feet and tugged his coat. Finally he squared his shoulders and spoke. "I think we both know what your parents would like for us," he said. "I don't think it's much of a secret with anyone in your family."

When he paused to get her reaction, it was all Nina could do to nod. No, it wasn't a secret. Even little Stella was aware of what was going on. By now everyone accepted it as a fact. Everyone, that is, but Nina herself. Panic suddenly seized her as she realized how true that was. Despite telling herself, these past few months, that her future lay with Dante, now that the moment had come to commit herself, she didn't know if she could do it. She reached over and grabbed the table for support.

"I think the world of you, Nina," Dante said in an earnest tone, taking a step forward. Terrified, Nina took two steps back. Dante didn't seem to notice. "I admire what you've done with your life," he continued, just as sincerely. "You've taken advantage of every opportunity that's come your way. And, in addition, you've created opportunities for everyone around you. I know how much you've helped me, and, believe me, I'm very grateful."

While Nina struggled to catch a breath, Dante regarded her solemnly. "You're a very strong and resourceful woman, Nina," he told her. Then he blushed deeper and added more shyly, "You're also *molta simpatica*. Very nice." After another pause, he said, even more shyly, "I think you're beautiful, too." Nina felt as if she were going to faint.

"Nina, I want to ask you . . ." The door to the Nursery rattled again, and another blast of cold air cut off the rest of what he said.

Nina looked up in a daze, and Dante turned around, startled. "Excuse me, Miss Colangelo," said the wholesome young woman in the doorway. Her name was Alice and she was one of the newly hired staff. "I'm sorry to disturb you, but the seed bagging machine has clogged again, and we were hoping Mr. da Rosa could fix it."

Nina's legs were so weak with relief, they barely held her up. When Dante turned back toward her and asked, *"Cos'ha detto?"* she joyfully translated Alice's request. Although she was extremely thankful for this interruption, Dante seemed distressed. He glanced from Nina to Alice, obviously torn between attending to business and finishing their private talk. Nina was sure it had taken him a long time to gather courage for this meeting, and now that he finally had, he was reluctant to leave before he said what he came to say.

Nonetheless, she said, in as neutral a tone as she could manage, *"Bè,* Dante. Maybe you should go see what's wrong. If they try to fix it themselves, I'm afraid they'll only make it worse. You know you're the only one here who has the patience to fiddle with broken machines long enough to figure them out."

"Yes, I suppose so," Dante agreed, but without much enthusiasm. "I guess I'll go have a look." He turned to leave. "Excuse me, Nina," he said.

After he had followed Alice out the door, Nina gave a gasp and staggered over to her armchair to collapse. She was breathing as hard and as fast as if she'd run three times around the Nursery to get there. She'd been granted a reprieve, but it wasn't going to last. Not like last summer, when the inevitable question had been postponed by talk of vegetables. Now it was only a matter of minutes before it finally came up. Maybe an hour or two. A day, at the most. Whatever the precise moment turned out to be, however, it didn't change the fact. Within a very short space of time, Dante was going to stand before her and ask her to marry him. Then he was going to wait for her answer.

The problem was, she didn't know what that answer was going to be. What on earth was she going to tell him? When he stood there shyly, his soulful eyes lit with devotion and hope, how was she going to respond? Could she say that she thought he was as sweet a man as she'd ever met in her life, that she, too, thought the world of him, but that when she imagined being married to him, shivers ran down her spine? Could she explain to him that while she enjoyed his company and considered him a very good friend, she wasn't in love with him because she was already in love with Wim?

Gasping again, Nina buried her face in her hands. It was the truth, and she finally had to admit it. She couldn't avoid it any longer, couldn't ignore it, or disguise it, or smother it with self-righteous excuses. She was in love with Wim. And probably had been since the moment she'd looked up from the floor at Castle Garden.

It was more than just his blue eyes, although there was no denying their fascination and appeal. The same could be said for his blond hair, whose exotic fairness had literally seduced her. Nor was it simply his long-legged elegance, nor the amusement in his voice. Not just his remarkable calmness of character, not just his iron strength when he seized her wrist. It wasn't only the quiet confidence he always exuded, or his natural kindness and courtesy. It wasn't even his impressive tenacity in pursuing every goal he set his sights on. It wasn't any one of those qualities. Rather it was all of them. Wim Pieter de Groot was different from anyone she'd ever known, and she was heart and soul in love with him.

Lifting her head, Nina let it fall back against the chair, too discouraged to hold it up. Nothing was changed by her dramatic admission. The same obstacles still confronted her. Although she now knew what to call the powerful emotion drawing her to him, it didn't do her any good. Because even if Wim returned her love, and there was no real indication that he did, their future together was impossible.

He might be different from anyone she'd ever known, but that was precisely the problem. There were too many differences in their lives, and not enough similarities. As many times as she'd reviewed the situation, she'd come to the exact same conclusion.

From their languages to their looks to their dreams in life, they had no common ground. Just look at their occupations, for example, which on the surface were almost the same. But Wim sold flowers because he enjoyed doing business while Nina did business because she enjoyed the flowers. They were miles apart on every subject, and there was no bridge in sight. Besides which, Mamma would never, in a hundred years, approve of Wim, and if Papà ever found out what had happened in the Store that afternoon, he'd probably shoot him. So that was the end of that.

All of which meant she was going to marry Dante. When he stood in front of her and asked for her hand in marriage, she would give it to him with no further hesitation. It didn't matter that she wasn't in love with him, because she *liked* him very much. More important, they shared a lot, from their Sicilian backgrounds to their passion for plants. It would be an ideal union, and Dante would be a perfect husband, considerate, gentle, and faithful. There, she thought, getting out of her chair. That was settled. Once and for all.

No longer interested in Christmas roses, Nina pulled on her coat and went back to the Store. If she wasn't going to get any pleasure from her time off, she might as well go to work. Although the catalogue was done and delivered, there were always a thousand things to do. Nina was desultorily shifting through them in her mind when she pushed open the door to her office. And was instantly alert. Seated behind her desk, swiveled around toward the enormous windows, was Wim.

It wasn't a sunny afternoon at the end of the summer, and the gardens outside were brown and lifeless, but the sight of him in this setting brought the memory of that day rushing back. Not that it really ever left her. Whether filling her with guilt and shame, or filling her with longing, it was never far from her thoughts. Now, though, she could almost feel the sunshine in his silky hair and feel his lips sliding across her skin. Coming on the heels of her recent decision, the memory was extremely disturbing.

"What are you doing here?" she asked, shutting the door behind her, well aware that Gideon was in the office across the hall.

Wim glanced at her over his shoulder, the same way he'd done that day, but now, instead of a welcoming smile, the expression on his face was sober. "Another in a series of friendly greetings," he commented, swiveling the chair around to face her. He crossed his arms on his chest and let the chair rock back as he looked at her intently.

"Every time I come to Stamford, I come with the hope that you'll have reverted to the Nina I used to know," he told her. "All the way here on the train, I keep imagining that when you see me, the light in your eyes will take on a wonderful glow. Like it did that day . . ." His voice trailed off and he glanced at the floor, as if he, too, were seeing them there. Then he glanced back at her and lifted his shoulders in a shrug.

"But every time we come face to face, my hopes are crushed to dust," he said in a grimmer tone. "Instead of being pleased to see me, your reaction is almost the opposite. You can barely bring yourself to say hello." A smile briefly creased his cheek, but there was no humor in it. "Today, for instance, you couldn't even manage that."

"Look," Nina began, shifting from foot to foot. She'd made her decision, and she was determined to keep it, but that didn't mean she felt happy and comfortable.

"I am looking," Wim said, before she could go any further. Staring at her across the desk, he told her, "I see a beautiful woman. The woman who once gave herself to me with a passion so grand, I can't describe it. I see the woman with whom I shared the most exquisite moments of my life."

He paused, shrugged again, then added, "I also see a cold and empty expression where I used to see radiant life. You haven't just closed the window to your soul, Nina. You've slammed it shut in my face. And for no reason that I can understand." Shaking his head, he let his disappointment show. "Overnight we became enemies," he said. "Without a single word of explanation. All of a sudden you started hating me, and I haven't a clue as to why."

His vehemence made Nina more miserable. "We're not ene-mies," she denied, shifting again. "I don't hate you."

"No?" Wim's eyebrows lifted. "In that case, you've certainly done a convincing job of *pretending* to hate me. You've got every small detail perfectly tuned." He finally unfolded his arms and counted off each of those details on his fingers as he named them out loud.

"When I walk into a room, you immediately rush out. Or, if you're forced to remain, you cringe as far away from me as you can get. You can't even look me in the eye, unless I goad you to do it. And when I talk to you at length, and ask you dozens of questions, you respond with brief, vague answers, or, more frequently, not at all.

"You've turned against me completely, Nina," he said, his voice growing hard again. "And you won't tell me what happened to change you. You tossed me some nonsensical tale about a glass of wine, like a bone of appeasement to a troublesome dog. But you won't tell me the truth. You've left me to guess and wonder, in vain."

"I have told you the truth," Nina protested, her temper starting to flare. "I gave you a very good reason, but you . . ." She stopped suddenly and threw up her hands, her anger draining as fast as it had erupted. "Listen, Wim," she said, shaking her head, "I don't want to start this argument again. There's no point to it."

"No argument," Wim responded, raising both hands in a gesture of surrender. He let the chair thunk forward, then he stood up, too. "I'm worn out with arguing," he confessed. "It tires me as much as it tires you. So I give up. You win." His hands fell in defeat.

"I was wrong," he said with a touch of bitterness. "Apparently, I'm not as stubborn as you. Your persistence in avoiding me has outlasted my persistence in chasing you. Which means you get to keep your secrets, Nina. I won't bother you anymore. I promise you that." Reaching behind him, he picked up his topcoat and draped it over his arm.

"In fact," he added, "I didn't even intend to argue with you today. Really, I came to say good-bye. I'm sailing for Holland tomorrow evening," he stated with his usual calm. "I don't know how long I'll be gone."

"You're what!" Nina exclaimed, fright shooting through her. It was one thing for her to swear to herself that she was through with him forever. To think of a hundred wise and sensible reasons for the parting of their ways. But to know that *he* was leaving for good, that *he* meant never to return, was a blow she wasn't prepared to take. When she tried to imagine him boarding a ship bound for Europe, and that ship carrying him thousands of miles away, her mind went numb with dread.

"You can't just do that," she sputtered. "You can't just leave America. Especially not on a moment's notice."

A humorless smile creased his cheek again. "Certainly I can," he replied. "It's quite an uncomplicated process. I do it every year. I always go to buy bulbs at about this point in December, and I usually return in a month or six weeks. This time, however, my schedule is undecided. Unless—" he paused to study her more carefully. "Unless I can interpret your unexpected burst of concern as a sign that you'll miss me."

"Uh . . ." Nina stammered as a flush spread across her cheeks. His announcement had stunned her so much, she'd let her emotions slip past her guard. "I only meant to say, um . . ." she mumbled, struggling to regain her stony composure. "What I meant was, it's an odd time to be traveling. After all, tomorrow is Christmas Eve."

The faint light of hope in Wim's eyes faded, hardening his usual irony and amusement. "Christmas is for families, Nina," he told her mockingly. "Those of us unencumbered by such trappings are free to go about our business as we please. It's really quite a blessing to be at sea over the holidays," he went on in the same cynical vein. "One is spared the endless offerings of plum puddings and mincemeat pies and the endless rounds of off-key carols. To say nothing of being spared the obligation of shopping for all those gifts. Yes, indeed," he said. "It's a refreshing change. I highly recommend it. Perhaps you ought to try it, too."

Nina heard the underlying austerity in his tone, and she remembered the flash of longing she'd caught on his face at the party on Long Island. His demurral didn't fool her one bit. Despite his professed relish of passing Christmas aboard a ship, she knew that, come the day after tomorrow, he'd much prefer to be in the warm circle of a family than amongst a group of strangers. The realization wrenched her heart.

Nevertheless, she couldn't let that affect her, she reminded herself, fighting back the urge to reach out her hands. She couldn't be moved. As soon as even one corner of her resistance was lowered, she knew her entire resolution would tumble to the ground. "No, thank you," she said stiffly. "I'd rather stay home on Christmas."

"Yes, of course you would," Wim agreed, his voice softening. He dismissed his suggestion with a flick of his wrist. "You're quite devoted to your family, I know. You're never happier than when surrounded by a swarm of sisters or when hugging and kissing dozens of cousins. Isn't that so?" Without waiting for her to answer, he continued in a dryer tone.

"In fact," he said, "the usual allotment of aunts, uncles, and so on doesn't seem to satisfy you. You seem compelled to recruit extra relatives. To fill vacant positions, so to speak. For example, there's your adopted grandfather, Don Alberto." He gave a little shrug. "Perhaps he's not everyone's ideal of a benevolent grandfather," he conceded, "but there's no mistaking his admiration and affection where you're concerned. What more could you ask for?"

With an aching heart Nina watched while he fiddled with his coat, giving it a vigorous shake. She could easily forgive the sarcasm in his voice. In truth, she hardly heard it. She could only remember his quick description of his own grandfather, a man who refused to meet him. It was plain as day that Wim was hurting. "Nothing more," she murmured. "I couldn't ask for anything more."

In the middle of brushing off his coat, Wim paused to give her a suspicious glance. Reassured that she was being sincere, he gave the coat another shake. "Then there's that da Rosa fellow," he said. "He handily fills the roles of son to your father and brother to you and your sisters. That was a smart choice as well."

Whether the thought occurred to him spontaneously, or whether he somehow sensed the alarm suddenly pounding with her pulse, Nina never found out. But all at once he stopped stock still and let the coat fall lifelessly across his arm. His brow furrowed deeply, and for a long, tense moment he fixed his stare on her face.

"Or perhaps I've got it wrong," he said in his even tone. "Perhaps brother isn't the role you've selected for Dante after all." His voice remained low, but it sounded much rougher as he forced the words out of his mouth. "Perhaps you're planning to expand your family even further," he suggested. "To a husband and children. *Bambini.* Isn't that how you call them?"

Nina didn't respond. There was nothing she could say. Besides which, it was impossible for her to speak. Her throat was full of tears. So she just stood there, woodenly, her lips pressed tightly together. The blush that had started to fade now came surging back, a brilliant scarlet.

The silence, this time, was even longer and tenser as Wim continued to study her face. Unable to meet his eyes, Nina could only glance at him. It was enough to shock her. There was no amusement in his expression now. No trace of his lopsided smile. For that matter, his expression wasn't even calm or composed, and there was no sign of his usual confidence. During the one single moment that Nina glanced over at him, the deep, tearing pain inside him was showing.

Nearly choking, Nina looked away. When she looked back, his expression was haggard. Somehow he'd managed to contain those awful feelings, to lock them safely away from view. With iron will, he'd succeeded in regaining his normal control. But the effort had left its mark. He seemed drained, his blue eyes sunken, the square lines in his face angular and sharp. And when he finally spoke, his tone was light, but the undertone was lethal.

"So that's the secret," he said. "That's what you couldn't tell me. Am I right?"

Again Nina didn't respond. If she moved, or even whispered, she knew she'd burst out crying. So again she just stood there, her heart burning with anguish and hot tears flooding her soul.

For another moment Wim waited. Then he shrugged and brushed past her. "Merry Christmas," he said quietly as he shut the door behind him.

Nina heard it click closed. She heard the finality as the latch was engaged. It was over. Wim would never walk through that door again. This time he was gone forever.

For some curious reason the tears didn't pour out. Now that she was alone, Nina didn't collapse to the floor, racked in sobs. Instead, the grief seemed to congeal inside her, blocking out all feeling, turning her numb. She continued to stand there for perhaps ten minutes, not thinking about anything at all. For ten minutes, she just existed.

Then slowly the shock receded and the little tingles of pain grew sharper. She made her way around her desk to her chair, sitting down and turning to look out the windows. It was nearly dark, but she didn't light the lamp. She was afraid the brightness would hurt even more. Pulling her coat more tightly around her in an attempt to ward off the winter chill in her spirit, she, too, waited. Waited for the pain to go away.

It will, she told herself dully. It will go away. Maybe not tonight or tomorrow, but someday it'll be gone. *Il tempo lenisce ogni ferita*, Mamma always said. Time heals all wounds. It was better this way, she tried to convince herself. It was better to get it over with now.

After all, what was her love for Wim built on but a few magnificent moments of passion? It was built on the silky touch of his hair, on his fair looks, and his charm. On the memory of looking up into his eyes and being stunned. It was just fascination. Just momentary intrigue. Just desire.

Over the years that desire would quietly extinguish, until she was left with nothing except the differences between them. It would end, this love. Sooner or later it would be gone. Without a doubt, it was better to let it die right now. To rid herself of this burden. That way the comfortable friendship she had with Dante could carry her contently through the rest of her life.

There was a slight rap on the door, and then the handle turned. Despite the rationalization she'd just made, Nina's heart leapt and she spun around. But it was Dante who was silhouetted in the doorway as the light poured in from the hall. Dante whose curls caught the glimmer this time. It wasn't Wim. As her racing heart slowed down again, the pain returned.

"Why are you sitting in the dark, Nina?" Dante asked as he went to light the lamp. "Is there something wrong with the valve or the wick? You should have called me."

"No, the lamp is fine," Nina said, blinking as bright light suddenly filled the room. Shading her eyes, she stood up and walked around to the front of her desk. It amazed her that she was able to speak normally, to make innocuous talk. "I was just thinking," she explained, leaning wearily against the desk.

"In the dark?" Dante repeated, turning away from the light fixture and coming over to stand near Nina.

Nina responded with an unintelligible murmur. Then, before he could press the point, she asked, "Did you fix the bagging machine?"

"*Si*," Dante answered, tossing his hand to show her how easily he'd done it. "It was just a few pumpkin seeds that spilled and got caught in the gears."

"Good," Nina said. Her eyes were used to the light, now, and she was able to lower her hand and look at Dante. For the second time in minutes her heart took a leap. This time, though, in dread.

Dante was standing in front of her, his hands twisting together and his cheeks very red. Oh, no, she thought, lifting her hand again. She massaged her throbbing temples. No. Not now. Please. I can't take it right this minute. Let him wait until tomorrow. At least until after supper. Please, let him wait.

But Dante didn't. "Nina," he began hesitantly.

She hesitated, too. "Yes?" she finally answered.

"It's about what I started to say to you before. You know, in the Nursery." He half turned and pointed over his shoulder with his thumb, so she'd know where he meant. "I mean about your parents," Dante stammered, the blush on his cheeks growing brighter. "About what they expect." His face on fire, he looked at her, as if begging for her help.

But Nina couldn't give him any. She was hugging herself again, holding in her growing terror. Not now, she kept repeating to herself, swaying back and forth. Not now. Not now. Not now.

"Nina, what I want to ask is . . ." Dante started again, taking a deep breath for courage. Nina's rocking stopped, and she braced herself against the desk. His words came out in a rush.

"I wanted to ask if you would be terribly hurt or insulted if I didn't marry you," he said. Then stepped back to wait for her reaction. When Nina just stared at him, her amber eyes huge, he held out his hands, pleading with her to understand.

"I like you very much," he explained. "I meant it when I said I think the world of you. And I meant it when I said I think you're beautiful and strong and smart. But you see," he added, "I'm in love with Serafina."

His words ricocheted around Nina's head for several minutes before they settled in her mind. He didn't want to marry her. He was asking her to release him. After all this time and torment, they weren't going to be joined in marriage. After all her excuses and rationalizations, after her long, sensible list of similarities, they weren't going to share a future. Nina's hand flew to cover her mouth when it dropped open. Then she burst out laughing.

"Nina, Nina," Dante fretted, taking a few steps closer. His hands hovered in the air around her, uncertain of how to stop her. She was doubled over with laughter, and her laughter was tinged with hysteria. "You *are* upset," he said miserably. "I'm so sorry.

I wouldn't want to hurt you for anything. What can I do? Please, tell me."

Nina just shook her head until she could rein in the gales of laughter. "No, no," she gasped, wiping the tears from her cheeks. "I'm not upset. Really." He didn't want to marry her. He wanted to marry her sister! Another fit of laughing seized her.

"Accidenti!" Dante moaned, taking two steps forward and as many back. "You're being brave to say that. But you're mad. And you have every right to be." He nodded. "You're the oldest and you should marry first. I should have said something right away."

"Right away?" Nina asked, gulping back the giggles again. "How long have you known?"

"Since Aurelia's wedding," he confessed timidly, afraid the news would trigger an uncontrollable attack. "Since the first day I met her."

"Madonna mia!" Nina exclaimed, swallowing more laughter and blotting her face on her sleeve. But as she thought back to that day, and others that followed, more laughter bubbled out. "I don't even have to ask if Serafina loves you, too," she said. "I should have realized that she was as taken with you as you were with her." She remembered the melancholy on her sister's face when Serafina found her among the cabbages. She'd thought Serafina was sensing her broken heart, but instead she was feeling her own. She had fallen in love with Dante, but Dante had already been chosen for Nina.

Nina shook her head while Dante looked at her anxiously. "You two are perfect for each other," she told him. "Much better suited than you and I."

"You're just saying that," Dante worried. "You're just being generous and kind."

"No, I'm not," Nina denied quite forcefully, holding up both hands and waving them. "Believe me, I would never lie to you about something like this."

"Davvero?" he asked, hunching toward her, hardly daring to hope.

"Really," she answered with a definite nod. "Yes. Really and truly."

Watching the relief light up Dante's face was like looking at the paintings in church. A celestial glow illuminated his classic features, giving him the aura of someone who'd been blessed. On impulse Nina threw her arms around him and gave him a gigantic hug. Then she planted a hearty kiss on each of his cheeks and held him off for fond inspection.

"You're going to make me much happier as my brother-in-law than you ever would have as my husband," she said with another laugh. "But mind you," she added, shaking him with mock ferocity, "treat my sister well, or I'll be after you!"

"Of course!" Dante replied, aghast at the very suggestion. "Serafina means more to me than anything else. Without her, life's not worth living. I'd hurt myself before I ever hurt her."

The smile remained on Nina's face, but the pleasure that had prompted it faded. The pure love ringing in his voice brought a renewed stab of pain. She felt as strongly, loved as deeply, but Wim had gone for good. Her love wasn't going to end in a festive wedding, but in a long, wretched wait for the pain to disappear. Giving Dante's shoulder a final pat, she said, "Congratulations." She sounded a little sad.

"Grazie," Dante responded. "Thank you very, very much."

After Dante left her alone, after he'd gone off to tell Serafina the rapturous news, Nina remained where she was. Leaning against her desk, her coat wrapped tightly across her chest, she thought about what had just transpired. The tremendous geyser of relief and light-headedness that Dante's words had released had died down to a shallow puddle. She was still very glad he didn't want to marry her, especially since he was in love with Serafina. But his sudden withdrawal from her future left her feeling somewhat lost.

With a shaky sigh she wondered what would have happened with Wim if Alice hadn't interrupted Dante in the Nursery. How would she have reacted when she walked into her office an hour ago if she knew then what she knew now? Would she have greeted him in a more eager manner, just to start with, or would the same argument still have applied? Would she still have believed that there were too many differences between them and not enough linking their lives?

After a long time Nina stood up and went over to turn off the light. It didn't matter what might have happened. It was useless to second-guess herself. She *had* stood silent when Wim had entreated her. She *had* let him walk away. And now he was gone. To Holland and who knew where else. She would never see him again. So all she could do was wait.

Christmas went by and so did New Year's and the Epiphany while Nina continued to wait. But the pain didn't diminish. Mamma's Saint's Day was the twenty-seventh of January, five weeks to the day since she'd last seen Wim. Although they had another feast, Nina felt anything but gay. In fact, the sight of so much happiness made her feel worse than ever.

Orazio was especially attentive to his Angelina, who rewarded him with affectionate kisses. Touched by this display of devotion after twenty-six years of marriage, Serafina slipped her hand into Dante's, underneath the table. He clapped it to his leg. Across from them, Luigi Tagliaferro cast his stolid gaze on Lucia, who smiled demurely in return. Nina could only huddle in her chair and wish the evening would end. She forced herself to smile, but inside she felt cold and hollow.

It wasn't that she wanted everyone else to suffer along with her. Quite the contrary, she was very pleased that Dante and Serafina were in love with each other, because she liked them both immensely. They really were a perfect match. And she found Luigi's plodding courtship of Lucia rather sweet, especially since the massive lockmaker had somehow managed to soften her sister's sharper edges. However, it all left her feeling desperately lonely. As the winter wore on, that loneliness made her morose.

Despite her preoccupation, though, she managed to keep a dutiful eye on business, appearing in her office every morning and inventing tasks for the increasingly idle staff. There wasn't that much to do. During January, eleven orders trickled in. The first week of February that number doubled. Don Alberto was impossible to be with as his mood seesawed between being extremely irritable and extremely worried.

"Do you think there's too much information?" he wondered one day, barging into Nina's office. He slumped down in the chair in front of her desk. "Do you think they got bored with all the reading they had to plow through? Do you think they gave up and went back to their old catalogues?"

Sighing, Nina put down the 1896 Farmer's Almanac that she was leafing through and looked at him. "I don't know," she answered as she had the last dozen times he'd posed the same questions. "I think it's too early to tell."

"That's what you keep saying!" the don snapped, sitting up straight in the chair and stamping his cane on the floor. "For God's sake, Nina, it's February the *eleventh* already. If the time isn't right now, it never will be. Just ask yourself when you made your seed orders in the past. Ask yourself if you hadn't sent them in by this date." Without giving her a moment to reply, he banged his cane down again and supplied the answer himself. "You always had your seeds in hand by February eleventh!" he practically shouted. "You were ready to plant them by now!"

Nina sighed again. "Yes, that's true," she conceded, trying to be patient. "We always ordered early. But don't forget, gardening is our occupation, not our hobby. All year round and every day, we're thinking about plants and lawns and seeds. The average customer, though, doesn't start thinking about his gardens until there's some sign of spring to remind him. After all, most people don't have a big, modern greenhouse to work in while the weather outside is still bitter."

"They don't need greenhouses," Don Alberto replied testily. "They can start the seeds on their windowsills. It's a well-known fact that the majority of seed catalogue customers are women, anyway. They're home all day and love to fidget with pots and trays. It's a perfect time for them to be sending in their orders."

"Well, I don't know what else to say to you," Nina responded, flinging out her hands, exasperated. There was a limit to her tolerance, these days, and Don Alberto was rapidly using it up. The way she felt right now, she didn't care if the Blackwell Seed Co. went out of business tomorrow. "People will either send for seeds, or they won't," she said unsympathetically.

"Bah!" the don retorted, storming out of her office.

The next day, however, the mailman brought forty-two orders, and Don Alberto's spirits started to rise. On the thirteenth of February, fifty-seven more orders arrived. The day after that it was sixty-eight, and the day after that it was one hundred and ten. On

Sunday, the sixteenth, there was no post, but Monday's mail held one hundred and ninety-four. Don Alberto cackled with glee.

"You see?" he exclaimed, rushing in to pound a fist on Nina's desk. "Didn't I tell you it was only a matter of time? People are always procrastinating. Waiting till the last minute. You watch," he predicted with a grand flourish of his cane. "The orders will come pouring in from now on."

A year ago Nina would have laughed delightedly at the don's brazen change of tune. Three months ago she would have smiled and shaken her head. In her present state, however, she lost her temper. "You did not tell me that!" she cried, jumping up to jab a finger in his direction. "You've been driving me mad with your doubts and dire speculations. At this time last week you were ready to declare the whole thing a failure. So don't pretend you knew all along that this would happen."

Startled by her outburst, Don Alberto took a step back. Under normal circumstances he would have responded with a furious eruption of his own. Today, however, unlike Nina, he was feeling good, so instead of barking at her, he simply complained, "You've been awfully touchy lately," he told her, thrusting his jowly chin forward. "I can't make a single comment without getting some snippy response from you. Every time I open my mouth, you jump down my throat."

Nina knew the don was exaggerating a good deal, but she also realized she'd been rude. Her nerves were rubbed raw by her loneliness, yet she was flailing out at anyone who got too close. The same thing was happening at home. There was only one person she really wanted to see, but she never would again. She'd made the decision to banish him from her life, and he'd gone away for good.

Somehow she'd better learn to live without him, she told herself. And soon. Or she'd lose her friends and family, too. Taking a deep breath to regain her control, she said, stiffly, "I'm sorry."

"No, you aren't," the don returned, starting to sulk. "Don't think I don't know you after all these years, Nina. You can't fool me with a few polite words. Something's got into you, and it's turning you inside out."

When Nina didn't respond, but stood there chewing her lip, Don Alberto plopped himself onto the chair in front of her desk, an aggrieved expression on his face. "You've been acting like this ever since Christmas," he grumbled. "You've been acting like a wounded bear."

"I'm sorry," Nina said again, this time a little bit more contritely. She felt bad that she'd let her mood affect her basic manners. "It isn't fair—"

"I'll say it's not fair," the don interrupted indignantly. "First de Groot went off to Holland, and then you turned into a foul-tempered fishwife. And all in the space of a week." He fixed Nina with a baleful gaze. "I'd like to know who I'm supposed to talk to," he said, "Mrs. Watkins? The girls who fill the orders?"

Nina's fragile hold on her composure snapped under the twin pressures of Don Alberto's self-pity and his reference to Wim. Who was *she* supposed to talk to with him gone? Who was she supposed to share her life with? Who was she supposed to love?

"Talk to whomever you like," she answered the don roughly as she crossed the room and snatched her coat from its hook. "But I have better things to do than to sit here, idly gossiping away the day." Yanking on her coat, she stomped out the door.

"I wasn't gossiping!" the don protested, jumping to his feet and shouting down the hall behind her. "I was talking about business!"

"I don't have time to talk about business!" Nina yelled back as she descended the stairs. "I'm too busy doing it! I'll be in the Nursery if you need me for anything else."

As soon as Nina opened the outside door, her annoyance started to fade. The stinging February wind hit her face and cooled her hot rush of anger. She immediately regretted having lashed out at Don Alberto when, really, he'd done nothing more offensive than be his usual self. It was she who was in an unusual frame of mind. Perhaps not a fishwife, as the don had accused, but certainly foul-tempered and bearish. On top of all her other anguish, now she felt ashamed of herself as well.

Being embarrassed about her mood didn't improve it, however. When she arrived at the Nursery to find Dante scrubbing down the benches, her greeting was glum. In fact, she stood just inside the door, hesitant, trying to decide whether to stay or leave. She hadn't counted on anyone being there, and she wasn't sure she could cope with the company.

"Hello, Nina," Dante called out as he bent over a bucket, wringing out a sponge. He glanced up at her. Then straightened and looked again. "What's wrong?" he asked, letting the sponge fall back in the suds. His eyes grew large with concern. "You look like someone's just cut off your feet," he said. "What's happened?"

In a quick attempt to dispel his worry, or at least to distract his attention, Nina gave a bright, little laugh, though it sounded false and tinny even to herself. She followed that with an airy wave of her hand as she declared, "No, no. Nothing's wrong. You just caught me by surprise. My thoughts were a thousand miles away when I walked in, never expecting to see you here. Somehow, I thought you'd be working on the new addition with Papà and the carpenters."

"E bè," Dante said, hanging his head. "I got too cold," he confessed. "My fingers got so numb, I couldn't hold the hammer." His shrug was apologetic. "It's my first full winter in America, you know. I'm not yet used to these temperatures."

Nina waved her hand again. "I don't think any of us are," she reassured him. "Around this time every winter, we all start dreaming about being in Sicily, where the sun is warm and glorious."

With a rueful nod Dante agreed. "Not like here," he said, gesturing at the dreary scene beyond the glass walls. "By ten o'clock I was so cold, my knees were knocking together. That's when your papà sent me in here to do a good cleaning before the benches get too full of plants. Really, we should have done it sooner than this, but we've all been busy putting the addition on your house. Even with the carpenters there to give us directions and to do the finish work, it's taken a lot of time."

"But it'll be wonderful when it's done," Nina said, keeping the conversation on a safe subject. She still hadn't gone beyond the doorway. "Once you and Serafina get married and move into it, you'll be glad you took the time to do it right. Both rooms are so big and light, you two will feel like you have a whole house to yourselves. You'll be able to hold balls in your bedroom, if you want to."

Dante smiled and flushed. "I don't know about that," he said shyly, "but we'll certainly be very comfortable." Then he shook his head. "I still can't believe Don Alberto suggested we do it," he said. "And as if that weren't enough of a gift, he went and hired his architects to design it and his carpenters to help us build it." About to shake his head again, he stopped and looked at Nina more shrewdly.

"Although," he added, "I suspect it was you who put the notion into his head. It seems more like you than like him. You can never rest until you've made sure everyone is taken care of. It wouldn't surprise me a bit to know you've been whispering in *il padrone*'s ear."

Nina's laugh was more genuine this time as she threw up her hands in surrender. "I confess," she said. "But my motives weren't as completely pure as you'd like to believe. It was either build an addition, or Bianca, Lucia, and I would lose our room. We'd have had to sleep standing up, or stacked up on top of Stella's dolls. It would have been pretty crowded with six of us together."

Horrified by the thought of such a situation, Dante's face flamed. "We wouldn't have displaced you!" he exclaimed. "Serafina and I were planning to rent an apartment in town."

"*Fff*." Nina dismissed that idea with a flick of her wrist. "It's much better like this. The addition is a hundred times nicer than any tenement you'd ever find. It's better that you live at home." With more force in her voice, she declared, "Families should stick together."

His bright flush fading, Dante agreed again. "You're right," he said. "I'm just glad Don Alberto could be convinced of it, too. From the way he acts with his sons, though, I never would have thought that he'd give much value to family life." Pausing a moment, he toed the bucket of soapy water. "You know," he said, leaning sideways against the bench, "just when I think that man was born without a heart or a bit of human charity, he'll do something like this, and I'll totally reverse my opinion.

"It makes me think that somewhere behind all that growling and snapping, there's a man who, in his own blunt way, is very decent." His eyebrows raised, and he shook his head. "I think I'm actually getting fond of him."

Nina gave another laugh and finally walked partway down the aisle. "I know what you mean," she said, leaning against a bench, too. "Don Alberto has a way of growing on you. And after eight and a half years he's grown on me a lot. In fact, he's become extremely dear." She felt comfortable with Dante. Now that there was no longer the threat of marriage between them, she could relax in his presence. "That's why I'm mad at myself for arguing with him just now," she confided.

"Ah." Dante lifted his hand in enlightenment. "Now I know why you looked like thunder when you first walked in."

With a grudging nod, Nina said, "I guess I'm feeling very guilty because this time he didn't even provoke it. It was all my fault." She rubbed her forehead. "What if I caused him to have another heart attack?" she asked, almost to herself.

For another moment Dante just stood in sympathetic silence, but when Nina slouched against the bench, absorbed in distant thoughts, he gently prodded her to go on. "I'm sure you didn't mean to do it," he said. "Something else must have been bothering you."

Suddenly realizing that she'd revealed too much and had opened herself up for scrutiny, Nina came erect, tossing her head and flinging her hands through the air. "It wasn't that bad," she amended. "Just a little tiff. I think I'm probably tired. Yes, that's it," she decided. "I didn't get much sleep last night. I don't know why, but maybe I drank too much coffee after dinner."

There was another silence as Dante again waited for her to continue. But Nina just shifted her feet. Casting a quick glance over her shoulder, she wished she hadn't moved away from the door. She was looking everywhere but at Dante when his soft voice came across the space between them. "You didn't have any coffee last night," he reminded her. "After supper you started to scold Rossana for not doing her schoolwork, then, in the middle of your lecture, you got up abruptly and went to bed."

While Nina scratched her chin and wondered what she was going to say next, Dante spoke again. "Serafina thinks that you miss the Dutchman," he said. "She thinks that's why you've been out of sorts lately." Hesitating only a moment, he added, "She's usually right about things like this."

Nina felt her heart start to beat harder, but still she tried to evade his probing. "*Bè,* Dante . . ." She let her voice fade away and lifted her hands in an elaborate gesture.

Though he flushed a bit, Dante refused to be deterred. "Serafina thinks that you and the Dutchman are two peas in a pod," he told her. "That you're both strong and smart and full of confidence. That you both have big dreams and the wills to pursue them. She thinks you both are going to have extraordinary lives."

This time Nina didn't say anything at all as she stood in the aisle and prayed for an escape. Dante's sweet words were like salt on her wounds.

"Serafina thinks that the Dutchman is the only person you know who you can really match wits with. Except maybe for Don Alberto, and he isn't nearly as charming. She thinks it gives you great pleasure to be with him and that you're feeling unhappy because he's away."

"*Va bene!*" Nina burst out, holding up both hands to stop him. "All right. All right. I miss him." She shut her eyes a minute and took a gulp of air. It was a relief to finally say those words out loud. In fact, to even say them to herself. "Yes, I miss him," she repeated more evenly, opening her eyes again and taking hold of the bench. She looked at Dante, meeting his steady gaze.

"I miss him," she said, nodding in agreement. "I like him. Very much. But that's beside the point. Because, Dante, don't you see? Serafina is dead wrong about our being similar." Steepling her hands, she shook them in front of her. It was suddenly very important to make Dante understand. Maybe then it would seem more real to herself.

"We're not two of a kind," she said. "Nothing about us is alike. From the countries of our birth to the cast of our complexions, there's an entire world that separates us and makes us different from each other. We have different languages and different customs and different points of view. And it doesn't matter that we both have big dreams, because those are different, too. It's the day-to-day details that count between two people, and when all is said and done, ours simply aren't the same."

Seeing the doubt on Dante's face, she shook her hands more desperately. "Look," she said. "You proved it yourself. You didn't call him by name. You called him the Dutchman. Which is what he is. Just as I'm a Sicilian." Throwing up her hands in despair, she said, "We're not two peas in a pod, at all. We're completely different vegetables."

"It takes all kinds of vegetables to make a garden," Dante insisted.

Nina shook her head. "Maybe so," she said without conviction. "But potatoes know better than to grow among the tomatoes, and onions won't do well among the beans."

"But potatoes and beans do well together—" Dante started to say, but Nina cut him off.

"It's no use," she said, her hands falling to her sides. "It would never work. My family ignores him, and his friends look down their noses at me. He's a stranger, Dante, and we're better off the way we are."

"But you miss him," Dante protested, unwilling to accept her argument. "He makes you happy."

"My family also makes me happy," Nina replied. "So does gardening. Up until now that's been enough. It will be in the future, too."

"But—" Dante started again.

And again Nina cut him off. "Do you have another sponge?" she asked, slipping off her coat. "I'll help you scrub."

Dante sighed. Then he lifted his shoulders in a helpless shrug. "You sweep the benches," he said. "I'll do the scrubbing."

An hour later when the Nursery door rattled open, Nina was midway down the fifth bench and Dante was at the far end of number four. They both looked up to see Don Alberto arriving in a cold gust of air. "Good afternoon," Dante called out, lifting the sponge in greeting.

"Hello, hello," the don answered absently, making a beeline for Nina's aisle. He scuttled along, supporting his bandy legs with his cane. Several yards in front of Nina, he came to a stop and thrust out his chin. "Have you finished with your snit, yet?" he inquired.

Abashed and ashamed, but just a touch irritated by his tone, Nina dipped her head. "Yes, I am," she answered. "I'm sorry that I yelled at you."

"Never mind that," Don Alberto said, impatiently brushing off her apology. "It's just that you didn't give me a chance to tell you what else came in today's mail."

Nina set down her brush and turned to look at him fully. He was standing with his legs splayed out, very pleased with himself, pausing for dramatic effect. Nina felt another twinge of irritation. "Oh?" she prompted.

"Got a letter from de Groot," he announced.

"You what?" Nina exclaimed, taking a great stride forward, her heart beginning to pound. "What did he say?" she demanded. She held out her hand as if to receive the letter. Then she remembered that she was finished with Wim, that she'd decided their relationship was impossible. She remembered that just an hour ago she'd explained this to Dante in a tone of utter finality. She quickly stepped back.

"Uh, I mean, what did he have to say?" The words were the same, but this time she said them with all the indifference she could muster. While she picked at a stain on the potting bench, she peeked from Dante to Don Alberto to see if they'd noticed her strong reaction. Although she caught Dante staring at her, he hastily averted his eyes, becoming interested in what he was scrubbing.

Don Alberto was not so discreet. Nor so shy. "Aha!" he pounced. "Knew that would get your attention."

It was all Nina could do to keep herself from shaking him as the don preened before her victoriously. "Yes," she conceded as calmly as possible, giving up on the stain and on her show of indifference as well. "You have my attention. Now, what did Wim tell you?"

"It's not so much what he told me, as what idea his letter put in my head," Don Alberto said in the same dramatic tone. Then he let his comment hang there.

Eyebrows knitting in genuine puzzlement, Nina took a small step forward. "What do you mean?" she asked. "What idea? Why can't you tell me what he said?"

Don Alberto settled himself in a grand pose with both hands on top of his cane. "I can tell you," he said. "Although there's not that much to report. First he thanked me for my letter."

"You wrote to *him*?" Nina demanded, taking a larger step toward him.

"Well, yes," the don admitted, shifting a bit. Then he looked annoyed. "Don't interrupt me, Nina," he scolded. "I *had* to write to him. Had to know where the devil he was and when the devil he was coming back. Couldn't take much more of the present situation. You've been going around with your jaw on the ground, and I've got no one to talk to."

Clamping her hand on her hips and shaking her head, Nina muttered, "That's just fine. It's just what he needs to hear." In a louder voice she asked, "And what was his response?"

"As I already told you," the don answered her, "he didn't have much to say. Just wrote that he didn't know when he was returning to America. That he was thinking of spending some time in London."

Pain twisted Nina's heart, and her stiff posture wilted. "Oh, I see," she said, wrapping her arms around herself. London. Geographically, it was closer than Haarlem, but somehow it seemed much farther away. She turned toward the bench, mechanically reaching for the brush.

"Don't you want to hear my idea?" Don Alberto asked. He sounded annoyed again, irked that Nina had lost her interest.

"Yes, of course," Nina replied, politely turning back to the don. She was having trouble concentrating on what he was saying, though. London. Wim was leading a life of sophistication that was the ultimate wedge between them.

Waiting for some spark from Nina, Don Alberto finally lost his patience. "Bah!" he snorted. "You don't even care that I've decided we're going to Holland. Decided that if de Groot won't come here to see us, we'll go there to see him."

"Uh-huh," Nina said.

Don Alberto shook his cane at her. "Wake up!" he ordered. "For God's sake, Nina! Didn't you hear what I said? We're going to Holland! I've got it all figured out. We'll go as soon as your sister gets married to da Rosa, so they can come along as chaperones."

Although there was a small sound as Dante's sponge splashed into the bucket, and a slightly louder one as he disguised a choke inside of a cough, Nina only nodded. "*Si, si. Va bene,*" she agreed. Then she noticed the cane being brandished in her face. And suddenly his words sank in.

"We're what?" she exploded, her hands flying up. "What on earth are you talking about now? I'm not going to Holland. What a ridiculous idea!"

"It's not ridiculous at all," the don countered, delighted at this show of spirit. "You haven't heard the best part yet." He was about to pause for more dramatic effect when he saw the storm building in Nina's face and realized that wouldn't work. "The best part is," he quickly told her, "I've decided to expand. We're going to do a fall catalogue, too. And offer spring-blooming bulbs."

Nina gasped. "You can't be serious!" she cried. "You must be joking!"

"Same formula as the seed catalogue," he went on, ignoring her exclamation. "Lots of varieties. Lots of information. And lots of designs for bulb gardens. That's why we've got to go to Holland. We've got see everything in bloom. Don't have time to do trial gardens, the way we did with the seeds. Can't plant them until next fall, and they won't come up until a year from May.''

"This is crazy!" Nina said, clutching her head. "We can't just go traipsing off to Holland."

"Why not?" Don Alberto asked, enjoying himself immensely. He leaned his back against a bench and tapped his cane against the floor. "Give me one good reason."

Nina's hands spread out as she contemplated the trip with horror. "Because," she said, too overwhelmed to think straight. "Because, well, we don't speak Dutch." She threw up her hands. "For heaven's sake!" she shouted. "Holland's a *foreign country*!"

"Of course it is." Don Alberto chuckled. "But we've got a guide. De Groot will show us around. And he'll be our agent for the bulbs we buy."

"No," Nina said, shaking her head emphatically. She was through with Wim. Positively. No matter how much it hurt or how much she missed him. To go to Holland was nothing short of insanity. Seeing him again would only prolong the agony.

"It's the best way, Nina," the don coaxed. "The bulb district is just a tiny area, so we'll be able to see every variety of bulb that's grown. It'll be easy for you to plan your gardens, and it'll be easy for your sister to make her paintings. Perfect, eh?" he said. Before she could respond, he looked beyond her shoulder at Dante and asked, "When are you two getting married? The daffodils start blooming around the end of March. I'd like to leave here in a month."

Though Dante glanced uncertainly at Nina, he answered *il padrone* as best he could. He wasn't sure he understood the question. Actually, he wasn't sure he believed what he heard. "We marry when we finish to build, Don Alberto."

"Finish to build?" the don repeated. "Oh, you mean when the addition is done?" He waved his cane like a magic wand. "In that case, we'll hire more carpenters," he declared. "Be done in no time. And send Serafina to town to Lyman Hoyt's for the furniture. Have 'em deliver it and send me the bill."

Dante was too stunned to respond, but Nina had no trouble finding her voice. "No," she said again, balling her fists at her side. "I won't let you bribe Serafina and Dante into going along with your crazy scheme. And I won't let you bully them, either. It's their *wedding*, for heaven's sake," she told him, shaking a fist in his face. "They don't want to gallop through it. They want to treasure the memory for the rest of their lives."

"I never said they should gallop through it." Don Alberto was indignant. "I was just offering a little help. They can have a party like the one your cousin had. And then they can have a honeymoon in Europe. A month or so of looking at tulips and daffodils. What could be more memorable than that?"

"No!" Nina shouted, slamming her fists against her sides. "No to the honeymoon! No to Europe! And no to another catalogue! It's all wrong, do you hear me? None of us has the time or the strength to do another catalogue. This was supposed to be fun. Remember? Besides, we're Sicilians. We don't belong in Holland."

For another twenty minutes Don Alberto presented his case, and for another twenty minutes Nina adamantly rejected it. In her frenzy she failed to realize what motivated the don. That he enjoyed Wim's company and meant to engage it the one way he knew how. By doing business. The only thing she was aware of was that the entire prospect filled her with panic, and that under absolutely no circumstances would she allow herself to be flattered, cajoled, or threatened into making the trip.

However, she wasn't immune to guilt. It was a tool that Don Alberto had recently discovered, and one he didn't hesitate to employ. First he made his face red and angry, then he clutched his heart. In less than an instant the expression on Nina's face changed to alarm. It took only another minute for her to capitulate. Chortling, Don Alberto went back to the Store to get Gideon started on the travel arrangements.

=22=

Despite Don Alberto's money and machinations, the addition didn't get finished until April the eighth. A week later, in a quiet family ceremony, Dante and Serafina were married. On the seventeenth, they embarked for Holland. The newlyweds were blissful, completely involved with each other. After spending the last few weeks fretting, Don Alberto was in an excellent mood. Nina stewed.

Her spirits started to lighten only when they docked in Rotterdam. Even in the hustle of the huge port, there was the sense of being somewhere new. Watching the burly dockworkers in their blue smocks and big wooden shoes, Nina felt a stir of excitement. Later, winding through brick streets lined with storybook houses, she felt the excitement grow. Young boys with baskets of winkles and brined herring, hawking their wares in Dutch, increased her excitement even more. Maybe, just maybe, this would be an adventure after all.

They boarded a train in the late afternoon, early evening really. But the sky was as clear at half past seven as it was in the middle of the day. "What wonderful light," Serafina remarked with an artist's awe.

"Fifty-two degrees north," the don told her authoritatively. "Same latitude as Newfoundland."

Her pretty brow wrinkling in puzzlement, Serafina looked at her sister for an explanation. Nina shrugged. "Just enjoy it," she advised.

She took her own advice. Leaning back on the velvet seat of the first-class compartment, she watched the country chug by. In the beginning it was mostly bridges and canals, watery highways jammed with boats of every size. Gathering speed, they raced past a few villages and fields before arriving in The Hague. Although it was the seat of the government and the site of the royal palace, neither the king nor the queen was there to meet them. After half an hour, the train chugged on.

Just past The Hague came Leiden, and just past Leiden the scenery changed. The clusters of brick buildings gave way to paper-flat fields, and the fields erupted in color. Nina moved to the edge of her seat. Transfixed, she stared out the window as arrow-straight bands of reds, yellows, pinks, purples, and blues flashed by, creating the effect of someone flipping through a brilliant deck of cards. Neatly boxed by grass-covered dikes, or by silvery streaks of canals, the fields of tulips and narcissus and hyacinths were a stunning spectacle.

For kilometer after kilometer the bands of flowers continued. Sometimes they lay perpendicular to the tracks, sometimes horizontal, but all the bands were exactly the same width, all were vivid, all were perfect. Occasionally the fields were punctuated by a plain, brick rectangle of a building. Drying sheds, probably, Nina decided, remembering the one for cabbages on Long Island.

Or occasionally there was a thatch-roofed farmhouse, or a windmill with its canvas sails full. Here and there was a pocket field of lush, green grass with a stout cow or two grazing on it. But mostly there was just the sky, only now turning rosy with the lowering sun, and the tidy fields of blooms in stripes of dazzling colors.

The resplendent view was briefly interrupted as the train whizzed through the bulb district towns. "Lisse, Hillegom, Bennebok, Heemstede," the conductor called out in turn. Little towns, but proper and dignified, like tiny versions of the bigger cities. They had the same winding brick streets and narrow brick buildings, with the same steep tiled roofs and unshuttered windows. The same lovely lace curtains relieved the architectural austerity, as did the profusion of skinny chimneys and the prevalence of charming mansards or stepped gable facades that looked like real-life advent calendars. It was all the same, only smaller.

At nine-fifteen they pulled into Haarlem, and Nina saw another difference. The narrow brick buildings in this elegant city were not only bigger, they were also grander. The stepping-stone gables were more pronounced, and the mansards had frillier trim. This was a wealthy city with a rich history of merchants and artists. Now it was the bulb capital of Holland, and, therefore, of all the world.

Completely captivated, they drove through the twilit streets, across a drawbridge spanning a canal. Long, low boats with round, snub bows lined both banks. Budding elm trees lined the shore. They clomped straight through the Grote Markt, a vast market square that was empty of vendors at this hour of the evening, but was guarded at the far end, nonetheless, by an imposing Gothic church. Behind it, they turned right, then squeezed down a thread-wide street. At a small hotel called the Maartens, the carriage stopped, and they were there.

Don Alberto was signing the register when a familiar voice spoke up from a few feet away. "At last," it said. "I was beginning to fear you'd taken the wrong train."

Nina spun around, her heart suddenly pounding, to see Wim

lounged against a fluted column. She'd spent the entire ocean voyage preparing herself for this moment, getting ready for the first time she'd see him, and though she thought she'd sufficiently steeled herself, it took only an instant to know that she hadn't. The memory that she thought was so clear and true was nothing compared with reality. She would never be able to totally capture his long-legged grace or remember, exactly, the square, clean lines of his face. That lopsided smile would never be as endearing in her mind as it was when Nina saw it in person.

And his eyes. Those startling blue eyes. No matter that they were etched forever in her memory, they still never ceased to take her by surprise. Only now, finally, she knew what color they were. They were the same blue as the fields of hyacinths she'd seen at dusk from the window of the train. Vibrant blue, deepened by the darkening sky.

But though Nina stared at him, Wim only glanced at her. Instead, he went straight to Serafina and pressed her hand in both of his. "Congratulations," he told her. His voice was warm and sincere. "You can't know how delighted I was to hear the news of your marriage." While Serafina blushed and looked confused, he let go of her hand and turned to Dante. "Congratulations," he repeated, grasping his hand now. "I wish you a lifetime of happiness."

Though Dante blushed, too, he wasn't nearly as flustered as his wife. "*Grazie,*" he responded, giving Wim's hand a firm shake. "Thank you very much." After only the slightest of pauses, he added, "I wish the same for you."

Wim's eyebrows rose imperceptibly and, for a moment it almost seemed there was a wistful light in his eyes. But then Don Alberto finished at the register and turned to clap him on the shoulder, and it was hard to know if the light had ever been there.

"Well, de Groot," Don Alberto trumpeted. "Here we are. The executive staff of the Blackwell Seed Company in Holland. What do you think of that, eh?"

A familiar crease appeared in the corner of Wim's mouth, and familiar amusement filled his voice. "I think it's quite the most remarkable feat I've ever seen," he said. "I don't know how you managed to get your managers to consent. It can't have been an easy task, for example, to separate your Head Gardener from her gardens."

"Took a bit of doing," Don Alberto admitted. "As you've

guessed, she didn't want to come, at first. Finally got her to agree, though.''

The crease got deeper still. ''I won't even ask what methods you employed,'' Wim said. ''Although I must confess that I'm very pleased you persisted. It's going to be thoroughly enjoyable showing her the fields of tulips in bloom.'' Holding up a hand, he checked himself. ''Showing all of you the *bloembollen*,'' he graciously amended.

''But particularly Nina,'' he murmured, almost under his breath. Turning toward her at last, his smile disappeared. He settled himself more carefully on his long legs, as if bracing for the worst. His gaze was serious as it swept her face, but when he finally spoke, his voice was soft. ''Welcome to Holland,'' he said. ''I'm glad you've come.''

Nina had rehearsed this moment a hundred times as well. A hundred times she'd practiced a cool and impersonal greeting. But when it came right down to her turn to speak, she found herself responding in a completely different fashion. ''Thank you,'' she said, without hesitation. ''I'm glad to be here.''

Again Wim's eyebrows raised imperceptibly and a look of surprise crossed his face. But he hadn't achieved the success he had by letting opportunities escape. ''Good,'' he said, recovering instantly and closing the space between them. ''I'll do my best to make sure your visit is memorable.''

Slipping her hand through his arm, before she had a chance to flee, he said, ''We'll start right away with a taste of Dutch food. Just a small meal tonight, I'm afraid. It's a bit past the dining hour, but I've persuaded the kitchen to stay open and to keep a pot of soup warm.

''It's *erwtensoep*, this evening,'' he went on chattily, as he led them down the thickly carpeted hall. ''That's a traditional pea soup. And I'm sure they'll serve it with some smoked sausages and, perhaps, a nice dark bread.'' Pulling open a huge wooden door, he motioned them inside.

''Don't worry about your baggage,'' he told them as they filed in. ''The porter will put it in your rooms. They're very good in this hotel. That's why I always stay here.''

About to follow the others into the dining room, Nina stopped short in the doorway. ''*You* stay here, too?'' she asked, pointing her finger first at him and then at the floor. ''You're staying here *now*?'' Under the same roof as her, is what she meant. The idea seemed so intimate, it sent a shiver along the top of her skin.

"Yes, I am," Wim confessed, his smile reappearing. "I have a room on the fourth floor." He took advantage of the moment before someone turned around to brush the back of his hand across her cheek.

Nina's eyes blinked, and she took a deep, trembly breath, but she didn't move away. "And on what floor are our rooms?" she asked, her voice husky and rough.

"The second." Wim sounded regretful.

Unable to speak again, Nina just gave a nod, then turned forward and continued into the dining room. It was long and rectangular with pale green wainscoting and frosted glass chandeliers. The requisite hand-tatted lace hung from high arched windows, and potted palms in majolica urns stood on mahogany columns of various heights. Dante was holding out a red velvet chair for Serafina, and Don Alberto was tapping his cane impatiently when Nina slid into her seat, breathing hard. Wim sat down next to her. Was she imagining it, or were the scrubbed spots in his cheeks a shade rosier than usual?

When he spoke, however, his voice was calm. "*Goeden avond,*" he said to the waiter who stood beaming by their table. "*We zijn nu gereed voor de soep.*"

"*Ja,* meneer de Groot. *Ik zal het meteen brengen.*"

"Eh? What?" Don Alberto asked while Serafina and Dante watched in round-eyed silence. "What did that fellow say? Is he bringing us a bottle of wine?"

"You shouldn't drink spirits, you know that," Nina reminded him, pulling her napkin into her lap. She was trying to ignore the fact that Wim was only inches away, but even without looking at him, his presence was a powerful force. "The doctor told you not to."

"Bah!" the don grumbled but without his usual rancor. "The doctor isn't here, thank goodness, and I mean to have a glass of wine to toast the occasion."

"Perhaps it might be more appropriate to do it with beer," Wim suggested. "That's our native wine. Quite fine, too, I might add."

Don Alberto nodded decisively. "Good," he said. "Beer it is."

Smiling again, Wim raised his hand. "*Ober!*" he called to another waiter who was idling by the kitchen door. Except for theirs, all the tables were empty at this hour. "*Breng ons wat pilsjes alstublieft.*"

Almost instantly, five glasses of golden beer appeared, each topped by several inches of creamy foam. Eyeing it with anticipation, Don Alberto lifted his up and declared, "This is going to be an outstanding sojourn, I can tell. Here's to all of us in Holland, together."

"To us," Wim echoed, lifting his glass, too. "*Proost.*"

"*Salute,*" Dante chimed in as he and Serafina followed suit.

Then, glasses in the air, they turned to look at Nina, who hadn't moved since the don had spoken. Feeling their eyes on her, Nina hastily raised her beer. "To us in Holland," she said, but there was amazement in her voice.

An uninitiated observer might have found Don Alberto's toast perfectly normal, but to Nina it sounded nothing short of stunning. His brief words held a measure of affection she'd never before heard him express. Looking from face to face, from Serafina to Dante to Wim, Nina realized that right here at this table were the only people in the world Don Alberto liked. The four of them were his family, connected by business and a love of plants. And for the duration of their stay in Holland, his family was reunited. She took a swallow of tangy beer. The discovery moved her deeply. It also added a new dimension to her chaotic feelings for Wim.

Before she had time to consider this extraordinary situation any further, a bowl of thick, steaming pea soup was set in front of her, distracting her attention. First she looked at it suspiciously, then she took a whiff. Finally she dipped in her spoon and lifted some up to her lips. "It's good!" she exclaimed, after a tentative sip. She took a larger taste. "Very good." Across the table, as if awaiting her signal, Dante and Serafina began to eat. They nodded in agreement.

"Heaven be praised," Wim murmured as he handed Nina a basket of crusty brown rolls and a plate mounded up with rich, yellow butter.

"Damn good," Don Alberto concurred, hunching over his bowl and shoveling spoonfuls of the smoky-flavored soup into his mouth. "Stick-to-your-ribs food. Just what you need on an evening like this one. There's a bit of bluster in that wind."

"It's blowing in off the North Sea," Wim explained. "And there's nothing higher than a house to blunt its strength. A good

deal of Holland is below sea level, you know. We just keep
building dikes to hold back the waves.''

"I was looking at the dikes from the train," Don Alberto
remarked, accepting the bread from Nina, picking out a roll, and
passing the basket on to Dante. "Wouldn't mind seeing one up
close." He dunked the roll in his soup and took a dripping bite.
"What are you planning to show us tomorrow, de Groot?''

"Maybe he's got business to do," Nina cut in before Wim
could answer. She'd broken open her roll and was slathering it
with butter, but now she paused to look at the don, somewhat
alarmed. Despite the rush of emotion she'd felt when she'd first
seen Wim in the lobby, and despite her moving recognition of Don
Alberto's affection, she hadn't completely forgotten her resolutions, or the reasons why she'd made them. The fact remained, it
was better if she spent as little time as possible in Wim's company.

"We mustn't impose on his hospitality. If he just points us in
the right direction, we can find our way by ourselves."

"Nonsense," Don Alberto scoffed while Dante and Serafina
looked doubtful.

"Nonsense," Wim agreed, brushing a bread crumb from Nina's
sleeve. His action had the desired effect. She turned sharply to
stare at him. "I did my business this winter," he told her with a
slight arch of his eyebrows. "While you're visiting in Holland, my
time is wholly at your disposal."

Nina looked away as abruptly as she'd turned to look toward
him and fiercely buttered her roll.

Plunging his into his soup again, Don Alberto nodded in
satisfaction. "What do you have planned for tomorrow?" he
asked once more.

"I've arranged with one of my suppliers to give you a tour of
his nursery," Wim replied. His voice remained level and calm,
though he seemed to breathe a small sigh of exasperation as he
stared at the back of Nina's head.

"It's just a short drive from Haarlem and quite typical of a
bulb-growing operation. Henk van der Veen has mostly single
early tulips, which have the advantage of being in bloom at the
moment. So I think you'll find it beautiful, as well as interesting
and informative. And in addition, Albert, you'll be able to get a
first-hand look at a dike. Henk's property is a grid of dikes and
canals.''

"Windmills, too?" Serafina asked hopefully, a spoonful of soup halfway to her mouth.

"Definitely windmills," Wim assured her. "Holland would come to a dead stop without its windmills."

Nodding as she swallowed her soup, Serafina looked pleased. "Good," she said. "I want to do some sketches. They're so graceful and lovely, I've already decided to use them in the cover painting."

"I wish to see the tools," Dante spoke up. He'd finished his soup and was mopping the bowl with his bread. "I think they should be very excellent to make the rows so tidy. It is possible to see?"

"It is possible," Wim replied as another smile creased his cheek. "But I think you'll find that it's the Dutch personality that makes the fields tidy as much as the excellent tools."

"*E bè.*" Dante shrugged, accepting Wim's explanation.

"And you, Nina?" Wim asked. "Is there anything special you'd like to see?"

Without turning around, Nina shook her head. "That's fine," she answered in a muffled tone, intently studying her roll.

Wim shook his head, too. "I'm glad you approve," he said. "Now, may I also suggest that you check your hair? Your pins need rescuing again." Nina dropped her roll, and her hands flew to her head.

Over the next few weeks it began to seem that Don Alberto's scheme was not so farfetched after all. Maybe doing business *was* the basis for congenial companionship. It certainly appeared to be true in this instance. With bulbs as a common denominator, the don's "family" enjoyed themselves, the sights, and each other quite a lot.

Serafina was enchanted by the light and the colors. By the picture-perfect scenes. By the way every view seemed to come with its own natural frame. The horizons were never distant in Holland—they were always well defined. If not by a dike running across the skyline, then by a farmhouse squatting under its low, thatched roof, or by a march of windmills, or by an upright, even bit of woods.

For his part, Dante relished touring the nurseries, learning about the bulb cultivation. He liked hearing about how the soil had been prepared, and he liked seeing the equipment used. He found the lath for marking out the exact rows very interesting, as well as the rolling drum which laid planting guides across them, but what fascinated him most of all were the hoes with three slender prongs for weeding between the young plants. They looked like delicate claws. He blushed with pleasure when Henk van der Veen gave him one to keep.

The don was equally as fascinated with the bulb sheds, where the harvested plants would be turned into money. He inspected the peeling tables, where women and children would remove the old growth from the bulbs, and the stacks of drying racks, where the bulbs would nestle all summer, like coins in a safe. He paid careful attention to the large, wooden sorting machines that sifted the dried bulbs through frames of various circumferences. The bigger the bulb, the more it was worth. He immediately memorized the sizes, storing away such information as the fact that eighteen centimeters for an amaryllis was considered premium.

As for Nina, she found all of it fascinating, but what she really loved were the flowers. She loved standing in the middle of a field with thousands of tulips bobbing in the crisp breeze around her. Each one was a flawless cup of satiny petals, its color clear, pure, and exquisite. And though few of them had any perfume or odor all of them smelled as clean as spring. The fields of hyacinths, on the other hand, were so fragrant they nearly made her swoon. The sweet, clovelike scent and the masses of bloom convinced her that she was in the closest thing to heaven that existed here on earth.

For Wim the fields, the seedhouse, and the tools, even the view, were nothing new. In fact, some of them were more familiar than he cared to remember. But what thrilled him beyond his power to describe it was watching Nina among the flowers. He remembered sitting in his office in New York, imagining just such a moment, but his imagination had been inadequate to envision the radiance of her expression. It was impossible to capture the combination of ecstasy and awe on Nina's face. She would walk down a row, completely absorbed, oblivious to all else but the flowers. Occasionally she would stop and brush her fingers across one. Her gesture was almost reverent.

As the days went by, the inexplicable wall she'd thrown up between them began to crumble. Wim breathed another sigh. This time, though, of relief.

23

"I was amazed when I looked at the calendar in the lobby and realized that you've been in Holland nearly three weeks," Wim said one morning. It was a lovely May day, and the dining room windows were open. The breeze fluttered the palm fronds, and sunshine filtered through the curtains, making lacy patterns on their table. "Time has flown by. Coffee or chocolate, Nina?"

"Chocolate," Nina replied promptly. "It's too delicious to resist." She helped herself to slices of cheese and sausage from the platter that the waiter held out, then added rolls, butter, black currant jam, and pickles to her plate. "We should buy several tins to bring home, don't you think, Serafina?" she asked, happily building a breakfast sandwich. "Benedetta, especially, would enjoy it."

"Uh-huh," Serafina answered as she stared at the jam pots, trying to make a choice.

"Try the *cilege*," Dante suggested, seeing her dilemma. "It's *buonissima*." Smiling gratefully at her husband, Serafina reached for the cherry.

"Perhaps you could do some shopping in Amsterdam," Wim said, "I thought we might take the train there today. As it's less than an hour away, it should be a pleasant excursion. A small intermission in your bulb tour, so to speak. Besides, it would be a shame if you were to leave Holland without seeing our most famous city. Chocolate, Serafina?"

"Yes, please," Serafina said, settling down a twist of bread studded with coarse salt and caraway seeds and holding out her cup. "The Baedeker guidebook says that the Rijksmuseum in Amsterdam has an impressive collection of paintings. Is that true?"

"Absolutely true," Wim confirmed. "Some of the Rembrandts are breathtaking. Dante?"

Dante waved his finger. "No, *grazie*," he declined. "I like better *caffè*."

Wim put down the chocolate pot and picked up the coffee. "Of course, the real glory of Amsterdam is the city itself," he went on, filling Dante's cup. "The sixteenth- and seventeenth-century mansions are magnificent, and the canals are a sight to see. There are hundreds of them. Almost more canals than streets. It's a city that can be toured either by boat or by foot."

"It's a perfect day for a walk," Nina said, quickly latching on to that idea. As much as she loved her sister and appreciated her talent, the idea of spending a bright spring day inside a museum wasn't very appealing. Nor was she particularly intrigued by the prospect of sitting motionless on a boat. The past three weeks had completely renewed her spirits, and she was brimming over with energy.

"A boat is probably more idyllic, but feet give you more control," she explained, trying to justify her preference. "When you're walking, you can stop to look at things whenever you like." As she took a bite of her sandwich, she glanced across the table. Suddenly remembering Don Alberto's age and his cane, she quickly chewed and swallowed, then amended, "Although a boat would be ever so much more comfortable."

"It's entirely possible to do some of both," Wim said, following both her glance and her thought. He dipped his head toward Serafina. "And to visit the Rijksmuseum, too. Coffee, Albert?"

"No," Don Alberto replied rather tonelessly. "Get that fellow to bring me some tea, will you, de Groot? I feel a little bit off. Knew I never should have eaten all those raw onions on the herring yesterday. Tasted awfully good at the time, though."

Her sandwich lifted, about to take another bite, Nina stopped and studied the don more closely. His confession of ill health had cause a spark of concern. Looking at him now, that concern turned to alarm. His face seemed puffier than usual, his baggy skin washed out and pallid.

"What's the matter?" she demanded, letting the sandwich fall, forgotten, to her plate. "You don't look well at all. Should we call a doctor? Wim," she said, twisting toward him in her chair. "Do you know a good doctor in Haarlem, or should we ask them at the front desk?"

"Don't be ridiculous, Nina!" Don Alberto lashed out before

Wim could answer. Irritation made him sit up straighter and put more life in his voice. "I told you what the matter was. I don't need some sawbones to tell me the exact same thing. It's the onions." Slumping back in his chair, he added, "I'm too old to be tearing around the countryside like I've been doing, eating as if I were twenty again. Going to stay in, today, and put my feet up."

"Good idea," Nina agreed immediately. His familiar grumpiness reassured her somewhat but didn't put her completely at ease. She knew better than to press him, though. Instead, she feigned a yawn. "A day of rest is just the ticket," she said. "We've been running ourselves ragged since we arrived. Amsterdam can wait for another time."

Her act didn't fool Don Alberto for a minute. "For God's sake, Nina," he snapped. "I have *indigestion*. I don't need an audience to see me through it. Fact is, what I need is some peace. Get out of here, all of you. Go to Amsterdam. I've seen dozens of cities, anyway. One more or less won't make any difference."

His unpleasant tone made it difficult to remain sympathetic, but still Nina gave it one more shot. "What if you feel worse during the day?" she asked, abandoning all pretenses. "What if you need a doctor or some medicines? I think we should stay here." Picking up her cup, she told him, "We won't bother you. We'll just be here if you need us. It isn't that necessary for us to see Amsterdam, either."

"Didn't you hear me?" Don Alberto nearly shouted. When people at the other tables turned their heads, he lowered his voice, but his tone remained harsh. "I told you to let me be," he growled. "I don't want any company. Besides, you came here to see Holland, not to sit inside a hotel playing nursemaid. Now, go on. Go to Amsterdam and leave me alone."

Exasperated, Nina plunked down her cup, splashing chocolate on the saucer and on the white damask tablecloth. "*Va bene*," she said, out of patience herself. "We'll be glad to oblige. In fact, we're practically on our way."

"*Bè, Nina*," Serafina spoke up. She dabbed her pink lips with her napkin, then smoothed it into her lap. "I'm not sure Dante and I want to go to Amsterdam." Beside her, Dante choked on his coffee and looked at her in surprise. She flicked him a warning glance, then turned back to her sister. "I think you and Wim should go ahead without us."

"Ah. *Si, si*," Dante agreed, suddenly understanding. When his

wife gave him another glance, he hastily added, "*Vogliamo un po'
di tempo da soli, Serafina ed'io.*"

But Nina understood, too. And she was completely uncon-
vinced by Dante's explanation that he and Serafina wanted some
time on their own. Her sister was less interested in being alone
with her husband than she was in Nina being alone with Wim. "I
thought you wanted to see the Rijksmuseum," she said darkly.
"What about the Rembrandts?"

Serafina had the grace to blush, but she didn't back down.
"There's a museum here, too," she said. "And I can go through
it at my leisure. Nobody else really wants to see the paintings, so
I'd just be a nuisance. You and Wim will have a better time by
yourselves. Besides," she said, "I've been wanting to make
sketches of the Grote Markt ever since we got here, but I've never
had the chance. This would be the ideal opportunity."

"It seems that no one wants us, Nina," Wim said. Without even
looking at him, Nina could see his crease of a smile. "We'd better
remove ourselves."

Half an hour later they emerged from the hotel. "Shall we walk
to the station?" Wim asked. "It's only fifteen minutes. Or would
you prefer to take a hack?"

"Walk," Nina answered shortly. She felt she'd been maneuvered into this situation, and the trick made her cross.

"Walk," Wim repeated, setting off at a comfortable pace.

It didn't take long for Nina's annoyance to lift. It seemed to fly
up in the warm, spring air and float away. Within two blocks of the
Maartens Hotel, the bounce returned to her step and she began to
enjoy herself. It was impossible not to enjoy the blond children
running past them, their clogs clomping on the bricks, or the
vendor cajoling them from the corner as the aroma of his grilled
sausages filled the street. She couldn't help but enjoy the ancient
buildings that leaned forward or sideways, thrusting their droll
facades toward a cobalt sky. Mostly, though, she enjoyed the man
by her side.

In a sudden flash of insight she realized that Wim was as
quintessentially Dutch as the country itself. He was arrow straight,
practical, and unquestionably solid, like the tall, brick buildings or
the dikes or the neat little towns. But he was saved from austerity
by his handsome face and his sense of amusement, like the
brilliant bursts of tulips saved the flat fields or the whimsical

gables saved the plain, angular buildings. Like Holland, he was open and forthright. But like Holland, he revealed only a little.

Another thought made her stop so suddenly that a man coming up behind her with a red kerchief around his neck and a basket of cheese on his shoulder nearly ran into her. "*Oei! Neem me niet kwalijk,*" he apologized cheerfully, readjusting the basket and skirting around her.

Startled by her unexpected stop, Wim halted several feet in front of her. "What is it?" he asked, coming back toward her. "Did you forget something? Shall we go back to the hotel?"

"No, I didn't forget anything." Nina tossed her hand over her shoulder, dismissing that notion. "It just occurred to me, though, that we've been in Holland for three weeks, and that you've shown us bulb fields and drying sheds and windmills and canals, you've fed us pea soup and brined herring and apple pancakes and beer, you've translated for us, you've guided us, you've explained Dutch customs and ways, but you've never once," she held up a solitary finger, "not once shown us where you lived as a child. You never even mentioned it." She saw his face starting to tighten, and she shook her head. "I know you didn't spring full-grown from the Maartens Hotel."

It took Wim a few moments to respond, but Nina didn't move. She didn't know why it seemed so important for him to answer, but it did. Almost holding her breath, she watched him carefully. She could practically see the thoughts churning through his mind. Because although he was very kind and generous, gladly giving his help or his time, sharing himself was a different story. For all his calm and friendly manners, he was really a very private person.

While she waited, Nina answered her own question. She suddenly knew his response was a test. It was a measure of how much she meant to him, of how close he wanted to get. A carriage drawn by a small, broad horse squeezed by them, and an apple-cheeked girl walked past carrying a market basket almost bigger than herself. It was filled with potatoes and new baby beets, a loaf of dark bread and a bunch of tulips.

Finally he spoke. His voice was rough and tense. "It's not much to see," he said. "But I'll show you."

He led off again, though this time his pace was brisk. Nina had to hurry to keep up with him, taking two steps for every one of his. She was breathing hard, but she knew it wasn't from exertion. It was from a sense of excitement building quietly within her.

Something was about to happen. She wasn't sure what it was, or how it would affect them, or even if she would have forced it as she had if she'd taken the time to mull it over. It had all come about so quickly, she hadn't had time to think.

Walking rapidly, they crossed over a pretty wooden bridge that spanned the River Spaarne. On the other side they twisted and turned down narrow streets, going farther away from the city's center. Wim didn't say a word, except to give her an occasional direction. Nina didn't talk, either.

The houses got smaller and not as high. Their gables were plain, without any drollery. When Wim finally stopped, they were standing in front of the third house in a row of seven, each one a square, brick box with two square windows and a simple wooden door. "This is where I lived with my parents and brother," he said. He didn't point, merely tipped his head.

Nina felt keen disappointment cut through her. He was right. There was nothing much to see. It was an anonymous building in a working-class neighborhood that gave no hint of the life that had been lived inside. Nor was Wim's reaction much more telling. His face was a mask. The only thing she could say was that he seemed out of place, too tall and too elegant to belong here. Other than that, she knew no more about him than she had at breakfast that morning. Whatever it was she'd been anticipating hadn't happened after all.

Lowering her gaze, Nina murmured, "Thank you for showing me."

There was another moment of silence as Wim seemed to struggle with his thoughts again. Then, again, he finally spoke. "If you like," he said, in that same terse tone, "I can take you to see the farm near Lisse where my grandparents live. After my father and Hans died, my mother and I went there to live, too."

Nina's head shot up and her excitement surged. "Yes," she answered instantly. "Yes, I'd like that very much."

"It means we won't be able to go to Amsterdam," he warned. "You may not get another opportunity."

"That doesn't matter," Nina said with a flick of her hand. "I'd much rather see the farm."

They walked back through the city to the railway station, but instead of boarding the express train to Amsterdam, they took the slow train south. As it tootled along, stopping at every town, Wim remained wrapped in his silent thoughts. Nina didn't mind, though. As before, she waited. In the meantime, she occupied herself, as she had on her first day in Holland, by looking out the window of the train and watching the fields of tulips flip by in bands of vivid color.

Twenty kilometers later, in the town of Lisse, Wim rose and motioned for her to disembark. On the platform he spoke to a young boy loitering about, then pressed a coin into his hand. The boy took off running, and a few minutes later a carriage appeared. "It's a bit far to walk," Wim explained as he helped her get in. "The roads are muddy, too."

He had nothing further to say while they drove out of town, past the fields Nina had seen from the train. There weren't many houses now, only blue sky and tulips. Tulips and blue sky. At this slower speed and closer range, though, Nina could see individual flowers and not simply a brilliant flash. She could see the creamy, rich texture of the petals, the tidy perfection of their shape. Tulips, too, were quintessentially Dutch, she decided, neat and matter-of-fact, but brightened by their extraordinary hues.

Interspersed among the bands of color were bands of green leaves and headless stalks. Those were the tulips that had already had their blooms cut off so energy would go toward producing a bigger bulb. At the ends of the rows sat heaps of the flowers, now limp and lifeless. For Nina, it was a painful sight.

After a while the carriage turned into a long, straight lane, more like a wide path, really, that ran between two fields. At the far end of the lane a low, stone house was hunkered, its thatched roof hanging down like an ominous brow. Behind it stood a shed. Farther away a windmill turned. There were no trees around any of the buildings, no hedges or fences or walls. There was nothing to break the chill north wind when it blew, nothing except the house and the shed and the windmill. Despite the mildness of the day, Nina shivered.

As they drew closer, Nina could see that the yard around the house was empty save for an old wagon and a barrel. The yard itself was dirt, packed hard by decades of clog-shod feet tramping back and forth. Not so much as a blade of grass relieved the flat, gray surface. Nina shivered again. Even their poor cottage in Sicily had had flowers planted in rusty tins along the window ledges.

When they stopped in front of the house, a woman emerged from the open door. Nina knew at once she was Wim's grandmother. The resemblance was striking. She had the same long, lean build and the same handsome face, though hers was lined and weathered. Even the scrubbed cheeks were the same, albeit somewhat faded. But that's where the similarities ended, because she had none of Wim's amusement. Her blue eyes weren't the color of hyacinths at dusk; they were the color of the winter sky. And when she recognized Wim in the carriage, the corner of her mouth didn't crease. But come to that, Nina realized, looking from grandmother to grandson, neither did Wim's.

"*Daag, Grootmoeder,*" he greeted her, his voice emotionless, his expression blank.

"*Daag,* Wim," she responded, not moving forward. She was wearing an old white apron over a worn brown dress. Wooden shoes stuck out beneath the hem. Her hair was pulled tightly behind her head, nearly white with a tinge of yellow. She stood with her arms folded across her chest, almost as if she were trying to decide what Wim wanted.

Rather than tell her, though, Wim got out of the carriage and reached back to help Nina descend. He paid the driver and said a few short words, then waved him on his way. Nina felt a twinge of panic as the hack drove off, leaving her in this cold, lonely place. Although they were surrounded by fields of bright, beckoning tulips, in this packed dirt yard she felt trapped. Glancing again at Wim, she could see that he was feeling so, too. For some reason that discovery settled her down, and she was able to face the squat, stone house and *de grootmoeder* more calmly.

"*Ik heb een vriendin ter kennismaking meegebracht,*" Wim finally said, explaining to his grandmother that he'd brought a friend to meet her. Putting his hand under Nina's elbow, he steered her across the yard. "*Dit is mejuffrouw Colangelo,*" he introduced. "*Zij komt uit Amerika.*"

For another instant Nina fought off the urge to pick up her skirt and run. Instead, she took hold of herself and held out her hand. "How do you do, Mrs. de Groot?" she asked. Turning to Wim she said, "Will you please tell your grandmother I'm honored to meet her?"

A shadow of a smile creased Wim's cheek at last, but it was accompanied by a cynical gleam. Without comment, though, he did as he was requested. "*Mejuffrouw Colangelo zegt dat het haar een genoegen is kennis met u te maken,*" he translated.

Sweeping Nina with an impersonal gaze, the elderly woman

shook her hand. *"Hoe gaat het,"* she said in a voice as level as Wim's but without his usual warmth. *"U komt van ver. Kom binnen en ga zitten. Ik zal u wat te eten geven."*

Rather than translate this time, Wim interpreted. Raising his eyebrows slightly, he said to Nina, "I told my grandmother that you were from America, and she thinks you've come from there today. She's suggested that you come inside for rest and refreshment." With a shrug he gestured toward the door, adding, almost under his breath, "Don't expect too much."

The muttered remark did nothing to boost Nina's confidence. "Perhaps it's too much trouble . . ." Her voice died as she looked around for an escape. The battered wooden door didn't seem welcoming.

"We're already here," Wim replied, scooping up her elbow again and propelling her toward the house. "Besides, it's nearly time for lunch. My grandfather will be in from the field any minute now." As he pushed open the door and stood back to let her enter, the cynical smile reappeared. "Are you regretting having forfeited a pleasant trip to Amsterdam for this?" he asked, almost taunting.

About to step across the threshold, Nina hesitated for a fraction of a second. Then, lifting her chin, she declared, "Not at all." And strode purposefully into the house.

Once inside, however, she faltered. In the first place, after the bright sunshine outdoors, the interior light was dim. But what really struck her a stomach-wrenching blow was how painfully stark it seemed.

That there was just a table, some chairs, and a cupboard was something she could understand. In Sicily, they had almost no furniture themselves. But in the height of tulip season, there were no flowers on the table. Nor were there any pictures on the walls or any collections of mementos. The dishes on the shelves were lined up like soldiers, and the washrag was folded precisely on the edge of the black iron sink. Even the air was austere. There were no smells of something delicious cooking.

"Ga zitten," de grootmoeder commanded, pulling a chair away from the table and smacking its seat. Hastening to obey, Nina crossed the room and sat down.

She didn't move from that spot for the better part of an hour. She didn't speak and she wasn't spoken to. Not that she felt particularly excluded, because nobody else was speaking, either.

At least, not much. Wim asked his grandmother a few perfunctory questions, and she supplied him with a few perfunctory answers. After a time Wim's grandfather entered.

He was a tall man, too, though more heavily built than Wim. His square face was less refined, but it was ruggedly appealing, and, like his wife's, it was weathered by wind and life. Also like her, his hair was almost totally white, both on his head and around his chin. His upper lip, however, was clean shaven. Age might have slowed his step somewhat, but it hadn't stooped his shoulders. The impression he gave was of being exceptionally strong and hale.

It also seemed to Nina, as she watched him shake hands with Wim, that *de grootvader* had a softer light in his blue eyes than did *de grootmoeder.* Although his greeting could hardly be termed effusive, he appeared genuinely pleased to see his grandson. After he washed up and seated himself at the table, however, the conversation was as meager as ever. Long, blank silences bracketed the few brief questions.

Lunch, too, was rather spartan. Just bowls of milk and thick slices of bread. In a wash of homesickness, Nina thought about lunch in Stamford. She thought about the laughter and the chatter and the family warmth. Swallowing another mouthful of the milk soaked bread, she also thought about the plates of steaming pasta and tender vegetables. When they finished eating, Nina jumped up to help with the dishes, few though there were.

"Don't bother," Wim advised her as he rose, too. He slid his chair up snug to the table, spacing it exactly halfway between the corners. "She has her own system," he explained in the same toneless voice he'd used throughout the meal. "She'd prefer to do it herself."

Nodding uncomfortably, Nina followed his lead, sliding her chair under the center of the table. Then she stood there. After a moment she shifted from one foot to the other.

"Why don't we go for a walk?" Wim suggested. "I'll show you the fields. The Duchesse de Parme tulips are just coming into bloom."

Nina didn't need to be asked twice. "Excellent idea," she said, whirling and practically bolting for the door. She felt that if she stayed another minute in the gloomy quiet, she'd probably start screaming. Once outside, she took big gulps of the fresh, warm air and feasted her eyes on the colorful fields.

"This way," Wim said, exiting after her. He pointed toward the path that led behind the house.

Whirling again, Nina dashed down the path, half walking, half skipping, taking a lunging step then skittering back to keep from running.

"It seems that bread and milk agrees with you," Wim remarked. "You're full of energy."

It was such a relief to hear the irony in his tone, Nina nearly cried. "I've been sitting all day," she told him, both hands flying as she spoke.

"Of course," Wim agreed, wryly accepting her excuse. He knew better, but he didn't contradict her.

When they entered the field, Nina's spirits rose even further. Band upon band of Duchesse de Parme tulips filled her entire range of vision. Each band, exactly one meter wide, was packed with fiery red tulips that seemed to have been dipped in molten gold. Nina gasped in delight and reached out her hand.

Wim viewed them with considerably less awe. "My grandfather's been growing them all his life," he said, brushing aside a flower that leaned into the path. "His father grew them, too. The owner of the farm got a few bulbs from the breeder when they were developed in 1820." Lifting his eyebrows, he added, "It's the highlight of our family history."

"It's a good highlight," Nina insisted, stroking one of the lustrous blooms. "They're gorgeous."

"You'd be calling them names other than gorgeous if you had to get up at dawn to snap their heads off," Wim told her with undisguised roughness. "The earlier, the better. When they're really cold, the blooms snap off easily. Once the sun warms the stems, though, they have to be cut." He swatted one hand across the mass of flowers, then jammed both hands into his pockets.

Subdued by the harshness of his gesture, Nina didn't immediately reply. She didn't stop admiring the tulips, though, or enjoying the spectacle before her. At a moderate pace they continued their walk down the packed-dirt path that ran between the vivid field and a slash of a canal. A long, flat barge was nudged against one bank, and a few lily pads floated in the center.

While she walked, Nina tried to imagine what Wim was like at eight years old, when he first came here to live. She could just see a long-legged boy with blue eyes too big for his face. In her mind, she saw him standing in this field, the red and gold tulips crowding against him as he grew taller and taller with each passing season. And every year that went by, he had to bend lower to do his job.

Another thought flicked through her head, and she came to a sudden stop. "Who snapped the tops when you left the farm?" she asked. "When you got your clerical position, who took your place here? Who does the work now?"

Hands still in his pockets, Wim glanced at her over his shoulder, but he didn't break his stride. "*Grootvader,*" he answered, pronouncing the single word clearly.

Hurrying to catch up with him, Nina said, "But how can he do it all by himself? After all, even though he looks to be in the best of health, he isn't a young man anymore. Isn't it too much?"

In response, Wim just shrugged.

Nina's eyebrows knit as she digested his answer. Such indifference among families puzzled her. "Surely you can help your grandparents now," she said, her tone almost reproving. "I don't mean that you should come work in the fields, but with all your success, couldn't you afford to hire someone who would?"

Wim finally stopped and turned to face her. Afraid she'd spoken out of turn, Nina stopped, too, flushing guiltily. Then she met his gaze, and the flush became a shiver. The light in his eyes was as bleak as she'd ever seen it.

"Yes," he told her. "I could afford to hire someone. For that matter, I could afford to hire dozens of workers. I could do more than that, as well. I could buy them some furniture. A comfortable chair or two. Perhaps a divan. I could stock their larder, filling those empty shelves with herring and vegetables and ham. Or I could even buy this piece of land for them, so they could make the profit on the bulbs themselves. Easiest yet, I could give them a sackful of florins so they could spend them however they please.

"But quite frankly, Nina," he said, his voice as stony as his face, "they don't want any of those things from me. They won't accept my help. Nothing. Not a scrap."

Another chill swept through Nina with his words, though she didn't remove her gaze from his face. "They won't?" was all she could whisper.

For a long moment Wim remained grim and forbidding, then his expression softened. "Listen, Nina," he said, taking one of his hands from his pocket and picking up one of hers. When he felt how cold it was, he picked up the other and chafed the two together. "Not all families are as loving as yours. You have no idea how lucky you are."

She did know, but she didn't interrupt. In fact, she held her breath. This was the moment she'd been anticipating since she'd confronted him on the street in Haarlem this morning. She knew it was. She could hear it in his voice and see it on his face. She could see his emotions rubbing together, even as he rubbed her hands. Not daring to breathe, she waited.

It took a while as Wim struggled to form his thoughts and to force himself to say them. "They didn't want us here," he finally blurted out, plunging right into the middle. He stopped chafing her hands but didn't let go, just let them hang loosely, entwined in his. There was a distant look in his eyes, as if he were gazing into the past. Then he inhaled slowly and started at the beginning.

"When my father and brother died in a flu epidemic, we had nowhere else to go," he explained. His voice was even again, but very quiet. "My father's savings went to pay for the funerals. After that, my mother and I were penniless. My mother tried to find work, but there was none to be had. Nothing respectable, at any rate. Not for a widow with a child." He paused a moment and briefly shut his eyes, again reliving the memory.

"*Moeder* sold all our possessions, one by one," he continued, "but that only postponed our fate, it didn't change it. We managed on our own for a few more weeks or months, but eventually it came to an end. When all that was left were our clothes and a couple of books, my mother brought us here."

Pausing again, Wim looked back down the path to where the stone house squatted ominously. He stared at it a moment, then turned abruptly away, releasing one of Nina's hands, but tugging the other. "Come," he said. "Let's keep walking."

Nina complied without hesitation. Nor did she object to the hand wrapped around hers. Quite the contrary, she gave it a squeeze. "I can't understand why they didn't want you," she said, shaking her head. She tried to keep her tone mild so she wouldn't upset him, but her voice trembled with indignation.

Both the outrage in her tone and the sympathy in her grip touched Wim and brought a smile to his face. It was a sad smile, but it was a smile, nonetheless. "They didn't want us for essentially the same reason that my grandparents van Dijk didn't want us," he said. "Because my mother was from a different class, and that made them suspicious."

"You can't be serious!" Nina stopped short again. She made no attempt to moderate her indignation now.

"Oh, but I am," Wim replied, tugging her into motion once more. Bitterness tinged his voice. "My mother's parents disapproved of my father because he was poor, and my father's parents disapproved of my mother because she was rich. Or at least she was before she married." He shook his head, too, his disgust apparent.

"It just goes to prove that rich or poor, educated or illiterate, people are all the same. They're all afraid of anyone who is different from them. Different clothes, different addresses, different accents . . ." He flung his free hand through the air.

"For most people those petty differences are cause for the utmost alarm. Never mind character or morals or individual traits." He dismissed them with another fling of his hand. "If a person doesn't live a life identical to yours, quick! Pull up the drawbridge! The enemy's coming!"

When, after several seconds, Nina made no further comment, Wim glanced at her and saw her staring straight ahead. Thinking that he'd frightened her with his vehemence, he consciously smoothed out his tone. "That's why I like your Don Alberto so well," he told her, calm again. "I know he has very little patience, and he can sometimes seem like a spoiled child, but he judges people on their own merits, not on something silly, like the cost of what they're wearing."

"Yes, that's right," Nina agreed because she had to say something and her mind was spinning too fast to make any other remark. Pull up the drawbridge, Wim had said. He might have been talking about her. Wasn't that what her resolutions were all about? Hadn't she banished him from her life because he was different? Even while she'd acknowledged his kindness and his sense of humor, she'd rejected him because his hair was blond instead of dark. Because he'd been born in Holland, not Sicily. Because his life wasn't identical to hers.

Nina shivered again, from shame this time. She was no better than Wim's grandfather van Dijk, the wealthy Haarlemer who'd cut off his daughter forever because she'd married a working-class man. She wasn't even as good as his stern grandparents de Groot, who, despite their disapproval, had at least taken in the homeless mother and son.

And she was certainly beneath Don Alberto, her grouchy

padrone, who had clasped her to his thorny heart. At a time when most Americans regarded Italian immigrants as only slightly less loathsome than the Plague, the don had unofficially adopted not only her, but her sister and brother-in-law as well. Together with a Dutchman, they were the people he thought of as his family. Though she'd always been grateful for Don Alberto's patronage, now Nina felt unworthy.

"Are you all right?" Wim asked with some concern. They'd come to the far end of the field, delineated by a path running perpendicular to the one they were on. Beyond them lay another field of Duchesse de Parme tulips, and beyond that was a little copse. Wim stopped on the cross path and studied her curiously. "You're unusually quiet."

"No, no. I'm fine," Nina reassured him. She lifted her head and made a pretense of looking around. "Isn't it pretty?" she murmured, barely seeing the tulips. Then realizing how inadequate that sounded, how trivial a response it was to his story, she turned to look at him. "I was just thinking about what you said," she told him truthfully.

Her reply seemed to satisfy him, because he faced forward again and started down the path beside the far field, pulling her with him. He didn't comment on her remark, however, only saying, "There's an ancient ruin on the other side of the woods. It's a sort of castle, a tower really, that a medieval knight supposedly built to keep his family safe. I used to play in it as a boy, whenever I could get away, but I haven't been there in years. What do you say? Shall we go exploring?"

"Definitely," Nina decided. She needed an adventure to clear her head. "I've never been in a castle before. Even a ruined one."

They had traversed the field and were threading through the woods when Wim spoke again. It was shady and cool underneath the budding trees. A carpet of old leaves, bluebells, and moss muffled their footsteps and the sound of his voice.

"My mother was an extraordinary woman," he said. His words came slowly and haltingly as he reached back into his past. "No matter how dismal and desperate our situation, I never much minded while she was alive. It was only afterward . . ."

His words died away, but Nina could hear his grief still, the wrenching sorrow of a sixteen-year-old boy who'd been left in that joyless stone house without anyone in the world who wanted him. The pain of it seared her heart.

"I'm so sorry," she whispered, gripping his hand hard again. "I can't even begin to imagine how terrible it must be. If all my family were to die, I don't think I'd be able to survive."

"Oh, you'd survive," Wim said with complete assurance, quickly returning to the present. "You especially, Nina. I don't doubt that you'd cry an ocean of tears, but they wouldn't last forever. One day you'd wipe your eyes, pick up your hoe, and start working in your garden again. You have a magnificent spirit. It's too strong and vibrant to be defeated."

Giving her hand a little shake, he told her, "You can no more surrender your passionate embrace of life than you can keep your cherished flowers from blooming. That's why—" He cut himself off before he could finish the sentence, clamping his mouth closed and turning his head to one side.

But his words flooded through her, filling her with warmth, making her heart swell with pleasure. At this moment, in this woods, Wim's irony had fallen away, laying bare his genuine emotions. Nor was there any denying that one of them was deep admiration. Nina looked at him, at the clean lines of his profile, and wondered what else he'd been about to say. " 'That's why' what?" she asked.

He waved his hand in dismissal. "Look," he said, pointing ahead through the thinning trees along the edge of the copse. "There it is. There's the castle."

24

Nina let Wim distract her. Although what he'd told her was moving and sad, what was more moving was the fact that he'd told her. He'd taken her into his confidence, showing her feelings that had probably been buried for years, feelings no one else had ever seen. This calm and charming but private person had opened the door to his life and had invited her in. It was an act of tremendous trust, one that touched her deeply, one that made her nighttime resolutions seem foolish. But at the same time it almost overwhelmed her. Willingly, she looked where he was pointing.

Beyond the woods lay a wild meadow, dotted with buttercups at this time of year. In the center of the meadow sat an immense brick structure, round on one side, square on the other, and probably thirty feet tall. Here and there a slit of a window was cut, and a massive door sagged on its hinges ten feet off the ground.

"That's not a castle!" Nina exclaimed, her knot of emotions suddenly unraveling in laughter. She looked back to Wim. "Castles have turrets and moats," she chided him, her hand swirling through the air to describe what she meant. "They have buttresses and wings and walls that stretch on forever with what-do-you-call that edge along the top that looks like a crown."

"This architectural wisdom from a woman who's never been in a castle before?" Wim responded, arching his eyebrows, though his crease of a smile appeared. It was obvious from the way his eyes lost their tightness that her laughter had changed his mood, too.

"For your information, signorina," he told her, "this is a *Dutch* castle. Plain, practical, and very, very solid. The walls are more than a meter thick. Besides," he added, "it does have a moat. At least it used to in the days of dragons. The depression is still there, though the water has long since drained away. Come on," he said, giving her hand a tug. "I'll show you."

Feeling as she did, Nina would have gladly followed him almost anywhere, but this scene intrigued her on its own. After the chill and eerie quiet of the woods, the meadow was sunny and warm and open. As they swished through the hem-high buttercups and rye, Nina understood why Wim used to come here as often as he could. "That bit of forest is like a barrier, isn't it?" she said. "The world behind it seems very far away."

"It *is* far away," Wim corrected. "As long as we stay on this side, though, nothing from the other side can bother us."

Nina felt another shiver run through her as she again got a glimpse of his past. It only lasted a moment, though. Then the magic of the meadow took hold of her, and she had the sensation of floating. The bees and the crickets buzzed and whirred. Somewhere in the distance a bird was singing. Other than that, there was nothing from horizon to horizon. Just the blue sky, the old castle, and them, hand in hand. Not even a tulip field indicated man's presence. In a neat and organized country, this little pocket was wild and forgotten.

As they approached the castle, Nina could see that it had been abandoned for ages. The roof had caved in at some point in history, and the bridge to the door was gone. Beneath it, the dried-up moat was strewn with rocks and rubble. Someone, a youthful Wim, no doubt, had collected a pile of it and stacked it against the wall for stairs.

Now he shed his jacket and laid it on the ground, then gingerly climbed up the pile, testing each ancient stone as he went. The top of the stack was four feet below the doorway, but Wim hoisted himself up with ease and grace. In one nimble motion he was in, turned around, and seated with his legs dangling over the edge.

"It's still safe," he called to Nina, leaning down and extending his hand. "Come ahead. I'll help you when you get up here."

Once again Nina followed him without hesitation. He'd said that nothing from the other side could bother them here, and nothing from the other side did. Her senses of logic and reason lay on the other side of the woods, along with her arguments and resolutions. They were beyond the copse, back in the world where the past and the future resided. Here, in this hidden meadow, only the present existed. Only these moments in the sunshine with Wim.

It didn't matter what she thought in this meadow. It only mattered what she felt. And right now, seeing him sitting in the doorway of a castle, his hand stretched out to her, she felt as if she were under a spell. Glowing, no, nearly bursting with emotions, she clambered up the rocks toward him.

When she got to the top of the pile, she looked up and raised her arms. Above her, Wim smiled at her innocent gesture. Nina smiled in return. Bending closer, he put his hands around her, lifted her through the air, and settled her in the castle door beside him.

"*Eindelijk,*" he said, not releasing his hold, but still smiling, his face only inches from hers.

"*Eindelijk?*" Nina repeated, staring at him and wondering, as she always did, why the tiny dot on his nose took her by surprise. "What does that mean?" she asked, not really caring about his answer. She could feel his hands pressing against her, feel the heat of his hands through her clothes.

"Nothing," he replied, his hands sliding slowly down her sides. "It's not important." They reached her waist and paused a moment, fitted into the curves. Then they started a slow ascent up her back. Nina hunched her shoulders and rolled her head as his fingers left ripples of pleasure in their wake.

Wim's smile deepened when her chin tilted up, revealing the smooth, tender skin underneath it. Just a small, soft hollow above the lace collar circling her throat, but as luscious and tempting as cream. Not even trying to resist, he leaned forward and brushed his lips against it, leaving a kiss as light as the stroke of a feather. "It's only important that you're here," he murmured while his lips moved higher. His voice ruffled the lobe of her ear.

Another shiver shot through Nina, though this one radiated heat. She felt his breath tickling the side of her nose while his tongue traced the shape of her mouth. She would have gasped at the exquisite feelings it caused, but her mouth was suddenly sealed by his.

His kiss was gentle at first, just a suggestion, a hint, just the warmth of his lips on hers. But it seized Nina in the pit of her belly and spread through her like a fire gone wild. Flinging her arms around his neck, she strained closer to him, and he responded with equal ardor. His arms wrapped her into a crushing embrace, and his lips no longer just grazed hers sweetly. His kiss was deep and hungry.

When they finally broke apart, their breathing ragged and hoarse, Nina sagged weakly against him. While she waited for her racing heart to slow down and for the throbbing in her body to subside, she heard Wim speak, his words almost lost in her hair. "Welcome to my castle," he said. His voice was low and rough, but the amusement was there. "I hope you're enjoying your visit."

For the second time since they entered the meadow, Nina's feverish emotions dissolved in laughter. Pushing herself back in his arms, her gaze swept down the rubble staircase before coming to rest on his face. "Actually," she said, her own face illuminated with happiness, "I'm more than a little afraid I'll lose my balance in this precarious position and go tumbling into the moat. Kissing you is a dangerous occupation, I've found."

Wim laughed, too, in sheer delight, enchanted as much by her shining expression as by what she said. Wrapping his arms more tightly around her back, he told her, "I won't let you fall. I only throw enemies into the moat. Never the people I—" He broke off suddenly, a shadow crossing his face. Then he shook his head as if to clear it. "Never beautiful maidens," he finished in a light tone, though it sounded somewhat forced. "I have a policy against it."

Nina hardly heard his last remark, however, because she was listening to what he *didn't* say. Her heart started racing again and her mouth was dry with excitement. "You did that once before, today," she told him. Her hands slid away from his neck and down his chest as she leaned farther back in his arms to peer at him. "It isn't like you to leave anything uncompleted. Least of all, your thoughts." She jabbed her finger into the monogram on his shirt and demanded, "What were you going to say?"

But as he did before, Wim dismissed her question, this time by grabbing her finger and kissing it. "Maybe you're right," he said. "This isn't the safest place to sit. Besides, the view from the third floor is better. Let's go inside so you can see the rest of the castle."

Nina shook her finger at him. "Wim—" she began.

"Nina," Wim interrupted, grabbing her finger again and using it to pull her hand around his neck where it had been. He forestalled any further protests by leaning forward once more and sliding his lips and tongue across her mouth.

His tactic worked. At least for a moment. Nina's eyes shut and her head arched back as shocks of pleasure burned through her body. For a moment she let her fingers twine through his silky hair and let her nose fill with the clean scent of his skin. For a moment. Then, as she twisted to get closer to Wim, her dangling feet sailed out through space and banged into the four-hundred-year-old wall.

"*Aiou!*" she cried, breaking off the kiss and digging her fingers into Wim's arms for balance. "Yes, let's go inside," she decided, a shaky laugh chasing away her jolt of fear. This position was perilous in more ways than one. "It's got to be safer in there."

"All right," Wim agreed, although he neither released her nor rose. Rather, he pulled her to him again and rubbed his nose slowly along her jaw. "In a minute," he murmured, nestling a moist kiss behind her ear. He blew it dry with an unhurried breath.

Gulping in some air, Nina felt herself flush. Her skin was hot and tingling inside her clothes. "No, now," she insisted, though her voice was little more than a whisper, and she was nearly powerless when she tried to push him away. "Let's go inside, now."

With a sigh Wim unwrapped his arms, but he let his hands glide up her back one final time. Unable to stop himself, he leaned forward for one final kiss. "All right," he agreed again, savoring the taste of her full red lips and the feel of her smooth, round cheeks next to his. She was as warm and vital as the sun. "Let's go," he said reluctantly.

Inside the castle it was dark and damp, but Nina welcomed the chilly gloom. In the moments that she stood at the end of the deep doorway, waiting for her sight to readjust, she was able to regain her composure, too. Sort of. Although she could breathe more regularly, and the strength returned to her limbs, she could hardly be considered normal. On a normal day she didn't swish through a meadow in Holland to explore an abandoned medieval tower. On a normal day she didn't pass the spring afternoon in a magical world, completely alone with Wim. Yes, the castle air cooled her heated skin, but it didn't put out the fire.

"Step carefully," Wim advised, taking hold of her hand to guide her. "No one's lived here for over eighty years, and some of the floorboards are rotten."

Nina nodded but didn't respond. She wasn't thinking about floorboards now, her attention was riveted on the hand gripping hers. Or, to be more precise, on the man whose hand it was. The instant he'd touched her, shocks had rushed through her body again. Part of it, she knew, was her senses, as her dubious composure was overcome by desire. But another part of it was her emotions.

With every minute that passed, their intimacy deepened and she could feel her excitement growing. It had started this morning, on the street corner in Haarlem, when she'd asked him about his past. Her anticipation had built as he'd taken her from Haarlem to Lisse, to meet his grandparents, to see the farmhouse where he'd spent his youth. She thought it had culminated in the field of Duchesse de Parme tulips when he'd told her about his life. She thought she'd gotten as close to him as possible when he'd taken her into his confidence. Now she knew something else was going to happen. That hadn't been the end, as she'd thought, but rather, it was just the beginning. Her nerves prickled where their hands were joined.

"As far as I can tell, the family used the first floor for drawing room, dining room, and parlor," Wim said, leading her into the middle. "The kitchen was in the cellar."

Nina nodded again and looked around obligingly, though she

really didn't register what she saw. The first floor was a vast open space with two huge fireplaces, each one big enough to stand in. The thick, curved walls had been plastered once, but now the plaster was crumbling. Debris littered the wide wooden floorboards.

At the far end of the room there was a narrow stone staircase. Wim led her up the steps to the second floor. Dark and cold and a large, single room, it was very similar to the first. "I think the family slept here," Wim said. Nina gave another nod.

When Wim poked open a hatch on the top of an even narrower set of steps, however, sunlight suddenly blinded her. And as she climbed out onto the third floor, Nina was genuinely enchanted. It wasn't any more royal than the other two floors. In fact, it was a jumble of roof rafters and broken tiles. But there was something about the way the tall walls, with their ragged, torn tops, seemed to circle the sky that instantly captivated her.

"It's wonderful!" she cried, pulling her hand out of Wim's so she could run to the window and look out. The meadow lay thirty feet below her, like a tiny kingdom full of buttercups. She turned back to survey the open-air room, seating herself on the deep sill. After the chill of the other two floors, this one was delightfully warm. Only the merest breeze stirred the baking rays of the sun, trapped inside the walls.

Those thick, solid walls not only kept the sunshine in, they also kept everything else out. There was a sense of privacy in here, a sense of security, that was greater than any Nina had ever felt. The copse had blocked out the rest of the world, but this roofless, round room was a world of its own.

"I thought you'd like it," Wim said, crossing the room to stand in front of her. Reaching out, he brushed a tendril of hair from her face. Then he smoothed his hand over the thick waves rippling loose from her bun.

Nina's breath caught in her throat and she felt her excitement surge. She was conscious of his closeness in every pore in her body. He filled all her senses to overflowing. In this secluded spot there was no one else but them. They were the only two people in this world.

"I've never come here with anyone before," he told her, continuing the slow strokes. His fingers curved to comb through the waves.

The effect was mesmerizing. Shutting her eyes, Nina rolled her

head with the motion of his hand. Rills of pure pleasure coursed
down her spine. It wasn't only his touch, though. Not solely the
ravishing rake of his fingers that caused the wonderful feeling. It
was also his words. Once again he'd shared a secret with her. He'd
drawn her closer to him, drawn her into his private world. Nina's
eyes opened suddenly. That reminded her.

"You were about to say something to me," she prompted him,
lifting her hand to his wrist to stay his fingers. The delicious
sensation distracted her and made it hard to think. "You were
going to tell me something else."

Wim paused only an instant, just a slight hesitation, then he
pried loose her hand and gripped it in his own. Unhindered again,
his other hand finished its sweep, halting only when it came to her
bun. "Was I?" he murmured, disentangling his fingers from her
hair and extracting her pins one by one. He dropped each one to
the floor.

Nina swallowed hard. His deliberate movements sent shivers of
longing running through her. She shut her eyes again, this time
trying to concentrate. "Yes," she responded in a shaky voice. The
last pin came out and her hair cascaded free. Wim grabbed a dark,
shiny fistful, again twisting his fingers through the strands. Nina's
head tilted back and she inhaled sharply.

"Before," she whispered, clinging desperately to reason, while
wanting to give in to her feelings. "In the doorway."

"Mmm," Wim answered, bending slightly to slide his lips
across her upturned face and to place warm kisses on the tender
lids of her eyes. "I forgot." With the tip of his tongue, he
followed the curve of soft skin below her lashes. A strand of his
own silky hair brushed her brow.

Lifting toward him on the sill, her body throbbing and hot, Nina
nearly succumbed, after all. She nearly let herself be consumed by
desire. Nearly. Then, through the swirl and rush of burning
feelings, a cold shaft of intuition made her freeze. She had no idea
where it came from, or why she knew it was true, but she was
suddenly certain he was lying. After his scrupulous honesty, all
afternoon, his excuse now sounded discordant.

"No," she said, putting both her hands against his chest,
separating them, but not by much. His face wasn't far away. The
rosy spots on his cheeks were flaming, his blue eyes were
startlingly bright. Through the linen of his shirt, she could feel his
heart beating as hard as her own. She took a deep breath. "You

didn't forget,'' she said. ''You were going to tell me something. What was it?''

Wim didn't move right away, and he didn't respond. The sun glistened in his blond hair and filled the room. He was so still, a robin landed on the ragged edge of the wall above them and a monarch butterfly fluttered in through the window. Then he pulled his hand out of her hair and, with the other, cradled her face. The light in his eyes was still unusually bright, but it was softer, even a little bit vulnerable.

''That I love you,'' he said simply. ''I was going to tell you that I love you.''

Nina knew that that's what he was going to say. Practically since the copse she'd been certain that was the thought he'd left unfinished. Without precisely spelling it out in her mind, she'd known all along that her anticipation had been building toward this instant. But now that he'd said it, now that his words were ringing in her head, she couldn't completely absorb it. Those words which she'd been waiting for with such tremendous excitement were meaningless sounds in her ears. She just sat there, staring up at him.

Then something inside her exploded. He loved her. Her heart started hammering. It was banging wildly. Torrents of joy swept through her. Leaping up, she flung her arms around his chest and smashed herself against him in a hug.

''*Caro mio!*'' she cried. ''*Ti amo!* Oh, Wim! I love you, too!''

For an instant Wim was startled by her ardent assault, then he started laughing. At first it was a staccato laugh of immense relief, then it became deep and rich with jubilation. Wrapping his arms around her, he lifted her off the floor and swung her through the air. ''Maria Antonina Colangelo,'' he declared. ''I love you more every minute. You never cease to delight me.''

Clinging to him with all her might, Nina threw back her head and laughed, too. She felt light-headed. She was so happy she could scarcely contain it. She was on the top of the world with Wim Pieter de Groot, whose blue eyes were etched in her heart forever. Wim. He loved her.

Still laughing, they spun around the room, clasped in each other's arms. It was an exultant dance, set to music only they could hear, the crescendo of their love. Then Wim's foot caught on a block of bricks, he stumbled, and they collapsed in a sprawl on the floor. It took them only a moment to recover from the fall, to realize nothing was broken. Nothing, that is, but the giddiness.

Nina's laughter suddenly died as she became aware of their position. One of Wim's long legs was wedged between hers, the other was jammed up against her. She could feel the strength in his body as it pressed next to hers, feel his flesh underneath his clothes. Staring into his eyes, bright and gleaming again, she saw he was no longer laughing, either.

"Nina," he said. His voice was little more than a rasp.

In response Nina strained closer to him, eagerly seeking his mouth. She welcomed the feel of his lips crushed against hers and the demanding thrust of his tongue. She relished the sensation of his fingers burying in her hair and dragging down the small of her back. Craving more, much more, she slipped her hands under his shirt and gasped with pleasure when he undid hers.

Her yearning grew sharper, her need more urgent, when she felt his bare skin beneath her hands. Lost in a swirl of desire, she wasn't satisfied until he entered her body. Not until she felt him deep inside her. Not until indescribable thrills shot through her, again and again, chills that were blazing hot. Not until those thrills ebbed away, leaving a shimmering glow. Only then, gulping for breath, did she relax in Wim's embrace.

"You're wonderful," he told her, his lips near her ear. His chest was heaving, too. "No wonder I love you so much."

Lying in the sunshine, in the crook of his arm, Nina started to laugh again. It was, by no means, a derisive sound. Quite simply, she knew of no other way to release the wonderful emotions swelling her heart.

"You know," she said, leaning over to place a nibbling kiss on his marble white shoulder, "I think I've been waiting to hear you say that since the day we met in Castle Garden. I think I fell in love with you the instant I looked up from the floor." Giving another laugh, she ran the heel of her hand down his chest. "And now, nearly nine years later, I've finally heard those wonderful words. On the floor of another castle."

Wim laughed, too, and rolled up on his side, leaning toward her. "Which only goes to show how noble our love is," he said. Then immediately added, "Although I think we should consider elevating it from the floor. At the risk of sounding like a princess, I'll have to say this mattress is exceedingly uncomfortable."

"There are a few peas under the mattress," Nina admitted with a giggle, sliding her hand up and down his side. His skin looked so delicate, but his body was taut and strong. "Though I have no complaints about the pillow." She turned her head sideways, rubbing her face against that porcelain skin.

Gazing across at her, Wim smiled with pleasure but didn't immediately respond. He let his own hand wander, trailing up her leg and over her stomach to trace the firm, round shape of her breast. Still smiling, he watched Nina's eyes drift shut.

"Tell me something," he murmured, brushing long strands of hair away from her throat. "You have to satisfy my curiosity."

"Uh-huh," Nina answered dreamily, nudging her nose underneath his chin.

"If you've been in love with me since Castle Garden," he asked, "what was all that business in Stamford this fall? Why did you turn against me?"

Nina's eyes opened. For a moment she stared at his neck. Then she rolled on her back and looked at the sky. "Oh, that," she said flatly.

"That," Wim confirmed. He waited patiently for an answer.

It took a little while. Nina's mouth worked as images from beyond the copse intruded in this perfect world. Bleak images and unpleasant memories. She saw Gideon and Bianca in the Nursery and herself sobbing in her old chintz chair. She remembered her sleepless resolutions and her realization that she and Wim were doomed by their differences. She remembered pulling up the drawbridge and retreating to the safety of what was familiar. Suddenly shivering in the warm sunshine, she turned toward Wim, seeking reassurance.

He wrapped his arm around her back and pulled her against his chest. Sensing her distress, he laid a tender kiss on the top of her head. "I finally decided it was Dante," he told her. "But as soon as Albert wrote to me, I knew that wasn't so."

"In a way it was, though," Nina said slowly, her voice muffled and hesitant. When she felt Wim stiffen next to her, she raised her head and quickly added, "Not that I was ever in love with him. Not that I wanted to marry him. But I knew Mamma and Papà wanted me to. Don't you see, Wim? It was because he was Sicilian."

She shook her head. "I mean . . ." Stopping short, she let her head fall back against him. She didn't know what she meant. Her reasons, which had seemed so clear and logical in Stamford, seemed hazy and absurd in Holland. Had she really rejected him because his hair was blond while hers was dark?

"You mean because we're different," Wim said, supplying the rest of the sentence. His voice sounded stony and remote. "You mean because we have different backgrounds, you felt our love was impossible."

Without lifting her head, Nina nodded miserably. "Yes," she admitted.

For a long moment Wim lay rigid. Then he clasped her to him fiercely. "Nina, why on earth didn't you tell me this?" he exclaimed. "Why didn't you talk to me about it? Why did you just withdraw? Didn't you trust me even a little?"

Her face still against him, Nina could only shrug. "I don't know," she said, as perplexed as he. "It all made sense at the time."

Another minute passed and neither of them moved. He held her tightly, his hands splayed wide across her back. With her head against his chest, she could feel his heart beating steadily. Finally he spoke, his voice calm and even.

"Does it still make sense?" he asked. "What are you thinking now?"

Nina raised her head, at last, and pushed back in his arms so she could look into his eyes. "Now I think that I love you," she told him. "That's what matters most. Somehow we'll make everything else work out."

As soon as she said the words, she knew they were completely true. She loved him and he loved her and they had a world of their own. The confusion and anguish that had seized her fled as quickly as they had come. She was sure again. Sure and serene and happy. The magic of the day had returned.

"We'll let down the drawbridge," she decided. "We'll build a bigger one if we have to."

The tension in Wim's body melted away as he hugged her again and burst out laughing. "I'd be lost without you, Maria Antonina," he confessed, covering her cheeks and forehead with kisses. "Without you, my life would be dreary and boring."

Nothing else interrupted their blissful state, nothing else punctured the glow. Not his grandparents' cold farewells, not the suspicious glances their crumpled clothes got on the train. Nothing at all. At least not until they walked into the Maartens Hotel and met Serafina in the lobby.

As soon as Nina saw her sister's face, she felt herself turn cold with fear. Tears were streaming down Serafina's cheeks and she was wringing her hands together. "What is it?" Nina cried in a horrified tone as dozens of grim possibilities occurred to her. "Are you hurt? Are you sick? Have you been robbed? Has something happened to Dante?"

"No, no, no." Serafina waved away each of Nina's questions. "Is neither of us," she said, the words choking in her throat. "We're fine. It's Don Alberto."

Her hands half extended to comfort her sister, Nina froze where she was standing. "Don Alberto?" she whispered.

"It wasn't indigestion," Serafina explained through her tears. "He had another heart attack. Oh, Nina!" she cried, throwing herself into the outstretched arms. "He's terribly sick."

=25=

For the tenth time in as many minutes, Nina looked over the rail of the steamer and scanned the busy pier. She tried to convince herself it was the ambulance she was watching for, but she knew it was Wim she wanted to see. For the tenth time, though, neither one broke through the crowd. Turning back, she opened her paper fan and waved it in front of Don Alberto. "Better?" she asked.

Slumped in a wheelchair, Don Alberto only grunted. Speaking was too much effort. Suppressing a sigh, Nina fanned more diligently. He looked awful. His baggy face was looser than ever and his thin chest was sunken and skinny. Only his brown eyes were still sharp, though now they seemed more tired than hard.

Overwhelmed by compassion, as she had been continually this past month, Nina leaned down to place three fingers across his wrist. It was a ritual they'd established during the harrowing bedside vigil, a compromise between her need to express sympathy and his dislike of syrupy sentiment. But disguised as an act of checking his pulse, Don Alberto tolerated her touch. Right now it was a little weaker than it should be, "thready," the doctor called it. Fresh worry knotted Nina's stomach.

"Bad?" the don asked, seeing her expression.

Not answering him directly, Nina gave a little shrug. "It's so hot," she said by way of an excuse. "This must be a record for the last week of June." She laid her hand on his forehead to see if he was feverish.

"Stop that!" a voice shouted. "Take your hands away from him instantly!"

Jumping back in shock, Nina saw Edward and Reginald striding down the deck, and a stern looking nurse striding at their heels. Her rapid heartbeat slowed to a dull thud of dread.

"Haven't you done enough damage already?" Edward demanded as he got nearer. He didn't look at his father, slouched below eye level in the wheelchair. Instead, he focused his venomous gaze on Nina. "Was it another one of your arguments that caused my father's heart attack?" he asked, stopping in front of her. "Another stupid dispute over plants? More than likely, your querulous Latin temperament provoked him once too often."

"No," Nina protested, though not very strongly. Edward's slur was insulting and his assumption wrong, but still, she was racked with guilt. As she'd sat by Don Alberto's bed, these past five weeks, she'd blamed herself for his illness a thousand times. Now, under Edward's accusing stare, the guilt came surging up once more. Her mouth dry, she tried to rebut his charges. "It was the trip," she said. "I think it was too much strain."

"*You* think?" Edward sneered, crossing his arms on his chest, striking an imperious pose. Despite the heat of the day, he was wearing a dark wool three-piece suit. "Since when are *you* qualified to make medical pronouncements? If you're like most Italian immigrants, you've never even been to school."

Although Nina flushed at his vicious tone, she managed to maintain her control. She had no intention of vindicating his bigoted opinions about her temper. Before she could respond to him, however, Reginald spoke up.

"She may be right about that, Edward," he said, looking over his father's head, too. Even though he was the center of their righteous fury, both men treated Don Alberto as if he were invisible. "It probably was a strenuous journey. Far too big an undertaking for someone of Father's age and health. He never should have gone."

Amazed, Nina looked at Reginald. She wouldn't have suspected he was capable of such reason. If anything, the petulant expression on his face had grown even more self-indulgent since the last time she'd seen him. He'd inherited his father's jowly features, but while Don Alberto's bagginess seemed a sign of character, Reginald appeared merely puffy and overfed.

"But I'm sure it's her fault," Reginald added, not returning Nina's stare. "I'm sure she coaxed Father into making the trip. She has him bewitched, wrapped around her grubby finger, as it were. She even convinced him to bring some of her relatives along. You know how *they* are. Brothers and sisters and cousins all over the place, and only too happy to spend Father's money. The cousins, of course, came home weeks ago, as soon as Father got sick and the fun was over."

Nina's free hand retracted reflexively, burying itself in the folds of her skirt, even though it had been months since her strong fingers had been stained or grubby. And she found Reginald's slurs nastier than Edward's, his assumptions more infuriating. Whatever goodwill she had felt toward him evaporated instantly. It was back to the usual hostility. But it was also back to feeling guilty. Because the fact of the matter was, Reginald had hit closer to home than his brother.

It was true that Dante and Serafina had returned to the States three weeks earlier. Not because the fun was over, but because Don Alberto insisted they go. No one knew how long it would take the don to recover sufficiently to travel, and Dante was needed in the trial gardens. Serafina should be with her husband. The don had sent them ahead with Wim, who had left Nina behind in Holland with the greatest reluctance. But problems had arisen in his office, and it was either return to New York or risk ruining the business.

As wrenching as it had been to watch Wim leave, in a way, Nina had been just as glad. Although her heart soared when he entered the room, and she felt desolate when he left it, he was the source of her searing guilt. She hadn't "coaxed" Don Alberto to go to Holland. Quite the opposite, she'd been against it. However, Don Alberto made the disastrous trip to the Netherlands because Wim was there, and Wim was there because of her. So Reginald was right. It was her fault. She hadn't used Don Alberto for his money, but he'd been used, nevertheless, pulled into the middle of a situation of her creation.

More piercing than her remorse at having instigated the trip, though, was her shame at her behavior once they'd arrived. Increasingly captivated by Wim and his country, she hadn't paid proper attention to her don. She'd failed to notice that he was tired, that the miles of tulips were taking their toll. She'd let him eat the wrong foods and drink his fill of the rich Dutch beer.

And on the morning that his heart had started to give out, she flounced out of the hotel in a huff. As he'd lain in his bed, pain ripping through his chest, she'd lain in an abandoned castle in the sun, naked and blissful in Wim's arms. How could she have been so selfish?

"Well, your free run is over, miss," Edward said, nodding in agreement with his brother. "No more European junkets for you and your family. You'll do well to remember that you're servants. You're dismissed. We'll take over from here."

A wave of humiliation rolled on top of her guilt and turned her flush a deeper red. But unlike last year, when she'd fled down the stairs, thoroughly intimidated, this time she didn't budge. It might be that she was responsible for Don Alberto's heart attack, but that didn't mean she was going to compound her injury by leaving him alone with his sons. For better or worse, she knew the don still preferred his adopted family to the one that had been born to him legally.

"I'm staying with him," she stated, gripping one handle of the wheelchair, daring Edward to pry her away.

A flush rose in Edward's face, too, but it wasn't one of guilt or shame. It was pure fury at being defied. He pointed a rigid finger at her. "Maybe you didn't hear me," he said. "Your services are no longer required. Or maybe you didn't understand me. How do you say 'go away' in your language? Scat! Ffft! Go! Go! Go!" He made whisking motions with his hand.

"You've always been an idiot, Edward," Don Alberto spoke up at last. All eyes finally looked down, startled by his voice. It was weak but full of contempt. "You were an idiot as a boy. A bigger idiot now. Maybe *you* didn't hear Nina. She's staying."

Edward's face got redder and the lines around his eyes stretched tight, as did his voice when he responded. "I'm sure you're grateful for her ministrations, Father," he said, sounding a bit patronizing, as well. "No doubt it was a comfort to see a familiar face in a foreign country, but you're home now and you can have proper care. We've hired Miss Pennycroft to look after you. She's a certified nurse." Gesturing to the woman behind him, he added under his breath, "Not an immigrant gardener."

Turning his head only minimally, Don Alberto gave the nurse an assessing look. Miss Pennycroft had steel-gray hair drawn into a tight bun under her white cap and an imposing bosom stuffed into her white shirt. "You're fired," he told her. "Don't want you near me."

"Father!" Edward cried as Miss Pennycroft snorted.

"Don't worry, Mr. Blackwell," she said, addressing Edward. "I'm used to difficult patients. We'll soon come to an agreement." Smiling grimly at Don Alberto, she moved forward with the intention of taking her rightful station at the back of the wheelchair.

Nina, however, had other ideas. Her face was burning red and her pulse was pounding, but her expression was fierce and protective. They'd have to haul her away by her hair before she surrendered Don Alberto to this dragon. Stepping sideways and seizing the other handle, she planted herself behind the don. Miss Pennycroft halted abruptly.

Seeing the standoff, Reginald took his turn. "Miss Pennycroft has excellent credentials, Father," he said, his tone nearly as condescending as Edward's. "She knows just what to do to get you back on your feet and feeling spry. You're uncomfortable now, but once you get home and settled, you'll be glad to have someone of Miss Pennycroft's ability to help you."

Again barely turning his head, Don Alberto rolled his eyes to glare at his younger son. "I had a heart attack, Reginald," he told him. "Didn't lose my mind. Know perfectly well what I want and whom I'm glad to have around. And it isn't that woman. Get her away from me before I have her arrested."

In the tense moment that followed, nobody moved. Miss Pennycroft's hand was still outstretched, and Nina's still gripped the wheelchair, her knuckles white. Don Alberto still glared at Reginald, Reginald stared at his brother, and Edward's hard gaze flicked between Nina and his father. Down on the pier, travelers called greetings to friends who were meeting them. Stevedores shouted to sailors and porters yelled to stevedores. Out in New York Harbor a tugboat tooted. But in these few square feet of deck it was very quiet.

"It seems I've come at just the right time," a familiar voice intruded. "I was afraid I'd be late."

Nina felt her heart jump again, this time in excitement and relief. Looking away from the nurse, she saw Wim coming toward them. His blond hair was shining, and he looked fresh and clean in a light summer suit.

"I was held up in traffic," he continued, reaching Don Alberto and picking up one of his hands to shake it. "A wagon overturned on Tenth Street and had everything tied up in knots. We couldn't move forward or backward until it was cleared away. You're looking much better, Albert," he went on without a pause. "A little color in your cheeks. I wouldn't be surprised if the sea air did you good."

Turning to the brothers, he held out his hand. "Wim de Groot," he said, shaking first Edward's and then Reginald's hand. "We met at your father's birthday party last summer." Without giving the startled men a chance to respond, he went around behind the wheelchair and took Nina's place.

"Let me," he said, smoothly pushing the chair forward. "Your legs might be wobbly on land after ten days aboard ship. We'd better go, though. I noticed the ambulance arrive as I was coming up the gangplank."

Just like that. In less than two minutes they were walking away from Miss Pennycroft and away from the tense scene on the deck. "Good to see you, de Groot," the don muttered. Then he slumped deeper in the wheelchair, worn out by the confrontation that had just taken place.

"*Very* good to see you," Nina echoed softly. She didn't want her voice to carry. After a moment of uncertainty the brothers were trailing along behind them. But it was good to see Wim. Although it made her feel guiltier still, the sight of him renewed her spirit.

The past weeks had been grueling, especially after the others had gone and she'd been left by herself to guard the don and to fear the worst. He hadn't recovered quickly, as he had last year, but had hovered near the edge for days on end. Even when he had finally diagnosed himself fit to travel, he was weak and fragile and had no appetite. Nina hadn't known whether she should insist they stay longer or should hurry them home. The responsibility was enormous.

On top of everything else, Don Alberto still had his mind on business. Or, to be more precise, had expected her to be concentrating on the Blackwell Seed Co. So, in between the shafts of guilt and the bolts of terror, Nina had cabled Gideon with instruction. daily and had daily received his reports. On her own, in a completely foreign country, Nina had had to take care of a sick, old man and, from a distance, a struggling, young business. It had made her feel desperately alone and scared.

She'd missed her warm family and the contentment of her familiar routine. She'd missed seeing her gardens making their springtime show. But most of all, she'd missed Wim. She'd longed to find comfort in his arms. Because whatever else happened in the future, or had happened in the past, for one perfect afternoon in Holland, she had loved him absolutely and entirely. No qualifications or reservations.

Now, as he rolled Don Alberto down the gangplank and across the broad wooden boards of the pier, just his presence gave her strength. "You rescued us," she told him. "I don't think I've ever felt quite so relieved as when I saw you on deck. You looked wonderful."

"You, on the other hand, looked ferocious," Wim replied. His voice was low, too, but, as always, amused. "Both of you. If that nurse had had any sense at all, she would have jumped directly overboard." He gave a quick glance behind him to make sure the brothers were still out of hearing, then turned forward again in time to steer Don Alberto around a steamer trunk the size of a pony.

In an even lower voice he added, "You also look extremely tired. Both of you, again. Can I persuade you to rest a few days in New York, like sensible people, or will you drag yourselves home immediately?"

"Home," Nina and Don Alberto responded at once and in chorus.

Wim's crease of a smile appeared. "As I thought," he murmured. "You're one more stubborn than the other. Ah, well." Shrugging in resignation, he told them, "I can go with you as far as the train, but unfortunately, I can't accompany you to Stamford. The buyer for a major account is arriving from Chicago later this morning, and I have to spend the next day and a half separating his checkbook from his closed fist."

"'Course," Don Alberto agreed, nodding wanly. They'd reached the ambulance and the attendants were springing forward to meet them. "Got to take care of business first," he said as the white-jacketed men scooped him up and put him inside.

"Of course," Nina said, echoing again. There was no enthusiasm in her tone, though, only keen disappointment. "Business first."

A shadow crossed Wim's face. "Listen, Nina," he started to explain. Then the brothers were upon them, and Miss Pennycroft shifted her feet a few yards away. In the end all he could say was, "I'll be out bright and early on Thursday morning. I promise." But between Tuesday and Thursday were forty-eight hours.

The first thing that happened when they reached the station was that Edward and Reginald admitted they weren't accompanying them to Stamford, either. Nina's eyes opened wide in surprise. No wonder they'd tried to force Miss Pennycroft on their father. It was a way of fulfilling their obligations without inconveniencing themselves. Her respect for them dropped even further.

Not that Nina wasn't just as glad she didn't have to suffer their company, but it meant that for another hour and a half, she was all alone, again, with the increasingly weak don. For another hour and a half the burden of his life lay heavily on her shoulders only. For another hour and a half she watched him anxiously as he dozed and woke. And for another hour and a half she felt her disappointment grow.

Until Wim had said good-bye in New York, Nina hadn't realized how much she'd been depending on his presence. From the moment he'd appeared on the deck to the moment he left her at the station, she'd leaned on him, if not physically, then emotionally. Those last weeks in Holland had left her drained. She was strained to the breaking point. She needed help. She could have overcome her guilt and forgotten her shame if only he'd fastened himself to her, as he had that day in Castle Garden, and stayed with her until she was safe. But he didn't.

Instead, she transferred her trust to the first people who came bursting through the door to help them when they arrived in Stamford. To Orazio and Dante. To her family. "*O finalmente! Papà!*" she cried, throwing herself against her father. His huge hug and the well-remembered feel of his bristly mustache as he smacked kisses on each of her cheeks confirmed it. At last she was home. She moved out of his embrace and into Dante's.

They carried Don Alberto out of the train, drove up Newfield Avenue to the estate he'd built in the middle of nowhere, then carried him up to his bed. Mrs. Watkins had some consommé

ready in the kitchen. However, Angelina was more direct. She
brought a bowl of *pastina in brodo* to his room.

"Eat," she urged him, holding the bowl of aromatic broth and
tiny pastas in front of him.

Don Alberto let her feed him a few spoonfuls of soup while
Orazio, Dante, and Serafina stood at the foot of his bed, watching
him closely. Every time he swallowed, they smiled and nodded
encouragingly. Fishing through a valise for his medicine, Nina
smiled, too. It was good to be home.

Finally Don Alberto shook his head, refusing the dripping
mouthful that Angelina held out. "Enough," he said.

"Tsch," Angelina clucked, returning the spoon to the bowl.
She shook her head, too. Not enough to keep a bird alive, Nina
could practically hear her saying to herself. Out loud, though,
Angelina said, "Sleep now. I bring you more later." When the
don gave a brief nod and let his eyes drop shut, she shook her head
again. "*Che peccato,*" she murmured. What a pity. Turning, she
shooed her family out the door.

Twenty minutes later Nina sat down to lunch. It was hard to
believe it was only noon. It seemed as if a lifetime had passed
since the steamship had nudged into the pier this morning. What
a difference between breakfast in the stately dining room aboard
ship and lunch in this noisy country kitchen, her sisters all vying
for her attention. Laughing, Nina did her best to respond to each
question and comment. It was *very* good to be home.

"I don't know why you had to go to Holland," Angelina
declared as Rossana cleared the table of salad plates and brought
out a huge bowl of strawberries. "It was too much for Mr.
Blackwell to be among all those foreigners. I'll bet you didn't get
a single decent thing to eat the whole time you were away." She
lifted a shoulder in disdain. "What do the Dutch know about
food?" she sniffed. "No wonder the poor man got sick."

Nina's laugh faltered and this time she didn't answer. She
wasn't really sure, anymore, what the answer was. Why *did* they
go to Holland? What purpose was served? There was no chance
they'd do a fall catalogue this year. That project was indefinitely
postponed. So what else was there?

She vaguely remembered walking through the bulb fields and
inspecting the drying sheds, taking pleasure from the moment and
from the camaraderie of her companions. But that was before

disaster had struck. Before Don Alberto's heart had betrayed him. Now the memory was faint and unreal.

After lunch Nina went to the Store, where she was greeted by cheerful smiles from the staff and tall piles of papers on her desk. Just as she was surveying the scene in dismay, Gideon walked in and said, "When you're finished with that lot, there are more in Mr. Blackwell's office." He lifted his eyebrows. "Welcome home," he added archly.

"Thanks," Nina muttered, collapsing in her chair. She felt overwhelmed. And hot. Swiveling her chair around, she yanked open the windows.

"I know there are a number of problems that require your immediate attention," Gideon went on, "but I think you ought to let me schedule an appointment with the accountant for first thing in the morning. He wants to talk to you. Something about the quarterly statement not balancing."

Nina swiveled back to face him. Had his expression always been so sly, or had she just forgotten? "All right," she agreed without protest.

"Well, actually, he wanted to talk to Mr. Blackwell," Gideon amended. "But I suppose that's out of the question at the moment?" His voice held curiosity, a desire for gossip. Sympathy, however, was utterly absent.

Suppressing a wave of uneasiness, Nina nodded. "Ten o'clock," she said, adhering strictly to business. "Have him come here."

"You should also make the pansy seed order fairly soon. The word is out that some of the varieties are in short supply. There's a letter from Ames Brothers to that effect." Gideon pointed toward the piles with the tip of his pencil while he scanned the pad in his hand for further notes.

Feeling increasingly weighed down, Nina pushed the piles around until she spotted the letter he'd mentioned.

"The printer has written twice asking for a delivery date," Gideon continued. "He says he can't do a rush job again, and he wants you to give him sufficient time." He flipped the page with the flat end of his pencil. "There was a problem with the plumbing in the Nursery two weeks ago. The plumber was in, but I'm not sure it's fixed satisfactorily. Better speak to your brother-in-law."

For the next ten minutes Gideon went on in a similar vein, reciting a list of near crises that all clamored for her concentration and decisions. Propping her elbows on the desk, Nina massaged her throbbing head. Her chest was tight, creating the sensation of suffocating. How was she going to get through all this?

After a moment she became aware of the silence in the room. Gideon had finished. Looking up, she caught his eyes darting away. "Or perhaps," he said, holding out the pad, "none of this makes any difference." As before, there was a question in his tone—in fact, the same one.

Another moment passed while Nina considered the question. What was the fate of the Blackwell Seed Co.? Would Don Alberto recover and the business continue? Her hands clutched her head harder and a cold knot formed in her stomach. Or would he die and his seed company dissolve?

Nina straightened up in her chair and folded her arms on her desk. "Of course it makes a difference," she told Gideon. Her tone was brisk. "We'll have to solve all these problems as quickly as we can. I'll get to work on them this instant." If she could keep the business running, maybe it would keep Don Alberto alive, she thought, although she didn't say it out loud. Gideon shrugged and went back to his office while Nina attacked the piles with determination and purpose.

By seven that evening, the piles barely dented, her spirit flagged considerably. Who was she fooling? This was a formidable task. Maybe Edward was right. An uneducated Sicilian immigrant had no right to attempt it. Throwing down her pencil, Nina tilted back in her chair and closed her eyes. They were burning and tired. When she finally bestirred herself, half an hour later, it was to close the windows and leave the office. Whatever happened next would have to wait until tomorrow.

On her way home she stopped at the Big House to check on Don Alberto. Dr. Taylor had visited, and he'd left a nurse. A pleasant-looking woman this time, who was sitting on a chair outside Don Alberto's bedroom, crocheting booties for some baby she knew. "Good evening," she said, nodding at Nina without missing a stitch. "If you're Miss Nina, he's sitting up waiting for you. Go right in." Nina did.

Don Alberto was, indeed, sitting up, but he needed half a dozen pillows to support him. Leaned back against them, he looked shrunken and old. The cold knot retied itself. Was it simply because he was wearing a nightdress instead of a suit, or did he really look worse than he did this morning?

"How's the business?" he asked at once, though his voice seemed thin and small.

Squaring her shoulders, Nina walked across the room and sat down on the edge of his bed. "It's fine," she told him, knowing as soon as she said it that he wouldn't be satisfied.

Sure enough, irritation filled his face. It was just a shadow of the ill temper that used to grip him, but it was annoyance, nonetheless. "Don't you treat me like an imbecile, too," he ordered in that same faint voice. "Tell me everything." Again, Nina did as she was instructed.

More or less. Although she talked for twenty minutes straight, she edited the accounting as she went along. Some situations she condensed, some she glossed over, and some of the more minor problems she eliminated altogether. The really amazing thing, though, was that as she described certain problems, solutions presented themselves. Suddenly they didn't seem insurmountable.

Don Alberto listened to her without interrupting. Occasionally he gave a soft grunt or a brief nod to signal he'd heard, but mostly he just lay there, his eyes half closed. And after she'd finished her report and was sitting quietly, unsure if he was awake or asleep, Don Alberto lolled his head to one side, cocked open an eye, and mumbled, "Doing a good job."

If it had come from anyone else, Nina would have accepted the compliment for what it was. But in the don's mouth, it sounded unnatural. "No, I'm not," she burst out, wringing her hands in her lap. Her momentary confidence disappeared. "I'm doing a terrible job. I'm just stumbling forward, guessing what to do, and constantly praying that my guesses are right."

Both of Don Alberto's eyes opened, and he slowly lifted his head. "How do you think everybody else in business does it?" he demanded. "They guess, too," he answered for her. "After a while your instincts get honed, but you never stop guessing." He let his head fall back against the pillows. "That's what makes it fun," he wheezed, almost out of breath. He recouped for a few seconds, then said, "Ask de Groot if that's not the truth."

"*Ufa*," Nina said, with a flap of her hand, dismissing Wim's testimony along with Don Alberto's explanation. "You're just saying that," she told him. "I'm sure that there are dozens of things that I'm doing wrong, but you aren't feeling well enough to correct me." After a moment's hesitation, she gritted her teeth and forced herself to add, "Perhaps you'd prefer to have one of your sons take over. After all, they're both experienced businessmen and could make the necessary decisions easily. I won't be upset if you'd rather have one of them. I understand. Truly, I do.''

Don Alberto's head raised off the pillows again, and he gave her his strongest stare yet. "Bah!" he scoffed with nearly normal vehemence. "You've got more sense than both of them put together. Why the devil would I want them around here to gall me when you're doing the job better?" Having delivered himself, he sank back on the bed.

This time his praise had more of an effect. Nina felt her heart swell and a warm glow suffuse her. Still, she wanted to make absolutely sure. "But I'm an immigrant," she reminded him. "I've never been to school. And I'm a woman, to boot."

Without moving from the pillows, Don Alberto shook his head. "Thought you were too smart to let them get to you," he said. His voice was weak again, but still impatient. "Didn't think you were paying attention to their damn fool snobbery." He took a shallow gulp of air before continuing.

"Being an immigrant's nothing to be ashamed of, Nina," he told her. "If it weren't for immigrants, America would still be a wilderness inhabited by buffalo." Pausing for breath again, he gave a slight shrug, "Might be better off that way, but it wouldn't be the United States. Everyone in this country was an immigrant once, so don't let my beastly sons con you into believing differently. Their grandfather was a sailor from Liverpool who jumped ship in Boston. Didn't even bother to immigrate legally."

"I never knew that," Nina said in surprise. "In fact," she said, even more surprised, "I don't know anything about your life before I met you."

"Don't like to talk about it," the don mumbled. His eyelids were flickering. He'd used up nearly all his strength. "Don't trust people. No one."

Nina rose from the bed as if stung, feeling guilty for having overtaxed the don. Again. "I'd better go," she said. "I'll see you in the morning." She started to turn away.

"Wait," Don Alberto commanded. As Nina turned back, he stretched his hand out feebly. "Got to tell you something," he said, his voice barely audible. Bending closer, Nina took his hand in hers, remembering to place three fingers across his wrist.

"I trust *you*," he told her. "Always have." He gave his head a slight shake again. "Don't know what all the fuss is about men and sons," he said. "Much rather have a woman like you for a daughter."

It took Nina a moment to respond. When she finally did, the tears in her throat made her voice husky. "You'd better close your eyes and hold your nose," she advised him.

His brow furrowed in suspicion. "Why?" he asked.

"Because I'm about to kiss you," Nina answered. "And I know how much you hate it."

An amazing thing happened next. As Nina hovered above him, the bags under his eyes wrinkled and his jowls jiggled. Don Alberto was actually smiling. "Go ahead," he whispered. "I'm tough."

The tears were rolling down her face when Nina leaned over the pillows and pressed her lips to his cheek.

By the time Nina fell into her own bed that night, she was more exhausted than if she'd turned over the entire kitchen garden by hand. Her body ached with fatigue, and her mind was swimming dizzily. Holland seemed extremely far away and a long time ago. She could barely remember the afternoon in the castle. The wonderful combination of sunshine and euphoria was lost out of sight behind a distant clump of trees. The only thing that was real was Stamford, right here and now. Her family, the Blackwell Seed Co., and Don Alberto.

The memory of her visit with him this evening was still vivid when she finally shut her eyes. His frail appearance. His faint voice. His rare smile of affection. The last thought she had, before sleep sucked her away, was that from now on, she was going to dedicate herself to business, for Don Alberto's sake. He believed in her abilities. She was the only person he trusted. She wasn't going to let him down. Not ever again.

By noon on Wednesday her vow was being severely tested. The stack of mail on her desk not only didn't diminish, it actually grew. Her meeting with Arnold Willio was difficult. The stout accountant wasn't used to dealing with women. At first he didn't want to tell her anything. Then he started scolding her because the books didn't balance. A quick lunchtime call on Don Alberto fortified her determination, however. The don looked even smaller than he had last night. More helpless. More dependent on her.

Nina spent the afternoon slogging through the piles, dictating letters to Gideon, straightening out messes. At half past seven she went to see Don Alberto, and while she fed him six ravioli from the plate Mamma had left for him, she recounted the day's events. As he had yesterday, he merely nodded or grunted. But tonight when he muttered, "Good job," Nina didn't protest. Rather, she took it as a spur to work even harder.

She was in her office at half past seven Thursday morning, again whittling away at the piles. By ten o'clock she'd cleared enough space on her desk to lay out a pad and a few folders and start making a schedule. "Defining the boundaries" was what Don Alberto always called it. She was deeply absorbed in the task when she realized there was someone else in the room. Startled, she raised her head sharply.

"*Mi dispiace,*" Benedetta apologized. She was holding a steaming pot of coffee in one hand and a plate of almond biscuits in the other. A cup and saucer were stuck in each of her pockets. "I didn't mean to scare you," she said. "But I didn't want to interrupt anything important, either."

"No, no." Nina dismissed her sister's concern with a wave of her pencil. "Coffee's just what I need right now. And your biscuits look delicious. How dear of you to think of me."

Benedetta pushed a pile of mail out of the way, then set down the coffeepot and the plate and unloaded her pockets. "You're working so hard," she explained.

"*E bè.*" Nina shrugged.

She'd finished three of the biscuits and was on her second cup of coffee and fifth page of notes when she again heard someone entering the room. Thinking Benedetta had returned to bring her another selection of sweets or to retrieve the dirty dishes, Nina glanced up casually. And was really startled. Wim was coming through the doorway.

For a moment her mind went completely blank as she tried to place him. That shimmering blond hair and handsome face were wholly out of context to the pounds of seed and projected sales that were gripping her attention. But it was only an instant before her memory flooded back, her memory of an abandoned tower and joyous love. Her heart leapt and her cheeks turned warm.

"Hello, Nina," he said, closing the door to the office behind him. "Sorry, I'm late. I missed the early train by two minutes, then had to wait over an hour for the next one."

"Hello," Nina responded uncertainly. "Are you late?" While she hadn't exactly forgotten he'd promised to come today, she hadn't exactly remembered it, either. Actually, she was still a bit confused, seesawing between one world and the other.

One corner of Wim's mouth lifted up in a smile. "Only two minutes," he answered, crossing the room. "Or over an hour, depending on how you look at it."

As Nina watched him coming closer, her confusion grew. In which world did she belong? Which one was real?

"I also stopped at the Big House to see Albert," Wim continued, rounding her desk. The smile disappeared and his expression became sober. "He hasn't gained very much, has he? In fact, he looks and sounds even weaker than he did on Tuesday."

"No, he hasn't gained," Nina answered, suddenly focused. The pieces fell back in the puzzle. The picture was clear. Her world was her family, the Blackwell Seed Co., and Don Alberto.

"I'm afraid the ocean voyage set him back," she told Wim, eyeing him uneasily as he settled himself on the edge of her desk, one foot on the floor, one swinging free. "I should have insisted that we stay longer so he could rest and get stronger, but he was anxious to get home, and since I was too, I let myself be persuaded." She inched her chair back. The way Wim was sitting, his leg brushed against hers. It distracted her.

"I hope you aren't blaming yourself, Nina," Wim gently admonished. "I know how you like to assume responsibility for half of creation. But this time you've done more than any one person should be expected to do."

"*E bè.*" Nina shrugged as she had before.

"Never mind the modesty," Wim said, leaning forward to tap his finger on her knee. Nina drew in a breath. Those blue eyes never ceased to thrill her. "If someone awarded medals for situations like this, you'd get a dozen, I'm sure. You've been exceedingly brave."

Nina was starting to shrug again when he leaned further toward her. She froze with her shoulders hunched up and her amber eyes wide. Her heart was beating very hard as she watched his face coming nearer, as she saw the clean lines, the rosy cheeks, the tiny dot by the bridge of his nose. He was going to kiss her, she knew that, but she didn't know if she wanted him to. She had less than a fraction of a second to make her decision.

At the last instant she turned her head sharply. His kiss glanced off her hair. For another instant he froze, too. Then he sat up straight.

"Now what?" he asked in a very quiet voice.

Her shoulders were still raised, and her eyes were still wide as she turned her head back to meet his gaze. Her heart was still banging, too. "I don't know what you mean," she answered him.

"Good grief, Nina!" Wim exploded, thrusting his hands in the air, then letting them slap against his thighs. "Are you going to start this charade again? I thought we'd left that nonsense behind us. I thought we'd learned to act like adults."

Finally dropping her shoulders, Nina pushed her chair farther away. "Look," she said a little desperately. "I'm very busy right now. Can we talk about this later?" It was hot in here. Suddenly finding it hard to breathe, she swiveled her chair around to raise the windows. They were already open. The trial beds, freshly tilled and planted, stretched out below.

"No, we can't talk about it later," Wim answered her bluntly. "Not tomorrow or next week or next month or in three years, but right now." He reached out and grabbed her chair, dragging it back to where it had been. "Of course you know what I mean," he told her, spinning the chair around so she faced him again. There was unusual agitation in his voice, a stirring ring. "And very fortunately," he added in the same tone, "this time I know what you mean, too. You mean that you're pulling up the drawbridge. You mean you've decided I'm your enemy."

"No," Nina protested, holding up both hands. "No, I'm not pulling up the drawbridge. I don't hate you. It's just that . . ." She stopped and clutched her head, pressing hard against her temples. It was just that what?

It was just that she had to choose between the two worlds pulling her apart. She couldn't live in both. She didn't have the strength. Her hands fell away and landed in her lap. She chose the world she was sure of.

"All right," she conceded, meeting his gaze again. "Maybe that is what I'm doing. Maybe I am retreating. And you can say that it's petty and shameful of me. You can despise me for being ignorant. But I can't help it." She lifted both hands and spread them out, palms toward the ceiling.

"I can't do anything else, Wim," she said, shaking her head.

"Our lives are too diverse. I don't hate you, but I can't overcome the differences. The whole situation is hopeless."

"Hopeless?" Wim sprang to his feet and stalked to the window, then whirled and stalked back to pound his fist on the desk. "How can you say that, Nina?" he demanded. "How can you so blithely condemn it? I thought we'd discussed this backward and forward. I thought we'd decided the differences didn't matter."

"That was in Holland," Nina retorted, jumping to her feet, too. With her emotions so raw and her nerves so strained, all she needed was one spark to set off her temper. And he'd just supplied it. "To be more precise, it was in a fairy-tale castle hidden in a magical meadow," she reminded him. "We could say anything we wanted to there because we were protected by the copse. We were in a place of make-believe where nothing could hurt us.

"But this is where I really live," she said, swinging her arm around the room. She encompassed the gardens outside and the overflowing desk and the leftover coffee and the almond cookies on the blotter. "That was one afternoon." She shook a single finger at him, then banged it on her pad. "This is forever."

"You're being dramatic," Wim said in disgust. He whirled again and stalked to the window. Turning to glare at her, he said, "You're overreacting."

"No," Nina denied, shaking her head. "I'm not being dramatic. I'm being practical. Isn't that what you want? Aren't those the traits you find desirable? Practicality and common sense and logic? Use some logic now, Wim," she goaded him. "Look at this situation realistically."

"I am," Wim replied, crossing the space between them in two strides. He planted himself in front of her. "When two people are in love with each other, as we are, the *logical* and *practical* and *sensible* thing for them to do is to get married. Not to quibble over silly differences. Not to fight about whether they eat pasta for lunch or pickled herring. There's room on a plate for both."

Nina had spun away from him, about to stamp her foot and shout that he was oversimplifying, when one word penetrated the roil inside her. Married. Spinning back, she stared at him in shock. Because in all the long nights that she'd lain awake, that word had never once formed in her mind. During all the heart-wrenching arguments that had taken place inside her head, that word had never once been spoken. She'd skirted around it, thinking about love and the future. Even about a life together. But she'd never come right out and named it. Married. As in Mrs. Wim de Groot.

"Well?" he demanded, glaring back at her, but reading the surprise on her face perfectly well. He knew she'd understood his angry proposal, and now he wanted to know how she meant to answer it.

"No," she said. This time she shook both her hands and her head, so there would be no mistaking her reply. No. It was too much to consider. Too enormous a change in her life. She had enough decisions to make. Enough problems to solve. One more would be too many. "No," she repeated.

Again Wim read her expressive face perfectly, and this time he drew in a breath to compose himself. "You're tired, Nina," he told her, holding out his hands in a gesture of reasonableness. "You've been under a dreadful strain these past six weeks and you're under tremendous pressure still. Don't come to any rash conclusions. Think about this calmly."

But Nina wasn't ready to be reasonable. "*You* are the one who does everything calmly!" she shouted, batting away his out-stretched hands. "I'm not calm. I'm dramatic. Remember?" Her finger pointed at him accusingly, then jabbed into her upturned palm. "You see?" she demanded. "Everything about us is different. We're total opposites. Our marriage would be a constant conflict. We'd spend the rest of our lives fighting not only with everyone around us, but also with ourselves. It's better that we realize that now and go our separate ways before we ruin each other forever."

Wim didn't respond immediately, just stood there watching her face. His hands stung from her slap, and his heart stung from her rejection. It was an effort to remain understanding.

"You're tired, Nina," he repeated with deliberate evenness. "Maybe you were right. Maybe we should have kept this for later. I'll come out to see Albert again on Sunday. Perhaps by then you'll have reconsidered." He turned and walked calmly across the room, opened the door, and calmly exited.

Nina watched him leave, listened to his footsteps recede down the hall, then get lost in the clatter of Gideon's typewriter. When his absence was irrefutable, she crumpled into her chair and buried her face in her hands. What had happened? What had she done? Nothing made sense right now. She felt both jittery and utterly drained.

Wim was probably right, too. Without a question she was tired.

Exhausted would be more accurate. But that didn't change the facts. The inalterable truth of the matter was there were too many differences between them. There had been before the afternoon in the castle, and they were still there after it. Nor would any weighty references to drawbridges make them disappear.

Her mind reeling, she forced her hands away from her face and clutched the edge of the desk. She had to get back to work. Somehow she had to concentrate. This was where she lived, she reminded herself, as she had just reminded Wim. With trembling hands she picked up her pad and tried to make out the blur of notes on the page. Her world was her family, the Blackwell Seed Co., and Don Alberto. And that was her final decision.

But before Wim came to Stamford again, her world got considerably smaller. Don Alberto went to sleep on Thursday night and never woke up on Friday.

=26=

Nina stood between her father and Dante, gazing across the cemetery lawn. Twenty feet in front of her was a hole in the earth. Don Alberto's casket rested at the bottom of it. Nina knew it was there, even though she was too far away to actually see it. And even though she desperately wanted to dash across that bit of grass and drop to her knees beside the grave, she remained where she was.

A dignified black velvet rope was stretched between two dignified stanchions, and Nina was standing behind it. Its purpose was to separate the servants and employees from the family and important guests. To Nina, it felt like barbed wire.

By the side of the grave a dozen or two chairs had been placed, but they were occupied by Edward and Reginald, their wives and friends. There had been no chair for Nina, the one person in the world Don Alberto had trusted. Nor one for Dante, nor Serafina,

nor Wim. As much as it hurt to be roped off from the don, it hurt
even more to know that Don Alberto, in his final moments, was
being roped off from the people he had loved. The beastly brothers
were at the helm.

The minister's words drifted across the lawn, a nasal-voiced
eulogy of the don. A spark of anger flared in Nina as she listened
to the glowing testimonial. What gave this man the right to make
definitive pronouncements about Don Alberto's life when he'd
never even known him? Don Alberto had never once set foot
inside the minister's church and Reverend Talcott had never once
visited the don at home. And if he had, Don Alberto would
have found the minister's sermons pompous and annoying and he
would have made fun of the man's watery eyes. Thus, the portrait
Reverend Talcott was painting now bore little resemblance to its
subject.

But the spark died away, and Nina's attention wandered. She
was unable to sustain her anger. Or any emotion, for that matter,
even her grief. Inside, where she was usually vibrant with feeling,
she felt nothing. These past five days were a blank. Since Friday
morning there had been a hole in her life as ugly and as gaping as
the grave. So while Dante kicked his toe into the grass on one side
of her, and Orazio beetled his bristling eyebrows on the other,
Nina gazed across the lawn, Reverend Talcott's meaningless
words passing over her head.

Instead, she found herself absently thinking that the cemetery
landscaping was dull. Just a tree here and there, a few clumps of
bushes, a bare stone wall, and the grass. Don Alberto would never
tolerate such an uninspired site to rest in for all of eternity. She'd
have to do a little planting this fall when it was cooler. Maybe put
out some pots of annuals until then. Four-o'clocks. He always
liked those, enjoying the fragrant trumpets of flowers that opened
up in the evening. And snapdragons. And a pot with lobelia and
toadflax spilling over the side. And . . .

Her musings were interrupted by motion all around her. The
service was done. On the other side of the rope the small group
was filing past the grave and dropping handfuls of dirt on top of
the coffin. On this side of the rope, however, people were moving
purposefully toward the carriages. They had to get back to the Big
House and prepare for the reception that followed. Only the
Colangelos lingered an extra moment while they said their own
silent prayers. They could afford not to hurry, though. They

weren't needed at the Blackwell estate today. And perhaps wouldn't be ever again.

Finally Orazio turned away from the grave and solemnly offered his arm to Angelina. Dante turned, too, and offered his to Serafina. Pressed against the rope, Nina stood alone. Completely dazed, she didn't know which way to turn.

"Come, Nina," a familiar voice said, and she felt her hand lifted and slipped into the crook of Wim's arm. "I'll walk you to the carriage."

Nina followed him obediently, glad to be given a direction, though a flicker of surprise pierced through the fog she was in. "Where were you?" she asked, glancing up at him. "I didn't see you anywhere."

"I was right behind you," Wim answered. He hadn't released her hand entirely, but rather, kept his fingers curled around two of hers. "Next to Maria Stella." They walked quietly for a few more yards, then he added, "You didn't think I would miss Albert's funeral, did you?" His voice was subdued, but incredulous.

"No, no," Nina reassured him, but vaguely, as if she were having trouble concentrating on what she was saying. Which she was. "But I find it strange they didn't let you sit near the grave," she said with similar detachment. "After all, you're a successful businessman, and you look very American."

Glancing at him again, she nodded, confirming her observation. "If it weren't for your hint of an accent, anyone would think you'd been born in a mansion on Fifth Avenue."

"You make that sound more like a curse than a compliment," Wim responded. There was a touch of amusement in his remark, despite the grim set of his jaw.

"No, no," Nina again denied, though there wasn't any energy in her voice this time, either.

"Well, in this instance, I think it's probably the case," Wim conceded, "It's certainly no honor to be associated with *them*." He cocked his head toward the drive up ahead, toward six carriages hung with black crepe and gauze. Teams of black horses, bedecked in black harness and plumes, were hitched to them, and groups of ladies and gentlemen, bedecked in black silks and veils, were getting into them in order of importance. Even this was a social occasion.

"They would have let me sit with them, you know," Wim told her. "They looked me over and pointed me to a chair. But when

I saw you were standing behind that rope, that's where I went, too.''

As it had before, faint surprise filtered through Nina's daze. Enough, at any rate, to make her stop walking, which made Wim stop, too. "Why?" she asked, looking up at him again. "I would have thought you'd want to be as close to Don Alberto as possible. I wouldn't have thought it mattered who else was or wasn't in the vicinity.'' Her eyebrows knitting, she regarded him quizzically.

"You did come to pay your respects to *him*, didn't you?" she asked.

"I did," Wim answered promptly. "Absolutely. I came to let Albert know I'll never forget him. But you see, Nina," he explained, tapping on the back of her hand with his finger, "I don't believe his spirit is trapped inside a box in the ground. And I certainly don't believe it was hovering among that bunch of hypocrites, or was listening to the mealy-mouthed rubbish that minister was spouting.

"In my opinion, if Albert's spirit was present anywhere today, it was stationed right about here." This time he tapped her shoulder. "If Albert bothered to come today, at all, I know he would have put himself as close to you as he could get." Lifting his brows, he said, "So that's where I put myself, as well."

For a moment Nina's surprise continued to grow. Then something thawed inside her. A sensation of comfort spread through her, a tender feeling, a sad sort of tranquility. "You sounded almost like Don Alberto just then," she said, her voice husky and low. Because along with the comfort, there also came the searing pain that it soothed.

"You're never so rude, no matter what you're thinking. You have the best manners of anyone I know. Only Don Alberto would insult people, or scoff at them, or call them names at will."

"Then it worked," Wim said. A hint of a smile creased his sober expression. "It was his way of letting me know he was listening. You see? I knew Albert would be wherever you were." About to turn again and tug her along, he seemed to change his mind, remaining, instead, as he was. Sympathy shone in his eyes.

"He always will be, too, Nina," he told her, running his finger down her cheek in the approximate path of a tear. "You can count on that. He'll always be there. You'll never lose him."

A rush of emotion choked off her voice, making it impossible for Nina to answer. Wim's words had awakened the feelings in her heart, but now, all at once, they were too much for her to cope with. After the first comforting wave of tranquillity, the pain was coming faster and hurting her more. No matter what wonderful things Wim said about his spirit on her shoulder, Don Alberto was gone forever, and she missed him terribly.

It was awful to think she'd never see him again. Never see his pouchy face, or see him hustling along, his head and shoulders thrust forward, his skinny legs pumping. It hurt to know she'd never argue with him again, or share a pot of tea and a cozy horticultural chat. No more Sunday dinners in the Colangelo kitchen or lunches in New York restaurants. No more staff meetings, or business discussions, or exhausting sessions that stretched her mind and imagination to their limits. And no more surges of triumph and pride when they accomplished what they'd set out to do.

It may have been true that Nina was the only person in all the world that Don Alberto trusted, but it was also true that, in all the world, Don Alberto was the person who believed in her the most. He was *il padrone*, the don, her generous patron. And her exacting mentor, her cranky companion, and her dearest friend. Now he was dead. A sob came up in her throat and came out in an anguished gasp.

"*Coraggio,* Nina," Wim said, gripping her hand. "Isn't that what you say in Italian? Doesn't it mean 'have courage'? In Dutch, we say '*Kop op.*'" He shrugged, settling her hand more securely on his arm. "It's all the same thing. It all means that life goes on. No matter how dismal today seems, the sun will rise tomorrow." Squeezing her fingers harder, he looked at her steadily and said, "You must believe me. It will."

As she bit her lip to contain her tears, Nina could only nod. There was no comfort in his words now, no melancholy sense of tranquility. In her head she knew that what he said was undoubtedly right, but that didn't make any difference, because it was in her heart that she hurt unbearably.

"Come," he directed again, starting to walk but keeping his eyes fixed on her worriedly. When he saw that she was managing, that she was putting one foot in front of the other, he turned forward and continued talking.

"Your family is waiting for you," he said, looking at the carriages where her parents, sisters, and brother-in-law sat. Nine people. Nine pairs of eyes watching them cross the lawn. Nine expressions ranging from curious to suspicious. Nine Sicilians regarding the Dutchman. Wim gave a silent sigh while he counted his allies among them. Two. Dante and Serafina, with two more possible neutrals. Maria Stella and Benedetta.

He made no further comment as they continued toward the drive, their footsteps almost soundless on the lawn. Then, a few yards short of the carriage, he stopped again, and again Nina was faintly surprised. Tilting her head, she looked at him. He was studying her.

"What do you intend to do now?" he asked.

Simple as it was, the question confused Nina. Glancing uncertainly between Wim and the carriage, she tried to form an answer.

"There's a reception at the Big House," she mumbled. "Not for us, of course. But Mamma cooked and Benedetta made cakes, and I think that some of the staff will come by." She rubbed her forehead, struggling to think of what else would happen and who else it would happen with.

"No," Wim said, giving her hand a gentle shake. "That's not what I meant. I didn't mean today. I meant what you intend to do about the future."

"Oh." Her voice sounded flat as Nina pulled her hand free from his clasp. Turning, she gazed across the cemetery lawn. Workers with their sleeves rolled up above their elbows were unceremoniously shoveling dirt into Don Alberto's grave. It was hot, and one of them paused to wipe his brow. After a long moment she turned back and looked at Wim, though the light in her eyes was distant and unseeing. "I don't know." She shrugged. Then she looked at the grass.

Worry clouded Wim's clear face again as he took note of her drooping shoulders. "I'll be out for a visit in a few days' time," he said. "We can talk more about it when I come again." Then he guided her the rest of the way to the carriage and helped her climb onto the seat, where her family swallowed her up.

The question was taken out of Nina's hands, however, before the day was out. When the knock sounded on the front door, she was crowded into their rarely used parlor with Gideon, Mrs. Watkins, five gardeners, a stableboy, three of the girls from the Store, and all of her family. Scattered around the room were remnants of Angelina's refreshments, although the cup of coffee balanced on Nina's knees was barely touched and the slice of orange cake on her saucer was only nibbled.

No one remarked on the knock, not on an occasion like this. In fact, Nina, absently listening to Alice tell Salvatore Cascio about baseball, hardly heard it, let alone saw Lucia get up to answer it. But the next thing she knew, the buzz of conversation in the room had stopped, and everyone was staring at the doorway. Somewhat startled, Nina turned to stare, too.

Edward's butler was standing there, a man whose expression was almost as arrogant as his employer's. Reed thin, with a nose like a beak, his high voice suited him perfectly. "Mr. Blackwell has asked the following persons to come to his house at half past five in the evening," he announced. Then he drew a folded paper from the breast pocket of his jacket, crackled it open in the deepening silence, looked down his long nose, and read the list.

"Mrs. Amelia Watkins. Mr. Gideon O'Shea." He enunciated each name deliberately, as if it were distasteful in his mouth. "Mr. and Mrs. Dante da Rosa. Mr. Orazio Colangelo." Here his haughty pose faltered as his tongue got tangled in the Italian. "And Miss Maria Antonina Colangelo," he finished, a bit garbled.

After refolding the page and replacing it in his pocket, he regained his crisp composure. "Half past five," he warned, casting his eye around the room. Then he turned on his heel and left.

"Well!" Mrs. Watkins was the first to break the silence. "What do you suppose that show of theatrics was all about?" she wondered, plumping herself up indignantly.

"*E bè*," Orazio responded, shaking his shaggy head. "No good," he decided and made a slashing gesture across his neck.

"Going to sack us all, eh?" Gideon spoke up. There were red spots of anger in his cheeks and bitterness in his tone. "Didn't even wait for the old man to get cold before they wielded the ax."

"I always said those two were a heartless pair," Mrs. Watkins declared. Yanking her blouse across her ample bosom, she looked around the room for a witness. Finding neither Mary nor Fiona, she settled her gaze on Nina.

"Didn't I say that to you more than once?" she demanded. "Didn't I say that they're as cold as ice? And high and mighty!" she went on without waiting for an answer. "Well! Did you happen to hear that scarecrow tell us that Mr. Blackwell wanted us to come to *his* house? Their poor father dead not even a week and already forgotten.'' Her chest heaved in outrage.

''Yes, I heard,'' Nina said uneasily. A shiver had run down her back when the butler had uttered those words. Only a week ago, the ''beastly'' sons had been nothing more than unwelcome guests. Now they were the lords of the manor. It was an uncomfortable feeling.

A similar shiver ran down Nina's back when they were ushered into the library at the appointed hour. Edward and Reginald occupied the leather armchairs. Messrs. Brown and Haverford, Don Alberto's lawyers, were seated behind his desk. Somehow it changed the whole character of the room, though none of the furnishings had been touched. Yet. But it seemed neither like the peaceful sanctuary where Nina had spent hundreds of winter hours cozily reading, nor like the busy office where the Blackwell Seed Co. had been born.

''Thank you for coming,'' Mr. Haverford said as he glanced up from the papers in front of him. Peering over the rims of his spectacles, he gestured to six straight-backed chairs that had been carried in from the dining room. ''Please be seated.''

The small group filed in and sat down in a single line. They took their seats in the order they entered. Thus, Nina found herself wedged between Gideon and Mrs. Watkins and couldn't see any of her family without leaning out or craning her neck around Mrs. Watkins's bosom. Edward and Reginald were in perfect view, though they both chose to ignore the group's presence. And on top of everything else, the French doors were closed, so the room was hot and stuffy. With a pang, Nina remembered the staff meetings that had taken place here. This wasn't like any of them. Her uneasiness increased.

''We've called you here this evening to read the last will and testament of Mr. Albert Blackwell,'' Mr. Brown said. He wore spectacles, too, but where Mr. Haverford's slid down his long, thin nose, Mr. Brown's seemed riveted in place. ''You've each been named.''

On either side of her, Gideon and Mrs. Watkins sat up straighter, the scowls on their faces suddenly replaced by smiles. Nina shared their start of surprise, but she didn't share their pleasure. She greatly resented these men sitting behind Don Alberto's desk, in his library, on his estate, carving up everything he'd worked for all his life and doling it out piece by piece.

When Mr. Brown began to read the will, however, her resentment washed away in grief. Despite a certain legal tinge to the words, Don Alberto's voice emerged, clear as day. It was he who was doing the doling. She could just imagine him scratching furiously on his pad as he composed his will and figured out his final gifts. A lump rose up in her throat.

To every employee who'd worked for him at least a year, he'd bequeathed a full month's salary. Nina did some fast remembering and realized that included all the Italian gardeners, but not Alice or her comrades at the Store. She shrugged apologetically, sure that Don Alberto hadn't meant to die so soon and slight them. In their armchairs by the desk, however, Edward and Reginald cleared their throats and shifted their legs, as if to signal their patriarchal patience with these rewards to faithful retainers.

"'If Mrs. Amelia Watkins is still in my employ at the time of my death, I bequeath to her the sum of one hundred and fifty dollars,'" Mr. Brown read. Beside Nina, Mrs. Watkins gasped, then snatched her handkerchief out of her sleeve and started to dab her eyes. Mr. Brown glanced at her briefly but continued without a pause.

"'She deserves it for her perseverance, if not for her cooking.'" Mrs. Watkins's handkerchief hesitated, and her chubby face wrinkled in confusion. Nina actually felt a smile starting to form and hastily suppressed it. Even from the grave Don Alberto was being wicked.

"'Similarly, if Mr. Gideon O'Shea is still in my employ at the time of my death, I bequeath to him the sum of two hundred dollars.'" Looking like the cat that ate the cream, Gideon's eyes darted around the room. He waited to hear what else Don Alberto had to say, but Mr. Brown had nothing more to add. Gideon was good at his job. Period.

"'To Mr. Dante da Rosa, and to his wife, Mrs. Serafina Colangelo da Rosa, I bequeath the sum of five hundred dollars each.'" This time, Nina gasped, too. A thousand dollars was a veritable fortune. "'They are both smart and talented and deserve a boost,'" Mr. Brown continued to read. "'I hope this helps them establish a foothold in America.'" On the other side of the increasingly cross Mrs. Watkins, Nina could hear her sister crying softly. Nina's own eyes felt suspiciously moist, and the lump in her throat got bigger.

Mr. Brown adjusted his glasses as Mr. Haverford handed him

the next page of the will. Focusing, he went on. " 'To Mr. Orazio Colangelo, my groundskeeper for as long as I've lived in Stamford, I bequeath the sum of three thousand dollars.' " Nina's mouth dropped open, and she heard her father's feet shuffle. " 'He and his whole family have been exceptionally loyal and hardworking in turning a cow pasture into a showpiece. I've always enjoyed his wife's meals, too.' "

The tears spilled over and ran down Nina's cheeks. Dear Don Alberto, she thought. In his own gruff way he'd taken care of everybody. If Papà never worked again, he could live for the rest of his life without worry, a more than generous reward for freely given loyalty.

For the first time, Mr. Brown paused, giving Nina a long look. Afraid that she was making a spectacle of herself, Nina quickly wiped her eyes and mopped her cheeks with her sleeve. Her arm was still raised in front of her face when Mr. Brown looked back at the will and resumed reading.

" 'To Miss Maria Antonina Colangelo, my gardening companion and friend, I bequeath my entire property on Newfield Avenue in Stamford, Connecticut, including any buildings that shall stand upon it and any furnishings within those buildings.' " Nina's arm slowly fell away, and she stared at the two lawyers, disbelieving.

" 'In addition, I bequeath to her my one hundred percent ownership of the Blackwell Seed Company and any properties, monies, or other assets that shall attach themselves to said business. Both the estate and the seed company are the result of her imagination and hard work, and she is the rightful heir. I trust her to make them both thrive.' "

Again Mr. Brown paused to give Nina a searching look, but this time she didn't move. She couldn't. She wasn't even sure she could breathe. She had no idea how to react to this astonishing development, whether to laugh or cry or collapse. If Don Alberto had been there, she would have argued with him. He wasn't, though. Once again, he had the final word.

But if Nina had trouble trying to decide how to react, no one else had a similar problem. Mrs. Watkins was sniffing and attempting to draw her bulky body up self-righteously, while Gideon was looking at her with undisguised interest. The brothers, however, were the most direct. And the most vocal.

"Tart!" Edward cried, leaping to his feet and pointing a

quivering finger in her direction. "You conniving, manipulating little hussy!"

"Italian vixen!" Reginald chorused, also jumping up. He thumped his fist on the desk. "You've been working on Father for years, buttering him up with your oily Latin charm. God knows what disgusting and immoral lengths you went to to convince him to leave you his estate."

"Don't think you'll get away with this, Miss Immigrant," Edward said viciously, continuing to wave his finger at her. "Don't go running back to your macaroni friends, flaunting your new riches, because we are going to contest the will. We'll prove that you used your dubious wiles to seduce a sick old man, to shamefully trick and deceive him."

"Shameful," Reginald echoed.

"You and your family will wind up with nothing," Edward promised. "And *that* is exactly what you people deserve."

Total silence followed the outburst as Nina shrank back in her chair. Overwhelmed by all that had happened in the last three minutes, she didn't know what to do. Already stunned by the don's bequest, his sons' verbal barrage left her thoroughly shaken. Nor was there, anywhere in her field of vision, so much as a friendly glance. Mrs. Watkins was enjoying her discomfort, Gideon found it curious, and the lawyers had no expressions. Sitting in the stuffy room, Nina felt terribly alone and vulnerable. She put her hands in her lap and stared at them.

Finally she heard the sound of someone rising, then two footsteps that ended next to her chair. "*Vieni,* Nina," Dante said quietly. She looked up at him holding out his arm. "Come," he said in heavily accented English. "The air is very bad in here."

Despite his accent and despite the dirt stains on his fingers, Dante possessed indisputable dignity. His profile reflected ancient civilization. His manner was of a man at peace. Lifting her chin, Nina rose and put her hand on her brother-in-law's arm. Followed by Serafina and Orazio, they crossed the room, opened the French doors, walked out of her house, down the terrace steps, and home through her gardens.

27

Nina hated Mondays. They never used to bother her. Very often, in fact, she'd looked forward to them. If she were in the middle of planting, or had had an inspiration on her day off, she'd actually been eager to get back to work. But all that had changed now. Now she'd come to dread them.

Now Mondays meant the arrival of a new stack of mail. And that meant new problems and new demands and new bills that were way overdue. Don Alberto may have left his estate and business to her, but his miserable sons had fixed it so she didn't have access to the bank accounts that went with them. Not while the will was being contested. And it took money to make them both operate. More money than dribbled in from seed orders in the summer. As a result, every employee, from the gardeners to Mrs. Watkins to the stable lads, had quit. Everyone except Gideon, that is.

Gideon. Mondays also meant having to face him again, after thirty-eight blessed hours of not having seen him. In her determination to hold together the empire that Don Alberto had entrusted to her, Nina had marshaled every resource at her command. She'd enlisted her entire family. Even eleven-year-old Stella had been put to work filling orders. There were some things, though, that none of them knew how to do, and that's where Gideon came in. So Mondays meant having to be reminded, afresh, how dependent she was on his skills, and how deep her debt to him was growing.

Most of all, however, Mondays were the day after Sunday, which was the day Wim faithfully came to call. The day he always pleaded with her to accept his help and his love, and the day she always turned him down. With each succeeding Sunday it was getting more and more difficult, though, to refuse him.

If only he weren't so persistent, such a constant pillar of support, she might have found it easier to banish him from her life, once and for all. Which was the only sensible thing to do, she kept reminding herself. It didn't matter that he seemed to be an island of calm and comfort in the middle of a chaotic sea. Nor did it matter that her heart still leapt uncontrollably every time she saw him, or that, deep inside her, she was still in love with him.

No, none of it mattered. Because the fact remained, he wasn't Italian. He was a foreigner. The same as Edward and Reginald and Arnold Willis, the accountant, and the judge who'd sealed the bank accounts. The same as all the other mean-spirited Americans insulting her and her family and throwing obstacles in their path.

But on the other hand, Nina thought on a Monday in the middle of August, as she threw down her pencil and got up from her desk to go home for lunch, on the other hand, his persistent offers of help and love were very tempting. If she didn't watch out, someday soon, in a vulnerable moment, she was apt to accept one or the other. Or both.

Wim continued to occupy her thoughts as she cut through a garden on the way to the path. With a certain amount of irritation, she had to admit he had been right yesterday, when he told her that the estate was going downhill rapidly. The flowerbeds looked terrible. So did the lawn. She didn't know whether to ignore them completely and concentrate her small force on the business, or to follow her instincts as a gardener and at least try to keep the property neat.

She hadn't settled that dilemma, or any of a dozen others, by the time she pulled open the screen door at home. Feeling hot, tired, and provoked, she walked into the kitchen. And came to an immediate halt. As the screen door banged shut behind her, all thoughts of Wim, weeds, and business disappeared. Standing around the big wooden table in front of her was her entire family. Every single member. Nor were any of them eating.

"What happened?" Nina cried, frantically looking from one person to the next. Angelina was openly weeping, Orazio was beet-red with rage. Serafina was wringing her hands, and Maria Stella seemed confused and upset. In her usual chair in the center of the table, Bianca Maria was sitting with her head hanging down. Even so, Nina could see the blotched color on her cheeks and her red and swollen eyes. "What's going on?" she demanded.

In response Angelina began to wail. "Your sister," she sobbed, pointing at Bianca, whose hands were stuffed between her knees.

"What about my sister?" Nina wanted to know, quickly

crossing the room. She came to a stop beside her father. "Papà?" she asked.

"*È una disgrazia,*" Orazio muttered in a tone every bit as fierce as his bristling eyebrows. "She's a disgrace!" He turned away in disgust.

A cold suspicion crept across Nina's mind, a chilly hunch that she knew what had happened. But before she dared to put such a terrible thought into words, she had to have someone else confirm it. More desperate, she twisted to look at Serafina, but Serafina only shrugged, unable to answer. Nina's gaze moved to Dante, who wouldn't meet it, then to Lucia, who had a devastated expression on her face. For once, she had nothing to say.

Finally, nearly speechless herself as apprehension clamped off her breath, Nina gripped the edge of the table and leaned, stiff-armed, across it toward Bianca. "What's wrong?" she asked in a gravelly voice. "Why is everyone carrying on?"

For a moment, Bianca made no attempt to respond, then she slowly raised her head. Her fine oval face, framed by fashionable curls, no longer seemed young and fresh. Now it seemed old and haggard. Since breakfast this morning she seemed to have aged twenty years, her flirtatious innocence replaced by a mixture of resentment, defiance, and fear. Though her raw and puffy eyes attested to heartbreaking tears, she wasn't crying when she answered Nina.

"I'm going to have a baby," she said flatly.

Those were the words she had dreaded hearing, and they hit Nina so hard, she nearly collapsed. As it was, her arms got weak and wobbled. She heard her mother's renewed wails and her father's roar, but the sounds seemed very far away. Out of the corner of her eye she could see Benedetta cover her face with her apron, and Rossana shift uneasily beside her. Those scenes, too, seemed distant, though, as if they were happening in another room. Indeed, in another family. The only reality was the wooden table that separated her from her sister and Bianca Maria herself. The ugly expression was distorting her face and the ugly incident was destroying her life.

"Who's the father?" Nina asked, her voice more raspy than before. She could barely speak with the horror that was choking her throat. She already knew the answer, but she had to ask the question.

Bianca, however, only screwed her mouth shut in a mutinous grimace and glared at Nina from red-rimmed eyes.

"She won't tell us!" Orazio shouted, stepping up next to Nina to pound his fist on the table. "*Il bastardo!* I'll kill him if I ever get my hands on him! He refuses to marry her!"

Her father's voice was a lot more real now, and the rest of the room was coming back into focus. Still intent on Bianca, though, Nina didn't turn her head. Instead, she raised her eyebrows. "True?" she asked her sister quietly.

Again it seemed that Bianca wouldn't answer as belligerence and bravado filled her face. However, she finally tossed her head and confirmed it with a brief nod. Then all of a sudden she crumpled. Tears started pouring down her blotched cheeks, and both her chin and her shoulders sagged. Weeping silently, all alone in the midst of her family, she made a pathetic sight.

If Nina had been stunned before, now she was overwhelmed by pity. Her heart wrenching, she stretched her hand across the table, but Bianca Maria was out of reach. Nina's gaze flicked to Serafina, standing a few feet away. Serafina gave a nod of her own and moved over to comfort their sister. She put an arm around Bianca's shoulder, and Bianca fell against her, her body racked by hysterical sobs. It was an unbearable sound.

The horror and pity merged inside Nina, turning to searing wrath. Unlike her father, though, she knew who the *bastardo* was, and she meant to confront him this minute. Spinning away from the table, she went racing out of the house. By the time the screen door banged shut again, she was off the porch and halfway across their yard. Despite the heat and the heavy air, she picked up her skirt and ran. She didn't feel the hot August sun. All she felt was her sister's anguish and despair.

She reached the Store and bounded up the stairs, then dashed, full speed, down the hall. At the second doorway on the right, she skidded to a stop, grabbed the doorframe, and propelled herself into the office. "What do you think you're doing?" she demanded, her breath coming in great gasps, her chest heaving in exertion and rage.

Gideon jumped when she first burst into the room, then scowling, he returned to his task of packing the contents of his desk into a potato crate. "You're a sharp one, Nina," he replied, his tone more caustic than she'd ever heard it. "I'm sure you can figure out what I'm doing."

In a mocking manner he picked up his leather-bound diary, held it out for her inspection, then dropped it into the box. "See?" he said in a falsetto voice, as if he were talking to an idiot or a very small child. "I'm putting all my possessions into this nice little crate, so I can carry it away when I go. As soon as I'm done," he added in a growl.

The nastiness in his tone was only further fuel for Nina's fire. Choking and spitting with anger, she pointed her finger at him, shook it hard, and shouted. "You can't go anywhere! Not after what you've done. You've got to stay right here and marry Bianca. Now! Immediately! Her life will be ruined if you don't. You've got to take responsibility—"

"Don't you shake your finger at me!" Gideon interrupted in a scream. He whirled away from his desk, raising the book in his hand menacingly, his pale face mottled and contorted. "And don't tell me what I have to do, either. I'm through taking your orders, thank God. I'm fed up to the teeth with kowtowing to the likes of you. 'Yes, Nina,' 'No, Nina,' 'I'll do it right away, Nina,'" he mimicked. His hand lowered, but his expression remained vicious. "I don't know who you think you are telling me what to do."

For just an instant Gideon's unexpected explosion startled Nina, and his threatening gesture made her take a step back. But neither one intimidated her or in any way diminished her own angry purpose.

"I think I'm the sister of the woman you've just ruined. That's who!" she shouted in reply. "I think I'm the aunt of your unborn child."

She didn't point her finger at him again, but she did clench her fist and shake it in the air. "And I have no qualms about telling you what to do, in this instance, since you don't seem to know without being told. Your sense of morality seems to be completely lacking. The only decent thing is to marry Bianca and make her and your child respectable. And that's what you should do, before it's too late."

"Not bloody likely!" Gideon hurled the words at her even as he hurled the book in his hand into the crate. "Talk about ruined lives," he shrieked. "Mine would be a disaster! Imagine me," he banged his chest, "a well-bred and well-educated white man, married to that ignorant peasant tart. Ha! As if that would make her respectable."

His voice lost some of its volume, but if anything, it gained in virulence. "I'd be sacrificing my life," he snarled. "And for what? For a pack of half-breed brats and an Italian whore of a wife who gets fatter and uglier every year? For macaroni three times a day? No, thank you. That's not for Gideon O'Shea."

Nina reeled back this time, rattled to her core by Gideon's poisonous attack. She'd come to expect slurs and insults from the Blackwell brothers and their cohorts, and she'd even learned to turn a deaf ear to unpleasant remarks on the streets. But this tirade surpassed all the rest for sheer malevolence. This one was truly personal. These insults came from a man with whom she'd worked closely for fourteen months, united in a common goal. They came from a man who'd whispered sweetly to her sister and had held her close and kissed her. His bitter contempt for them turned her cold.

If she was momentarily speechless, though, the same couldn't be said for Gideon. Scooping out the contents of the top desk drawer and tossing it into his crate, he sneered, "How do I even know the brat is mine? If Bianca's lain down for me, who knows how many others she accommodated just as readily?"

At Nina's gasp his gaze flitted across her face. "It seems to run in the family, doesn't it?" he commented. "Though I suppose one can't expect anything more from your class of people."

"How dare you speak like that!" Nina sputtered, beside herself with fury. She'd found her voice again, but just barely.

"I dare plenty!" Gideon's voice was raised to a scream once more, as once more he left off his packing to thrust himself toward her. "The wonder is how *you* dare to preach morality after that little trick you pulled, seducing Blackwell into leaving you his estate."

He whirled back to the box again and threw in a pen, a cut-crystal paperweight, and an ivory-handled letter opener. "You might have fooled that crazy old man," he continued without pausing in his task, "but you can't fool me with your innocent airs. You're a clever bit of baggage, you are, Nina Colangelo," he told her, wagging his own finger in her direction. "You even managed to two-time your golden goose with that slick Dutchman. A nice piece of work," he congratulated.

"You're despicable!" Nina yelled, shaking both hands in the air. "A pestilence! An evil, wicked snake!" There weren't words to express her passionate loathing. Not in English or even in Italian.

"I'm glad you're going. I'm glad you're not marrying Bianca.

I wouldn't condemn my worst enemy to such a fate. I wish you'd left months ago, when your salary stopped," she told him, whisking her hands to get rid of him. "My only question is why you stayed as long as you did."

"Why?" Gideon repeated, slamming a final journal into the crate. "I'll tell you why!" he shouted. "I stayed because I thought I could cut myself in for a bigger slice of the pie. I thought you'd see how much you needed me and give me a percentage of the business. *That*'s why I stayed. But it was a gamble that didn't pay off. This whole house of cards is about to fall down. Then you and your sainted family will be out on the streets. Good-bye, easy living. Good-bye, Queen Nina. Good-bye, Blackwell Seed Company."

He grabbed the crate up under one arm and started for the door. As he passed the file cabinet, he reached out with his free hand, jerked open a drawer, and let it crash and spill onto the floor. "Good-bye!" he spat, pushing her out of his way and stalking out of the room.

"Good riddance to rubbish!" Nina shouted after him, poking her head out into the hall. Stiff with anger, she watched him disappear down the stairs, then listened until she heard him stomp out of the Store. She could have gone to the window in his office and watched him go down the path, but she suddenly slumped, her pounding heart slowing. She'd had enough. She was drained and spent and hot.

Turning back into the room, she surveyed the mess of files on the floor for a disinterested moment, then sighed and sank down to clean it up. With her back against the file cabinet, she picked through the papers, absently at first, and then with increasing dismay. She'd never seen any of them before, she realized, and she had no idea what they were all about.

Nina let a fistful of papers fall into her lap and let her head loll back on the cabinet. With every minute that went by, she felt more overwhelmed. Gideon's departure not only left Bianca in a scandalous state, it also left a huge hole in the business.

Not that she wanted Gideon back, she thought, lifting the papers to desultorily fan herself. Nothing on earth, no amount of shame or scandal, could make her believe Bianca Maria was better off married to that abominable creature. Nor did she want him in the company, no matter how valuable his skills. He was dangerous: dishonorable and treacherous and greedy. From now on she was going to rely only on people she could absolutely trust. And that meant that from now on, she was going to rely only on family.

"Nina?" a timid voice interrupted her thoughts.

Rolling her head, she saw Bianca standing in the doorway. She looked neither defiant nor old and worn now. Now she looked extremely vulnerable. "*Si, cara?*" Nina answered, inviting her in with a weary wave of the papers.

Bianca came in and knelt on the floor near Nina, then brushed some spilled papers into a pile. "Is he gone?" she asked, her voice hovering between hope and fear. Avoiding her sister's gaze, she studied the pile.

Nina nodded. "He's gone," she confirmed.

Her face threatening to break again, Bianca sat down abruptly. Tears were welled up in her eyes. "I only wanted to have some fun," she sniffled, extracting a soggy handkerchief from her pocket. "I was just bored and wanted to have a good time." She blew her already reddened nose.

"He was handsome and charming and he told me I was beautiful," she explained almost wistfully. "I didn't mean for it to go so far."

There was silence for a moment, then Nina said, "I know you didn't." Despite the understanding in her words, though, there was a certain note of doom in her tone. Intentions were beside the point. It was the consequences that had to be dealt with right now.

"My life is over, isn't it?" Bianca said, starting to weep softly again.

The silence was longer this time. Finally Nina shrugged. "No," she said. "It isn't over. But to be perfectly honest, the future doesn't look awfully bright."

When Bianca continued to cry, Nina slid over next to her and slipped her arm around her sister's slim shoulders. Leaning back against the desk, she held Bianca close. There was nothing else she could do. It was the only comfort she could give.

They sat like that for an indeterminate amount of time. After a while Bianca stopped crying, but she seemed reluctant to move. It was almost as if she knew there would be few moments like this one in the weeks and months and years to come. There would be very little solace or peace.

Nina didn't object, or chase her sister away. Rather, she laid her cheek against Bianca's curly hair and closed her eyes. There wouldn't be many moments like this one in her future, either.

Moments when she could yield to discouragement, when she could sit on the floor and just be. When she didn't have to solve problems or make decisions or accept responsibility or slay dragons. When the only thing that was required of her was an encircling arm.

It was all too short a moment, though. Bianca raised her head and looked at her sister, her blurry eyes full of anxiety. "You won't tell Papà, will you?" she asked.

Nina's mind swam back into focus at the sound of Bianca's voice, hoarse from her sessions of sobs. The plaintive question was almost identical to the one Bianca had asked nearly a year ago, when Nina had interrupted Gideon kissing her in the Nursery. Piqued by that memory, she also remembered her horror and guilt as she'd equated the scene to Wim and herself.

It had been the same. The same secret meeting, the same glittering desire, the same seduction by looks and charm. She remembered collapsing into her old, chintz chair then, wondering if Wim's motives were really any different from Gideon's. She remembered her shame and disgust when she realized she'd been fooled by Wim's gracious manners.

Most clearly of all, though, she remembered writing Wim out of her life, after that, vowing never to have anything to do with him again. She should have kept that vow, she told herself now. The corners of her mouth turned down in a frown. She shouldn't have let her resolve weaken and drift away on the spring breeze. It was only by a miraculous stroke that she wasn't in Bianca's situation herself.

"Nina?" Bianca asked again. This time she sounded desperate. "Please say you won't tell Papà. Please. I couldn't bear to have anyone else know."

The frown disappeared from Nina's face, and she gave her sister a sad little hug. "No, I won't tell Papà," she promised, as she had last September.

Thinking back, maybe she ought to have done it then, but what was the point of doing it now? Gideon was gone. He couldn't be made to marry Bianca Maria, and all in all, she was better off that way. The only point to be made, the only lesson to be learned, was never to let it happen again. Never again trust anyone outside her family or "her own class of people." And that meant never again trusting Wim. No matter how tempting his offers were.

Another moment went by while Bianca soaked up Nina's

sympathy, then she raised her head again. "What if Papà guesses?" she asked, her brow furrowing in distress. "What if he puts two and two together? What if he asks you where you went when you flew out of the house just now, and how come Gideon suddenly quit? What will you tell him?"

Nina thought about the suspicious coincidences for a minute, then she made her decision. "I'll tell him that bad luck always comes in bunches," she said, letting her arm drop away from Bianca and leaning her head against the leg of the desk. "God knows it's the truth," she added. They'd had more than their share of bad luck lately. Their cup was brimming over. Could things possibly get any worse?

They could. As the month of August went by, Nina struggled to make sense of Gideon's file cabinet. Indeed, of all the tasks in the Office Manager's realm. So much of it was tedious or unintelligible that she very often found herself close to tears. How much more could she take? How much more could she do? She was only one person, and each day had only so many hours. Between the heat and frustration, she felt as if she were on the verge of shattering.

Just when she was about to throw up her hands, though, just when she was about to give up, Don Alberto's baggy face would appear in her mind, and her resolve would stiffen all over again. It would be a betrayal of his trust to walk away now, an insult to the memory of her patron and friend. Not only would it be rude to reject his very generous gift, but she'd also be letting him down. More than anyone else, he'd believed in her abilities and talents. More, even, than she had herself. And it was probably true that he'd started the Blackwell Seed Co. as much to give her an opportunity as to entertain himself in his retirement. After all he'd given her, she owed it to him to keep trying to make it work.

So Nina scrounged around and found a few more drops of patience and a few more minutes in each day. Her family rallied to her aid, but aside from admiration and encouragement, there was only so much they could do to help. Take the typewriter. When Serafina tried to master its clacking keys, the usually sweet young woman became nearly savage. Rossana took to it more easily, but she had already taken over the accounts, and once school resumed in September, her time was very limited.

In the middle of it all, in the middle of being stretched as tight as a violin string, Nina was summoned to court to give a deposition. For four long hours a swarm of lawyers poked and prodded her verbally, asking her questions about her relationship with the don. The questions were so sharp and incessant, and the lawyers were so quick to twist the meaning of her words when she answered, that by the time the whole procedure was over, she wasn't sure of what she'd actually said.

She left the courthouse on shaky legs, her head throbbing, and her mind in a whirl. For the rest of the day she was next to useless. She couldn't concentrate and she made stupid mistakes.

"What did your lawyers say in response?" Wim asked her on Sunday from his seat on the other side of her desk. He had his jacket off again and his shirtsleeves rolled up and his hands clasped behind his head.

Nina frowned. She wished Dante would stop telling Wim these things. This was family business. It wasn't any of his concern.

"Didn't they object?" Wim persisted. "Didn't they accuse the Blackwells' lawyers of badgering you or putting words in your mouth?"

Her frown deepened as she considered her options. She could ignore him, in which case he would heckle her until he had her attention. Possibly even reaching across the desk to seize her hand, distracting her with the thrill of his touch. Or she could out and out tell him to stop meddling in her affairs, in which case the discussion would end in an argument. They'd trade accusations for a while until one or the other of them would storm out the door. Then she'd spend hours feeling disconcerted and distressed, hours that she didn't have to spare. If she gave him just enough information, maybe he wouldn't pursue it any further.

"No, they didn't object," she said, picking up her pencil and drawing circles on her pad. "They weren't even there. One of their law clerks came in halfway through and took notes."

Her tactic didn't work. Wim didn't drop the subject. Rather, he rocked forward and leaned his arms on the desk to study her intently. "Don't you think you ought to consider changing law firms?" he asked. "I know it's the one that Albert used and you want to be loyal to him, but these men hardly seem to have your best interest in mind. In fact, from what I've heard so far, I would almost suspect that they *want* you to lose."

Nina's pencil scribbled harder as she considered her new dilemma. Should she cut this off now and risk the consequences, or should she answer him and continue to let him probe? Confounding the problem was a more difficult quandary, one that she'd been agonizing over all week. She was at the end of her rope, both in patience and in knowledge. She needed help and she didn't know where to turn to get it. If she were to keep this business going, she needed someone with real expertise. Fat Arnold Willis, the accountant, had been reluctant to talk to her since the day Don Alberto died, and her lawyers, as Wim had pointed out, were indifferent.

But questions arose on a daily basis, little details of doing business that she didn't know how to deal with. Did she dare ask Wim for assistance? And if so, could they keep it on a strictly impersonal level? Could he answer her questions, explain the mysteries, without interfering or assuming a degree of trust that didn't exist? Was he willing, in short, to be an employee? Nina took a deep breath. Well, she thought, there was one way to find out. Try it. If it didn't work she could always argue with him later on.

"My lawyers aren't allowed to say anything at a deposition. They told me that in advance," she explained. She'd better give him the information he wanted, if she wanted to get some from him in return.

"But that reminds me," she went on quickly, before he could give voice to the protest she saw forming on his face. "When I was at their office last week, I forgot to ask them a few questions about the insurance policy that just came in the mail." Keeping her tone as casual as she could, she said, "If that's something you know about, maybe you could save me a trip back into town."

Glancing up from her doodling, Nina saw his exasperated expression turn to one of hope and surprise. "As long as you're already here," she hastily added, so as not to convey the wrong impression. "I mean, we might as well talk about something useful."

"Might as well," Wim agreed solemnly, though the corner of his mouth had a suspicious twitch.

That did it. Nina put down her pencil, folded her hands on the desk in front of her, and looked him directly in the eye. "Listen," she said in a steady voice. "I need someone to give me advice. Not about what to do with my life, or whether or not to switch law firms, but advice, no, perhaps *instructions* would be a better word, about insurance policies and tax notices and all the other details that Don Alberto and Gideon used to take care of.

"I need someone to answer my business questions. And that's all. Do you understand what I'm saying?" She paused to make sure there was no mistaking her intentions. When his eyes narrowed slightly and his smile disappeared, she took that for a confirmation.

"As long as you insist on coming out here once a week, you might as well be that someone," she went on, her hands still folded and both her voice and gaze still steady. "I can't pay you anything right now, but when the will is settled, I'll reimburse you for your professional counsel. Whatever you think is fair."

"For heaven's sake, Nina!" Wim exploded, sitting up straight in the chair. "I don't want your money. You know very well I'm more than glad to give you advice, or instructions, or whatever you want to call it"—he flung his hand in the air—"but I'm not interested in a salary. I want to help you, not go on your payroll. Can't *you* understand that?"

Nina wasn't moved. All she could think of was Gideon, and how in June he'd grandly offered her his help for free. And how he'd spat at her, six weeks later, and revealed his true objective. To make himself so indispensable, she would give him part of the company. That's what happened when you trusted strangers, she reminded herself. They deceived you and fled. Now, though, she knew never to trust one again.

"I want to keep this on a business basis," she responded, her face strong and immobile. "Either this is a professional arrangement, or don't bother to come here anymore. You're wasting my time."

For a moment the only sound in the room was Wim's fingers drumming on the top of the desk. He stared at her, searching for a crack in her expression. But she looked right back at him, her gaze unnaturally calm and impassive. He sighed, his fingers slowing.

"All right," he agreed, lifting his hand to rub the back of his neck. "We'll do it your way. Where's the insurance policy?"

With a tight nod of satisfaction, Nina searched through the piles on her desk until she found it.

28

Against all odds, the Blackwell Seed Co. stayed afloat, and the 1897 catalogue went to press at the end of October bigger and more beautiful than the last one. Reluctant as she was to admit it, Nina knew she couldn't have done it without Wim. He'd arrived early every Sunday, though this was his busiest season, and had stayed until every bit of work was done. Several times he'd even brought along his bookkeeper and clerk to type up a stack of letters and to give Rossana some pointers. He'd answered all the questions on her weekly list, showing remarkable patience, thoroughness, and concern for her comprehension. He would have made a good teacher, Nina decided, choosing to focus on those traits and not on the affection with which his counsel was also delivered.

Troubling debts aside, both personal and financial, Nina felt a moment of pride when they sent the catalogue off to the printers. She felt a sense of tremendous accomplishment, of deep satisfaction, the same feeling of euphoria that had wiped out months of grinding toil last year. But it was only for a moment. The glow was short-lived. On November the second, Don Alberto's will was brought to trial.

The proceeding was brief. Almost farcical. From the instant she walked into the courtroom, flanked by her parents and Duute and her three oldest sisters, Nina felt the hope drain out of her. Every other person in the room was a white, male American, and their expressions ranged from contempt to suspicion. Except for her lawyers, Messrs. Brown and Haverford. Their expressions were blank.

All of a sudden Nina felt weak and shivery. She wasn't sure she had the strength to go through with this ordeal. She stumbled down the aisle, eliciting frowns from the courtroom officials, and collapsed on a chair in the first row while her family seated themselves, protectively, on either side of her. In front of her was a little fence and beyond that were her lawyers, but they were turned face forward now and didn't bother to greet her. Her sense of despair deepened.

The first thing that happened was the other lawyer made his opening remarks. His name was Hamilton, and he was short, stocky, and almost completely bald. "Your Honor," he said, bowing to the judge on his bench, "we will attempt to show the court that one woman, Miss Maria Antonina Colangelo, had undue influence on Mr. Albert Blackwell in the matter of his will. That through her manipulation and seduction, she was able to enjoy liberties above her station and to convince a poor, lonely old man to leave her an unimaginably large portion of his estate.

"We will show the court that this woman"—he turned to point an accusing finger at Nina—"this shameless woman preyed on Mr. Blackwell's delight in gardening, the innocent hobby of his retirement years. That she used her father's position as grounds-keeper, and her own willingness to root around in the dirt, to ingratiate herself to a man isolated on his country estate by his advanced age and ill health."

The blood ran cold in Nina's veins. Her mouth went dry and her heart pounded in her ears, blocking out the rest of Mr. Hamilton's statement. How could this be allowed to happen? How could this nasty man be allowed to distort the truth? Surely someone would stop him any minute now.

No one did. No one stopped Edward, either, or Reginald, in his turn, when each strode purposefully forward to describe how Maria Antonina Colangelo had stolen their father's affections while they were in New York City running his business and managing his properties. How she'd plied him with greasy Italian food, and God knows what other kinds of immoral favors. With chins stiffening bravely, they related many incidents of her brazen behavior, including the time she'd had the impudence to plop herself down at the head table when they'd given their father a lavish party to celebrate his seventy-fifth birthday.

Nor did anyone stop Arnold Willis when he squeezed his large body into the witness box and swore that Maria Antonina Colangelo never let Mr. Blackwell alone. That she was always at his elbow, telling him what to do, that she was always peering over his shoulder when they were discussing finances.

No one stopped the clerk from Lyman Hoyt's furniture emporium when he testified that Miss Maria Antonina Colangelo had come in with her sister and had bought two rooms' worth of furniture, then boasted how she'd get Mr. Blackwell to pay for it. Or the waiter from the Grosvenor who told the court that Miss Maria Antonina Colangelo lunched with Mr. Blackwell frequently, always telling him what he could or couldn't have to eat. Or the gardener Mr. Blackwell had fired after a week, who claimed Miss Maria Antonina Colangelo didn't like him because he was white.

No one stopped any of them. Not even her lawyers. Nor did they do much to rebut the villainous charges. No one mentioned the magnificent gardens that were her creation. Nor the business that had made Don Alberto's last year on earth enjoyable. No one mentioned the nearly nine years of friendship between them, nor the don's dislike of his sons. Nor the fact that, even so, he'd left them the bulk of his considerable estate.

It wasn't any surprise, therefore, when after a short deliberation, the judge announced his verdict. After all, who was he more likely to believe, two well-bred, well-respected American businessmen, or an immigrant Italian woman who had stammered on the witness stand, stunned by Mr. Hamilton's fierce grilling?

"It is the opinion of this court that Miss Maria Antonina Colangelo exerted undue influence over the late Mr. Albert Blackwell. That she used her wiles to persuade him to make a will favorable to herself and her family. This will is overturned."

It wasn't a surprise, but nonetheless, it was a tremendous shock. It hit Nina almost like a physical blow, as if someone had struck a fist against her heart, pounding out her breath and making her hurt. It was a shock to lose, in one instant, the business she worked so long and hard to preserve. It was a shock to know she no longer had a home. Not just the Big House but also the comfortable farmhouse where she'd lived with her family for almost the whole time they'd been in America.

Apart from her losses, though, apart from humiliating her and portraying her as grasping and sly, this judgment today also humiliated Don Alberto. It reduced his memory to that of a foolish and incompetent old man. To a doddering and gullible simpleton who wasn't capable of deciding how he wanted the fruit of his life's prodigious labors divided.

"*Che peccato*," Nina muttered, putting both hands on the rail in front of her and pushing herself to her feet. It was shameful.

Disgraceful. To think that Don Alberto's sons, his own flesh and blood, were responsible for this defamation. It turned her stomach to contemplate how they'd willingly, even eagerly, debased their father for the sake of material gain.

"Truly," Angelina agreed, rising majestically next to Nina. She cast a scornful look at the men on the other side of the rail, then said disgustedly, in Italian, "That pair of scoundrels never even liked Don Alberto's house. And they certainly don't need it."

"They don't want the seed company, either," Orazio added, standing up on the other side of his daughter. "All that work, and they'll probably just let it dissolve. What a pity."

Through the cold pain gripping her, Nina felt a sudden burst of warmth. She looked gratefully from her mother to her father, a look that swept in her sisters and Dante. Let Edward and Reginald have the estate. Let them have the company. She still had what was most important. She still had her family. Her loyal, loving, enveloping family who would never turn on her, viciously disowning her memory. Head high, Nina threaded out from the row, then linked arms with her parents and started down the aisle in a family mass.

"Just a moment, young woman," Edward's voice barked out.

Nina stopped and looked over her shoulder, her eyebrows raised. "Are you speaking to me?" she asked quietly. All her nervousness and dread were gone. The worst had happened. These arrogant men couldn't hurt her anymore.

Edward's humorless expression grew more disagreeable as he left the group of lawyers congratulating him and his brother. "Of course I'm speaking to you," he said, irritated by her composure. "I'm giving you notice to vacate my property."

There was dead silence in the courtroom. Every face was cocked in their direction, every person was rigid with curiosity. Nina slipped her arms free from her parents' and turned to face the man poised menacingly three feet away. "All right," she said in an even tone that belied the anger flickering inside her. "We'll be gone by the middle of the month."

"You'll be gone in forty-eight hours!" Edward snapped back, taking another step forward. "Do you think I'm stupid enough to let you and your family have the run of my property for two weeks? You'd loot it bare and wreak some of your hot-blooded Latin revenge. I'm not my father, you know. I won't fall for your tricks."

"Fff!" came a scoff from behind Nina's left shoulder.

Edward shifted his harsh gaze to Angelina, raked her with his eyes, then looked back to Nina. "And what, may I ask, was that sound supposed to mean?" he said.

Nina returned his supercilious stare. "It means you must think *we* are stupid," she answered him, "to mistake you for your father." She let her gaze travel from his face to his feet then back to his eyes, contemptuously measuring him as he had measured her mother. "You might be six inches taller than he was," she told him, "but you aren't even half his size." Turning again, she started down the aisle with her family.

"Just a moment!" Edward thundered, more enraged than before. "I haven't finished with you yet!"

Though Nina stopped again, she didn't immediately turn to face him. Rather, head up, she fought to control her own rage. What gave him the right to speak to her this way? To treat her as if she were his lowly subject or a common criminal? And what was wrong with every other man in the room? Where were their manners, if not their sense of decency? Why didn't someone tell Edward that he was being an evil bully?

"Can't face me, eh?" Edward sneered. "It doesn't matter. I don't care if you look at me, just so long as you listen. I'm placing guards around every building on the property except the one in which you reside. No one in your family, or anyone connected to you, will be permitted to enter without the express permission of myself or my brother. *Comprendee*?" he asked with malicious condescension.

Losing her fight, Nina whirled around to regard Edward with fury and scorn. "*Comprendee*?" she repeated scathingly. "What sort of ignorant gibberish is that? What's the matter? Can't you speak English?"

Dark red color flooded Edward's face, and the veins in his neck started to throb. "Very well," he snarled. "I'll tell you in plain English. Pack your wretched bags and leave! And if you have some item of personal property in any building other than your residence, state now what it is and how you can prove that it's yours."

While Edward tapped his foot, Nina scanned the Store and the Nursery and the Big House in her mind. "Nothing," she declared, flinging both hands away from her. She didn't want anything. Not a book, not a photograph, not even a copy of one of the catalogues.

She wanted no mementos of the times that came to this bitter end. "You and your brother can have it all," she told him. "All the objects and all the money. The things I'll take away with me are far more valuable."

"Little thief!" Edward pounced, moving another step closer. "I knew it! Now what are you stealing?"

Nina looked at him and slowly shook her head. Then she lifted a finger and slowly shook that, too. "I'm not the one who is stealing," she said with deadly calm. "You and Reginald are the thieves.

"You stole from me and you stole from my father and you stole from my sister and brother-in-law. And what is even more unforgivable is that you stole from your own father. What I take away with me, though, you can't possibly steal. Because I take with me my family. My memories of Don Alberto. And," she added, her golden eyes huge, "I take the truth."

This time when she turned and walked away, she didn't stop when Edward shouted at her.

"*Basta!*" Orazio slammed the palm of his hand down on the kitchen table. Everyone's cup jumped in its saucer. "Enough! I've had enough of this America. It's a strange land full of strange people and strange customs. It's not at all what we thought it would be when we came here nine years ago.

"It's no paradise!" His hand slammed down again. "It's a living hell! Not one day in all those nine years have we been welcome."

"*Bè*, Orazio," Angelina said more moderately as she dabbed her finger at a splash of coffee. "When the don was alive, we were welcome here."

"*Bè*," Orazio conceded, lifting his shoulders in a shrug. "Maybe here. Mr. Blackwell was a good man. *Riposa in pace*," he added, crossing himself.

"But nowhere else!" His voice grew fierce again and down came his hand. He didn't notice that Benedetta plucked up her cup just in time. "And now the don is gone. Instead, there are those *figli di puttane*!" he shouted, shaking his fist in the general direction of Stamford. "Those sons of whores!"

"Orazio!" Angelina warned, frowning. "The girls . . ." She gestured toward Stella and Rossana, who were clutching their cups and watching their father nervously.

"Some Americans have been nice, Papà," Benedetta said in a cautious tone. "Mr. Weed at the Union Market is always friendly. And Mr. Silliman gives us peppermints whenever we go into the Park Drugstore."

"And then he tries to sell us something we don't need," Lucia put in tartly.

"*A punto!*" Orazio's hands were as expressive as his words. "My point exactly! They want our money and they want us to clean their stables and tend their gardens, but they don't want us to live in their neighborhoods. They laugh at us, make fun of our food, our olive oil and pasta and wine. They call us names and cheat us, then accuse *us* of stealing.

"That's enough!" They all grabbed their cups as his hand slammed the table one more time. "I've had enough! I'm going home!"

For a shocked moment there was complete silence. Bianca Maria found her voice first. "Home?" she echoed in alarm.

"Home?" Stella repeated, bewildered.

"Papà." Nina spoke up. She'd barely said a word since they'd left the courthouse an hour ago. Now she knit her eyebrows, leaned forward with her arms on the table, and looked at her father intently. "Do you mean Sicily, Papà?"

Orazio gave an emphatic nod. "I mean Sicily," he confirmed. "Castel'Greco. The place where I was born and the place where I want to die." He shut his eyes briefly as a shudder ran through him. "I can't imagine being buried in this foreign place," he said with real horror. "Of resting among these strangers for all of eternity. I want to go back to the hills where I belong."

Although the idea initially startled her, the more Nina thought about it, the better she liked it. Leaning back in her chair, she rubbed her chin. After all, what was America without Don Alberto or the estate? What did she have here except bitter disappointment and humiliation? And where would they go now, if they stayed in this country? To another tenement? To a job in a factory that paid seven dollars a week?

Wouldn't it be better to return to Sicily? To a land where they were welcome and where they knew what to expect? She'd been happy there, happy among the wildflowers and the sheep and the stark beauty of the hills. She could heal her bruised spirit there, nourish her battered soul. Surrounded by her own people, she could be happy again.

There would be no daily stack of mail to contend with, no pressure to succeed. There would just be peace and the timeless ways of those ancient hills. Just her family and sticking her hands in the soil. It was exactly what she needed.

"I want to go back, too," she announced. "I think it's an excellent idea."

Not everyone was as sure. Although Serafina shot her a look of utter surprise, it was Benedetta who lodged the first objection.

"Our kitchen wasn't very nice in Sicily," she said, casting a glance at the big Glenwood in which she'd baked hundreds of loaves of bread, not to mention innumerable tortes and untold batches of *biscotti*. "As I remember, we had to cook on an open hearth. And do the washup outside."

"There was an outhouse, too," Rossana added glumly. "I was scared to go out to it after dark."

"An outhouse?" Stella asked in amazement. Her memory didn't reach across the Atlantic. As far as she could recall, life had always been lived in Stamford, more specifically, in the house they would leave forever, the day after tomorrow. "What about the bathtub? Where was that?"

"In a bucket," Benedetta answered, her jolly face despondent. "Mamma used to heat water on the hearth, and we'd take turns standing in the bucket and sponging down."

Stella sucked in her breath and rolled her eyes, though she didn't dare make a comment out loud. Everyone always spoke of Sicily with such reverence, but to her, it didn't sound very appealing. To hide her disappointment, she lifted up her cup and drained the last of her coffee.

"Don't forget to mention that we had to haul the water home, first," Bianca Maria put in. She didn't make an attempt to disguise her disgust. "Don't you remember all those trips to the piazza?" she asked, pushing her empty cup out of the way. "I used to think my arms would get stretched below my knees."

Stirring uneasily in her chair, Nina cradled her cup in both her hands. She *had* forgotten all those discomforts. Well, maybe not forgotten. Perhaps *overlooked* would be a better word. In her eagerness to regain the sense of innocence and contentment she'd known in her youth, she'd overlooked some of the harsher realities of life in Sicily.

"*Basta, ragazze*," Orazio ordered, spreading his arms out in front of him to stop the complaints. "We don't have to go back to

that miserable house. Or go to work for that miserable Don
Franco. With what I've saved in the past nine years, we can buy
our own land and build a big, beautiful new house. With a proper
stove," he added, making a grand flourish toward Benedetta.
"And running water." His flourish toward Bianca was also grand.
"It'll be the showpiece of Castel'Greco."

Relief rushed through Nina so rapidly, she nearly dropped her
cup. "You see?" she said, smiling from one sister to the other.
"It's perfect. The best of both worlds."

Although Orazio nodded in satisfaction, Dante looked dubious.
"Maybe," he said. He poured himself another cup of coffee and
stirred in a spoonful of sugar, carefully composing what he wanted
to say. Finally he set the spoon on the saucer and looked around
the room.

"I came from Sicily less than two years ago," he told them.
"My memory of life there is still fresh. There was a wealthy man
in our village . . ." He held up a hand. "Wealthy compared with
the rest of us, I mean to say," he amended. "But he had a fine
house, and he ate meat three or four times a week. Yet when his
child got ill, his first son, a good boy, there was no doctor. No
hospital. No medicine."

He picked up his cup and took a sip of coffee. When he set the
cup down again, he said, "The boy died. His fine house did him
no good."

In the silence that followed, Dante took another swallow of
coffee and again returned the cup to its saucer. "Life in Sicily is
hard," he said. "Even with a little money, there are no doctors or
schools. The villages are isolated. There are no opportunities."

"*Aiou!*" Bianca wailed, wrapping her arms around her chest
and rocking back and forth on her chair. "My life is over. I'll
never have any fun again. I'll wither away in a village in Sicily,
scrubbing clothes on the rocks in the stream, I'm doomed."

"Stop sniveling," Angelina commanded, finally entering the
discussion. She had been quiet until now, listening to everyone
else talk, a contemplative expression on her face. Now she reached
a decision. "Your life isn't over," she told Bianca, her voice
ringing with authority, her coral drop earrings trembling.

"Quite the opposite, this is the perfect solution for your
problem. No one in Sicily has to know you aren't married. We'll
make references to your husband. To a tragedy." Her hand waved

vaguely. "An accident. Maybe a streetcar. Or a runaway horse. Whatever." With another wave she dismissed the detail.

"After a decent period of mourning," she went on with her scheme, "you'll emerge as a respectable widow. And your child will be a respectable orphan. You can continue your life." Angelina brushed her hands against each other.

"*Ecco fatto*," she declared in a pleased tone. "It's done. We're going home."

It was indeed. They might make delicate hints to Orazio, but no one dared argue with Angelina. One by one they stood up to start packing.

Nina rose, too. Though Dante's sober words lingered in her mind, she was still glad they were leaving America. Life might be hard in Sicily, but it wasn't easy here. She was tired of struggling, tired of the constant battles. After her confrontation with Edward this morning, she felt exhausted, bled dry. She couldn't wait to return to the soothing solitude of the hills.

Just as she was shoving her chair under the table, the sound of footsteps hurrying up the back stairs made her freeze. A loud knock on the door made everyone else stop, too. Now what? What new torment had the beastly brothers devised? What edict were they imposing? What demand were they making?

The knock came again. Louder this time. More insistent. Dante was closest to the door. Drawing a deep breath, he went over and opened it. Wim came striding into the room.

"I've just come from the courthouse," he said, his usually calm voice rich with outrage. The rosy spots on his cheeks were bright against his pale white skin. "I can't tell you how shocked I was to find it closed up and the trial over when I arrived," he said, glancing from one stony face to the next. His gaze came to rest on Nina, standing up straight, her hands resting on the back of her chair.

"It's appalling. Disgraceful," he went on, advancing toward her. "The clerk told me what happened. He said the trial was finished in little more than an hour. That the judge never even left the courtroom to deliberate. That he made his decision almost instantly." Wim came around the table and stopped scarcely a foot away. "Is that really true?" he asked in an incredulous tone.

Nina didn't answer him immediately, just stared into his eyes. Those intensely blue eyes. Those eyes were America, too. They'd thrilled and astonished her the first time she saw them nine years ago. And they'd thrilled and astonished her every time since. Including today. She looked away, looked down at her hands on the back of the chair. Her knuckles were white. "Yes," she said in a low voice. "It's true."

"You don't have to accept this, you know," Wim responded at once. He didn't step any closer, but he leaned toward her, urging. "You must be able to appeal," he told her. "There can be a new trial, with a different judge presiding. This time there can be witnesses who testify on *your* behalf."

"*Ufa.*" Without looking up, Nina shrugged in dismissal. "What good would that do?" she asked, finally raising her eyes. "It would still be the word of two American businessmen against the word of an immigrant Italian woman."

"No, not *ufa*," Wim disagreed, shaking his head. "It would do a lot of good. I think that this time you'll win. Of course, you must get different lawyers," he quickly added. "Men who will truly represent you. Men who will respond to the Blackwells' lies and distortions. Nina, you've got an excellent case. It just needs to be properly presented."

"Too late," came a growl from the other end of the table.

Startled, Wim turned to find the source of the voice. He just caught Orazio scraping his chin with the back of his hand. It didn't take an Italian to understand the contempt. "Why too late?" he asked, his eyes narrowing.

"Too late," Orazio repeated. "Let them keep." With similar contempt, he flung his hand wide, encompassing the entire estate. "We are going home to Sicily," he said. "*Basta* America."

Wim's eyes opened wide. "Sicily?" His voice was shocked. "All of you?" he asked. "You aren't all going to Sicily, are you?" Disbelieving, he looked back to Nina for a denial.

She held his gaze for a pained moment, then again dropped her head. "Yes," she said. "All of us."

In the seconds that followed, Nina could hear Wim take a long, deep breath. Then she heard him slowly exhale. "Nina," he said. "I want to talk to you outside." His quiet words reverberated in the stillness of the kitchen. When she didn't move, he leaned forward and seized her by the wrist.

"*Che fa?*" Orazio cried, fists balled, springing forward to his daughter's defense. "What do you do? Stop! Take away your hand!"

"No, Papà!" Nina begged as she pried Wim's fingers loose from her wrist.

At the same moment Dante lunged out and grabbed Orazio's arm. "It's all right," he reassured. "He won't hurt Nina. I know him. Please, Orazio. You must let them talk in private."

For a single, tense moment nobody moved. Wim stubbornly remained at Nina's side, staring at Orazio, and Orazio, staring back, stayed taut at the end of Dante's grip. In between them Nina couldn't breathe. Finally Orazio relaxed and again flung out his hand. "*Va bene*," he granted, though with a certain amount of suspicion and a great deal of reluctance. "Go. Talk."

Wim's nod of acknowledgment was short, then he turned to Nina. "Coming?" he asked. He sounded grim.

Nina nodded, too, and led the way out the back door, snatching her shawl off the peg as she passed by it. Her breath was still tight in her chest, and her movements were awkward. In total silence she walked beside Wim as they descended the porch steps, crossed the yard, and started along the path. It was a gray and raw November afternoon, chilling her body the way the day's events had chilled her spirit.

Halfway down the path they suddenly stopped. Ahead of them was the Nursery, but it was no longer the welcoming sanctuary Nina knew. Now it looked like a prison. And even though she was on the outside, Nina felt like the prisoner. Two burly men, legs braced, arms akimbo, glowered at them, guarding the big greenhouse against her intrusion. Nina nearly burst into tears. Who was going to take care of all the plants inside?

"How can you let them do this to you?" Wim asked, reading her face as he always could. He kept his voice low, so only she could hear, though his breath made thin puffs in the air when he spoke.

Bending even closer to her ear, he said, "That greenhouse is yours. You designed it, you named it, you filled it with plants. And when he died, Albert gave it to you as a measure of his respect and affection. By moral right and legal decree, every square inch of this estate belongs to you." His voice rose slightly as he asked again, "How can you let them take it away?"

With a gasp to keep back the tears, Nina whirled and ran in the opposite direction. Clutching her skirt in one hand and her shawl in the other, she ran across the paths leading to the Store and to the gardens and to the library terrace.

Wim caught up with her on the wide front lawn, grabbing her arm and pulling her to a stop under a bare branched maple. Yanking her around to face him, he demanded, "Is that your only answer? To just run away? To run away from me? To run away from America?" His breath made bigger clouds now, which mingled with hers as she gulped for air.

"I know you better than that, Nina," he said, giving her a shake. "You're not a quitter. It's not like you to run away."

"Maybe I'm not running *away*," Nina replied, struggling to pry his fingers loose from her arm as she had pried them from her wrist before. This time it was useless, though. He wasn't letting go. She stopped struggling and looked at him. "Maybe I'm running *to* something," she said, her voice choked but intense. "Did it ever occur to you that I might be running *to* Sicily? *To* tranquillity and beauty? *To* peace and contentment?"

"Bah!" Wim scoffed, suddenly jerking his hand free from her arm after all. He spun away, stalked off several paces, then spun again and stalked back. "Beauty. Tranquillity. Peace," he mocked. "It sounds like a travel brochure. For God's sake, Nina!" he exclaimed, throwing up his hand. "Go there for a vacation, but don't go there to live!

"If you stay in Sicily, you'll be wasting your life. Wasting everything you've worked so hard for during your years in America. Not just this," he said, indicating the estate with a sweeping gesture. "Not just your gorgeous gardens, and the Nursery, and a seed catalogue that must be giving W. Atlee Burpee fits of envy.

"Not just the things you've created," he said, grabbing both her arms this time as he stared into her face. "But your education, Nina. The education that made those creations possible. You'll be wasting everything you've learned. Throwing away nine years of knowledge and experience. Throwing away your fluency in English and your ability to run a business. To say nothing of your vast knowledge of plants." He shook her again. "You'll be throwing away all that opportunity to waste your life as a peasant."

This time Nina was more forceful in her efforts to free herself. Placing the heels of her hands on his chest, she shoved hard. "I *am* a peasant," she retorted, taking a few steps back and rubbing her arms where his fingers had bit in. "A *contadina* from *Sicilia*," she said, lifting her chin. "And no matter how many silk and linen dresses I own, no matter what sort of pompous title I'm given, I'm still a peasant. And I'm going back where I belong.''

"Oh, Nina," Wim said in disgust. He started pacing up and down again, his feet kicking through the carpet of fallen leaves no one had had the time to rake. "Maybe you were a peasant," he told her, stopping short in front of her again. "But you aren't any longer. You've come too far. Gained too much. You can't empty these years out of your head. You can't give up your chance for success to go while your life away in some remote little village."

"Success!" Nina cried, tossing both her hands in the air. She too started pacing, scuffling in the leaves. "I'm sick of hearing that sound. I'll be just as glad to forget English and all your favorite words. *Sensible. Practical.* What are the others?" she demanded. Answering her own question, she shouted a few more. "*Business. Opportunity. Reasonable. Profit.* I can't stand them anymore!" Stopping short as he had, she shook her steepled hands in his face. "Do you hear me?" she yelled. "I never want to hear any of them again.

"I arrived in this country nine years ago, eager to learn." Though her voice lowered a little, her tone was bitter. "I was happy and trusting, and I believed what I was told. That success was desirable and business was the way to achieve it." She looked at him and shook her head, her face flushed from the cold and emotion.

"I don't believe that anymore," she said. "America has ruined my trust. It's slowly stolen away my happiness. I used to laugh all the time, and hum and sing. This morning, on the drive home from the courthouse, I tried to remember the last time I laughed." She shook her head again. "Do you know, I couldn't?" she said. There was amazement in her voice. And sadness, too.

Then she gathered herself up and started to pace again. "Enough is enough," she declared, her hand slicing through the air decisively. "I don't want success anymore. I want to be happy. I want to be left alone with my family and my gardens and the familiar ways of Sicily."

"Listen to me, Nina," Wim said, holding out his hands. His voice was lower, too, consciously calmer. "You've had a terrible blow today. You've been hurt. Insulted. Of course you're depressed, but please—" He paused until she stopped pacing and turned to look at him. "*Please* don't let them defeat you." Taking a step toward her with his hands still outstretched, he said, "You're better than they are. Don't let them win."

Nina sighed. A deep, weary sigh. "It's not just today," she said, glancing at his hands and glancing away. "It's every day. It's always a fight. Always a battle. I'm tired of it. Tired of the pain and the worries and the humiliation. I'm tired and I want to go home."

"Life's a fight," Wim said, lifting his hands in a helpless gesture. "Wherever you are in the world there are disappointments and heartaches and battles. But at least in America you have the chance for victory. Here you have opportunities, though you have to seize them. You have rights, though you often have to insist on them. And the terrible injustice that was done to you today can also be undone, in this America. You have to fight for it, but in the end you can get it."

There was silence as Nina let his words settle in her mind. Drawing her shawl tighter, she hugged herself against the dampness and chill. She was tired. There were shadows under her golden eyes, and her skin looked pale against the gray November sky. "No," she finally said, turning from him. "No. It's not worth it." She started to walk away.

"What about us?" Wim's quiet voice followed her as she rustled through the leaves. "What about our love?" he asked. "Can you just forget about that, too? Doesn't it mean anything at all that I want to marry you?" His tone was as even as it ever had been, but it was tinged by pain that Nina had never heard.

She stopped and turned again, ten feet away. "You shouldn't marry me," she told him mildly. "I wouldn't make you happy. Not after a while. Right now I'm just another one of your battles, and you're determined to be triumphant. But you'd soon find out that it was a hollow victory. You'd be dissatisfied with me as a wife, and you'd regret ever having fought the battle."

Still hugging herself, she shrugged. "You'd be better off marrying an American," she advised him. An image flashed through her mind. An image of a pretty pink and white woman standing next to him in a sunny seedhouse on Long Island. "Someone like Penelope Beale."

Wim's jaw tightened and so did his voice. "Don't you think I'm capable of deciding who I want to marry?" he asked a bit more brusquely than he meant to. "Don't you think I can tell which woman I love?"

Nina's eyebrows lifted, and a sad smile tugged at her mouth. "No," she answered him without anger. "Not in this case. Not if you're talking about me. You're not in love with me. I finally realized that. You're in love with an ideal that you've created in your mind. Maybe she has my face and body." She glanced down, almost as if she were confirming it herself. Then she looked back at him and went on.

"Your Nina is efficient and sensible, though," she said. "Your Nina knows about taxes and insurance. She enjoys doing business. She wants success.

"But that's not me," she said, shrugging again as her voice began to fade. "I'm not a businesswoman. I don't belong behind a desk in a linen suit. I belong in a garden, wearing old clothes, with my hands in the dirt." For a moment she looked at him with great regret, then her gaze slid away. With a final shrug she turned once more and started for the house.

When Wim called to her, anguish in his voice, she just shook her head and kept walking steadily. From where he stood, he couldn't see her hot tears. But she could feel them, streaming down her cold cheeks and searing her heart.

=29=

Watched carefully by Edward and Reginald, to make sure they didn't unleash any last-minute vendettas, the Colangelos left Don Alberto's estate on November the fourth. It was another raw autumn day, though some weak sunshine whitewashed the sky and cast thin shadows underneath the big trees on the lawn. In the wagon they'd hired at a livery in town, were eleven trunks full of their clothes, books, dishes, and linens, as well as a few odd pieces of furniture: two rockers, some plant stands, and a pretty cabinet. Everything else in the farmhouse Don Alberto had bought. After nine years in America, they didn't even own the beds they slept in.

Their faces were sober, very grave, as they climbed into two hired carriages and started out the drive. Benedetta was silently crying, her round cheeks wet and shiny. Stella's sobs were muffled against Angelina's bosom. Unspilled tears made Serafina's soft, brown eyes seem huge. Nina was past tears, though, and past anger, too. Her head against the carriage seat, her eyes straight ahead, she ignored the two men whose malice had brought about this end.

But as they drove past the Nursery and the Store and the Big House, Nina realized that she wasn't past the pain. It still hurt tremendously to think she'd never see them again, never start her first spring seeds in the greenhouses, or see the rose garden in bloom. For nine years, her entire adult life, she'd spent all her time and imagination turning Don Alberto's estate into its own world. Now, with the crack of a gavel, she was exiled from that world forever.

Never again, she thought, repeating a phrase that had gone through her mind hundreds of times since Don Alberto had died. Never again was she going to create a world that wasn't her own. In Sicily their land and their house and everything in it would belong to them. In Sicily she would be secure in her world, with her family, forever.

"I think you're making a mistake," Zia Gabriella said as she ladled *pasta e fagioli* into soup bowls and passed them along. Fabrizio and Ettore had carried a bench in from the seedhouse and attached it to the kitchen table to make room for their unexpected guests.

"You've had a bad experience," she continued, "but America can be good, too. Look what it's given us." Waving the ladle through the air, she indicated the large, comfortable kitchen. A drop of rosemary-rich tomato sauce fell on Claudia's sleeve.

"Mamma . . ." the sturdy young woman reproached.

"*O la.* Sorry, *cara.* Go quick. Cold water," her mother responded with another descriptive wave of the ladle. Claudia jumped out of the way.

"We had a nice house, too, Gabriella," Orazio said, accepting the bowl of hearty bean soup that Marina passed him. He put it down in front of him with barely a glance. "Then in the blink of an eye, that pair of jackals kicked us out." A bitter note crept into his voice.

"They stood there with their guards," he said. "Big brutes who urinated on the rhododendrons, like mongrel dogs. And they acted as if *we* were the thugs. To my dying day, I'll never forget the looks on their faces as we drove away.'' The look on his own face was cold and harsh. "It was as if they were sure that even the clothes on our backs were stolen from them."

"*Bè*, Orazio," Zio Sergio soothed as he spooned grated cheese on his soup. "Like my Gabriella said, you had a bad experience. Those two are evil. Scum. I put a curse on them. *Cornuto,*" he swore, sticking the spoon in the cheese dish and making the sign of the cuckold with his index and little fingers.

"But listen," he said, ceremony over, "not all Americans are like them. They aren't all mean. Take Mr. Beale and his family," he said, pointing in the direction of the house on the other side of the hedge. "They're decent people.

"You know what it is?" he added, wagging his finger wisely. "It's that we're different from the Americans. Their ways seem peculiar to us. But don't forget, we seem just as peculiar to them. It takes a little time for us to get used to each other." Zio Sergio was a big man with a barrel chest and an enormous eagle-like nose.

"That's the truth," Zia Gabriella agreed. She filled the last bowl and set it in front of herself. "You just need a little patience.

"After all, Orazio," she said, "you found a good situation once. Give it some time, and you'll find one again. Maybe even something out here, near us. Wouldn't that be nice? Long Island is full of potato and cabbage farms, so there's bound to be a position. If you like, we can ask Mr. Beale if he knows of an opening somewhere. Eh, Sergio?"

"Too late," Orazio declared, as he had several days earlier. "My mind's made up. We're going home." He dipped his spoon into the soup but just stirred it around without seeming to be aware of what he was doing. "Our trunks are in New York at the steamship office, and our tickets are in my pocket," he said, patting his jacket, as much to reassure himself as to show them what he meant. "Everything's set. The *Galileo Galilei* sails for Naples on the twelfth, and we'll be on it. All that we need is a place to stay until then."

"You'll stay here, of course!" Zia Gabriella replied at once, while Zio Sergio echoed her words. "Our house is your house for as long as you need it," she told them. "Actually," she added, "I wish you'd stay longer than you are. I wish you'd think this over more carefully.''

"No." Orazio shook his head doggedly. To avoid any further response, he took a mouthful of beans and pasta, though he hardly tasted the savory soup.

"Angelina," Gabriella pleaded, looking toward her sister. "Can't you talk to him? Can't you make him see reason?"

For once Angelina had little to say. She looked worn out, her majestic shoulders stooping. Her only response was to lift her hands and spread them out, palms up. "*E bè,*" she said.

While Zia Gabriella cajoled and Orazio resisted, Nina listened to the discussion without joining in. For one thing, she was too tired to talk. Almost too tired to eat. Today had been brutally long and draining. After months of days that had been long and harrowing.

But for another thing, she didn't want to think about what her aunt and uncle were saying. Like her father, she had her mind made up and she didn't want to change it. An image of Sicily shone in her mind. It was peaceful and heartening, like a beacon in a storm. It was what kept her going from hour to hour, kept her putting one foot in front of the other. Always trudging toward that wonderful light. To extinguish the beacon, to consider other plans, was more than Nina could safely handle. So she shut her ears, ate half of her *pasta e fagioli*, then collapsed on a pallet on the parlor floor.

After three days of moving from the pallet to an armchair to the kitchen table, then back to the pallet to start the round over again, Nina felt restored enough to venture outside for a walk. Actually, escape might be a more apt description of what she was doing. Because Zia Gabriella alternated her pleas for them to remain in America with discourses on Nina's unmarried state.

"Twenty-five years old and no husband," she would say, shaking her head and tsking. "My Aurelia's already a mother."

It was when Angelina started to look at her shrewdly, though, that Nina really got nervous. It was a look she hadn't seen in some time. Certainly not this past summer. Not even during the year preceding it. Not much, at any rate. Not since she'd become a businesswoman with a big salary and dressmaker clothes. Then, there'd been only pride and respect. But now that her business and salary were gone, now that she was just Nina again, that look was starting to resurface. Wrapping her shawl around herself, she went outside to escape it.

Outside wasn't as much of a refuge as she'd hoped, however. Just to start with, it was cold and windy. There was sunshine, but the sky was slate blue and the wind came whipping off Long Island Sound with nothing but flat, empty cabbage fields to stop it. It cut right through her heavy wool shawl and posed a new threat to her ever-perilous hairpins. One hand shot out from under the folds of her shawl and clamped on her head as she hurried away from the lifeless fields.

Nina found protection from the wind by the barns and the seed-house, though she didn't find refuge there, either. There, it was memories that cut through her shawl with a razor-sharp chill. As clearly as if it were happening right now, she could see herself walking between Don Alberto and Wim. She could hear the excitement in the don's voice as he talked about cabbages, and she could feel the excitement inside herself at having met Wim again after all those years.

She remembered peeking sideways at him in awe and fascination. And being struck by the thought that he was the essence of America. That he was fair-haired and smart and ambitious, just like America, and that, just like America, there was something about him that was foreign.

She should have put a stop to things, right then, she thought as she changed direction again, this time heading inland, away from the Sound and toward the road. Her pace was neither brisk nor plodding, but an aimless ramble, just fast enough to keep warm while she went on thinking. She should have stopped both Wim and Don Alberto in their tracks on that bright May day. If only she'd known, she could have forestalled all the heartache that was born among the wedding festivity.

"Miss Colangelo! Hello!" a voice boomed behind her, interrupting her brooding.

Nina stopped in her own tracks and gave a sigh. She wasn't sure she had the stamina to endure Harry Beale's heartiness right now. On the other hand, she couldn't very well ignore him, either. First off, she was walking down his drive, which meant she owed him the courtesy of a greeting, but second, she'd have to be deaf to pretend she hadn't heard him call out her name. Very reluctantly she turned to face him. And immediately wished she hadn't.

"So nice to see you, Miss Colangelo!" Harry proclaimed as he advanced across the lawn with his hand outstretched. "You remember my daughters, Penelope and Cecilia, don't you?"

Did she ever. Nina took in their dainty faces and fur-trimmed coats with a single glance. "So nice to see you, too," she murmured as she placed her hand in Harry's and let it be pumped. She nodded toward the Misses Beale and smiled wanly. They nodded and smiled wanly in return.

"We're just taking a stroll to settle an enormous breakfast. Eh, girls?" Harry said, chatting cheerfully. "Cook made my favorite today. Baked kidneys and eggs in a cream sauce. I probably ate too much," he admitted, patting the middle buttons of his double-breasted coat, "but I couldn't resist. In any event, I was able to convince my girls to keep me company while I walk it off."

"Only on the lawn, Papa," Cecilia reminded him. "Only twice around and then we go back in. You promised."

Throwing an arm around each of his daughters, Harry let out a roar of laughter. "So I did. So I did," he agreed. "My girls would rather be snuggled by the fire," he explained to Nina. "Delicate. Just like their mother. She can't take the cold and dampness, either." He gave his daughters another squeeze before releasing them and saying, "Might as well stay in New York every weekend, eh?"

"Oh, Papa," Penelope responded, cocking her head and scolding him sweetly. Maybe she disliked the cold, but the nippy air seemed to like her. It had painted her porcelain cheeks rosy pink and had faintly colored the tip of her nose. With her fluffy curls peeking out from under her fur bonnet, she made an utterly fetching picture.

"You know we come out because all our friends are here," she told her father. "What would we *do* if we stayed in town for the weekend?"

Letting out another roar of laughter, Harry grabbed her into another hug. "I was only teasing, honey," he apologized. "I know you have fun in the country even without going outside. Besides, it gives me a chance to catch up with Sergio and find out what's been happening on the farm. Oh, say!" he exclaimed, abruptly turning back to Nina.

"Your uncle told me about the Blackwell estate. Hard luck, eh?"

Nina looked at him a moment before answering, wondering if he were teasing again, if such titanic understatement were some form of American humor. When she decided that he was sincere, that there seemed to be genuine regret on his genial face, she nodded briefly and said, ''Yes. Hard luck.''

''Remember I was telling you about it last night?'' Harry said, looking from one daughter to the other. ''How Mr. Blackwell left his estate to Miss Colangelo, but the court overturned the will?''

Cecilia looked blank, but Penelope nodded. ''Yes, I remember,'' she said, staring at Nina, suddenly interested. ''What will you do now, Miss Colangelo?'' she asked.

Again Nina paused before answering, this time, however, to swallow the distaste in her mouth. Though Penelope's tone was perfectly civil, she hadn't asked her question out of sympathy or concern. Quite simply, she was curious to know the end of this gossipy story. Apparently immigrants' feelings were beside the point.

''We leave for Sicily next week,'' Nina finally responded, keeping both her tone and her expression flat and unreadable.

''What!'' Harry cried, his rubbery lips turning down in a rare frown. ''Going back to Sicily? Good heavens, you mustn't do that, Miss Colangelo. You mustn't let this setback make you give up completely.

''You and your father could find dozens of good jobs in this country, I'm sure. Mr. Blackwell might be gone, but I'd be glad to write you a letter of reference in his stead. For that matter,'' he added, holding up a finger as a better idea occurred to him, ''I'd be happy to help you find a position. Why, just off the top of my head, I can think of three, no, make that four people who are constantly complaining about their gardeners. I'll bet they'd jump at the opportunity to hire the two of you.''

''Oh, no,'' Nina replied quickly, shaking her head, more certain than ever. She clutched her shawl tightly to her chest. She didn't want a job and she didn't want Harry Beale's help and, most of all, she didn't want to stay in America. Yes, *she* knew she was a gardener first, but after she'd bought cabbage seed from Harry for two consecutive years, why didn't he think of finding her a job with a catalogue company? Why did he assume she was only capable of physical labor? Why did even ''decent'' people like the Beales believe that Italian immigrants were some sort of inferior species of human being?

Taking a deep breath, she squared her shoulders. ''Thank you, anyway,'' she said in her politest voice. ''But our plans are made.

We've already booked our trip. You see, we're quite set on spending some time abroad, and the south of Italy is so delightful in winter.'' She extracted her hand from under her shawl and held it out to Harry again with her brightest smile.

"It's been a pleasure doing business with you," she told him. "Perhaps we will again someday." After giving his hand a few firm shakes, she turned and winked at his pink and white daughters.

"Best hurry, now," she advised them in a kindly tone, making a gentle shooing gesture before tucking her hand back under her shawl. "If you stand here much longer, you'll catch a chill."

Without waiting for any of them to reply, Nina smiled again and continued on with her walk. Before she strolled away, however, she did get a chance to note the astonishment on all three faces. A sense of grim satisfaction put starch in her step. It was the first satisfaction she'd had in nearly a week. The first since she had, in essence, called Edward a liar and turned her back on him in the courtroom.

One by one she was turning her back on all these Americans. One by one she was walking away from everyone who demeaned her. One by one, including Wim.

His insult was far more subtle than the others, but it was an insult, nonetheless. Not content with who she was or where she came from, he'd changed her in his mind to someone else. He'd reshaped her in the mold of an American woman. A woman like . . . No, not like Penelope Beale, Nina corrected herself before she even thought it.

Walking along the country lane, a shadow of a smile slid across her face. At least that was one ghost she could finally lay to rest. There was no way that the sensible woman of Wim's imagination could possibly be mistaken for the fluffy female she'd just left on the lawn. He might not be seeing Nina Colangelo when he looked into her eyes, but she now knew for certain he wasn't seeing Penelope Beale, either.

With a shrug, Nina kicked at a fallen branch in the road. It wasn't much of a discovery, she realized. Too little, too late to do any good. Because it no longer mattered whether or not Penelope haunted her. What mattered was that when Wim looked into her eyes, it wasn't she he was seeing. What mattered was that for all his poetic speeches about drawbridges, he couldn't accept who she was.

Well, he had made his choice, Nina thought with another shrug. Now she was making a choice, too. She was choosing to return to Italy. She was turning her back on America and on the men here who couldn't accept her. All of them, from Gideon to Edward and Reginald to Harry Beale to Wim. She was walking away from America and walking toward Sicily.

That thought sustained her for the rest of the morning. It even helped her get through the rest of the day. And the next, and the next. On Tuesday evening, however, with only one full day remaining, another shock made that thought begin to crumble. It came after dinner, after the plates had been cleared, when they were just sitting around the table, dunking hard biscuits into their coffees.

"I have something to tell you," Dante suddenly announced. When everyone looked at him, he blushed bright red.

"Che c'e?" Orazio asked, his attention only half engaged. The other half drifted back to Ettore, who was teaching Rossana a card trick. "What is it?"

"I've decided not to go back to Sicily," Dante answered. Despite his blush, his voice was sure and firm. "Serafina and I are staying in America."

"What!" a chorus of voices instantly rose.

"What are you talking about?" Orazio's voice roared above the others. "What are you saying?"

Though his face got even redder, Dante wasn't intimidated by the outraged shouts. "You know what I think about life in Sicily," he said, wrapping both his hands around his coffee cup. "I've told you that I'm worried about schools and doctors for my children." He glanced at Serafina, who gave him an encouraging nod. Turning back to the others, to Orazio in particular, he leaned his arms on the table and hunched forward to continue his explanation.

"I haven't been in America for even two years," he said. "That's not enough time to make a fair judgment. Despite what's just happened, I'd like to give it a chance. More important, though," he went on, pushing the cup out of his way, "two years isn't enough time to have saved much money. I still can't afford to buy a decent piece of land in Sicily, so if I went back now, I'd be returning to the same situation I left. Onions and bread and wondering if my boots can last another winter.

"It's not what I want," he said, shaking his head. "Not for myself. And certainly not for my family." He sat back in his chair and looked again at his wife, reaching over to take one of her hands in his. "Definitely not for my family," he said. Serafina smiled.

"*Bè,* Dante," Orazio stuttered, too stunned to speak. He just spread out his hands and lifted his bristling brows.

Nina found her voice, though. It was shaky and hoarse and it was filled with horror, but it worked sufficiently to put words to her thoughts. "You can't stay here," she said, staring, eyes wide, from Serafina to Dante. "You'll break up the family. We'll be five thousand miles apart." She couldn't imagine life without her favorite sister in the immediate vicinity. It had been hard enough to adjust when Serafina had moved out of her bed and downstairs to her husband's. The idea of an entire ocean between them, however, turned her ice cold.

"Nina, listen," Dante said, leaning forward, arms on the table again. He wasn't blushing now, and his tone was very earnest. He seemed to want to make his sister-in-law understand more than anybody else. "I don't want to break up the family," he said. "God knows I hate the idea of separating Serafina from her parents and sisters." He lifted his right hand as if swearing that were the truth.

"But even more, I hate the idea of Serafina living in a dismal stone cottage," he said, searching Nina's shocked face for some sign that she heard him. "I hate the idea of her never being able to make paintings, because she is too tired from carrying water and wood. And because we have no money to spare for art supplies, even if we could find some place to buy them. I hate the idea of my babies dying because there are no doctors when they're sick, or growing up stupid because there are no teachers or books.

"Nina, please," he said, stretching his hands toward her across the table. "Please say you understand I don't want to break up your family, but I've got to think about *my* family first. Please say you don't despise me for that."

"Of course I don't despise you," Nina responded as she struggled to concentrate. She heard Dante's words, but they sounded distant and faint. It was almost as though she were reading his lips, as though she were watching him speak and gesture from very far away. She was having trouble believing this was really happening. She looked at her sister, and Serafina nodded again.

"He asked me first," she said softly, responding to Nina's unspoken question. "I told him I agreed. We have to think about our children." Her voice held the same plea for understanding that her husband's did.

"Don't you see?" she asked. "Life here will be much easier for them than it will be for us. If they're born here, they'll *be* Americans. They'll learn to speak English without an accent, and at school, they'll learn American ways. When they grow up, they'll just melt into this country. They'll be able to walk through any door that they choose." Lifting her shoulders, she said, "It's an opportunity we can't deny them."

Putting her head between her hands, Nina massaged her throbbing temples. Apparently this was happening. Apparently it was true. She was still having difficulty absorbing the enormity of it, however. She still wasn't quite sure how to react. She looked up. "I'll miss you," she said simply.

"O Nina!" Serafina cried as the expression on her face suddenly changed from responsible parent to vulnerable child. She jumped up and ran around the table to wrap her arms around her sister. "I'll miss you, too. All of you," she added, looking over Nina's head at the other members of her family.

"But you don't have to go," she said, squeezing Nina harder. "Nina, you especially. You could stay in America."

"Stay, Nina," Dante chimed in immediately. "Our children should know their Auntie Nina."

"No," Nina quickly responded, though she gripped Serafina's encircling arm with both her hands. "I can't stay here." While she was confused about the rest of it, she was certain of that.

"America isn't all bad," Dante coaxed from across the table. "Look, if it weren't for America, I'd never have met Serafina. If I'd stayed in my village, I would have missed the greatest happiness of my life."

Nina couldn't see her sister's face above her, but she was sure Serafina was blushing. Dante was again. It wasn't a blush of embarrassment, this time, but a blush of love. On top of her aching confusion, she now felt a sharp twist of loss.

"There are other good things about America, too," Dante went on. "And other people. Americans. I liked Don Alberto very much. And I like Wi—'' Just in time he saw Nina's eyes widen. ''I like other people that I've met,'' he amended.

''I like America, too,'' Benedetta suddenly burst out. She jumped to her feet, not to hug anyone, but to clasp her hands together and beseech her father. ''Papà,'' she begged. ''Please, please, please, don't make me go back to Sicily. Please. I'd much rather stay here.''

In an instant Orazio was on his feet, too. ''What's going on?'' he shouted, shaking his fist. ''What kind of nonsense is this? We're *all* going back. Nobody's staying.''

It was Dante's turn to rise. He didn't leap up in frustration or rage, rather he stood up slowly. A strong, steady man with a strong, steady purpose. ''No, Orazio,'' he said, meeting his father-in-law's eyes. ''Serafina and I aren't going back. We're staying in America. Our future is here.''

Pausing, he turned to look at Benedetta, who was still standing, though her head was bent and tears of disappointment were trailing down her cheeks. ''And if you'll let her, Benedetta is welcome to make her home with us. I know you don't want to lose her, but she'll be happier here. Try to understand that when you make your decision.''

Benedetta's head shot up, and hope filled her round face. She cast a glance of immense gratitude toward Dante, then turned to stare at her father. ''Please, Papà,'' she urged as hard as she dared.

Before Orazio could answer, though, Lucia spoke up. She didn't rise but sat quietly in her chair, her hands folded, resting on the table in front of her. ''I think you should know that I've decided to stay, too,'' she said.

Gasps of astonishment greeted her announcement. Over the years, Lucia had been the Colangelo most critical of America. It was inconceivable that she, of all people, would want to stay.

''Luigi Tagliaferro has asked me to marry him,'' she explained. ''I'm going to accept.''

''*Figlia mia*,'' Angelina wailed, leaning toward Lucia, bewildered. ''Why? Why?'' She lifted up her hands. ''I don't understand. Do you love him desperately?''

''Desperately?'' Lucia permitted herself a hint of a smile. ''No. Luigi doesn't inspire any grand passions. Ours won't be a marriage like Serafina and Dante's. But he's a good man and we'll be content. After all, Mamma,'' she said, a panicky twinge in her voice. ''I'm twenty-two years old now. Nearly twenty-three. I know I can have a husband and a home here. How do I know what I'll find in Sicily?

"Besides," she went on, forcing herself to sound more positive. "Serafina will be here. And maybe Benedetta. And Zia Gabriella and all her family." She nodded at her uncle and cousins. "It won't be as if I'm here all alone." She nodded again, to herself, this time. "I'll be all right," she said. "You can't have everything in life. This is the best choice for me." It was at that moment, sitting erect and accepting reality, that Lucia achieved the majesty she'd always imagined she had.

Through many pots of coffee, and far into the night, the discussion went on, sometimes shouting, sometimes sobbing, pro and con. In the end Orazio relented. Benedetta and Lucia were allowed to stay. There was nothing he could say about Dante's decision but to eventually give his grudging blessing.

After her outburst, Nina fell silent. She just listened to the arguments and the pleas that went on all around her. She still couldn't believe the family was being torn in half. That her beloved family, the refuge to which she was retreating, was being yanked apart, dissolving before her very eyes.

It had never occurred to her that if she made the decision to return to the life she once led, the life she remembered might no longer be there. She had just assumed that if she went back to Sicily, everyone else would, too. It was a staggering blow to realize that although she'd decided to stop the world, the world had kept on turning.

=30=

"Nina, be a good girl and pour another glass of wine for Signore Mazza," Angelina said.

Nina stopped still with her fork in midair, her mouth open in anticipation of the *coniglio all'agrodolce* balanced on its tines. Then her mouth closed and she set the fork on her plate. "Yes,

Mamma,'' she said, pushing away from the table and standing up.

There was nothing in either her tone or in her dutiful demeanor to suggest the annoyance that was flaring up inside her. The carafe of wine was sitting in front of their guest, only inches from his glass, while she was sitting at the other end of the table. Was it really that necessary to have her wait on him?

She walked around to where Domenico Mazza sat, a tall, leathery man who smelled of tobacco and sheep. When she picked up the carafe and poured the dark red wine in his glass, he made sure to avoid contact with her, either by glance or by touch. In fact, he almost seemed to cringe from her presence.

Yet Nina, as well as everyone else at the table, knew that as soon as Sunday dinner was over, this taciturn shepherd would pull Papà aside. In true Sicilian fashion he would tell her father that he was a forty-one-year-old widower with a house, land, and two hundred and ninety-seven sheep. That he and his helpers milked the sheep every day and turned the milk into pecorino cheese, which he either aged with black peppercorns or sold fresh at the Saturday market in Noto. He would assure Orazio that he made a good living, that he was healthy, respected, and could read and write his name. Then he would say he was looking for a wife.

At age twenty-six Nina was strong and still young enough to bear him sons and help with the sheep. With Orazio's permission, he'd like to marry her. That's what he was going to ask, everyone knew it. What no one knew, though, was how Orazio was going to answer.

Nina finished filling Signore Mazza's glass, set down the carafe, and started back to her seat. "And your father?" Angelina prompted, her eyes narrowing in reprimand. Again, her command stopped Nina in mid-motion. This time, she was less successful at hiding her exasperation. The tumbler in front of Orazio was still half full. Besides which, the carafe was well within his reach, too. Impatiently Nina retraced her steps, snatched up the carafe, and dumped some wine in her father's glass. He looked up and glared a warning. She ignored it and plunked the carafe back on the table.

Two chairs down, Stella sucked in her breath, waiting for the explosion that was bound to follow. That sound was just what Nina needed, though. It punctured her irritation and restored her sense of humor. Granted, the situation was deadly serious, but she could now see that it was also just plain ridiculous. Returning to

Laura Simon

her seat, Nina passed behind Stella and gave her sister's braids an affectionate tug.

"So, Signore Mazza," she said cheerfully as she settled back in her chair, whisked her napkin into her lap, and picked up her fork. "I understand you have sheep. What breed are they?" She ignored her mother's black glance as she had ignored her father's glare, and just took a bite of the *coniglio* while she waited for Domenico's answer. The sweet and sour hare was cold, but it was still delicious.

"I have two hundred and ninety-seven sheep," Domenico answered earnestly. "One hundred and twenty of them are milking ewes. They're good sheep. Farfalla, my best milker, gives me two liters a day." The only thing was, he addressed himself to Orazio, as if the question had come from him instead of from Nina.

"*Bè*," Orazio responded, taken a bit off guard. "Good. *Bravo.*" He didn't seem to know what else to say.

Not so Nina. "Have you ever considered upgrading your herd by introducing another breed?" she asked as if they were having a real discussion. "I've heard that farmers in Puglia are having a great deal of success with the Altamurana and Lecesse breeds. Of course, those sheep are raised for their wool. For mattress production, you know." Taking another bite of hare, Nina suppressed a smile. Who would ever have thought Don Alberto's monologues on the wool industry would come in handy?

"My sheep are milkers," Domenico told Orazio, doggedly refusing to look at Nina. He seemed a little puzzled by what was happening. Since when did unmarried women engage unmarried men in conversation? Especially about livestock? Especially at their father's table?

"*Si, si*," Orazio acknowledged, shooting Nina another warning glare. "I've been thinking of running a few sheep myself. Nothing much. Just for family use."

"You might want to experiment with the Sopravisana breed, Papà," Nina said, a bit more grimly. The situation seemed less and less humorous. She was getting tired of all the warnings, and she was getting tired of being disregarded. "They're a triple-purpose sheep that's raised extensively in Tuscany and Lazio," she went on, determined not to be silenced. "Milk, meat, and wool . . ."

"Nina, we're ready for the greens," Angelina interrupted.

The only sound in the kitchen was a small hiss when Stella

sucked in her breath as she had before. This time, for sure, sparks were going to fly. Angelina, elbows on the table, was leaning toward Nina, an unmistakable scowl on her face. Nina, poised with her fork in midair again, was scowling defiantly in return.

It's hard to say what might have happened next. Certainly two strong wills were set to collide. But the tense scene was suddenly shattered as, from the other room, came the earsplitting sound of a baby's wail.

"*Accidenti*," Bianca Maria murmured, shoving her chair away from the table. She stood up wearily to see what Giacomo wanted now. Ever since he'd been born, nearly two months before, he'd been fretful and sickly, rarely sleeping more than an hour at a time. Consequently, no one else did, either.

It was worst, of course, for Bianca, who looked pale and drawn with dark smudges of exhaustion under her eyes. But sitting there with her fork in the air, Nina realized that they were all affected. Everyone was tired and worried, and everyone's temper was short. She put down her fork. This wasn't the moment to be campaigning against Domenico Mazza's prospective proposal or to be protesting age-old modes of behavior. Without another word, Nina got to her feet and began to clear the plates. Angelina gave her a grateful look.

Although nobody asked her, Stella got up and began to clear, too. She helped Nina scrape the plates into a bucket for the pigs, then stacked the dirty dishes in a galvanized tub. Later, they would carry it outside to do the washing, since the new house still hadn't materialized. Orazio had spent most of his savings buying the farm of his dreams, where, in addition to the pigs, there were several dozen chickens, eighteen goats, two burros, some cattle, and a fine stand of olive trees. Indoor plumbing, however, would have to wait a while.

"If we were back in America, this wouldn't be happening," Stella grumbled, but softly, so only Nina could hear.

"Which wouldn't?" Nina whispered back. The smile pulling at her mouth was both amused and sympathetic. Poor Maria Stella. She was having the hardest time adjusting of anyone.

Orazio had reembraced Sicily with a force that astonished them. He seemed to swell up or grow taller, to become a new man. It was as if he'd been dormant all his life, quietly building up energy, and now he'd burst forth.

As for Angelina, she seemed content. She was enjoying the

status that came with owning their farm, a big and prosperous one by Castel'Greco standards. Not that they saw many people, living a mile, uphill, from the village, but in church she was treated like a grand signora. For Angelina and Orazio, this would always be home. It was worth waiting for a sink to be back among friends, relatives, and familiar ways. And in such triumph. But Stella, poor Stella. For her this was a foreign country.

Now, as she flipped Stella's braid away from the edge of the washtub, Nina whispered again, "What would be different in America?"

"All of it," Stella answered in the same low grumble. Clutching a few dirty forks, she waved her hand through the air. "If we were back in America, Giacomo would go to a doctor. And we'd have a proper kitchen. And that smelly, old man wouldn't dare to think he could marry you." Clattering a few dishes to cover up her criticisms, she declared, "You're a hundred times better than he is. But because he has 'two hundred and ninety-seven sheep,' everyone's treating him like he's some sort of king."

She shook the dirty forks under Nina's nose. "If we were back in America, *you* would choose your husband. Not Papà."

"*Ragazze!* The greens!" came Angelina's sharp reminder before Nina could respond. To be honest, she didn't really know how to, anyway. Everything Stella said was completely right. With the innocent clarity of youth, she'd assessed the situation and pinpointed the truth. Besides which, her fierce declaration of loyalty moved Nina tremendously.

In the end, Nina just patted Stella's shoulder, picked up the bowl of dandelion and mustard greens, and carried it to the table. There, she sprinkled them with a few pinches of coarse salt, then dribbled dark green olive oil, pressed from their own olives, over the top. A splash of vinegar, made from wine from their tiny vineyard, finished the dressing. She tossed the greens and served them, starting with Domenico Mazza.

When they'd finished eating, she and Stella again cleared the plates, then Nina carried over another bowl, this one filled with sweet white peaches and medlars from trees in their yard. The thought crossed her mind that if Benedetta were here, there'd also be a plate of almond biscuits made with their own almonds. But no sooner had the thought formed than she shrugged it away. Benedetta was better off where she was, Nina reluctantly admitted. So was Serafina. And Lucia.

After she made coffee and carried that to the table, after she poured a cup for Domenico Mazza and stirred in his sugar, after she gave the table a final clearing, and after she carried the brimming tub out to the well with Rossana's help, after she washed the dishes while Rossana and Stella took turns hauling up buckets of water, after the three of them dried the dishes and put them away until supper, after all that, Nina took a stroll across the yard. As soon as she rounded the corner of the barn, however, she picked up her skirt and ran as fast as she could

It was a perfect day in May. The air was clear and warm and smelled like the wildflowers in bloom all around her. There was bright pink valerian springing out of the miles of stone walls that divided the fields, and brilliant yellow mayflowers, and wild snapdragons, and thistles. Nina ran until she was out of breath, which didn't take long because the ground underfoot was rocky and steep.

When she slowed, though, taking great gulps of the clean, sunny air, she didn't look back, just kept going forward. Away from the squat, stone farmhouse whose stucco was crumbling, whose pink paint was washed out and faded. Away from her family sitting around the kitchen table inside, away from her father, gravely considering Domenico Mazza's marriage proposal.

Nina walked and ran for nearly an hour. Through the olive grove, across the uneven field where goats and cattle grazed among outcroppings of lava rocks and clumps of prickly pear cactus. Over endless stone walls, built by endless generations of *contadini*, engaged in the endless task of clearing the ground. Hiking up to the top of the hill and skidding down the other side on her heels.

This was the Sicily she remembered and loved. Here, in the ancient hills where flowers bloomed in abandon. Here, where the sky was a dark, rich blue. Here, where despite centuries of peasants wresting out a living, there was something about the land that remained untamed and wild.

Her flight wasn't entirely aimless. Though she stopped frequently to admire the view, the spectacular gorge cutting a swath through the hills below her or a pure white morning glory climbing up a dilapidated pole gate, she kept heading for one of her favorite spots. It was the ruin of a town destroyed by the great earthquake of 1693, a town that had prospered hundreds of years before

Christ. There was nothing left now but the bare remains of a couple of walls, a few foundations, and utter solitude.

That's what she wanted most at this moment. Peace and quiet. Because despite the fact that their farm sat on the top of a hill and the only thing they could see was a sprawling patchwork of rocky fields, despite the fact that they rarely had visitors, or that their trips to Castel'Greco, a meager collection of houses and a church, were infrequent, and despite the fact that they went even less frequently to Noto, a little city built of golden sandstone in a lusciously Baroque style, despite such seeming isolation, Nina was hardly ever alone.

Morning till night, she was busy working with her mother, hauling water, heating it, washing dishes and laundry. She helped Angelina prepare meals, helped her make cheeses and preserves. Together with her sisters, she cleaned and mended, fed the chickens and pigs. These days she even took a turn at cradling Giacomo in her arms, patting his back, singing him comforting songs. When the day was finally over and she crawled into bed, Bianca was next to her. And so was everyone else. Mamma, Papà, Rossana, Stella, and baby Giacomo together in the same room. It was the only room there was, besides the kitchen, that is.

Nina had gradually come to realize that *this* was the Sicily she'd left nine years before. Granted, they owned their own land now, and there was plenty to eat, but all day, every day, was consumed by the business of living. Anything they wanted, they had to find or make for themselves. There was no coal man, no ice man, no dairy or butcher. If they wanted a fire, they had to gather the wood. If they wanted bacon, they had to raise a pig, slaughter it, and cure its haunches. They all worked hard and they all worked together and they all worked for the good of each other. It was life in its most elemental form.

As Nina scrambled up a sheep trail and emerged on a plateau, she wondered, not for the first time, why she'd ever imagined she'd be free to putter in flower gardens when she returned to Sicily. Where she got the idea that she would pass her days creating enchanting gardens, in which she would then pass languid afternoons quietly reading. The only flowers here were the ones that bloomed wild from late winter through June, before the sun baked down and the sirocco winds seared the hills. The only garden here was the one where they grew the vegetables they ate. Aside from a bougainvillea twined over the well, there wasn't time to fool with any others. There wasn't time and there wasn't irrigation.

Breathing hard from the climb, Nina picked her way among the ruins until she found the one she was looking for. It was the half-exposed slab of an old foundation, bleached nearly white by three hundred years of sun beating on it. Growing amidst the rocks and ancient rubble all around it was purple flowered vetch, tiny daisies, and bright yellow *fiori di maggio*.

With a sigh of relief, Nina threw herself down, startling a lizard who was sunbathing on the hot rock. It skittered sideways a few feet then froze, blinking its goggle eyes and sticking out its tongue. Giving it only a brief glance, Nina lay back on the spot it just vacated and flung her arm across her brow. The sky whirled above her.

No, Nina decided, continuing her thought, the gardens of her memory weren't in Sicily. They were in America. It was there, in Stamford, on Don Alberto's estate, that she'd spent her days with her hands in the dirt. It was there, under Don Alberto's patronage, in his library and on his grounds, that she'd come into her own as a gardener, that she'd blossomed, so to speak.

Growing up in Sicily, she'd had only a fascination with flowers, but then, as now, she'd spent her days cooking and scrubbing and caring for baby sisters. It wasn't until they'd emigrated, until her sisters got old enough to take over her tasks, until such luxuries as running water and coal deliveries freed her to help her father, it wasn't until life evolved beyond the elemental, that she'd been able to turn her fascination into an occupation that she loved.

Shutting her eyes and sliding her arm across them, Nina miserably admitted that she missed America. Although the Sicilian hills were gorgeous and the pace was less frantic, there was no question about the fact that it was also less stimulating. In an odd sort of way, she missed the flurry and commotion she'd been so determined to escape. Not all of it, mind you, not the typewriter and ledgers. But she missed the challenge of confronting and solving problems, and she missed the glow of pride and satisfaction she felt when her ideas were realized.

There was more, much more that she missed. Little things, of course, things she'd taken for granted, things like ice cream and gas lights and Ivory soap. But there was also a certain feeling of self-worth that she missed, the feeling that she had the right to choose her goals and had the time needed, every day, to work at achieving them. She missed the subtle sense of being looked up to for leadership. Yes, there had been enormous responsibility along with it, but there'd also been respect. She missed that. She missed it a lot.

Before leaving America, exhausted and bitter, she'd imagined that it would be wonderfully soothing to fall into the familiar routine of old Sicilian ways. And for a while they had been reassuring, the welcome home had been heartwarming, but once she'd gotten some rest, some of those old ways had begun to seem suffocating.

Take this business of Domenico Mazza, she thought, rubbing her arm across her eyes. Even Stella could see it was both ludicrous and frightening. Ludicrous to think that a woman who'd run her own company could become the drudging wife of an illiterate shepherd. Frightening to think that it wasn't even her decision to make. That someone else, her father, had control of her fate. Not that she was going to marry Domenico no matter what Papà decided. No matter how flattered she was supposed to be that a man who owned two hundred and ninety-seven sheep would be interested in an old maid like her.

She'd rather die a spinster than marry someone like that. She couldn't. It was too late. She wasn't a peasant anymore. Even if she wanted to, she couldn't undo what she'd learned. Wim had been right, she couldn't empty those years in America out of her head. A pain twisted through her. Wim. Ah, Wim. Most of all, she missed him.

Nina rolled over on her stomach and rested her cheek on the sun-warmed slab. She barely felt the heat, though, barely felt the afternoon sun on her back. What she felt, instead, was empty and cold. These days she always did, when Wim entered her thoughts.

What on earth had she been thinking of to believe she could just walk away from him? That she could put an ocean between them and still be happy? Even in those terrible times last summer, even when she'd had her mind set hard against him, she'd never been able to stop her heart from leaping in pleasure every time that she saw him. And even when she'd provoked arguments with him and stormed away, she'd looked forward all week to seeing him again on the following Sunday. She'd looked forward to his startlingly blue eyes and his ironic sense of humor, to his loyalty, his calmness, and his straightforward honesty.

Slipping her hand under her cheek to cushion it from the stone,

Nina now wondered if her reasons for rejecting Wim had been realistic, or if they'd simply been the result of an unfortunate series of experiences. If the differences between them had really been insurmountable, or if she'd simply been reacting to Don Alberto's death, Gideon's betrayal, and the Blackwell brothers' treachery.

Her sigh spread a warm breath across her fingers. She'd never know the answers to those questions. It was too late for them, too. It was too late for all of it. She'd made a choice, and now she had to live with it.

Despite the unhappy thoughts stirring in her mind, Nina must have fallen asleep, because the next thing she knew, it was very late in the day. Gasping, she jumped up. She had to hurry home and help with supper. Brooding and daydreaming weren't going to get a meal on the table.

Still groggy, she stumbled and skidded back down the sheep trail, hauled herself over stone walls, and ducked under gates. Then, with the refreshed feeling that comes from an afternoon nap, Nina grabbed her skirt up in both hands and ran across the rocky fields. The sun was setting almost directly in front of her, throwing long, purple shadows under gnarled and weathered trees.

She went past the gorge, without stopping to admire it, and through the pastures where the goats and cattle had been grazing earlier. She was nearly home, climbing up the last hill, through a field lush and red with poppies, when a figure appeared, silhouetted above her. It was the figure of a man, black against the streaky sunset sky.

The first thought she had was that Orazio had come to find her. She quickened her pace, taking longer strides. As she hurried, one hand clutching her skirt up so she wouldn't trip, she used the other hand to shade her eyes while she squinted ahead. No, it wasn't Papà. The man was too tall. Could it be Domenico Mazza, coming to claim his bride?

Nina stopped abruptly and let her skirt fall. The thought was distressing, but it vanished almost as soon as it came. No, it wasn't Domenico, either. The man was too lean, and he carried himself too gracefully.

Picking up her skirt, Nina started walking slowly, still shading her eyes. A tiny hope crept into her heart, and she started walking faster. There was something about his posture, something about the way his jacket was slung over his shoulder. Was she imagining it? Was it a distortion of light? Was it like the shadows that stretched reality into purple fantasy?

Her heart started beating harder and the hope swelled until she felt almost giddy. Until she wanted to laugh and to cry and to shout all at once. She walked faster. And faster and faster. Then she started to run, and he ran, too. In the middle of the field of poppies, on a hillside in Sicily, Nina ran into Wim's embrace.

His arms closed around her, crushing her to him as he spun with the force of their impact, swinging her through the air. Nina clung to him as tightly as she could, not letting go, even when they collapsed in a heap on the ground. Until this very minute, she hadn't realized just how much she'd missed him.

Until she felt his hands spanning her back and cupping her head, she hadn't realized how much she'd missed his touch. Until she pressed her nose against his neck, she hadn't realized how much she'd missed the clean scent of soap that was part of him. And until she felt him breathing hard against her as they sprawled in the poppies, she hadn't realized how much she'd missed being in his arms. How much she'd longed for him. How desperately she'd wanted him to hold her. With a small cry she strained even closer.

In response Wim buried his fingers in her hair, then pulled her head back until his lips found hers. He kissed her, not deeply, because his breath was still coming in gulps, as was hers, but he kissed her again and again. He kissed her lips and her cheeks and her brow. He put kisses on her eyelids and on the lobe of her ear. Then he turned so she could kiss him, too. On his chin, on his nose, on the spot where his smile made a crease.

They kissed each other eagerly. Hungry, quick kisses, until their breath came back and their mouths met again. This time his kiss was long and thorough. This time his lips lingered on hers, and his tongue traced their imprint. This time Nina could feel his nose rubbing against hers, could feel a lock of his silky hair tickling her forehead. And this time she could feel his kiss radiating through her, filling the emptiness, warming the chill.

When he finally broke off and trailed kisses across her face, they weren't frantic pecks, but slow, savoring caresses. With deliberate and exquisite lack of haste, he rolled his head so his cheek pressed against hers, so his mouth was by her ear, so his breath was soft on her neck. While one hand was still splayed across her back, the other hand, feather light, combed through her hair.

"Marry me," he urged. "Marry me, please, Nina, and never leave me again."

A shock ripped through Nina, shattering the sensuous spell. She slid abruptly away and stared at him, eyes wide, over the top of a broken-off poppy. Those were the first English words she'd heard in nearly six months, and that fact, as much as their meaning, cleared her head in an instant. They startled her, bringing America into focus, banishing the nostalgic haze that was starting to form around her recollections.

"What did you say?" she asked, the English awkward in her mouth as well as in her ears. Inching farther back, she looked at him more carefully. At his cornsilk hair and his marble white skin. At his blue eyes, the color of hyacinths in a northern twilight, at the spots on his cheeks, rosy and scrubbed.

They were completely different, she and Wim, she thought, remembering the questions she'd asked herself only a few hours before. One was the product of ancient sunbaked hills, full of secrets and traditions, the other of the hard-won polderland, flat, practical, and cool. Wasn't that why she'd left him? And had anything really changed?

"I asked you to marry me, Nina," Wim replied, returning her careful stare. Apprehensive, he reached out to smooth back her hair, to let his fingers slip down the side of her face and gently tip up her chin. "I'm asking you to come back to America," he said. "To be my wife. I'm asking you to share my life and to let me share yours."

Though his words sounded like music now, though her heart cried out to accept, now they weren't in Holland, weren't in a fairy-tale castle, in a magical meadow. She'd learned a lot since then, in the harsh school of experience, and she wasn't about to let the euphoria of the moment fool her into believing it could last forever. She wasn't about to risk getting hurt again.

So, as much as she wanted to fling herself back into his arms, she pulled his hand away from her face instead, then sat up among the smashed poppies and regarded him seriously. "Please don't think I'm not extremely flattered," she told him, wrapping her arms around her knees as she hugged them to her chest. "I know you've made a long and difficult journey to find me, and I don't doubt that your intentions are completely sincere, but I can't help wondering," she said, raising one hand to rub her brow, "I can't help wondering if your proposal is such a good idea."

"What!" Wim sat bolt upright, one hand swiping out, decapitating a bright crimson flower. "What are you talking about?" he demanded. "I can't believe you can say that. Not after the greeting you just gave me. Not after those kisses." He leaned forward to tap his finger on her knee. "Nina," he told her, "you were every bit as glad to see me as I was to see you. How can you possibly deny that it's true?"

"I don't deny it," Nina replied, shaking her head. For once his explosion didn't trigger her temper, too. She wasn't angry or tense, and she wasn't rejecting him. Not really. What she was doing was trying to find the answers to her questions.

"Of course it's true. I *was* glad to see you. I was overjoyed. What's more, I still am. But don't you see, Wim?" she implored, unwrapping her arms to hold out her hands. "Don't you see that it isn't enough?

"It isn't enough to have a few blissful moments, like the one in Holland, or this one now." Her hand swept out, too, not in exasperation, though, but to encompass the beauty around them. The sky was turning fiery and fierce, lending drama to the red of the poppies. "It isn't even enough to have a few passionate thoughts. Or yearnings. Or desire. Or heartache when we're apart." Her apologetic shrug dismissed those enormous emotions.

"Marriage is forever," she said simply. "It's all the time and every day. And in order to be happy, we have to be able to get along. We have to agree on the daily details, have a common pattern to life. Otherwise, we'll feel like strangers in our own home. We'll argue and bicker. Don't you see?" she said again as she again held out her hands. "I'm afraid there are too many differences between us. I'm afraid we aren't enough alike."

"We *are* alike, Nina," Wim responded, seizing her hands and not letting go, even when she pulled. "Don't *you* see?" he asked. "We're very much alike. We're both smart and tough and incredibly stubborn. I wouldn't be here now if I weren't. Moreover," he added, giving the hands he was holding a shake, "you wouldn't be, either."

"That's not what I meant," Nina said, finally yanking her hands free. How could she make him understand what she did mean? What could she say to make him understand her fears? Before she could explain it, though, before she could find the right words, he plucked up a poppy and did it himself.

"I suppose you're talking again about me being blond and you being dark-haired,'' he said, wagging the fragile flower in front of her nose. "I suppose you're talking again about pancakes and pasta. About the fact that you were born in Castel'Greco and I was born in Haarlem. Isn't that right?''

"Well, yes,'' Nina answered a little warily.

"Well, no,'' Wim contradicted, flinging the flower away. "It's not right. It's all wrong. It's a poor excuse.'' He wagged his finger, instead.

"It doesn't matter where we were born,'' he told her. "Because we left those places behind. Once upon a time you were a Sicilian and I was a Dutchman, but that isn't the case any longer. Now we're both Americans.'' Pausing, he waited for her response, but when she only looked at him, he said, "Tell the truth, Nina. Now that you're back, are you really glad to be here? Is it the paradise you remembered, or is it beautiful scenery and a stifling existence?''

For a long time Nina didn't have anything to say. She just fingered the poppy petals at her feet without really feeling them. He'd guessed it exactly, almost as if he'd been here himself. Maybe he had, she suddenly realized. Maybe Holland and Sicily weren't that different, after all. Maybe the abandoned castle was no different than the bleached ruins of the village. And maybe toil in the bulb fields was no different than toil in these ancient hills. She picked a poppy and held it to her nose, even though she knew perfectly well it didn't have a scent.

"No,'' she admitted, finally turning to rest her chin on her knees. "It isn't the paradise I remembered. You were right. I'm no longer a peasant.''

Wim reached out and seized her hand. With the poppy in her fingers, he brought it up to his lips. "Come home with me,'' he urged, placing a kiss on her knuckles. "Come back to America where you belong.''

Nina let the flower fall and clutched his hand. She didn't want to let go, didn't want his touch to disappear. But still she hesitated. There was still something wrong. A brooding question still lurked in her mind. She turned her head again, cheek on her knee. Her quiet pose gave no sign of the emotions tearing her inside.

"Nina, I love you,'' Wim said softly.

His tender words drifted down and settled around her. But instead of soothing her, instead of swelling her heart with joy, they formed a cold knot that twisted in her stomach. Pulling her hand free, she sat up straight. "Do you?" she asked, peering through the fading light. "Do you really?"

It was Wim's turn to take his time before responding. In the Sicilian twilight his eyes were nearly as purple as the long shadows. Then he answered her, his voice calm, but with a resonance that came from deep within him. "Yes," he said. "I really love you."

Nina swallowed hard and let her head fall back. Why? she thought, looking at the sky. Why couldn't she just let herself go? Why couldn't she give into her longing and throw herself into his arms?

"Of course, you were quite right when you accused me, during our last battle in Stamford, of falling in love with an ideal I'd created of you." His voice was still calm, but its ironic undertone had returned.

Nina's head snapped up and her eyes opened wide. In time to see a smile creasing his cheek. "I knew it!" she cried, thrusting a fist in the air. Before she could shake it in anger and vindication, though, he snatched it out of the air and trapped it between his hands.

"Perhaps it would be more accurate to say you were partially right," he corrected himself. "Perhaps I should say you were right in stages."

"You should say what you're going to say," Nina retorted, trying to shake her hand loose from his grip. "Stop speaking in riddles and stop telling me pretty lies." She rose up on her knees and swatted at his wrists. "Let go," she ordered.

"No," he refused, grabbing the other hand.

"Wim," she threatened.

"Nina," he countered. His smile deepened. "You know, I've always liked hearing you say my name. Ever since that day in Castle Garden, it's delighted me whenever you've said it. In Holland, it's just an ordinary name, but in your voice, it sounds exotic and exciting." He shrugged.

"Maybe it's your lovely accent," he speculated. "Or maybe your magnificent manner." He tossed his head and attempted to mimic her. "'Wim,'" he tried. "No," he decided with another shrug. "I can't do it. It doesn't feel the same. When you say it, I feel extraordinary."

Nina stopped struggling and looked at him. Though a faint hope was nudging her heart, suspicion was still furrowing her brow.

"That's what I wanted to tell you," he said. "About the way you make me feel." He wasn't smiling now, and there was no irony in his tone. Instead, she heard that remarkable resonance again. "I wanted to tell you that you were right. I did create an ideal. But, Nina, I promise, I fell in love with *you*. I might have crossed the two in my mind, but I never did in my heart. And that's where it counts."

He felt her fists open against his hands, and he smiled again, not mocking, though, not amused, but fond. "I fell in love with the woman whose hands are always flying," he told her. "With the woman whose face is animated by the emotions inside her. Despite what it seems, I fell in love with the Nina who digs in the dirt. Not the one behind the desk, but the Nina who makes gardens as beautiful and bursting with life as she is."

He let her hands go now, but they didn't fly as he'd described. Rather, they fell to her sides. She didn't move them. She didn't move at all. She just knelt in the poppies, hardly daring to breathe.

"You know," he said, reaching up to rescue a hairpin, "I thought I was helping you. I thought I was helping you by teaching you the value of business and success. By teaching you the virtues of being practical and sensible and all those other words you've come to detest." He held out the hairpin for her to take, but she ignored it, staring into his eyes. Reaching up again, he slipped it securely in place.

"I even had the temerity to think I was setting a good example," he said. Now his smile was rueful. "I thought I was showing you how a poor immigrant can rise to success. I imagined that my experiences, the way I took advantage of opportunity to build a prosperous business, would somehow inspire you. I thought I was helping you to succeed, too."

There was a moment of silence while Wim searched her face. Nina's eyebrows knit. She knew that he wanted her to say something, but she wasn't sure what. While it wasn't his nature to boast, it wasn't like him to be humble, either. Finally she cleared her throat.

"Thank you," she said politely. "You did help me. You're a very good teacher. You taught me about taxes and invoices and using my mind to think with instead of my emotions."

Ha! she thought, after she'd said it. That was one lesson that had stuck very well. It was exactly what she was doing now. It was why she was kneeling here, staring at him, with her hands at her sides, instead of circling her arms around his neck and rubbing her cheek against his shiny hair.

"Did I teach you that?" Wim asked, grimacing in apparent chagrin. His hand made an erasing motion. "It was a mistake. I apologize. Forget that lesson. The lessons you taught me were far more valuable." When she blinked in surprise, his tender smile reappeared.

He slid two fingers down the side of her face, ending under the point of her chin. Lifting it up, he told her, "You are a very good teacher, too. Unfortunately, I'm not as apt a pupil as you. It took me too long to learn my lessons."

Letting his hand drop away, he took a deep breath. "I think I finally did, though," he said. "I hope so. I hope I finally learned to think with my heart instead of my head. I hope I know now what's important in life. Not business and profit, but happiness and love. I hope I've finally learned that that's the true success."

Nina's heart was banging so hard, she had to press her hands against her breast to contain it. She bit her lip, afraid her excitement would spill over before Wim had finished. He'd paused for another breath, but she knew he had more to say, and she wanted to hear it. Every single word.

He didn't disappoint. Not this time. His words sent shivers down her spine.

"It was your example that was the inspiration, Nina," he told her. "I had only to watch you to be inspired. I just had to look as you went about your day, reveling in your family's adoration, reaping pleasure from your flowers. I only had to see the glorious spirit with which you approached life, to realize that satisfying the needs of the soul is more important than satisfying the needs of the pocket."

He lifted his shoulders in a helpless shrug. "I had only to watch you, Nina. And to know how you make me feel. That was the most important lesson you taught me," he said quietly. "You taught me that I need you to make me feel alive."

"*Amore mio!*" Nina cried, her emotions finally bursting free. She flung herself forward and grabbed him into a hug. "I love you! I love you! I love you!" she shouted, joyous laughter mingling with her jubilant declaration.

"*God dank!*" Wim exulted as his hands gripped her back. "Thank God for that! I was afraid I'd lost you through my own stupidity." He rolled his cheek along hers, holding her tighter.

"If only I hadn't left you in Holland to take care of Albert by yourself, or at the train station in New York when you came home, none of this would have happened. You never would have shut me out or returned to Sicily in despair. Isn't that so? Aren't I right?"

Squashed against him, Nina only nodded, rubbing her nose against his clear, clean skin. It didn't matter. It was over and done with. What was more important was the way she felt now. The way happiness made her feel as if she were floating. As if the only thing that anchored her to earth was the clutch of his arms and the press of his lips.

Wim's hands ran the length of her back. "Nina, my Nina," he murmured, planting kisses on her brow. "Thank God for my Nina. I promise you, it'll never happen again. From now on, all your burdens will be mine to share, no matter what else. From now on, Nina, you come first."

It didn't seem that Nina could feel any happier, but every word he said made her float even higher. "*Caro mio!*" she rejoiced, weaving her fingers through strands of his silky, blond hair. She arched back her head to receive his kisses on her throat. Gasping with unparalleled pleasure, her hands slipped down his cheeks and his jaw and his neck. And halted. It was his tie she was holding.

She didn't stop feeling happy. She didn't fall out of love. But her feet were suddenly back on the ground. In a field of poppies, to be exact. Placing her hands flat against his chest, she pushed him back a few inches and looked at him shrewdly. In the dusky light at the end of the day, his eyes were unusually bright and his lips looked bruised. His hair was disarrayed, and the tie she was holding was askew. However, it was still silk, and it was still handmade expressly for him.

"Somehow," she said, cocking her head, "somehow I have a difficult time imagining you tossing your business to the winds. I can't quite see you shedding your finely tailored suits to spend the rest of your life holding my hand and picking posies of violets." She peered at him more intently, her suspicion growing as his eyes crinkled and his cheek creased.

"Somehow," she said, "I suspect you'll find a way to turn these lessons you've learned into a profit."

The crease lengthened and his smile spread. "Now that you mention it," he said, ducking forward to put a kiss on her nose, "I do have an idea I want to discuss with you." He leaned forward again and brushed his lips across her mouth. "But it can wait," he added softly. He outlined her mouth with the tip of his tongue, then blew it dry with a breath.

Despite the thrill that it caused, despite her ecstatic sigh, Nina flattened her hands and pushed again. Harder. "I think we better discuss it now," she decided, despite her husky voice and her racing heart.

Wim gave a laugh, though it, too, sounded hoarse. "All right," he agreed, raising his hands in surrender. He fell on his side in the poppies and propped himself up on an elbow.

"Simply put," he said as Nina settled back on her heels, "I've bought a seed catalogue business. Quite a good one. And I want you for a partner."

"You've what!" Nina exclaimed, springing to her feet. "Of all the gall!" she shouted. "Your pretty speech was just so much dandelion fluff. You *still* think I belong behind a desk, buried in piles of paper. You *still* think I'm just being obstinate, or I'm a child who doesn't know her own mind. You don't take me the least bit seriously, do you?"

Rolling forward, Wim grabbed her around the knees. When she toppled into his arms, he pinned her close to him, speaking into her ear. "If I didn't take you very seriously, I wouldn't have come five thousand miles to propose to you," he told her. "Either partnership. Marriage or business. Now, after that harrowing trek in the donkey cart from Noto, can't you at least listen to what I have to say before you reject me?"

Nina stopped struggling to free herself and leaned stiffly against his chest. "Go ahead," she said grudgingly. Because she refused to look at him, though, she didn't see his smile.

"Thank you," he acknowledged, cautiously loosening his grip. When she remained where she was, he let her go and fell back on his elbow.

"It wouldn't be like before," he said. "There wouldn't be the piles of paper for you to sort through by yourself. Albert was building a business you could run after he was gone," Wim explained as his fingers crept along the rigid shoulders leaning against him. "He threw it all in your lap in an attempt to make you self-sufficient. Like throwing a puppy into the water to teach it to swim.

"But this would be a business we could share," he went on. "Each of us contributing what we know best. I can take care of all those desk details you despise. As you know, I'm good at them.

And you can concern yourself solely with the seeds and the gardens, a process that I find mysterious and overwhelming. Neither of us can do it alone. But together it would be enjoyable as well as rewarding.''

His fingers reached the middle of her back and started to creep up her neck. "What do you say?" he cajoled. "We'd make a perfect team, Nina. There isn't the conflict you imagine. We complement each other. Rather than tearing us apart, our differences make us stronger. Partners. Husband and wife.'' He paused a moment and so did his fingers. Then they started inching through her hair. "Are you interested?" he asked.

Nina tried to ignore his fingers, and the whispery feeling they left in their wake, as she forced herself to think his proposals through carefully. Practically. Sensibly. She suddenly started laughing. Too late for that, she realized. She was already hooked. He was right. They were a team.

"When do we get started?" she asked, twisting around to look at him. Laughing, too, he pulled her down on top of him.

"You gave me a turn," he admitted, wrapping her in a giant hug. "For a moment I thought my investment was wasted. And that Dante and Serafina would be out of work."

"Dante and Serafina?" Nina shoved away from him again, sitting up to stare in astonishment. "What are you talking about?" she demanded. She banged her hand on his chest. "Are you trying to tell me you've involved them in this scheme, too?"

With another laugh Wim caught her hand. "Of course," he answered. "It's a cardinal rule in business. When you find excellent people, hire them on the spot. They're in Stamford right now. Serafina's dreaming up catalogue covers, and Dante's getting the trial gardens started."

This time the shock stopped Nina still. Her entire body felt quiet. She wasn't even sure her heart was beating. After a moment she took a tentative breath. "Stamford?" she asked. Her voice was very small. "Do you mean you've bought Don Alberto's estate?"

Wim let go of her hand and sat up, too, draping his arms over his upturned knees. "No," he replied, his eyes fixed on her face. "I bought his business. *You* own the estate."

It was nearly dark now, but Wim could see her golden eyes grow huge. Another affectionate smile lit his face as he explained. "When Albert's will was overturned, by law his prior will was reinstated. And much to his wretched sons' dismay, this one, too, named you as heiress to his property in Stamford, and all the buildings on it. Unfortunately, the seed company wasn't started at the time Albert made that bequest, so the business went to his sons.''

Still smiling, he reached out and picked up one of her limp hands. ''Our partnership, however, should rejoin them. For good.''

It took Nina a few minutes to digest what Wim had told her, to be aware that he was holding her hand. ''I'm sure they'll contest,'' she said, groping for some flaw in this incredible news. ''The judge will overturn this will, too.''

''Unlikely,'' Wim replied, picking up her other hand. ''So unlikely, in fact, even Edward and Reginald recognized the futility of their suit. They sputtered a bit, then withdrew it. Get used to it, Nina,'' he advised, tapping her hands together to get her attention. ''You own the estate. You're a capital partner in our enterprise.''

It was another minute before it really sank in. But when the shock wore off, sheer elation took over. Throwing back her head, she laughed and laughed. She laughed as she hadn't laughed in months. Since before Don Alberto had died, at least, maybe even longer. She laughed until tears squeezed out of her eyes and streaked down her cheeks, until she gasped for breath and until her sides ached. She laughed until the bad times and the bitterness were completely exorcised, until the world was set to rights again. Until she felt her heart overflowing with life and love.

''You were right again,'' she acknowledged when her laughter finally subsided. ''Your immigrant theory was dab on the mark. De Groot and Colangelo have blended into Blackwell. Put together a Dutchman and a Sicilian, and chances are, you'll get an American.''

Slipping into his embrace as a half moon peeked over the horizon, Nina nestled her head on his shoulder, another soft laugh escaping. ''What a sensible man I'm going to marry,'' she announced in complete satisfaction.

Above her, Wim smiled his crooked smile and laid his cheek on her hair. ''What a lucky man,'' he corrected.